SLASHTAG

Jon Cohn

Paperback ISBN: 979-8-9880619-0-8

Cover Artist: Covers by Christian www.coversbychristian.com

Illustrations: Delaney Cohn

Editor: Lyndsey Smith, Horrorsmith Editing www.horrorsmithediting.com

To my wife, Delaney, the only person I know who would voluntarily participate in Slashtag.

CONTENTS

CHAPTER ONE

Dire California is a dead town. The headstones are made of crumbling saloons and mining supply stores eaten from the inside with dry rot. A vestigial sheriff station stands in shambles, housing nothing but rats and sand for nearly a hundred years. And yet, the hollow buildings are only placeholders for the people who lived and died in Dire. Their bodies all lie together, buried throughout a house on a hill that's been feasting on their souls for the past eighty years, and might continue to digest them for another eighty more. It stands as a monument to the insanity of mankind, or perhaps, it's the house itself that is insane.

"Okay, this is straight up stealing the intro from *The Haunting of Hill House.*" I shake my head at the equally pretentious and vapid text in the email. "This whole line about the hotel surviving the past eighty years and lasting eighty years more, I'm pretty sure is copied word for word. Plus, the building's not even on a hill. Dire's a flat town in the middle of the desert."

"Are you talking about the Liam Neeson movie, or the Netflix series?" my brand manager, Maggie, asks from behind the faux-mahogany desk in her office.

"I'm talking about the actual book! You know, Shirley Jackson, the mother of modern ghost stories?"

Maggie gives me an exasperated look from under her tangle of wild red curls that says both, "I don't know," and "I don't care."

"I think you should seriously reconsider their offer." Maggie taps a long, gold acrylic fingernail against my laptop screen, urging me to read on.

To humor her, I skim through the terribly written preamble and get to the part where the email actually explains the event.

You are hereby cordially invited to take up residence at The Propitius, California's most infamous haunted hotel, for Krentler Media's first-ever hybrid streaming event. This one-of-a-kind experience will be televised nonstop on the KMC network, while simultaneously giving viewers an interactive experience on Social.com. Join in with six other celebrities as you solve puzzles and hunt for clues in the infamous Propitius Hotel, home to the twentieth century's most heinous mass murderer. But beware, only those that survive the event can earn a ten-million-dollar donation to their charity of choice and become the official spokesperson for Social.

"Why exactly did you think this would be a good idea?" I ask. "You told me that, according to your algorithms, my target demo hates horror, or really anything that promotes critical thinking. Wouldn't a bunch of spooky puzzles feel wildly off-brand for me?"

"That's true, generally speaking," Maggie says, consulting the tablet in her hand. "Our data says that girls ages twelve to forty aren't typically looking for that kind of content in a lifestyle influencer. These are... special circumstances."

"And by 'special circumstances,' you mean my fans don't want to see me enjoying life and would much rather watch me be the victim in a horror story. Is that about right?"

"Have you seen the things people are currently saying about you online?" Maggie waves circles around my face with her open hand. "You, as a brand, are in very real danger here. This isn't a simple oopsie daisy.

A lot of people are really sick right now, and they're all blaming Tawny Howlett."

Maggie isn't the most comforting person in the world, but at least she's honest. In the last twelve hours, the world has slowly become aware that a batch of NatFit, a new meal-replacement drink, was tainted to the point where several dozen people have ended up hospitalized with a rare parasite only found in Venezuela. Unfortunately, my face is plastered across every single bottle as their trusted spokesperson, making me a convenient target for their wrath.

"Nobody would actually believe I'd poison them on purpose. It's not like anyone would believe I'm sitting there at the processing plant, actually making this stuff."

"People are recording themselves shitting in trash cans on the street and tagging you as the receptacles. It doesn't matter what they *should* think. This is what's happening right now. As far as your options for damage control, I'd say you have three choices. The first is to do the haunted hotel, which, even without this incident, I would strongly recommend for brand exposure. Your second choice is to hop on the hashtag-vanlife trend and live out of a customized astro van for the next two months."

I feel a migraine coming on at the very suggestion. "I don't even want to know the third."

"That's because your third option is to drink a tainted bottle of NatFit on camera, then livestream the result for fourteen hours."

"I already told you I'm not living out of a van. I'm thirty years old with a sister to take care of. I'm not putting myself through something like that." *Besides,* I want to tell her, *I've already spent enough time trapped inside a van to last me a lifetime.*

"Okay—"

"I'm not going to livestream poisoning myself either, even if that is what people want to see."

"Well then. It sounds like that only leaves one choice." Maggie clasps her hands and gives me an obvious look.

For a moment, my heart flutters as a fourth option pops into my head, one that could solve all my problems. "What if I used this opportunity to just fade away? I could shut down the whole Lifestyle Guru business and let the world forget about me for a minute."

Maggie flicks her eyes up from her tablet and looks at me like a mother whose child just threatened to hold her breath until she either gets a pony or dies. "Don't be dramatic. Besides, hiding is the last thing you want to do right now. You publicly endorsed a tainted health drink, and now, millions of your fans are out for blood. As of right now, three of the ten top trending hashtags across the entirety of Social are hashtag-TawnyToilet, hashtag-Nastyfit, and hashtag-FlushTawny. Staying silent simply isn't an option for you here. You need to make an apology to your audience, and then you need to put forth an act of contrition. Something big enough to drown out the people who blame you for poisoning them. Historically, if you don't come out with some sort of apology within the first twenty-four hours, people are going to assume you're being disingenuous. If you wait any longer than that, they'll assume you had a PR person write your apology for you, which is even worse than not apologizing at all. I'm telling you this as your brand advisor and as your friend, you need to get ahead of this as fast as possible."

To be clear, Maggie is *not* my friend. Her career depends on me staying in the spotlight, which means her job is to manipulate me into doing what's best for my brand, usually to the detriment of my mental and emotional health. Depending on the day, it's either a curse or a blessing that she's so damn good at what she does.

I close my eyes and take three deep breaths, counting to five on each inhale and then again on each exhale. It's one of the breathing exercises I frequently use to open or close my videos. Unlike the magic crystals or copper-infused balance bracelets Maggie has me peddle, this breathing technique actually does help me to become more present. It gives me a few moments to stop myself from blurting out that I'm glad NatFit accidentally tainted an entire batch of their drink and to double down on the idea that this is an opportunity for me to claw my way out of the spotlight, once and for all.

My phone buzzes on the table next to my laptop. It's a text from my sister, April. "Shit. I'm supposed to go see a movie with her today."

"Well, that's going to have to wait," Maggie says.

"I know." I'm already halfway through typing out that I'm stuck in a damage control meeting. I think about my sister, how all of this might affect her, and it helps to slow me down from making any rash decisions. "Okay, fine. You win. I'll just keep peddling cruelty-free moisturizers on live streams for the rest of time. So, in order to keep my channel alive, I'm guessing I need to get started on writing that apology video?"

"Already have it finished." Maggie taps around on her tablet a few times and brings up a document. "We're going to have you focus on giving the most sincere apology for the situation. You're deeply sorry for the pain you've caused, and you're going to be more involved in quality control in the future, and blah, blah, blah. I've marked the points in the video where it would help if you could get emotional, if possible. You can cry on command, right?"

I read through the statement. "This apology makes it look like this whole thing is my fault. It doesn't even mention anyone in the company being responsible for accidentally making thousands of bottles of Ex-Lax."

"Of course it doesn't. If you said anything negative about NatFit or its employees, you'd be violating your non-disparagement clause. Right now, you're only an enemy to the public. If you say anything about the company that might put them in a negative light, you open yourself up to a potential lawsuit as well."

As I've learned time and time again by this point, the more famous I get, the less freedom I have. "So, you're saying, even though this group of idiots created an entire shipment of product that makes people crap themselves in public, I'm supposed to take all the blame, even though I've never met any of them."

"To be fair, none of their faces are on the bottles insinuating that if they buy the stuff, they'll lose twenty pounds and have perfect skin. You're not just peddling makeup anymore, Tawny. This is something that people chose to put inside of their bodies, and they did it because you made them believe it was safe and healthy. Whether or not you invented the drink is irrelevant. You're the face of NatFit."

"That's only because you told me to!" I can't help but snap at her. "I said in the beginning...it's one thing to sell makeup. That's something I'm an actual expert on. I never pretended to know the first thing about health drinks. You said NatFit was going to be the next big thing and that partnering with them would be a major step in my career!"

"I don't have a crystal ball. I just make the best decisions I can for you based on the information I have. On paper, they seemed like a solid bet."

I shake my head and rub a tear of frustration out of the corner of my eye. "I just don't understand why I'm the only one getting the blame, here."

"Because there's nobody that people love to point their fingers at more than women who are perceived as powerful. White men can fail as many times as they want and still be bulletproof. As a woman, you get one, maybe two, chances in your life to win people back over, and you have to do it while showing that you are simultaneously flawed and perfect. Otherwise, they're going to call you Tawny Toilet for the rest of your life. So once again, you can either go buy a van, drink some poison, or suck it up and spend a weekend in a haunted house with a bunch of other celebrities. Those are your options." Maggie's eyes are bugging out of her head, and her freckled cheeks are turning almost as red as her hair. "After the apology video, of course."

"All right, fine. I'll make the apology, but I'm going to need time to figure out what comes next."

Maggie sighs, though at this point, I can't tell if it's from relief or frustration. "I really think the haunt is your best option. I don't want to have to deal with the smell of you not showering for the next sixty days."

I read the apology letter again. It's full of lines like *I'm so sorry to have broken your trust*, and *I vow to do whatever it takes to make things right*.

"I'm taking a pass at this apology. There's no way I'm reading this thing word for word."

Maggie runs her tongue along her teeth as her lips curl up in a sneer. "How about this? You've got a lunch meeting scheduled in an hour with your 'boyfriend'," she says, using air quotes.

"D-wreck? I can't deal with that dipstick right now. Can we reschedule?"

"Not a chance. Meeting with D-wreck is the best thing for you. Our numbers show he's currently in the midst of an uptick. Plus the two of you in public having a meal will show people that you're not hiding. Just try not to look like you're having too much fun."

"That shouldn't be a problem," I say, cringing at the thought of spending any amount of time with that thirty-year-old child.

"If you're serious about re-writing the apology—which, for the record, I think is perfect as-is—D-wreck should be your first stop anyways. I swear to God, that man has more lives than a cat."

"I guess that's true," I concede.

"Plus, he was the first person announced to be taking part in the show. If anyone can convince you to join, it's him."

The migraine that's been brewing all morning starts to throb behind my eyes. "Of course, he's going to be part of it. Why wouldn't he want to spend a weekend making everyone's lives more miserable than necessary."

I look back to the invite, with the plagiarized description and iconic photo of the massive Victorian-style hotel. Then, across the top of the page, I re-read the name of the event. "Do you really think anyone's going to take a show called *Slashtag* seriously?"

"Probably, why?"

I shrug my shoulders in creative despair. "I just think it's probably the dumbest fucking name I've ever heard in my entire life."

CHAPTER TWO

From: Casting@Krentler.media
To: Board@Krentler.media
CC: Lucy.K@Krentler.media
Subject: Paperwork Signed

Gentlemen of the Board,

I'm excited to confirm our first subject has signed their contract to participate in *Slashtag*. Derek Sarecki, AKA D-wreck, is a multi-generational influencer who has been producing content for over fourteen years. He has over 24 million subscribers and will guarantee an extremely entertaining performance for his fans. Our analysts predict he could bring in as many as 80% of his followers to tune in for at least a portion of the show.

Additionally, we feel his followers fit in perfectly with our most coveted demographic, as they typically have a high tolerance for violence and demonstrate a distinct lack of empathy for others.

Carol

CHAPTER THREE

It takes forty-five minutes to drive eleven miles. Not bad, considering it's almost noon in LA. I park my car and walk up to Natural Organics, one of the fourteen restaurants where my PR team has approved for me to be seen. D-wreck is sitting at a table on the outdoor patio, with a fast-food bag in front of him. He's talking to a couple of boys, probably somewhere in their early teens. They're trying to look casual while asking for a selfie with him, though they're practically dancing in place with excitement.

D-wreck grabs a handful of fries from his plate and tosses them at the kids. "Eat those off the floor, and maybe I'll take a picture with you." It takes all of three seconds before he stops the boys from shoving dirty fries into their mouths and waves them around the table to take a picture with him.

I understand why Maggie set us up, from a business perspective. While his numbers with teenagers are as high as ever, he's starting to lose the followers that are closer to our age. The idea is, by putting him with Tawney Howlett—the squeaky clean lifestyle guru— I could help him evolve his teenage prankster image into more of an adult with a child-like sense of humor.

According to Maggie's research, semi-incompetent yet charming adult men are up twelve percent from last year. After getting to know him over these last few months, I believe he could do it, if he really tried. D-wreck's pretty bro-ey, but he's not a total lost cause. He needs to let his hair grow out a bit, ditch the baseball cap and tank tops, and lose a little bit of the toning—dad bods are in again. If he did all that, he could stand a chance to get a hosting gig on a reality competition series, or something like that.

In return for renovating his brand, I get to continue to sell the lie that I not only know how to handle my own life, but I can also bring out the best in someone else too. Of course, all that was before my reputation took a nosedive.

D-wreck shoos the kids away when he sees me, then rises to give me a hug. It's one of the three public greetings in which we've agreed to engage.

We haven't even sat down before I drop my phony smile and tell him, "I need your help."

"I bet. It sounds like you're having a pretty *crappy* day," he says, with a goofier grin than the twelve-year-olds with whom he was just talking.

"Come on, man. I'm dealing with some serious, uh...serious—"

"Shit?" he says, bringing the sentence to the natural conclusion I'd struggled and failed to avoid.

"Can you at least look like you have an ounce of compassion? You're supposed to be on my side, remember?"

D-wreck waffles at the suggestion. "I don't think that kind of reaction is on-brand for me, at least not yet. Based on our calendar, I'm not supposed to start seeming more mature for at least another two months. Besides, potty humor is timeless."

I try not to look at his face, and instead, my eyes land on his half-eaten burger. "Did you seriously bring In'N'Out to an organic vegan restaurant?"

He takes a big bite, pretending to savor every moment of it. "Hell yeah, I did. Have you seen the menu in there? It's brutal."

D-wreck may be an asshole, but he's not wrong. I try to look forward to ordering a beet salad with vegan feta, but I can't stop staring at his meal. My stomach growls, reminding me that, in my crisis, I've forgotten to eat anything today.

"Is that burger animal-style?" I look around at the half-populated café, trying to see if anyone has their phones pointed in such a way that they might be filming us. The constant threat of being recorded in public creates low-grade paranoia and, after a while, either starts to develop into a sixth sense or leads to a mental breakdown. Sometimes, if you're lucky, it does both. "Can I have a bite?"

D-wreck's smirk turns to genuine shock. "Wow, you're just saying 'fuck it' to all the rules today. If you want to risk it, get down with your bad beef-eating self."

It's been four years since I've been allowed to be seen eating meat. After my last makeup brand was heavily marketed as being cruelty-free, I was invited to become involved in a number of charities protecting wildlife foundations. At the time, Maggie decided my image as a health-focused role model and animal activist would be improved if I were perceived as being a vegetarian.

"Screw it. Even death row inmates get to splurge on a last meal. Can you just look around and let me know if it seems like anyone could be filming me right now?"

D tosses his hands out to his sides, gesturing generally around the restaurant. "I mean, everyone has a phone and a Social account. The entire world are paparazzi."

My hand flies up to my face, and I rub my thumb against a scar on my chin hidden under concealer. The urge for total image self-destruction comes crashing back to me with such force, it takes everything I have to push it down and not let the heat of the moment get the best of me. I let out a long, controlled exhale. "Fine. Can you just, like, take a really big bite and describe it to me?"

"This whole thing is really getting to you, huh?" For the first time in as long as I can remember, D-wreck almost sounds like someone who actually has a shred of compassion for their supposed girlfriend.

"I've never had people hate me like this. The worst backlash I've ever gotten was that one time I called Kei Sentra 'he' after they came out as non-binary, and that only trended for, like, three hours, until Landon Keating got caught defacing a bunch of his own movie posters."

"Oh yeah, I remember when that happened. Not your thing...the poster thing." He brings the burger up to his mouth and takes a huge bite, causing my empty raging stomach to let out an audible grumble. "That was hilarious," he says, with little bits of masticated meat soaring out of his mouth.

"Everyone's blaming me for this NatFit thing. I've lost almost two-hundred-thousand followers in the last twelve hours. What do I do?"

D-wreck's eyebrows raise in tentative excitement. "Are you asking what I would do in your situation?"

I already regret asking. "I guess."

He leans back, finding a comfortable position in these rigid metal chairs. "I'd roll with it. These chicks buying your low-cal-whatever drink are all trying to lose weight, right? Sounds to me like you just did them a favor."

"Oh, fuck off."

"No, seriously. Just reframe it to a golden ticket situation. Only a few lucky winners will get to lose five to ten pounds overnight. Then just add a disclaimer like, 'we do not recommend taking this product before trans-continental flights.'"

"I'm serious, D. You've been in trouble more times than I can count, yet you still have almost twice my followers. How can I fix this?"

He finally drops his grin, swallows his food, and shakes his head. "I don't know. Our situation is different. I'm a straight white dude that's been doing dumb shit for fifteen years. At this point, whenever I get in trouble, I mostly just shrug and say, 'ain't I a stinker?' As long as I don't sexually harass anyone, it seems like there's basically nothing I *can* do to get canceled. People expect me to act like an idiot, and I've learned to grow thick skin. When the shit really does hit the fan—pun intended— I just push through until people find someone else to get pissed at." He quickly looks to either side, then leans in, like he's about to share some top secret information. "Look, it sounds like you already know what to do. You give your court-mandated apology, you take your lashings, and then you move on. Personally, I can't think of a better way to make an ass of yourself than by being spooky roomies with me on this *Slashtag* show."

I shake my head and sigh. "When did Maggie call you?"

D-wreck checks the time on his phone. "I'm guessing somewhere around the exact moment you left her office."

"I already told her I need some time to decide. I have some very real concerns with putting myself into that situation."

"Come on, you have to do it. For the first time in, like, ten years, you've shown the world that you're not perfect. Big stinkin' deal. Come on the show. We'll get the"—he catches himself fast enough to change his next word—"pants scared off us. Then halfway through, you fake some sort of revelation that all the health and meditation crap on your site is giving you strength for a second wind. By Monday morning, you'll be even more popular than ever."

"I don't know. I have to talk to April."

D shoves a handful of fries into his mouth, letting a few fall from his fingers during the journey between the white paper bag and his face. "All I'm saying is, everyone loves a redemption story. If you play your cards right, you could even become a Final Girl and win this thing."

Despite the tightness in my chest, I feel the faintest trace of a smile curl up at the thought. D-wreck is one of only a few people who knows about my secret love of horror movies. Dangling the moniker of a Final Girl in front of me is a cheap shot, but I'd be lying if I said it wasn't at least a little tempting.

"So, what does that make you? The comic relief that dies in the first half?"

He scoffs at my suggestion, feigning indignation. "Hell no, I'm going for Final Boy."

I shake my head. "That's not really a term."

"I know," he says with smug confidence. "I'm going to claim it during the show."

"What if..." I pause, momentarily horrified I'm even going to say this out loud. "What if I don't want to recover my image?"

"You saying you want to go full scorched Earth? Throw a couple middle fingers at the world and show up in some *Dripfeed* listicle in two years, about people who publicly fucked up their lives?"

I honestly don't know how to answer the question. It's been so long since I've had to actually make a difficult decision for myself, I feel like I'm drowning in a sea of bad options. D-wreck makes a come-back sound so simple. For him, I'm sure it is. He gets to float through life, stumbling from one idiotic scheme to the next, failing ever upward. In my experience, catastrophe tends to be the tip of the iceberg.

"I just don't know if I have the strength to—"

Something hairy brushes up against my leg, and my already tightened muscles spring into action. Gasping, I leap to my feet. I forget where I am, all the people around me. My metal chair shoots backward, and an animal lets out a yelp of surprise. There's a large dog on the patio, about knee height, baring its teeth at me.

I've already made a scene, but I don't care. To get away from the animal as fast as possible, I leap behind the chair, putting it between me and the dog.

"Sorry about that," some lady says at the table behind me. "He's friendly, I think he just saw some fries on the ground and wanted to sneak a treat." She turns her attention to the dog, who has forgotten all about me and is making quick work of D-wreck's discarded fries. "Come here, Bruno. That's a good boy."

You're a good boy, aren't you, Clarence? a voice from my childhood echoes in my head, reinforcing my belief that things can always get worse. By the time I can feel my lungs circulating oxygen again, I realize I'm still hiding behind a chair.

"Okay, well, that was weird," D-wreck says. "Feeling a little jumpy today?"

"I just...I don't like dogs."

"Definitely keep that part out of your apology."

"Thanks," I say, kicking myself for letting my guard down.

"Seriously, everyone loves dogs."

"I know, I'm fine. It just snuck up on me."

As he rambles on and on about the eternal popularity of dogs, I can't help but run a finger along a series of small oblong scars across my thigh. "You know what? I think this may have actually helped after all."

CHAPTER FOUR

From: Ron.M@Krentler.media
To: Lucy.K@Krentler.media
Subject: Techbounce Article

Lucy,

My grandson just sent me this article from some website called Tech-bounce about us. I don't like it. In the article they claim they even reached out to us before publishing, which means somebody knew this was going to print and didn't do a goddamn thing about it. You're going to get this article down within the hour, and then you're going to find the idiot that let this happen and fire them immediately.

Article pasted below...

Ron

Techbounce Presents: Everything You Need To Know About Social's Founders

When the news broke nearly a year ago that every existing social media website would be folded into one mega platform called Social, people thought it was a piece of viral marketing for a new movie, or possibly a very early April Fool's joke. It seemed especially odd, since Social's parent company, Krentler Media, also announced the purchase of a wide array of other user-based sites like Reddit, LinkedIn, even fringe platforms including Parler and 4chan.

And yet, somehow, not only was it all true, it was just the first step in a series of moves that—through brute force—would make the new network the most-used social media platform of all time. Once the ink was dry and Krentler Media had spent a staggering $1.6 trillion in acquisitions, they announced that every platform, other than their newly formed Social, would cease to exist and that all users would need to merge the data from all of their other accounts over to this new monopolized meganetwork.

But what exactly is Krentler Media, and how did one man go from an arms dealer to the God Emperor of the internet? It's no secret that William Krentler began his career at Harmine Defenses, taking over as CEO in the mid-80s after 20 years with the company. By the year 2000, Harmine Defenses had grown to become one of the largest and most profitable defense contractors in the world.

Here's where the story gets weird. In 2014, Ron Morrison Jr., an Arizona Supreme Court justice, retired from his life-appointed seat in order to partner with Krentler for a new business venture. The two men founded Krentler Media, and with it, the Krentler Media Channel, or KMC as it's more widely known. While the channel had some scripted content, it mostly served as a platform for right-wing politicians and pundits to share what were then-controversial topics.

Leading up to, and after the 2016 election, Krentler Media exploded in popularity and expanded its board to include well-known film producers like Charles Menuscha and legendary Raconteur Hotel chain magnate, Joseph Bartlett.

In the wake of the 2020 election, Krentler Media made a hard pivot away from politics, radically changing the content on the KMC network to focus on unscripted reality programs. More importantly, they launched what would soon become the one Social network to rule them all.

The question we keep asking is, even with all the resources at their disposal, how could Krentler Media possibly come up with the money to buy out not just one, but all existing social media platforms? And more importantly, why would a former arms dealer and Supreme Court justice even want to be involved in such a project? We've reached out to representatives at Krentler Media, but so far, they've had no comment. We will post updates as we learn more.

CHAPTER FIVE

As soon as I get home, I make a beeline for the bathroom. On top of the anxiety of my little Social empire crumbling, I'm still feeling shaky and embarrassed from the dog incident at the restaurant. Any time I leave my house or put myself in front of a camera, there are about a dozen mental checkboxes I have to hit, preparations in order to protect myself and my image. I let myself get distracted today, and now, I'm afraid to see if there's a new trending hashtag of me cowering from a pooch. It only serves to reinforce how bad of an idea it is for me to go on *Slashtag*.

Behind me, the sound of an electric hum approaches from the hallway—my sister April is resting her chin on a curious fist. I feel a slight loosening in my chest at her bright smile.

She looks just like me, if I were in an electric wheelchair and was allowed to eat real food like a normal person. We both have slightly dark complexions from our father's side. Our eyes are green, though hers are speckled with these little bright spots people always say have a hypnotic quality to them. I'm taller than she is, though I think that's mostly due to stunted growth from getting stabbed in both her kidneys when she was ten.

April keeps her dark hair short and doesn't have to bother with hours of makeup application every morning. She's comfortable in her skin, in an effortless way that I am not, even though I'm the one famous for my "natural beauty" line of products. April's smile comes with ease, despite every day being a literal battle of survival for her. Her face is slightly blotchy, but in her defense, she doesn't have to use a regimen of eleven products on her face every night. Also, she gets to eat chocolate and shellfish.

Our scars are our biggest differences. I've got the bite marks on my thigh and two cuts on my face. The one on my chin is somewhat easily concealed by makeup, and a strategically placed wave of hair rides across my forehead and tucks behind my ear, hiding another one. Her scars aren't visible, aside from the wheelchair she spends almost her entire waking life in.

"Whatcha doing?" she asks, pretending as if my entire life weren't on fire right now.

"I've poisoned half of my fans, the world hates me, and I have to shoot an apology video. Other than that, I'm just dandy."

April scrunches up her eyebrows. "I'm guessing now's probably not the best time to tell you I've turned to crack and owe my dealer a hundred and fifty thousand dollars?"

Even at my lowest, April can always bring a smile to my face. "What have I always told you about doing crack? I make enough money for you to get the good stuff."

We both laugh.

"I don't mean to tell you how to live your life, but if you're about to shoot an apology, shouldn't you be putting on more makeup? I'd imagine you'd want to look your best for something like that."

"I'm going in a different direction." I scrub off all the concealer from my scars and take alcohol wipes to my eyelids and lips, making sure to get every inch of Howlett-brand makeup off my face. By the time I toss the wipe away, it's nothing but a mess of brown and red smears.

"Is this some sort of a creative new branding strategy?"

"Something like that. I had a thought today and figured I'd run with it."

Once satisfied that I've sufficiently de-beautified myself, I head into my yoga studio and turn on several ring lights in the room. Without my makeup or any camera filters to soften my face, I appear shiny and reflective against the harsh light.

April follows me into the room, holding a piece of paper she's fished from my purse. "Is this the apology you're going to give? It's a little harsh, don't you think? This thing reads like you were at the juice factory, laughing maniacally while pouring gallons of rat poison in the tank."

"Yeah, I'm not saying any of that. How do I look?" I ask.

"You want an honest answer?" Her raised eyebrows say more than words ever could.

I nod. "That's all I need to hear."

"Have you run this new idea past Maggie yet?"

I set up a tripod and attach my phone so it points at an angle accentuating the scars I've never shown to anyone outside of my family. The ring light hits every uneven groove of gnarled tissue, heightening the contrast between each mound and divot on my damaged face. "It's better to beg forgiveness than ask permission, isn't that what they say? Besides, Maggie works for me."

"But does she, though? Sometimes it seems like you pay her to tell you what to do. I don't even know what kind of relationship that is."

"Well, today, I'm the one in charge, and she's just going to have to deal with it." I close my eyes and inhale, count to five, then do the same with my exhale.

"So, if Maggie didn't inspire you to do this, who did?"

"D-wreck," I try to say casually, knowing my sister's feelings about him.

Concern hangs heavy across April's face. "I don't know if that D-wreck is a good influence on you." She wags her finger at me like we're in a fifties sitcom. "Anyways, I thought *you* were supposed to be the one rubbing off on *him*."

"Yeah, well, I'm already ankle-deep in shit. How much worse can it get?"

April weighs the question for a second. "I guess you could be waist-deep. Or neck-deep. That would be way worse."

"Well, if that happens, then you'll be stuck with having me around the house more often. Can you hit record for me?"

April rolls up to the phone, using the joystick on her electric wheelchair to guide her, and hits the red button.

"Hello to all my fans, and anyone else who has been unfortunate enough to drink one of the tainted bottles of NatFit in the last twenty-four hours. I've been instructed to make an apology video, but first, I want to start by telling you a story. Most of you have never seen my face without makeup before, and in the last few years, you've probably never even seen what I look like behind filters. Hell, I'm not even allowed to post my own content without it passing through several levels of approval and touch-ups. But this is what I actually look like, and these are my scars. When I was twelve years old, I was walking home through a park and got attacked by a dog. It tore up my face along my jaw here, my forehead above my right eyebrow, and another place I'd rather not show on camera. I'll never really understand why the dog attacked me, and not a day goes by in my life that I don't think about it.

"It took me five years of practicing makeup daily until I reached the point where I could completely cover up the scars and make myself look like the person I wanted to be. I got a job at a beauty counter at Macy's and started doing makeup tutorials on YouTube, mostly for practice. Now, here we are, all these years later, and I can't even think of the last time I posted anything just for me. I wanted to share this story, not to try and garner pity from any of you, but to illustrate a point that sometimes bad things happen. I can't go back in time and change what happened to me. It's something I've learned to live with, even though it affects me every day. Each morning, I have to wake up and look at this in the mirror and make the choice that I'm going to be okay. And some days, that's really hard.

"I'm horrified to think of what many of you are going through because you made the decision to believe in me, and I let you down. I know a lot of you are looking at my face on that bottle right now, as you're suffering through what I understand to be an extremely aggressive form of food poisoning. I realize that after you recover from this, you may recall this horrible experience you've had whenever you see my face. I get it. I also have a negative reaction every time I see this face.

"So here's my real apology. I'm truly sorry that something bad has happened to a number of people who drank NatFit. But just like that day when I was twelve, this is something that's happened, and there's no way to go back and undo it. If that means you don't want to watch my videos or buy my products in the future, I completely understand.

"Unlike, unsubscribe. Call me Tawny Toilet, or whatever you want. I promise to do better in the future to make sure something like this never happens again. Thank you."

I step forward and turn off the recording.

"What do you think?"

April's face is frozen in surprise. "I mean, it's something. I can't believe I'm saying this, but do you maybe want to try one where you read the scripted apology?"

"You think it's too honest?"

April stares at my feet while twirling her hair. "It's both too honest and not honest at all, in all the wrong places."

"Obviously we can't tell the real story of how we got our scars, but it's close enough that I feel like at least some of the sentiment comes through, right?"

"I already told you, I don't want you to say anything about it as long as it can come back to haunt us. It's not just your story to tell, and we already know the Pandora's box we open if we bring it up. I understand that you lie for a living, and I'm fine with it, but this affects both of us, and I'm not okay with you opening up this door again, especially in front of millions of people." There's something else that's on the tip of her tongue. She would never say it, but I know we're both hearing it.

Good dogs keep their mouths shut.

The look in her eyes snaps me back from whatever temporary insanity I was just experiencing. "Of course, I'll delete it right now." I tap the little image of the trash can next to the video. "You really think I should just go with Maggie's version of the apology?"

April snorts out a laugh. "Heck no. That thing's even worse than what you just shot. How about we use hers as a template and write something that doesn't sound like it's coming from a corporate robot?"

I check the time. "Are you sure? Shouldn't you be at the movie right now?"

While I may not be excited for *Slashtag*, April—and what seems like the rest of the world—are extremely hyped for it. In anticipation of the event, theaters have re-released *Murder Mansion*, a disastrous reboot of a campy classic based on the hotel where *Slashtag* is to take place. It starred the upcoming *Slashtag* cast member Landon Keating as a serial killer, delivering one of the most gonzo performances since Nic Cage in *Vampire's Kiss*.

"It's only fun if we're seeing the movie together," April says. "If I watch it alone, I won't have anyone to gripe to about how they ruined the whole thing with the demonic amulet sub-plot. Half the fun is having someone for me to complain to. If you're telling a story based on a real person, you can't just give him magic powers."

"I know," I say, hearing her once again start up on a soapbox rant she's given at least a hundred times.

"I wonder if they're going to find a way to force the amulet into *Slashtag*. I bet you a hundred dollars they do. Hollywood always doubles down on the dumbest ideas."

"Probably." I regret bringing up *Slashtag*, not because of her strong opinions on the movie, but because of what I've neglected to mention. I can only give her one-word answers as a ball of guilt forms in my stomach, which I try to ignore.

But, of course, she senses my shift immediately.

Her eyes narrow. "You're not telling me something."

While I've become quite good over the years at lying to my audience, there's one person in this world who can always call me out in a second. "I need to tell you something. I was sort of invited to be on *Slashtag* today."

"You *what!*" she screams.

"I'm not doing it."

"Why the heck not?"

"For the same reason you didn't want me to talk about being attacked. This is a Krentler Media production. It's obviously a trap built purely to humiliate us."

"Wait, wait, wait, wait, wait," April says, pumping her open palms in the air and squeezing her eyes shut. "We've been watching horror movies every night and weekend for twenty years, including three separate films about this very hotel, and you're not even going to entertain the idea of being part of it?"

"You know who's on the board of directors. It's already hard enough having all our social networks monopolized by those evil pricks. I'm not going to throw myself at the mercy of whatever sick game they have planned."

"But Tawny, think of all the other people that are going to be there. Chef Costanza, Landon Keating. I mean, Britt Holley is going to be there. No offense, but these people are way more famous than you."

"So?"

"If they're bringing in Britt Holley, there's no way it can be that bad. Why would the most pampered reality star in America sign up for this if it wasn't going to be legit?"

I feel the ball of guilt grow heavier as April gets so excited that her chest starts heaving. If our roles were reversed, I know she would give anything to live out a horror movie on live TV.

"I know you think this is really cool, despite the people running it. You have to understand that, if I did this, it wouldn't be because of fun or social climbing. People are pissed at me all over the country. My role there would be as a whipping girl. It's a platform to take me down a peg or two in front of millions of people so that everyone can work out their aggression against me by watching me be the butt of some high-budget prank."

April's face shifts to one of actual frustration, something I rarely see from her. "Okay, so you're saying your act of penance is to hang out with a bunch of celebrities at a house haunted by one of our favorite slasher-movie villains and solve escape room puzzles? Jesus, what crimes do *I* have to commit to get invited on *Slashtag*?"

"You're missing the huge red flag planted right in front of the door. *Slashtag* is literally an event run by the worst humans imaginable. I don't want to have anything to do with Krentler Media."

April's fingers are twirling her hair so fast, she might just take off like a helicopter. "Look, even though the video you shot was really truly terrible—like, death by word-vomit asphyxiation bad—you did have one good point about how you have to make that choice to be okay. Nobody's going to disagree with you that the world is terrible and getting worse every day, but we can't let that stop us from living our lives. This isn't something we can just choose to avoid, like Chick-fil-A. In like, three days, Social is literally going to be the only platform out there. We're either going to have to make peace with the fact that it's run by a group of trash people or sit and stew in impotent rage until we lose our frickin' minds. I don't know about you, but I know what I'm going to choose."

I hate it when she uses my words to make me sound like I know what I'm talking about. Still, I've made enough concessions in my life already. "I just don't know if I can do it. Doing anything that directly supports Krentler Media's board of directors feels like a bridge too far. If there was any way for me to transfer this onto you, I would."

I do feel a little bad for complaining about the event itself. Hosts aside, it really does sound like something tailor-made for my sister. She already believes she could enter a horror film at any moment and come out triumphant, and she's probably right. Even in a wheelchair, April is still tougher than ninety percent of the other cast members.

At one point in my life, I would have jumped at this opportunity, but being a fan of horror and puzzles were hobbies that ran counter to the interests of my target demographics. As I worked my way to become a brand representative of high-class makeup and yoga pants, Maggie became more and more restrictive of the pastimes I was allowed to enjoy. I can't quite pinpoint the exact moment I made peace with giving up my personality for an on-screen persona, though the last horror movie I remember posting about was *The VVitch*, if that gives any indication.

"Look, I know you're really excited about this opportunity, and you're going to think I'm making a huge mistake here. But I have to follow my gut. They want to put me on display in front of millions of people, when right now, all I want to do is disappear."

April nods, looking crestfallen. "All right, I understand. If you don't want to do it, I won't keep pushing."

"Thanks." We both share a moment of awkward silence. I don't want to let this ruin our night. "So, I need to get working on another version of this apology video. How about afterwards, we can watch *Murder Mansion* on the couch and just pretend we're on *Slashtag?*"

April's mouth rounds into a petulant curl. "Fine. But I get to gripe the whole time about the outlandish nature of the demonic possession arc."

CHAPTER SIX

From: Casting@Krentler.media
To: Ron.M@Krentler.media
Subject: Ms. Howlett

Hi Ron,

I just got off the phone with Tawny Howlett's agent and it's looking increasingly unlikely that she will be involved in the *Slashtag* program. As I'm sure you're aware, we are just 3 days away from the event and we need to secure our final cast member. I understand Tawny was your top choice. She scores very highly in affluent girls and gay men aged 14-40. Additionally, the number of her followers who are influencers themselves are likely to push viewership to their followers, opening her up to a much wider audience than the 19 million she currently has.

That being said, we have already announced that there will be seven cast members, and unless we lock someone in within the next 24 hours, we run a very real risk of being unable to fill that spot with a subject of comparable quality. I've spoken with our marketing team about finding a replacement that still pulls a similar demographic, and they feel confident there are a number of potentials who can fill her role. You can see a list of recommendations in the attached document.

Please confirm whether or not we can move forward on re-casting Tawny.

Thanks,

Carol

From: Ron.M@Krentler.media
To: Casting@Krentler.media

Carol,

We always knew she would be difficult to persuade.

Let me reiterate that Tawny is absolutely essential to our cast. If she were not, I wouldn't have gone through the effort of landing her in this controversy in the first place. It was my belief that the stick would be the most effective approach, but if that is not the case then I suggest we try the carrot. I'm giving you authorization to propose the secondary offer.

Please let me know when she accepts...

Ron

CHAPTER SEVEN

It ended up taking almost three hours for Tawny and me to write and film her new apology video last night. In the end, we struck what I think was a good balance between the insane apology Maggie had written and the even crazier one my sister had concocted. After posting it straight to Social without notifying Maggie, we both agreed to turn off our phones, pour a couple of tall glasses of wine, and mercilessly make fun of the abomination that is *Murder Mansion.*

Tawny made it maybe fifteen minutes into the movie before passing out, though after the day she had, I wasn't going to hold it against her.

When I got up and back into my chair this morning, she was still conked out on the couch, a true rarity for her. Normally, Tawny's the one up at the crack of dawn, waking me by grinding up her daily smoothie in the blender. All things considered, I decide it's maybe best if I handle breakfast this morning. No smoothies. Instead, I feel it's a good time to break out the big guns: scrambled eggs and a big honkin' plate of cured meaty goodness.

I push myself out of the chair, balancing on my bony legs as I reach up to shove the plate of bacon into the microwave. It's not like I'm totally paralyzed—I can stand or walk if I really have to. I just get exhausted easily, thanks to a pair of bum kidneys that haven't worked since I was a kid. Getting stabbed multiple times in an attempt to stop your sister from being kidnapped will do that to you, I guess.

I'm just about to surprise her with breakfast in bed when the door-bell rings.

The way our house is set up, I can see anyone at the door through a set of blinds around the corner. Standing in front of our home is Tawny's employee/boss, Maggie. I'm guessing she wasn't a fan of our video and is likely even less a fan of Tawny having turned her phone off. Maggie may be Tawny's kryptonite when it comes to standing up for herself, but I can safely say I have zero reservations about telling Maggie how I feel.

I take a second to prepare for her to come at me with a hurricane of stress and urgency. While I know it's her job and everything, she always treats Tawny's internet popularity like it's a life-or-death situation. It gives a bad name to those of us who actually have played a round of chess with the Grim Reaper.

Opening the door, I am surprised to see that Maggie is smiling. It looks unnatural on her. To be completely honest, I wasn't sure she even had the capacity to feel joy.

"Morning, Maggie. Isn't it a little early for house calls?"

Maggie's grin fades slightly when she realizes it's me at the door and not her client, but it's not enough to bring her back to a resting frowny face. "Is your sister around?" She butts her head into the house, hoping to bypass talking to me altogether. Her eyes narrow. "Do I smell bacon?"

"That vegetarian stuff is just for the public. In the Howlett house-hold, we go full-carnivore."

"Lovely. Where is she? I've been calling her all morning."

"Tawny's taking a mental health day. I'll be her representative for the time being. Did you not like the video?" It takes a modicum of effort to stifle a smirk. I don't know what it is about her, but I just can't help myself from acting like a brat around Maggie.

"Fuck the video. I've got bigger news. Actually, it's good that you're here. I think you may be just the person I want to talk to, after all."

Well, this is new. Maggie usually treats me like a sub-human parasite. Apparently, loving your chronically ill sister isn't popular on social media, and generally, Maggie works hard to make it seem like I don't exist.

"What's going on? You're never happy to see me."

"Well, today I am, and I have a feeling you're about to get pretty excited too. How would you like a new pair of kidneys?"

I feel like I've been kicked in the chest, promptly forgetting how to breathe. All at once, my mouth is too dry to even form a response.

"I'll give you a minute to pick your jaw up off the floor," Maggie says, while looking smug.

"What are you talking about?"

She pulls a phone from her purse, flashing an email in front of me with words that are far too small to read. It seems all the moisture that was in my mouth has traveled up into my eyes, making the whole world go blurry.

"After relaying the message that Tawny was reluctant to participate in *Slashtag*, they countered with this offer." Maggie turns the phone back to herself and scans the message until she finds a section to read aloud. "Here at Krentler Media, we understand that nothing is more important than family and understand Tawny's concerns regarding the health of her sister. It's our understanding—blah, blah, blah—doesn't want to leave her alone for too long...Here it is. In addition to Tawny's fee, Krentler Media is prepared to guarantee that her sister, April, will receive a new pair of kidneys, just for Tawny participating in *Slashtag*, with all medical fees included."

"But that's not how it works...You can't just promise someone new kidneys. There's a list."

"Honey, these are the same people who just bought every social media company in the country. You don't think they have the connections to get you a fresh set of kidneys?"

I'm absolutely speechless. All I can do is repeat my incredulity in clipped phrases.

Now Maggie is the one smirking. "Do you maybe want to go get your sister now?"

"Yeah, um. Can I just see that again?" I ask, even though I never really saw it the first time. Maggie hands me her phone. I scroll back up to the top and start reading the email. I'm about halfway through, when Maggie interrupts me with another heart-stopping surprise.

"By the way, did Tawny mention the *Slashtag* offer to anyone else?"

I shake my head. "Just me and D-wreck. Why?"

Maggie reaches back into her purse and pulls out a stuffed animal. It's a black dog with a brown beaded eye missing. "I found this on your doorstep. It had a note attached that says, 'Can't wait to see you.' Do you know what this is about?"

Yes. It's just like all the other gifts our stalker has sent us over the last two decades.

"No," I say. "Not a clue. Listen, I'm going to go get Tawny and let you tell her the good news. Can you do me a favor, though? Get rid of the toy, and don't say a word about it to her, okay?"

CHAPTER EIGHT

I'm sitting in a limousine, heading out for the desert with nothing but a Lululemon sports outfit and my phone. Though I still can't believe it, I'm on my way to participate in *Slashtag*.

After eighteen years of waiting, a decade of donations and constant attempts to pull every string I possibly can, I've finally been offered the chance to repay my sister for saving my life. At that point, there was no deliberation to be made, no question of the morality of working for the devil. Everyone has a price, and they found mine.

For the next few hours, I have nothing but time to stare at my phone and read people's comments to Maggie's PR blitz promoting my upcoming appearance on *Slashtag*. From what I understand, as soon as I arrive at the location, I will lose access to my phone for the duration of the three-day event. I might as well soak it all in now. Responses so far are a curious mix of both my supporters and detractors, for once coming together to celebrate my impending humiliation.

Scrolling through comments is far and away the worst part of my job. Typically, I receive two kinds of comments to my posts. The first are the ones intended to make me feel worthless, denigrated, and frequently in danger for my life. Many of these comments are from what appear to be straight white men who range in eloquence from, "I'd bang her if she wiped all that skank shit off her face," to the classic "Get fucked and die." These ones are easier to reconcile, as they're mostly from incel trolls just looking for attention. It's the comments from women that are typically a bit more well-thought-out and biting. A few of them I still replay in my head at night, the words forever burned into my head.

IMO Tawny Howlett is a bad person. She is out of touch, selfish, self-obsessed, materialistic, and rude. She has no humility and lacks self-awareness.

Somehow, the only comments I find worse than trolls are the ones from kids who find me inspirational. For as much as I think about all the hate people have for me around the world, what makes me feel even worse are the comments from young girls who think my social media identity is the real me, that my meticulously crafted lie of a lifestyle is one they could realistically attain. I've lost count of the number of young faces in YouTube comment sections making posts like: *Tawny inspires me to be my best and most beautiful self.*

Each video that goes up on my channel has thousands of these types of comments, and at a certain point, I have to stop looking at them before it makes me want to throw up. If only some of these people knew me in real life, they would see there's absolutely nothing here worth all their praise. I'm just a girl who can do a pretty good job of putting on my own makeup, with an entire team of storytellers and visual effects artists working around the clock to turn me into an idea of a person who literally can't exist in the real world.

All it really took was being okay with giving up the person I used to be...

"Are you just going to stare at your phone this whole ride, or are we here to party?"

I pull my head out of my phone as D-wreck grabs a bottle of champagne from a mini fridge. Sitting next to him is Kawaii Kiki, one of the few participants I actually had to research prior to heading out on this adventure. Apparently, she's extremely well known in the cosplay circuit. It's a fandom that completely eludes me. While I may be mostly up-to-date on horror releases, I couldn't tell you the first thing about trends in video games, superheroes, or anime.

Kiki is a small Asian girl, probably no taller than five feet, with bright pink hair and an even brighter orange dress. She's wearing a neon purple fuzzy overcoat that reminds me of Marla Singer's jacket from *Fight Club*—if the jacket had been made from the skin of the old McDonald's mascot, Grimace.

At D-wreck's suggestion, Kiki drops her phone into one of her coat's massive pockets and lights up with excitement.

"Fill it to the top!" Kiki exclaims, making her shoulders dance.

D pours champagne into three flutes, and we all hold them out in a toast.

"To whatever the hell we've all gotten ourselves into!"

"I'll cheers to that." I take a sip of the drink and feel a rush of tiny bubbles tickle my nose.

Kiki manages to drain her entire flute in one big gulp.

"So, on a scale of one to six-six-six, how scared are you guys for this?" she says in a slightly adorable Australian accent. "I'm, like, the biggest baby when it comes to horror. I can barely even handle some episodes of *Black Mirror*, and those aren't even that bad."

"I'm actually pretty excited," D says. "I hear there's a hidden spider-themed whorehouse, and it's my mission to find it. Though, I guess I'm gonna have to at least pretend to be freaked out once I'm inside."

"Yeah, I know that game. I'm gonna have to toss these before going in. Bad for my image." Kiki pulls a pack of Camel cigarettes from one of her bottomless coat pockets and tucks them into a cupholder. "D-wreck, do you like horror games? For some reason, even though I'm a wimp when it comes to movies, as soon as you put me in control of the character, it's a totally different story."

The two of them get into a lively debate over games I've never heard of. I can't help but notice that, as Kiki gets excited, she raises her tone at the end of each sentence, as if she's asking a question. It's not a big deal right now, but it's one of those pet peeves that has a chance of getting on my nerves quickly.

That glass of champagne has opened a floodgate, and Kiki is sharing every detail of her multitudes of fandoms. I know that the moment I leave this car, I'm going to be livestreamed non-stop for upward of seventy-two hours, and I was really hoping to be able to enjoy a quiet car ride to mentally and physically prepare myself.

It seems D-wreck and Kiki have other plans.

I check my maps app to see how long of a drive it is to the ghost town of Dire. We're still roughly four hours from our destination. Just as I'm starting to feel the first real bout of anxiety, I get a text from April that reads *Final Girl for life!*, followed by a gif of Buffy the Vampire Slayer smashing a skeleton with a sledgehammer.

I quickly text her back. *At this rate, I'm not sure I'm even going to make it to the house. I'm currently trapped in a car with Kawaii Kiki. She is a lot.*

Within ten seconds, I get a reply. *Hey, it could always be worse. You could be trapped in the car with Franklin Hardesty.*

I snort out a small giggle. She's referring to a guy from *The Texas Chainsaw Massacre* who is notorious for being one of the most obnoxious characters in the history of the genre.

The hardest part of this whole thing is going to be the inability to have any contact with April. Even when I have to travel for work, I don't think we've ever gone more than twenty-four hours without talking to each other.

Kiki brings my attention away from the phone as she leans over and places both her hands on my knees. "So, I have to ask, are you two really a couple? Like, for real-real?"

"Me and Tawny? Of course, we are. We are deeply in love." D-wreck answers for me, matching Kiki's conspiratorial tone. He looks around the limo before continuing. "I'll even let you in on a little secret. I'm pregnant."

Kiki rolls her eyes and leans back in her seat. "Okay, that's what I thought. This is all a PR thing, isn't it?"

"What gave it away?" I ask, appreciating what little time I have left to engage in an honest conversation.

"I mean, we've been in the car for, like, half an hour, and the two of you have barely even spoken. You're not even sitting next to each other."

"Whelp, you got us," I say, putting my hands up as if I were caught red-handed. "Just do me a favor and don't say anything about it inside the hotel."

"Moi?" Kiki says, feigning offense and clutching her hand to her chest. "I would never stand between the fake love of two people joined by the sanctity of public relations. I guess that's the only good thing about being a fetishized sex icon for nerds. It boosts my numbers to be eternally single. So do you guys, like, have all sorts of rules for your fake dating and stuff?"

I check back at my maps app. An upcoming crash on the freeway has added twenty minutes to our estimated arrival time.

Fantastic.

CHAPTER NINE

Dripfeed *Presents: From Reality Royalty to Scream Queen—Britt Holley's Newest Series Swaps Glam for Gore*

In the world of reality TV, few names are more recognized worldwide than that of Britt Holley. Britt became an overnight sensation at the age of 10 when she became the breakout star of the mother-daughter reality series Drama Mamas. After five years on the show, she got her first spinoff series, Welcome to Holleywood *moving from her home state of Texas to California to pursue her career in acting.*

While she never seemed to land more than glorified cameos in teen comedies, Welcome to Holleywood *rocketed her to reality TV stardom. Eventually, she met up with her future ex-husband, pop star Gage Preston, who went from an occasional cameo to full on co-star in her next series* Holleywooed. *The series premiered in 2016, chronicling the ups and downs of their relationship. The show ran for three seasons until their marriage ended; however, even that couldn't keep Britt from dominating our television screens. In 2020, the rest of her family made the move from Texas to LA to star alongside Britt in* The Beverly Holleys *on the KMC network.*

And now, in a move seemingly coming out of nowhere, Britt is gearing up for what will perhaps be the greatest challenge in her career—competing on the upcoming horror/reality hybrid series, Slashtag, *premiering this Friday on both the KMC network and simulcast as an interactive livestreaming event on Social. Aside from a brief role in the horror comedy* Chucky vs. Jason, *this will be Holley's first foray into the world of horror, and here at* Dripfeed, *we absolutely cannot be more excited.*

CHAPTER TEN

Our limo pulls onto a dirt road that ends in a massive chain link fence. Barbed wire runs as far as I can see in either direction. Several guards with hip-holstered pistols stand at attention on either side of a liftgate, which is operated by another guard in a box. He nods at the limo driver, and then moments later, we pass through the security station. Ahead of us is a huge, dilapidated sign reading: *Welcome to historical Dire California, Est. 1848.*

"Was that weird to anyone else?" I ask.

Kiki seems unconcerned. "What, the security? I don't know. I'd reckon that seems pretty normal for a location where a bunch of celebrities are filming."

"But what about the fence? Do you think they built it to surround the entire town?"

"Probably to hold back all of our adoring fans," D-wreck says after finishing off the last sip of his drink. "Oh man, I'm so fucking ready for this!" He looks over to me for confirmation, and his eyes soften for just a second. "You good?" he says, like a real boyfriend might.

"Totally." I give him a reassuring nod, even though my stomach is threatening to do a backflip. I quickly turn away so he doesn't have time to catch the obvious lie plastered across my face.

Through the window, I can see a line of crumbling wooden buildings. Each one has a faded or broken sign denoting general stores, an old bank, even a town jail.

At the end of the dirt path sits the main attraction, which stands out entirely from the decrepit ghost town. Whereas most of the buildings are made up of old, rotting wood, this building looks like it's been plucked from time. It's a massive Victorian-style hotel painted a crisp olive green, with rich red accents lining the windows, doors, and steepled wood-shingle roof. It stands at nearly triple the height of the rest of the buildings and stretches out wide enough that most mansions in Beverly Hills would be jealous of the square footage. On each of the building's corners stand tall, rounded spires. They're all identical, except for the frontmost left one, which rises an extra level from its counterparts.

I know the history of this hotel, of the hundreds of grisly murders that took place throughout the twentieth century. This building has appeared in movies, documentaries, and countless Reddit threads. I'd imagined that, upon seeing it in real life, I'd feel some sense of unease, dread, maybe even macabre revelry. Maybe I'm just too desensitized to horror at this point, but in the moment, the Propitius Hotel feels more like a Disneyland attraction than a historical house of horrors.

The limo pulls up in front, and moments later, the driver opens the door for us to step onto the dirt. I look over to D-wreck and Kiki, both staring in awe at the building—so much so that, for the first time in hours, Kiki's mouth isn't moving.

D-wreck turns to us with a devilish grin. "Let's goooooo!"

I wish I could muster the same level of excitement, but mostly, I just feel disappointed April couldn't be here to see this in person.

The front door to the Hotel swings open, and a blonde woman in a gray pantsuit comes rushing out to greet us. She's a little older than me, maybe mid-thirties, and has a perfect plaster smile—a hallmark of any good TV host. She's holding a large black tablet, and the juxtaposition of history and modern sensibility only furthers to pull me out of whatever emotion I'm supposed to be feeling.

"Welcome to The Propitius, and the first ever season of *Slashtag*! I'm Lucy, your host for the weekend. You three are the last to arrive, so I'm going to ask that you tie up any last Social posts or final messages to your loved ones now. When you're done, I'm going to need to collect your phones, and you won't be getting them back until after *Slashtag* is over."

There's only one person I want to message, but the knowledge this will be our last communication for the next few days causes my brain to go blank. The text I end up sending April reads: *About to step into the Murder Mansion and lose my phone. Remember, you have dialysis at 4 today, and the nephrologist tomorrow morning. Don't be afraid to ask Hector if you need anything at all. Love you!*

I wait in anxious silence for April to respond as D-wreck and Kiki post things to Social. By the time Lucy thrusts a bag out for us to drop our phones into, I feel mine buzz one last time. April's message reads: *Don't worry about me. I promise to hide all the valuables before the orgy ;). Love you sis, and don't forget we've been training for this all our lives. Now get in that haunted hotel and win this thing.*

I drop the phone into the bag, only to be handed a new one with my name etched across the back.

"Here," Lucy says. "Every contestant gets one of these. There's no service available, just a few apps to help during the show. Don't lose it."

"Does it have any games?" D-wreck asks while he fidgets with his.

"Save it for the cameras," she says, without a hint of amusement. "You got three apps. Notes, Flashlight, Camera. That's it. Everybody ready?"

"How do I charge it?" Kiki inspects it for buttons and ports.

"You won't need to," Lucy says. "It's designed to last you through the weekend."

I check my new phone, locating all the expected buttons, but am surprised to see a fourth app labeled: *For Tawny*. I tap it, and a message flashes in giant text across my screen. It's only there for a few seconds, but that's all it takes for such an intense shiver to run through me that I nearly drop the phone. By the time I recover it, the message is gone, along with the app entirely.

But the message remains clearly in my head, just as it has every other time I've received it from Him over the last eighteen years.

"I said, is everybody ready?" Lucy repeats. She's standing on the porch, next to the bright red door.

I want to turn and run away, to tell her that no, I am *not* now, nor will I ever be ready. This was a terrible idea from the second I heard it, and if I go in here, I'll be making the biggest mistake of my life.

I take a deep centering breath and remind myself why I'm here in the first place. "Yeah, sorry. I'm ready." I climb the stairs to the front porch and join Lucy by the door. As long as April gets her kidneys, I'll let them do whatever they want, and I'll take it with a grin. I won't say one nasty thing about the monsters running the show because, as the message reminded me, *good dogs keep their mouths shut.*

CHAPTER ELEVEN

THE RULES

Congratulations on being selected to compete in the first-ever Slashtag *event hosted by Krentler Media. You will soon be stepping into the most immersive—and expensive—haunted house experience ever conceived. As such, there are a few simple rules to keep in mind:*

1. *You will be on camera at ALL times, with one exception. For privacy, there is no video or audio recording equipment in the restrooms.*
2. *You will be expected to stay "in character" at all times. There are situations you will encounter during the event that will be upsetting, disturbing, and occasionally gory. While Krentler Media's aim is to create an intense horror experience for its cast and viewers, it may at times feel questionable whether you are experiencing reality or fiction. We ask that you kindly refrain from questioning if aspects of the experience are real or fake with other cast members, as it could damage the immersion of the experience.*
3. *Personal phones and smart devices of any kind are strictly prohibited. No smoking, vaping, outside food or drinks are allowed. We*

recommend wearing something comfortable, as you will not have an opportunity to change until filming has wrapped.

4. *Once started,* Slashtag *will continue uninterrupted until either a winner—or winners—is declared or 72 hours have passed, upon which all remaining contestants will be eliminated.*

5. *Krentler Media is not responsible for any accidents or injuries sustained at The Propitius. While many precautions have been taken to bring the hotel up to safety code, it is an old building, and it can be dangerous.*

6. *If you are found breaking any of these rules, you may be punished in a variety of ways, including immediate expulsion from the experience, forfeiting all donations to the charity of your choice and/or initiating an immediate permanent ban from using the Social platform.*

CHAPTER TWELVE

The entry hall to The Propitius is smaller than I expected from the pictures I've seen, and entirely different from the huge foyer depicted in *Murder Mansion*. The so-called grand staircase wraps around the left wall, just wide enough to climb single file. It forms an awning overhead leading into the hotel. In the center of the half-helix formed by the staircase hangs a sparkling chandelier that, while likely impressive in the 1920's, isn't terribly fancy by today's standards. The walls are covered in a crisp burgundy wallpaper decorated with a repeating pattern of golden fleur-de-lis. Aside from the corridor passing under the staircase, there are openings to my immediate left and right leading down stretching hallways lit by electric candelabras.

The lobby feels especially congested, thanks to the group of people packed into the space. Everyone is excitedly talking to each other, their voices reverberating off the walls and making the room feel even more claustrophobic. The whole situation is immediately overwhelming. Outside, this place felt just like any other old building, but now, it's starting to really hit me that I'm actually at the real Propitius hotel. And it's not just the building—my knees almost start to tremble as I recognize the famous faces all around me.

The first person I notice is a large Black man standing a full head and a half taller than everyone else in the room. He's Shawn Eamon, a former NFL player I remember being at the center of some controversy a couple years ago. Shawn is talking to Landon Keating, a movie star who has been famous ever since he was a child actor. I always imagined him to be at least six-feet, but in reality, he's barely five-six, made slightly taller by having his blonde hair balled up into a man bun. Landon's always been thin, but ever since he became the butt of a popular internet meme, his cheeks have become hollow, and his complexion is so pale he almost glows in the dim light.

Conversely, Britt Holley is exactly as glamorous as one would expect. She's been a reality queen for as long as people have been lining up to get exploited on TV. Britt's wearing a black low-cut bodysuit, showing off her cleavage, with a pair of white athleisure sweatpants custom-tailored to look just the slightest bit baggy. Despite the somber lighting in the room, her eyes are hidden behind an oversized pair of black Balenciaga sunglasses. I can only guess how much she was paid by these companies just to show up wearing these brands.

The last contestant almost makes me jump in comparison to the rest of the beauties. He's wearing a large rubber mask of a bald man with cartoonishly caricatured features. Truth be told, of all the people here, he is probably the person I've actually spent the most time watching. Chef Costanza has made a name for himself by keeping his true identity a mystery. The recipes he's shared on his YouTube channel aren't only practiced by aspiring home cooks around the country; some of them have even appeared in Michelin-star restaurants, which only furthers the rabid speculation that he could secretly be a celebrity chef, like Michael Symon or Richard Blais.

I know I've had quite the career myself, but I feel like an amateur compared to some of this lineup of fame. These people are in movies and TV, considered by some to be at the top of the ladder in their respective areas. Then here I am, a girl who's pretty good at doing makeup and showing off yoga poses.

Lucy strides with confidence into the center of the room and claps her hands together. The cast immediately cut their conversations and form a circle around her.

"All right, everyone, I know you're all excited to get started, so let's get right to it. Welcome to *Slashtag*—the first-ever hybrid mega event from Social and the KMC network. I'm your host, Lucy Hodge, and I want to humbly thank you all for joining us." Lucy is speaking into a mirror on the wall at the base of the stairs, where I'm assuming a camera lies hidden. "I'm thrilled to announce that, just for showing up, each of you has earned a fifty-thousand-dollar donation to the charity of your choice. However, any contestants who manage to escape the hotel will earn an additional ten million dollar donation to your foundation from Krentler Media. That's right. This is a fully cooperative experience, which means every competitor who makes it out alive will be considered a winner. I know you're all itching to get started—"

Her words are interrupted by the sound of the front door clacking its deadbolt into place.

It's a cheap jump scare, but it seems to do the trick. Britt lets out a startled yip and throws her hand to her chest.

"Oh my God," she says, laughing at herself.

Landon laughs too, but it feels more *at* her than with her.

Lucy's plumped lips stretch into what I'm sure she believes to be a devious smile. "It seems someone else is excited for you all to be here too. The spirit that haunts this hotel has been trapped in these walls for over sixty years, and it's going to be up to the seven of you to either send his soul to hell, or die trying. Ladies and gentlemen, I give you the greatest serial killer of all time, Arthur Wilson."

The lights dim, and Lucy gestures over to the mirror, which fades from reflective glass into an opaque gray. A sepia-soaked video begins to roll. Saloon-style piano music accompanies the flickering screen, coming from hidden speakers all around us.

CHAPTER THIRTEEN

The Life and Death of Arthur Wilson, Part 1

A man in a brown tweed suit and bowler hat, with thick round spectacles, stands at the entrance to the Propitius Hotel. He inspects the walls, as if appreciating the recent construction of the building, then pulls from his coat pocket a small candy, which he pops into his mouth. The honky-tonk soundtrack eases back, and an over-the-top radio announcer's voice cuts in, sounding like he has come straight from a World War II propaganda video.

"The year is 1916. The Gold Rush has dried up in most places; however, business is booming in Dire, California, and none are seeing profits soar more than the Wilson Family. Arthur, son of town founder, John Wilson, opens his doors to The Propitius, a building which he claims will keep the town prosperous for generations to come. To the gold miners, their families, and local business owners, Arthur Wilson is the very embodiment of the American dream, a provider of comfort and luxuries found nowhere else in the western frontier. Why, even the hotel's name holds a promise of hope and a bright future.

"However, there also lurked a darker side. To the drifters, strays, and folks down on their luck, Wilson is better known as the architect to their American nightmare. Like his father, young Arthur had hopes of becoming a doctor, but it was said that while John was dedicated to the pursuit of preventing death, Arthur was much more interested in its cause."

Two men in white outfits, with aprons and rubber gloves, stand over a body. They're moving just slightly too fast, as if the film was recorded using an old crank handle that didn't sync up perfectly to real life. Cut to an insert of two pairs of gloves making an incision down a bare male's torso. One set of hands places a retractor clamp inside the cavity to hold the skin apart, while the other reaches around inside his body and handles a number of internal organs. Cut back to the two men standing over the body, where the taller of the two masked surgeons shakes his head in disappointment and points out of the room. Arthur hangs his head in shame and walks out of the scene.

"The Propitius became a hotspot for people to celebrate their windfalls or drown in their misfortunes. Having been in charge of construction, Arthur had drawn plans for the building, filling it with a number of hidden pathways and secret chambers. It was in these rooms he would perform gruesome experiments on drifters and deadbeats, away from the watchful eye of his father. Famously, he would cover up the smell of decaying bodies in the walls by having a number of cigar rooms strategically located throughout the property, which had air vents running to a number of common spaces."

A group of mustached men in vintage suits smoke large cigars in a parlor, followed by a shot of a pair of female guests walking down a hall. They stop and sniff at the air. Their noses shrivel up in disgust, and they pinch their nostrils. Behind them, an ovular hole appears in the wall, revealing Arthur Wilson sawing the leg off a corpse on an operating table. After a few seconds, the x-ray effect on the wall fades away, and the two offended women in the hall scurry offscreen.

Quick cut to a basement, where several police officers are standing over a dirt pit, shaking their heads in disgust.

"In 1928, a tank in Wilson's secret moonshine distillery exploded, leading to the discovery of thirty-two bodies buried underground. Though the authorities conducted an exhaustive search, Wilson was never found, and the Propitius Hotel closed its doors for good. Or at least, that's what they thought."

Cut to black. The music shifts from a saloon piano to an organ with accompanying gospel singers in the background. The orange sepia color tone fades away as a new cue card appears on the screen.

The Life and Death Of Arthur Wilson, Part 2: Sutter's Return

A black and white montage of stock footage plays: Martin Luther King, Jr. speaks at a podium, hippies dance in the mud at music festivals, and thousands of women march through Washington. Despite the quality of film changing, the canned radio announcer's voice remains the same.

"The year is 1965, and sweeping change is in the air as Americans across the country fight for civil rights and freedom of expression. While this remains a popular sentiment across a wide portion of the nation, there is another movement coming together in the form of The Church of the Eighth Sin, led by a man claiming to be one Reverend Arthur Sutter. Inspired heavily by the teachings of the Old Testament and traditional conservative values, Sutter builds a small but loyal following, preaching the opposite of popular progressive agendas. Sutter rebukes these modern sensibilities, citing his discovery of an eighth sin as his reasoning. He also bears a striking resemblance to an aging Arthur Wilson."

The left half of the screen is consumed by a stony-faced Arthur Wilson standing in front of the Propitius, while the right side features a picture of an older white man, with thin wisps of hair combed over his liver-spotted scalp. His eyes are hidden behind a similar pair of thick, black-framed glasses, and his mouth reveals a mess of crooked and missing teeth. While his wardrobe is different, consisting of a traditional priest's robe with a white collar, there is a metal pendant hanging from his neck, with a large jewel in the center. It looks almost identical to a trinket Arthur is holding in his picture.

The screen cuts to a video of the elder Arthur standing in a church, delivering a sermon to a large congregation of white people dressed in their Sunday best.

"My good God-fearing people, I have come here today to tell you of the eighth, and possibly most deadly sin of all, and that is the sin of defiance. I tell you there is no greater betrayal to your pact with God than to disobey his words and the words of those he has entrusted to speak on his behalf. I see young men and women every day in the news, going out and protesting for civil rights against the wishes of their good Christian parents. Indeed, there is far greater room in Hell than there is in Heaven, and Satan himself is ready with open arms to accept those who betray their fathers."

Cut to a shot of the now-aged Arthur leading his congregation into the town of Dire, before he stands on the front porch of the hotel. His arms are outstretched as if he himself were Jesus.

The radio announcer resumes. "And so, Arthur Wilson once again returns to the Propitius, ready to condemn a new generation of souls to be trapped forever in these halls. It's said that in the almost forty years he was missing, Arthur became involved in the occult and, among other things, discovered the secrets to mind control. He created eight glass statues representing each of the deadly sins. These statues were said to possess his congregation, forcing them to perform horrific acts upon one another as Arthur watched behind his network of hidden rooms."

The camera presses itself against a peephole, peering into a bedroom in which two men brutally beat each other, while a woman lies in bed with the sheets pulled up to her neck, screaming at them to stop.

"It's unknown why Wilson decided to end his torturous experiments, but one day, he gathered all of his followers into a single space and pumped in a toxic gas, killing ninety-eight members of his congregation. It was almost two months before authorities came to check on the property, where they found Wilson had taken his own life inside of a hidden room full of artifacts forgotten to the modern world."

CHAPTER FOURTEEN

The audio cuts out, and the video gives way to something more akin to a slideshow. Several photographs flash across the scene, showing the body of Wilson on the floor, clutching a pistol in one hand and his jeweled pendant in the other.

There it is. I can almost hear April groan. *Slashtag* is indeed going to be doubling down on the notion of a demonic amulet being a factor in Wilson's crimes. It's not enough to just have the ghost of a bloodthirsty maniac. Now we have to include the idea of satanic influences too.

Lucy takes over for the narrator, segueing into an explanation of what will be expected of us over the next three days. "It is said that through the mystical arts, Wilson was able to tether his spirit to this hotel using three totems, representing his body, mind, and spirit. It's your job to find and destroy these three totems before it's too late.

"You can find his body, or what's left of it, located in his private apartment." A human skull appears in the center of the mirror, then fades away. It's quickly replaced by a brass key, which splinters into three pieces before fading to black. "Of course, you'll need to reassemble the key to his room first. After that, you must find and destroy his mind."

A medieval-looking leather-bound book appears, with an octagon in the center. I have to squint to make out the colored symbols sitting at each of the points: red knife, a gold coin, and a green eye. The picture is replaced by a sturdy-looking wooden door sporting the same symbols.

"Find and destroy all eight deadly sin statues to gain access to Sutter's Sanctum in the tallest spire of the hotel."

For a second, a red glowing stone housed in a gold pendant appears on the screen. However, the image quickly begins to flicker. The chandelier rattles, and the bulbs surge to life. I have to shield my eyes from its blinding-white burn. Several of the bulbs pop, sending glass raining to the ground and prompting Britt to let out a burst of screams in quick succession. A moment later, there's a sound of electricity sparking, then the entire house goes dark.

This is the fun, safe kind of scared April and I used to live for, and it makes me feel close to her, knowing she's watching. A smile threatens to pull itself across my lips, until I remember the message I got on my phone moments before walking in.

"Uh oh," Lucy says, feigning surprise. "Looks like we blew a fuse. You know how these old houses can be."

"What does that mean?" Britt asks.

"It means you all better hustle your buns to get the power back on, before it gets *really* dark." Lucy presses a button on her tablet, and a harsh blue illuminates her face. "Sunset is roughly forty-five minutes away. I'd suggest you come up with a plan soon, unless you want to spend the weekend only using your flashlights."

"Hang on." D-wreck raises his hand. "Is there any way we can watch that video again? I kind of spaced out halfway through."

"We can't watch a video if there's no power," Kiki says in a way that just begs to be finished with, "you idiot."

"How does a mirror turn into a movie screen in the first place?" D-wreck retorts.

Footballer Shawn lifts a finger in the air and stares at his phone screen. "Yeah, I got caught up taking notes and missed some of that. Is there going to be some sort of a recap somewhere?"

"Glad you asked," Lucy says, pressing her fingers together like a Bond villain and cocking an eyebrow. "There may not be any power in the house, but I might be able to provide you with a little help...from the other side."

She wiggles her fingers. My phone vibrates in my hand. Suddenly, there are seven little lights glowing around the room. That is, until Britt screams again in surprise and drops hers on the floor with an echoing clack.

"Sorry, I'm so nervous right now."

"Probably not something you want to advertise," Landon says, in the ominous voice he used when he played Arthur Wilson in *Murder Mansion*.

I look at the alert on my phone. It directs me to a new app labeled *Mission Log*, showing a list of tasks we are supposed to perform. At the top of it reads: *Restore power to the hotel*.

"That's a little gift from me to you, along with one other special feature."

My phone buzzes again, showing off a new app called *Broadcast*.

"If you're ever lost or in a bind, each player gets to use one broadcast, in which they can immediately send a video out to all other players' phones."

"So, it's like a lifeline," Kiki says. "I guess that's better than nothing."

"Wait." Shawn scrolls through the app. "This doesn't tell us anything about how to turn the power back on. Where's the breaker?"

"Excellent question." Lucy begins to back out of the lobby into the hall. "I guess there's only one way to find out!"

"Or you could just tell us. That would actually make it two ways for us to find out," D-wreck says.

"I wish you all the best of luck and sincerely hope each of you survives your stay at The Propitius Hotel!" Lucy cackles as she backs around a corner, disappearing from sight.

"Wait, can't you give us a little hint? Like, maybe what floor it's on?" D-wreck follows her around the bend. "Whoa."

"What is it?" I ask.

He turns back to me, grinning ear to ear. "She's gone! Oh man, this is so cool."

CHAPTER FIFTEEN

Talking Tag: the Official Companion Podcast to *Slashtag*

Hey there, podcast fans! Can't get enough of *Slashtag*, even though it's airing twenty-four hours a day? Need a recap on what happened while you were asleep, eating dinner, or stuck at work? Or do you just want a deep dive into the insidious history of Arthur Wilson?

Krentler Media has you covered with *Talking Tag*, the official companion to the genre- and reality-bending mixed-media mega-hit show. Listen in with hosts Jon Menuscha and Nate Murray of *Making the Dough Show* and *Quarantine Scream Team* as they break down every major beat of *Slashtag* so you don't miss a thing.

Each episode will be uploaded once every few hours for the entire duration of the show to recap, theorize, and offer behind-the-scenes commentary from guests, including eliminated contestants, special effects designers, and even *Slashtag's* host, Lucy Hodge!

The first episode is available now, in which Jon and Nate break down the contestants and learn some behind the scenes secrets of the show!

Listen to the first episode now by going to www.slashtaginsider.com.

CHAPTER SIXTEEN

"Anyone know anything about circuit breakers?" I ask, trying to push the conversation forward without sounding too assertive. While I'm not terribly worried about being trapped in an extremely haunted house with no power, I *am* concerned about looking like I'm trying to take the limelight from some of the more famous people in the room. I have a feeling being an attention hog isn't going to do much to endear me to an audience that already hates me.

"Most modern hotels have breakers for each individual room, but I'm doubting this place is set up that way," Shawn says.

Britt steps up into the leadership role I assumed she would. "Let's also not forget, this is all a big puzzle, right? I'm betting this is just a way to get us to split up and explore the hotel."

"Wait, you want us all to split up?" Kiki almost sounds offended by the suggestion.

Beneath the rubber mask, Chef Costanza speaks up in a slightly muffled tone. "Britt's right. It will be a lot harder to navigate around here after the sun sets. Plus, I can't cook us anything for dinner if there's no power in the kitchen."

"All right, then," D-wreck says. "We split off into three groups, each taking a floor. Sound good?"

"Wait, before we do that, should we maybe go around the room and all introduce ourselves? I don't mean to offend anyone, but I'm not entirely sure who all of you are. I'm Britt Holley, star of reality shows like *Drama Mamas*, *Holleywooed*, and currently starring on *The Beverly Holleys*."

Kiki puts her hand in the air next. "I'm Kawaii Kiki. Professional cosplayer."

"I'm sorry, what is that?" Britt asks.

"I build costumes and accessories for pop culture conventions."

"Landon Keating, movie star, rock star," Landon says obviously, as if he were explaining to everyone that water is wet. "If nothing else, you probably know me for playing Arthur Wilson in the *Murder Mansion* movie, so I can probably help when it comes to some insight on him, or rather, his spirit."

"Chef Costanza, celebrity chef and mystery man by trade." He speaks with a slight New Yorker accent, though it's anyone's guess whether or not it's genuine.

"I have a question," Britt interjects. "Do you wear that mask all the time?"

"Yeah, any time I'm on screen."

"But, like, doesn't everybody already know who you are? Isn't your name Costanza?"

Several eyes cast a confused glance over to Britt.

Costanza answers slowly, as if he were speaking to a child. "No. It's because of the bald mask. You know, like George Costanza?"

She continues to stare blankly at him.

"Have you seriously never seen Seinfeld?"

Britt shrugs. "I don't watch a lot of TV unless I'm in it. Does this mean you're going to be wearing that mask all weekend?"

"You never know!" the Chef says, as if he were teasing what was coming after a commercial break.

"Shawn Eamon," the footballer says, raising his arm high enough that his fingers brush against the ceiling. "Pro, er, former pro football player."

I go next. "Tawny Howlett, makeup tutorial expert and lifestyle influencer. At least, I hopefully still will be by the time this is over."

Britt squints her eyes and stares at me intensely for a few seconds, then excited recognition sparks across her face. "Wait, I know you! You're trending! Tawny Toilet, right?"

I bite my lip and nod. "Yeah, that's me."

Finally, our last member raises his hand. "D-wreck. I used to do a lot of prank videos, but now I usually just stream myself playing video games and talking about pop culture shit. I don't know, at this point, I'm mostly famous for already being famous. Oh, also, Tawny is my girlfriend."

Everyone's staring each other down. Most of these people are meeting for the first time, and I can at least take a little comfort in knowing D and I will naturally be on a team together. It makes these opening hours feel like they will be a bit more bearable than they would if I were tethered to some stranger.

Britt grabs control of the room again, simply by opening her mouth. "Well, everyone, it's a pleasure to meet you all. Now that introductions are out of the way, maybe we should pair up and each pick a floor to search. D-wreck, you want to explore the first floor with me?"

My heart drops into my stomach, and the hairs stand up on the back of my neck. Did she not hear D say that we're an item literally five seconds ago? I look over at D-wreck, expecting him to correct Britt by saying he's already spoken for. He gives me a smirk and a half shrug, then takes a step over to his new teammate.

Kiki quickly claims Landon to scout the second floor with her, and in the same time span, Shawn attaches himself to Costanza to hunt for the basement. It all happens so fast, my head starts to spin. I'm suddenly back in fifth grade, watching as everyone gets picked for the kickball team until I'm the only one left.

What am I doing here? It turns out Krentler Media doesn't even need to do anything to leave me feeling vulnerable and humiliated. A group of my peers handled that just fine. My face grows hot, and I swear I can actually feel the schadenfreude grins of millions of Americans as I already get taken down a peg.

"Hey, Tawny, you want to come with us?" Shawn asks.

I look up at the towering man and nearly throw myself into his arms for inviting me along.

"That would be amazing."

Before joining his group, I turn to stare daggers at D-wreck for not stepping up, but he's already dedicating one hundred percent of his attention on his glamorous new partner.

"Thank you," I tell Shawn, subconsciously brushing the bangs across my forehead to make sure my scar is obscured.

Despite his imposing stature, his eyes are a soft gentle blue that cut through the fading light of the entry hall. I don't care if I'm a third wheel at this point. At least I'm part of a group. "Where do you think we should head first?"

We look around the room for any hints as to which direction we might find basement access. Before they have a chance to leave the lobby, I turn my attention to the local expert.

"Landon, you were in the movie about this place. Any idea where we might find the basement?"

Landon rolls his shoulders up and then back down in a fluid motion. The way he moves has a dreamy quality, like he's on muscle relaxants. He points down the immediate hallways on either side of the front door. "I think those hallways lead to the dining room and reception lounge, but I don't think you're going to find the basement there."

I point under the stairs, to the branching paths leading deeper into the house. "What's down these directions?"

"I don't know...Craft services? We filmed on a soundstage. I've never actually been here before."

"Fantastic," I say. "Well then, I guess the hunt is on. Should we all agree that once someone gets the power running, we all meet up back here?"

"Those of us that are still alive!" D-wreck gives his best Vincent Price impression while pointing his phone's flashlight up at his face. The shadows contour his features, making him look as spooky as possible. To really seal the deal, he follows it up with a bellowing laugh.

While it was clearly meant as a joke, the reverberating echo of his voice through all the dead space makes me shudder ever so slightly.

Britt semi-playfully slaps him on the shoulder. "Are you seriously planning on acting like a child the whole game?"

"I'm considering it."

"Well, let's try to remember, we still don't actually know what it takes to get eliminated yet, so make sure we all stick with our partners and keep an eye out for anything that seems off," Britt says.

I would, if only my partner hadn't abandoned me to cozy up to a future Real Housewife of Beverly Hills.

"We're in a hundred-year-old haunted house wired up to scare the shit out of us. What isn't weird about this place?" Kiki asks.

"Just keep a lookout," Shawn says. "And don't be afraid to take notes on your phones. Any detail can be important."

"Great idea, Shawn," I say a little louder than I should, taking a step toward him in hopes of making D-wreck jealous. "I just rewatched *Murder Mansion* to get ready for this, and I vaguely recall the basement access being found somewhere in the middle of the building. That way, guests wouldn't naturally wander down there."

"I was actually about to suggest the same thing," Shawn agrees. "Let's get to it."

We're not two steps out of the lobby, when we lose what little light we had coming from the entry hall windows. There's a real sense of claustrophobia setting in almost immediately. We pull out our phones and turn on the flashlights. The halls inside the house split continuously into branching paths, with no indication of where we're headed or where we've been. For a second, my lizard brain kicks in and starts screaming that I'll never be able to find my way back to the lobby, urging my legs to pick up the pace. Being inside this house has kicked all of my emotions into overdrive. As it turns out, I may not have to fake being scared for the cameras so much after all.

We hit a dead end, finding a pair of rooms with gold plaques affixed, noting them as the *Cigar Room* and the *Ballroom*. Neither of them lead to the basement, so we backtrack to the nearest intersection. We're about halfway down the hall, when Costanza stops dead in his tracks.

"What is it?" I ask.

"I thought I heard something. Like voices."

This is classic horror movie stuff. Obviously, this place is rigged with cameras and speakers and likely a small team of actors hiding in the walls, waiting to scare the pants off us. The thing is, I didn't hear anything, and a quick check with Shawn confirms he didn't either. I wonder if the spooky atmosphere is getting to Costanza too.

"Did you hear what the voices said?" I start to ask.

"No," he mutters before I can finish my sentence.

"Well, I'm officially creeped out," Shawn admits without a hint of sarcasm. As if making a trail of bread crumbs, he opens up his notes app and starts writing down the names of each room as we pass them. *Provisions, Barber...*

"I thought this place was a hotel." Costanza brushes dust off a red and white striped pole sticking out of the wall.

Shawn looks up from his phone to inspect the barber shop. "It's not that uncommon for hotels to basically have mini-malls on the first floor and then put apartments or guest rooms above. It was especially popular in the early twentieth century."

"How do you know all this stuff?" Costanza asks. "You study up on this place before coming here?"

Shawn shrugs, as if the answer is obvious. "Well, yeah, didn't you?"

"I watched *Murder Mansion*, just like Tawny."

"I'm more interested in the history and layout of the building. I figured it would be more helpful to focus on that, and less on the stories that will give me nightmares."

"Well then, how about you focus on this?" I point my flashlight to a plaque on a door opposite the barber shop.

Shawn smiles in relief. "Basement access."

We descend slowly, each wooden stair groaning under our feet. By the time we reach the underground level, the darkness is nothing short of oppressive. Instead of bringing light to the path in front of us, our flashlights are fighting against an all-encompassing force trying to close in around us. The movies, the documentaries, the ghost hunter specials, all suddenly catch up to me in a surreal moment of feeling like I've been here before. It's down here that Wilson committed some of his most horrific murders and buried dozens of bodies. I don't know if it's the splash of reality or the fact that it's at least ten degrees colder down here, but an intense shiver runs through me.

"Maybe I should go first," Costanza says, likely noticing my reaction

—along with millions of viewers at home. "In case anything jumps out at us."

I want to let him play the hero, but logic stands in my way. "I appreciate it, but how well can you actually see through the eyeholes of that rubber mask?"

"My peripheral vision isn't so good, but I'm pretty used to it. The hardest part is when the kitchen gets really hot, or when I have to be on set for a fourteen-hour day. The heat from lighting is the real killer."

Shawn continues the conversation. It helps keep us from freaking ourselves out too much. "I remember when you were a guest judge on Master Chef. I always wondered if they did any camera tricks or—"

"I'm not Gordon Ramsay. They didn't do any camera tricks."

"No, yeah. But in that episode, you were subbing for—"

"I'm not Joe Bastianich either. I promise, the bald head is just part of the rubber mask."

Just as we're getting settled into a rhythm, some unseen monkey at a command board presses a button and sends a collection of pipes over our heads banging together. It's loud enough to nearly throw me off balance. To my side, I see a flashlight whirl as Costanza falls to his knees.

"*Puta madre*, that scared the shit out of me," he says, with a Latino accent cutting into his Brooklyn attitude.

"Wait, are you—"

"I'm not Aarón Sánchez. I just got taken by surprise is all. Don't read into it."

I pan my flashlight around the basement level. If the first floor was a maze, down here, things are a full-on labyrinth. The wood floors are replaced with packed dirt at our feet. The walls are gray concrete, making it almost impossible for Shawn to find landmarks to jot down in his notes app.

As we continue down random corridors, the one thing that *does* seem to be changing is the height of the ceiling. Pretty soon, Shawn is hunching just to keep his head from hitting any of the metal pipes.

"Everything okay back there, Shawn?" I ask.

"Yeah," he says, convincing no one. "I'll be honest, I don't exactly love small spaces. Or the dark. Or scary things in general."

"No offense," Costanza replies, "but why are you here?"

Shawn takes a deep breath. "You know, I'm starting to ask myself that same question."

"So what *do* you like?" I'm trying to pick the conversation back up. "Aside from football."

"Actually, my real passion is cooking."

"No shit?" Costanza says.

Shawn lets out a nervous chuckle. "Yeah, it's a little embarrassing to admit, but I'm actually a huge fan."

"Of my channel? Get out."

"Hell yeah, man. That recipe video you did for prosciutto-wrapped sole with the beurre blanc and asparagus? That shit was inspired."

"The key is to make sure the sole sits on top of the asparagus—"

"So the prosciutto doesn't lose its crispy crust, sitting in the sauce," Shawn finishes for him. "My boyfriend, Danny, is more of a steak and potatoes kind of guy. Even he had to agree that dish was dope."

"You been cooking long?" Costanza asks, staving off fear and boredom as we meander aimlessly, occasionally trying to open unmarked locked doors.

I've accepted my role as third wheel, but all I really care about right now is getting the lights back on.

"Back in high school, I used to work at this restaurant with my mom after football practice and on weekends. Bussing tables mostly, but I learned a lot about cooking too. I don't know, it kind of left its mark on me. I like to think that in another life, I could have been a chef."

"Why didn't you?" I ask. "Football seems about as far from cooking as you can get."

"I mean, look, don't get me wrong. I liked football. It's just...I come from a small town in Alabama. When you look like me, you don't really get a lot of opportunities to get out and do something with yourself. My old man used to say you have to get the most out of the gifts God gives you."

"And God gave you the gift of being roughly the size of a Hummer?" Costanza jokes.

"Pretty much. Football just came naturally to me, kept me mostly out of trouble, even made me popular for a minute. And while it lasted,

I was able to make enough money to pay off all my parents' debts and stuff. I won't lie, that part was pretty cool."

We round a corner, and my senses light up. "Do you guys smell that?"

"We must be under that Cigar Room." Costanza stops at a door and presses his head against it as Shawn and I continue along the path. "Guys, can you come listen to this? I swear there's someone talking in here."

I press my head against the door and listen. Somewhere in the distance comes the low hiss of either a furnace or running water...I close my eyes and try to filter out those sounds, taking deep but quiet breaths and trying not to gag on the smell of old smoke.

Just as I settle into the silence, something slams against the door from the other side. I jump back, startled by the sudden force, wanting to laugh at my gullibility for playing right into another jump scare.

But something else catches my breath in my throat.

Along with the thump, I swear I heard the bark of a dog on the other side of the door. My heart races at the thought of a rottweiler snarling from just one room away, waiting to come and rip another pound of flesh from me.

No. I'm just getting a little overexcited. There's nothing down here but us and an army of unseen crew members.

"Hey guys, check this out." Costanza points his flashlight at another door a few feet ahead, with the words *Electrical Room* in tarnished brass. He turns the knob, and the door pushes forward an inch. "Door's not locked. That seems like a good sign."

At first glance, this doesn't look much like an electrical room at all. Almost the entire space is filled with a pile of antique wooden chairs. There's at least a hundred of them all tossed haphazardly on top of each other, creating an uneven landscape of junk that spans the room. Some of the legs are splintered or broken entirely, jutting out like spikes in a makeshift barricade. A solid portion of the chairs hang precariously on top of others, looking like they could collapse into a heap of scrap wood at any moment.

My first thought is that we've hit another dead end, but Costanza's flashlight catches a small, rusted breaker door on the far wall.

After surveying the room carefully, Costanza looks back at us with both hands on his hips. "Seems like we have two options. We can either try to climb over this mess to reset the breaker, or we can clear a path."

Without hesitation, Shawn attempts to pull one of the top chairs off the pile, but the first chair he grabs immediately snags onto another one, making it hard to separate them. He traces the point where the two chairs intertwine but discovers the other chair is pinned in place by two more. "This is way harder than it looks. It's like they're all connected."

"Can't you just give it a good yank? A guy your size, you could probably rip its legs right off," Costanza says.

Shawn shakes his head. "I'm not doing that. There's got to be at least a hundred chairs in here."

"Fine. I guess it's up to me, then." The chef warms up his gloved hands by rapidly rubbing them together. He then grabs an errant leg poking out of the pile and tests his weight by stepping on the back of it.

"Maybe I should do it," I say. "No offense, but I'm lighter than you, and I'm not wearing a big rubber mask."

"I can do it." Costanza slowly crawls onto the wooden minefield. "Just keep your flashlights pointed ahead of me so I can see where I'm going."

We do as we're told, keeping our lights trained in front of him as he carefully tests each spot before committing his weight. The wood creaks under his hands and knees, threatening to come crashing down at any moment.

He's almost there, when he lets out a gasp of surprise.

His hand flies up, as if he just touched a hot stove, and the sudden shifting of his weight causes his foot to crash down onto the wicker backing of a chair. Costanza yelps in pain, and his leg craters through the mesh. It plunges into the darkness below, ending with a loud crack. I can't tell if the sound comes from the splintering of wood or his bone. His ensuing shriek makes me worry it's his ankle.

"Costanza! Are you okay?" Shawn tries to angle himself closer by stepping on a chair, but it immediately crumbles beneath his weight.

"There's something down here!" Costanza shouts, his voice turning quickly to panic. "Underneath the chairs, I saw something move!"

I crouch and point my flashlight through the thicket of wooden legs and spines, but I don't find anything beyond a tangle of debris. From my vantage point, he's too deep into the pile for me to even see his leg.

"Maybe the chairs just shifted under your weight," Shawn says.

"I know what a chair looks like," Costanza snaps. "Something's moving down there."

I volunteer another explanation. "Could it have been a rat?"

"I don't know. Maybe." The chef hisses in pain, trying to pull himself up and out from the hole, but the wicker backing is gripping his thigh like a Chinese finger trap. "I can't get out. I'm stuck!" His breaths are coming in short quick bursts.

Combined with the poor ventilation of the rubber mask, I'm worried he could hyperventilate and potentially pass out from lack of oxygen.

"Try to calm down. See if you can take some slow deep breaths, counting to five on both the inhale and exhale."

His breath is amplified beneath the mask as he follows a few breaths of my guided meditation.

"You're doing great. Try looking again. Do you still see anything moving down there?"

He searches the dark crevices beneath him, this time moving his head in slow sweeping gestures to make up for his lack of peripheral vision. "No, I don't think so."

I have no idea what he could have seen down there—it might have been a rat, an actor hiding under some sort of trapdoor, or just a manifestation of his own paranoia. Right now, what's most important is getting him safely off of Chair Mountain.

"How does your leg feel? Can you move your foot at all?"

Costanza wiggles around a bit. "It hurts, but I can move it. I think it's mostly just scraped up." He takes a few more breaths, starting to calm down. "Yeah, I'm okay. Give me a second." Costanza reaches down and slowly pulls his leg back up and out of the hole, wincing the entire time as wicker splinters scrape at his skin. Once he's fully clear of it, he takes his phone from his pocket and turns the flashlight on, inspecting the hole.

"What do you see?" I ask.

"Nothing now, but I swear there was something down there."

"How's your leg look?"

He bends his knee a few times, then rotates his foot in a couple of circles. "Definitely got a few cuts, maybe a sprained ankle. Doesn't seem like anything too serious, though I won't know for sure until I'm off this pile of trash."

"Do you want to come back and let me give it a shot?"

"I'm almost at the control box. Give me a second." He's just out of arm's reach from the panel door, though he takes his last couple of movements much more carefully, relying solely on his good leg for stability. Costanza finally reaches the panel and swings it open, revealing a series of black switches. "This better work." He lays his palm against a whole column and slides them sideways at the same time.

Somewhere in the distance, there's a buzz of electricity. Moments later, a single bulb hanging from a chain on the ceiling yawns to life.

"Hell yeah!" Costanza shouts as Shawn and I applaud his effort. "Look at us, coming through with the first win. And man, does it feel good to be back in the light."

Even though we've only checked off the first in a long list of objectives, the lights push that claustrophobic feeling away and let me breathe just a bit easier. It takes Chef Costanza less than half the time to return to us, now that he can actually see where he's going.

Once he's back on solid ground, I'm able to get a better look at his leg. The black chef's pants hide any blood, but the bottom cuff is mostly shredded, and the ankle of his once-white sock is now red.

Costanza tests his weight on the foot. "As long as there's no sprinting challenges, I think I should be okay. Let's get back upstairs ASAP. It's freaky as hell down here."

From down the hall comes a rusty groan, followed by the ominous *clack* of a door slamming shut. I'm beginning to hate whoever is sitting behind the operating board of this show.

"Oh hell, what now?" Costanza mumbles.

We step out of the electrical room, and it takes less than a second to figure out what the issue is. At the end of the hall, a door has appeared, blocking us from leaving the basement. It's not just a simple wooden door either, not like most of the ones we've seen so far. This is a huge steel door that, as far as I can tell, came sliding down from the ceiling.

Shawn gives it a couple of shoves, but it doesn't budge.

"Well, this is just what we need," Costanza says. "Is this how they reward us for getting the power back on? Trapping us down here for the rest of the weekend?"

"Let's not give up hope yet," I reply, though I feel my heartbeat start to quicken. "I'm sure there's another way out. You guys remember that other door that was locked earlier?"

"You mean the one under the Cigar Room?" Costanza asks.

"Yeah. Maybe by restoring the power, some things in the house have changed." I try the door. It clicks open. "See? By blocking off one path, they opened up another. It's just like Britt said—one big series of puzzles."

As soon as I step through the threshold, I'm hit in the face with a blast of an acrid smell. It's got a hint of the cigar smoke, but it's mostly swallowed by something more intense—like an old burnt steak that's been charred to a crisp, then left in a small room to rot. The dirt on the ground is softer, like sand, and in the corner sits a rusted metal furnace with a grated door that makes me feel like it's grinning at me. Just above it is a hole in the ceiling about two feet in diameter.

"Guys, I think this is our way out."

"Up there?" Shawn says. "Yeah, naw. There's no way I'm going to fit through that. Besides, how would we even be able to climb up there?"

I don't have an answer for him, but something tells me this has to be the way. "We can definitely take another look around, but unless there's another door I'm not seeing, I don't know that we have much of a choice. The only other idea would be to go back into the electrical room and see if there is some sort of a trap door under all those chairs."

"I'm not going back in there," Costanza says. "Maybe there's a way to open the metal door from the other side?"

I turn my flashlight back on and look up at the hole in the ceiling, trying to find any sort of indentations to use as ladder rungs. It appears to be a solid brick chimney. "I can see light coming in from a room up there. It's no more than about ten feet, I think."

"Cool, so all we need to do is shimmy our way up ten feet of brick chimney, even though I have an injured leg and Shawn is literally too big to fit? Great plan, life guru."

"I'm thinking, okay? They wouldn't put us in this situation if there wasn't a way for us to get out of it."

"All right, so what's the solution? Without some help, I don't see how we're ever going to find our way up."

"I don't know. Maybe there's a clue in the furnace or something."

"Hang on," Shawn says. "I think you're onto something."

"About the furnace?"

"No, about what Chef just said. There's four other people in this house, and they told us from the beginning this is a team game. What if we ask them to help? We each get the ability to broadcast once to the rest of the group, right? I'd say this warrants a call for assistance."

Chef Costanza pulls out his phone. "Well, if I'm the genius who came up with the idea, I guess it's on me to be the one to make the call. Where should I tell everyone to meet?"

"Outside the metal door," Shawn says, as I simultaneously suggest they all meet in the Cigar Room.

"I already told you, I'm not going to be able to fit through that hole," Shawn says.

"I understand your point, but it's going to be much easier for them to find the Cigar Room than a random door in the basement. Remember how hard it was for us to even get this far? At least upstairs, they can follow a path based on the notes you took. If they can get a rope or something and pull me or Costanza out, then one of us could lead them back down to the door and see if there's a way to open it."

Shawn tightens his lips, his nostrils flaring. "Fine. But I'm not getting myself stuck in that chimney unless it's an absolute last case scenario."

"That's fine. Chef, are you ready to make the call?"

Mission Log

- ~~Restore Power to the Hotel~~

- Destroy Arthur Wilson's Body Totem
  - Unlock Arthur's Apartment
    - Find the key's knob
    - Find the key's shaft
    - Find the key's bit

- Destroy Arthur Wilson's Mind Totem
  - Unlock the door to Sutter's Sanctum
    - Destroy the Greed statue
    - Destroy the Sloth statue
    - Destroy the Wrath statue
    - Destroy the Envy statue
    - Destroy the Lust statue
    - Destroy the Pride statue
    - Destroy the Gluttony statue
    - Destroy the Disobedience statue

- Destroy Arthur Wilson's Spirit Totem

SOCIAL

CHAPTER SEVENTEEN

"What?"

"I said, can you hand me the soldering kit?" Hector asks.

"Oh, sure." I tear my eyes away from one of my dual monitors, find a wooden box next to me, and pass it over to him.

"You know, April, the world isn't going to end if you take the day off to watch *Slashtag*. It's not like we're going to get this controller finished today anyways."

I look at the mess of 3D-printed parts and electronic bits strewn across Hector's workspace. "Sorry, I'll do better."

"Seriously, it's fine if it takes an extra day to get this out. It's not like the other thirty backlogged orders are going anywhere anytime soon. Enabled Accessories isn't going to go under because it took us a little longer to build a couple of custom PlayStation controllers."

He has a point. When Hector and I founded our company, I didn't realize just how long it would take to build each custom controller for differently-abled gamers. Or how expensive it would be. Between the cost of parts, obscene shipping rates, and paying Hector's wages, I've estimated, at our current rate, we're losing somewhere between ten and sixteen dollars per sale. Since Tawny left to be on *Slashtag*, I've basically been entirely useless. This means we're probably closer to losing twenty dollars per unit. I'll admit, it's not the best business plan, but we're helping people, and my sister says that's all that matters.

"Look, I know you feel guilty watching Tawny instead of working, but do you seriously think she expects you to not watch the show? It's horror and puzzles—this thing's practically made for you. How about we take the rest of the day off and you show me how this show works?"

It's a pretty tempting offer. "Are you sure you want to stay? I know you can't stand this horror stuff."

"True, but it's the only thing people are talking about online. How will I be able to keep up at the watercooler if I don't tune in?"

I snort out a laugh. "Like we even have a watercooler."

"Let's call it a professional courtesy. What have I missed so far?"

I can't fight fate, and it's not often that someone gives me carte blanche to talk about horror. "Okay, so the power went out in the building, and everyone split up to find the breaker. Because my sister's a badass, her team found it and got the place running again."

"Who are these people on the screen? I don't see Tawny."

"That's because she's stuck in the basement. We're currently on the master feed, which is what the showrunners decide is the most interesting story for the moment. This is what you'd see if you were watching it on TV. Chef Costanza called the rest of the team to help him escape the basement via a chimney chute, and now D-wreck and Kiki are tying together bedsheets from a couple of guest rooms to make a sort of rope."

"What's the difference between the master feed and other feeds?" Hector asks.

"If you're watching on Social, you can click any of these buttons along the bottom of the screen to follow a specific contestant whenever you want."

I click the button that says Tawny's name, and the screen cuts to an overhead view of her sitting on a dirt floor with two men. "The big guy is Shawn Eamon. He was a football player before he got cut for being gay."

"I don't really know sports, but aren't there already a number of gay football players?"

"Yeah, but I guess none of them are openly partners with a member of the same team. It caused a whole fuss. His partner is like a Super Bowl MVP or something, so he got transferred, but Shawn got dropped entirely. He's spent the last ten minutes talking to Chef Costanza about food recipes. I guess they're both really into cooking. Honestly, that part's kind of boring, so it's fine that they've cut away from them. Once they get out of there, Tawny will probably get more interesting stuff to do."

"What are all these other buttons?" Hector asks, pointing to a drop-down menu.

"Oh, those are for individual rooms. I'm not really sure why anyone would want to look at live feeds of rooms where nothing is happening, but it's there anyways. There's at least one camera in every room, except the bathrooms." I click a tab that says *Basement*, which brings me to another drop-down series of buttons. "They were just in the electrical room before, so when I click it...Huh."

"What?"

I squint at the screen, unsure what to make of it. "That's weird. A minute ago, there was just one big pile of broken chairs in the room. Now they're all stacked up along the wall."

"Is that weird?"

"I mean, yeah. There's, like, a hundred chairs in there. How could someone move them all in five minutes?"

CHAPTER EIGHTEEN

D-wreck sends a rope made of bedsheets down the chimney. By the time it reaches us, the sheet is already black with soot. Fantastic. We're an hour into this thing, with no extra clothes, and I'm already going to be stuck looking like a coal miner for the rest of the weekend. Perfect timing to really show off my latest line of makeup.

"Tawny, you grab on first. We're going to pull you up," D-wreck calls.

"No pranks!" I shout, remembering the half-dozen times he's asked me to get into the passenger seat of his car, only to inch it forward every time I try to grab the handle. "I'm serious."

"Scouts honor," says the man who's never so much as been camping.

"I swear to God, if you let go when I'm halfway up, my ghost is going to haunt you for the rest of your life."

"What? I would never!" D-wreck says, in his most over-the-top impression of indignation.

"It's fine. We're all holding on," Britt chimes in from somewhere behind him. "Just hold on tight, and we'll pull you up. Don't worry, Tawny. We'll have you up in no time."

In real life, Britt is nothing special. She's just a person who won the fame jackpot, like the rest of us. Yet somehow, when she speaks, her clear confidence makes me naturally inclined to believe her. Even though she stole D-wreck away from me during the first minute of the game, I find it nearly impossible to stay mad at her.

"If I make it up all right, Costanza will be next, and then we'll figure out how to get Shawn out."

"You better. I'm the only one taking notes. Y'all are never going to figure out how to even find a bathroom without me." Shawn smiles with his whole face, so gentle that I wonder how he was ever a football player to begin with.

I shift my attention to the knotted bed sheets. There's a loop tied around the bottom to stick my foot in, and I wrap a section of makeshift rope around my forearm a few times for stability. "Okay, I'm ready!" Before I can even finish calling out, I'm jerked up hard toward the hole. The force of liftoff swings me like a pendulum, and I bang my hip on the furnace. A quick shock of pain forces a grunt out of me that reverberates up the chimney louder than I expect.

My ascension halts immediately, and a woman with an Australian accent calls down. "Everything all right down there?"

"Yeah, can you just pull a little slower?"

After a few more tugs, the team gets into a rhythm, pulling me up in measured increments. As I ascend into the dark chute, I do breathing exercises to distract myself from the black powder covering the walls. It's safe to assume this whole place has undergone extensive reconstruction to essentially make it more like a themed attraction than an actual piece of historical property, but part of me wonders if they bothered cleaning sections like this. If not, I'm scraping against the carbon remnants of God knows how many charred bodies baked onto the blackened bricks. My back scrapes against the wall, creating a cloud of soot that stings my eyes. My lungs ache from inhaling the stuff. I start to cough, which stirs up even more dust.

For a second, they stop pulling me. "Everything okay?" Kiki calls down.

"Faster," I wheeze. I'm hacking so hard I feel like I'm going to throw up. Wouldn't that be a fitting sight for all my food-poisoned fans?

The folks upstairs get the message, and now I'm double timing it up the chimney. I shut my eyes and use my free hand to pull my shirt up over my nose and mouth. A strong hand connects with mine, and with one solid pull, it yanks me out of the fireplace. I crawl on my hands and knees across the red-carpeted room, hacking up a lung in the process.

When I can finally speak, my words come out sounding like an eighty-year-old man's. "Water. Anybody got any water?"

"Here." Britt rushes over to a side table, then hands me a large glass bottle full of clear liquid.

I take a swig, and the dryness in my throat is immediately replaced by intense burning. My lungs are choking on ash, and now my throat is on fire from whatever I just drank. I force it down, knowing the alternative would be vomiting black sludge all over the rug. It takes a few more coughs before everything starts to settle down, and the burning in my throat calms to a roiling heat in my stomach.

"That wasn't water."

D-wreck grabs the glass bottle, which I now realize is actually a decanter. He takes a sniff, then swigs some back. "All right, now it's a party."

"Well, I'm glad you're enjoying it," I say. My mouth still feels like someone poured an urn into it. At the risk of looking unladylike, I scrape my tongue against my teeth to collect a layer of ashy gunk, then find a corner to spit in. A line of black fluid bungee jumps from my lips, only separating when it reaches my knees.

"You okay?" Britt asks.

"Yeah, just in desperate need of a shower. Really wishing they had let us bring a change of clothes. I feel like I'm covered in dead people."

D-wreck comes up behind me and places a hand on the small of my back. Despite our relationship being entirely fake, and me still being mad at him for ditching me, it still brings me a small sense of comfort to not be alone.

He then goes ahead and ruins it by saying, "When this is all over, would you mind giving my chimney a scrub too?"

"Fuck off," I say, but I don't pull away, instead letting his hand rub small circles around my back.

"Everything okay up there?" Costanza's voice echoes from the fireplace.

"I'm okay. I'd say to tie a bandana or something over your face, but this may be one of the few times where being fully masked may actually work to your advantage. Just try to keep your breaths shallow and shut your eyes."

The rest of the group sends the once-white linen rope back down the chimney, while I give myself another minute to recover in one of the burgundy leather wing chairs. The second round goes a lot smoother—not only does Costanza manage to avoid choking on ash, but the pulling team has also found a better rhythm and seem to have him up in half the time.

In the light of the Cigar Room, everyone is able to get a better look at the damage on Costanza's leg. Most of his scrapes are already drying, and though he has a bit of a limp, he swears he's already feeling much better.

Kiki lights up, remembering something. "When we were exploring the second floor, I saw a little shop called *The Apothecary*. I'm wondering if maybe we could find some painkillers for your leg up there."

"If you're offering, I won't say no," Costanza says.

"All right, I'm on it!" she says, then starts to rush out of the room.

"Wait," I say. "You should take someone with you. No one should ever be alone, just in case."

"I'll go with her," Britt offers. "We'll look for some bandages and other stuff too."

While they head out for their supply run, I turn my attention back to Shawn. "You still down there, big guy?"

"It's not like I have anywhere else to be."

Landon turns to me, D, and Costanza. "So, how are we going to get him out of there?"

"There's no way we're pulling him up," I say. "A man his size, plus his claustrophobia and all the ash on the walls...If he got stuck, he could be in very real danger of asphyxiation."

"What if we put soap on the walls?" Landon asks.

D-wreck shoves his oversized eyebrows together and nods. "Well, that's...an idea. I don't know that it would work for this scenario, but it gives me some great ideas for future pranks."

"I think our best bet is to head back down into the basement and see if that sliding door can be opened from the other side," I suggest.

"All right then, let's hit it." D-wreck claps his hands, then produces two thumbs up.

"I think you should stay here with Costanza to wait for the ladies to get back." It may be petty, but it goes a long way toward easing my salty feelings about D-wreck ditching me earlier.

"Why not have him do it?" D whines. He points a finger at Landon, clearly not understanding this is about retribution more than logic.

"He knows the house better."

"Bullshit. He already admitted he's never even been here before."

"Technically true," Landon admits, "but I understand the psyche of the building. I'm more attuned with its emotional and spiritual resonance. If I have to, I can step into the mind of Arthur Wilson to uncover the motivation of the door."

"I think its motivation is to be closed, bro. Not that hard to figure out."

Landon shakes his head dismissively. "Everything has a motivation. If Arthur Wilson had a reason for placing the door there, I might be able to tap into the logic behind it and deduce a psychological solution."

"Seriously, D, don't make a big deal out of this," I start to say, but my words get cut off by a loud reverberating crash coming from the basement. "Shawn, you okay?"

"Yeah," his voice calls back. "It sounded like it came from the electrical room. Can you guys hurry up and get down here?" There's a moment of silence before Shawn follows up by muttering something in surprise.

"What's going on down there?" D-wreck shouts into the fireplace. "Shawn? You still there?"

I feel a clammy hand on my shoulder and turn to see Landon looking at me with sudden seriousness. His dark eyes are burning with the intensity of *The Manimal*, a knockoff Batman-type he played in a movie.

"We're going after him," he says, clearly more for the cameras than me. He stalks dramatically into the hall, only stopping when I assume he realizes he has no idea where he's going. "Hey Tawny, why don't you lead the way?"

Once we reach the basement, Landon pauses and rubs his hands against the walls.

"Wow, it feels so much heavier down here. It's like the trapped spirits are trying to pull us down into their unmarked graves." Even if he does sound like a character from a cheesy movie, he's not entirely incorrect. Being down here does feel different; there's an almost palpable sense of unease making me want to get back upstairs as soon as possible.

"Hey, so my sister's a big fan of yours," I say to keep things light. "She made me promise I'd ask you a question about *Murder Mansion.*"

"She is, is she?" He seems clearly amused. "Sure."

"What's your feeling on the whole possession angle?"

Landon lets out a mocking laugh. "Do you mean in regard to the actual man, or the character in my film?"

"Both, I guess."

"I believe that the writer used the Amulet of Duriel as a storytelling device to bring the audience into the POV of the character, and it made for a wonderful metaphor."

"So you don't think Arthur Wilson was actually possessed by an evil amulet?"

"I think Arthur Wilson believed in demons. Whether you take that literally, or as an expression of conscience, is up to you."

I want to keep going and live out pretend interviews April and I have had together, but our conversation is cut short when we come upon the metal sliding door. Just like on the other side, there doesn't seem to be a handle of any kind.

"Shit," I say, realizing there's going to be more to this than meets the eye. It's quickly becoming apparent nothing in this hotel is built to be simple. I pound on the door a few times and call out Shawn's name but get nothing in response. My immediate concern is he's suffering from another potential panic attack.

"Let me try," Landon says.

I step back as he gently runs his hands along the edges of the door, then slowly presses his body and face against it. He turns his head to the side, holding his ear against the door, then begins to emit a sound that's somewhere between humming and chanting.

"What are you doing?"

"I'm absorbing the situation, attuning myself to the barrier and the spirit of Arthur Wilson so that I might understand it and, therefore, overcome it."

"And how's that working for you?" a voice from behind startles me.

It's Shawn.

I feel a wave of relief, immediately followed by a swell of confusion. "How the hell did you get out of there?"

"Come on, I'll show you." He leads us down a corridor to a door I swear wasn't there earlier.

We step into what I surmise to be the trophy room of a serial killer. The walls are covered in shelves filled with sealed jars containing an assortment of severed body parts. Swollen hands and feet float in greenish liquid, puffy and discolored. One jar contains a pair of eyes, while the one next to it houses a shriveled brain. On a lower shelf, there's a dead possum in a jar. Next to it are a series of possum fetuses in various stages of development. Each jar gets incrementally smaller, sort of like a Russian nesting doll for lunatics. In the center of the room sits a rusty metal table that bears a slight downward gradient leading into a drain in the floor.

The room is so overstuffed with every mad scientist trope that Shawn has to stop me from accidentally walking straight into a hole in the floor. He pulls me back from the brink, and I look down at an opened hatch, with a staircase on the other side leading into darkness.

"Remember Costanza said he saw something under those chairs? I think he was right. When I went back into the breaker room, all the chairs had been moved, and there was a hidden passage that led to here."

"What do you mean *moved?*"

"I can't explain it either. They were all just stacked along the wall."

While Shawn looks concerned, I'm genuinely impressed the *Slashtag* team was able to move all those chairs in such a short amount of time. I want to go see it for myself, but Landon can't tear himself away from the museum of horrors.

"This is fascinating." He presses his face against a jar containing what I guess is either a pair of severed testicles or possibly a massively underdeveloped set of kidneys. "How many people do you think died in here?"

"I'd prefer not to think about it," I say, bringing myself back to the actual reality of this building beyond the show. It once again gives me an opportunity to be genuinely disconcerted, without having to fake a reaction for the cameras. While the room is almost certainly dressed up with a bunch of fake organs made by a special effects team, it's also very likely that actual people were killed in here.

The bolts holding the metal table to the ground are just as rusted as any other fixture in here. I wouldn't be surprised if Wilson used to torture and kill victims on this very surface.

"I bet it's at least a dozen." Landon nods his head with unearned confidence. "And I bet he dissected a lot more than that."

Shawn waves a rolled-up piece of yellowed paper in his hand. "I found this on the table, by the way. I think it might be the first clue toward Wilson's totem."

"What's it say?" I ask.

"I haven't opened it yet." He turns the paper around to reveal a red wax seal holding it together. Pressed into it are the initials *AW*. "But that's not all. I also found this."

In his other hand, Shawn holds out a silver Zippo lighter.

CHAPTER NINETEEN

From: Casting@Krentler.media
To: Board@Krentler.media
CC: Lucy.K@Krentler.media
Subject: Potential Subject #5

Good afternoon, Gentlemen of the Board,

For our fifth subject, the criteria was to find a participant with mass appeal, who could also bring a dramatic flair to the event. I believe I've found an ideal candidate in a YouTube and television cooking sensation who goes by the name "Chef Costanza." Although his Social following is currently under 10 million followers, we feel he brings a number of elements that will more than make up for his relatively low subscriber base.

First, he's appeared on dozens of TV shows, including *Good Morning America*, *Master Chef*, and even *Dancing with the Stars*. For many of his guest appearances, single episode viewership tends to consistently draw upward of 600k extra viewers.

Second, his gimmick of keeping every inch of his body hidden from view makes him extremely mysterious and adds an extra layer of spectacle to the event. If we were to tease the unveiling of his identity during *Slashtag*, it could bring in a demographic who would watch purely out of curiosity to find out who is behind the mask.

While he guards his identity well, we have discovered his real name is Miguel Arroyo. One potential reason Miguel has been so keen on keeping his identity a secret is that he has a rather colorful history. At age 17, he was arrested for aggravated assault and attempted robbery. After being released just over a year later, he worked at a number of restaurants around New York City. Our sources have spoken to many of his former employers, who have all said that, while he is an incredible cook, he does not behave well under stressful situations and has been fired from multiple positions due to his propensity for emotional outbursts.

We believe that the combination of his mysterious TV persona tied with his history of volatile behavior makes Arroyo a wildcard, which could be an excellent source of entertainment.

Finally, by having him onboard, we solve the issue of food preparation for our subjects during the event. We recommend planning his arc to be a slow build, starting him out under the radar, then slowly nudging him in the direction of having increasingly temperamental outbursts. Potentially an ideal 4th or 5th elimination.

Let me know your thoughts.

Carol

CHAPTER TWENTY

"Hey man, I told you to keep your fucking mouth shut!"

I was hoping to return to the Cigar Room to congratulatory pats on the back and a collective *job well done*, but before I even reach the doorway, I can tell it's unlikely. From the sounds of it, D-wreck is making enemies faster than I can make friends. I knew it was stupid to believe he would actually look out for me here. He's been too busy flirting with Britt and treating this whole thing like one big joke.

"All right, what happened?" I step into a scene that doesn't surprise me in the slightest.

Costanza throws an accusatory finger at D, who is sprawled out on a lounge chair, laughing so hard tears are streaming down his face. "Your boyfriend's an asshole, that's what happened."

"I wish I could say that narrows it down. What did you do to him, D?"

"Oh no, I'm purely a spectator in this guy's mental breakdown. I was just sitting here, enjoying a fine bottle of hundred-year-old gin, when Costanza started cussing me out."

"The fuck I did. Why don't you tell them how you started it, you son of a bitch!"

D-wreck's eyebrows leap halfway up his forehead, and he gestures both his hands over to Costanza. "See! He's the one with the potty mouth!"

"You should have heard some of the things he said about me. Nobody's talked to me like that since I was a kid."

"Well, hang on," I say, trying to de-escalate the situation. "What kinds of things was he saying?"

Costanza shakes his head. "Personal attacks, racist shit, you name it."

"I'm not trying to take anyone's side here, but no one here knows who you really are, right, Costanza?"

"Yeah, so?"

"How could he possibly be making personal attacks against you, if he doesn't even know who you are?"

The logic doesn't seem to be sinking in. Costanza's chest is puffed out, like he's ready to throw a punch. "I don't know. How does he get away with ninety percent of the shit he pulls?"

"Yeah bro, what would I even have to gain anyways? If I knew who you were, I'd probably blackmail you into cooking for me or something. I wouldn't blow it just to get you pissed off without even having an audience."

Costanza throws his arms out to his side, as if he were being cruci-fied. "We're literally being broadcast to millions of people right now!"

"Oh yeah," D-wreck says, in a more muted tone.

I don't know why I feel compelled to continue defending D. Maybe it's just a force of habit by now. "You also mentioned earlier in the base-ment that you were hearing whispers, right, Costanza? D-wreck wasn't even with us then. I agree that it sounds like someone is messing with you, but I don't think it's him."

The room grows silent. Costanza is almost starting to relax, when D-wreck opens his big fat mouth again.

"Maybe they put a hidden speaker in your mask. You should prob-ably take it off and check."

I don't have to see Costanza's face to feel it burning red with rage.

Of all moments, Landon decides this is the best time to inject himself into the conversation. "Do you think it was Arthur Wilson?" he asks, his eyes sparkling with interest. "How was his timbre? Did he come from a place down here?" He lowers his voice and holds a flat hand in front of his belly button. "Or was it more gritty, like this?" Landon's hand turns into a claw that he holds at his chest as he adds some gravel to his tone.

"Don't you start with me," Costanza says. "I got respect for your movies and all, but I'm going to need you to back all the way off before I lose my cool."

Landon's eyes go wide in shock, and he recoils at even the first hint of confrontation. He retreats through the door and bumps into Britt and Kiki.

"Whoa there, looks like you've seen a ghost," Kiki says with a nervous laugh, then takes a minute to absorb the tension in the room. "Wait, did you lot actually see a ghost?"

"We're trying to figure that out," I say. "Costanza thinks D-wreck's taunting him, but I'm trying to remind him that we are all trapped in a very haunted hotel."

"Did you hear something from the other side? What did it sound like?" Kiki asks eagerly.

"It sounded like a guy's voice, okay?" Costanza says, his irritation clearly building again.

"I don't know if I can do anything about that, but if your leg is still giving you trouble, I think I found some pain relievers in the Apothecary." Kiki digs into a white canvas shoulder bag I haven't seen before. She pulls out a small brown pill bottle. Its label is faded and peeling from the corners. "Dr. Wilson & Sons Pain Prevention. Judging from the ingredients, I'm pretty sure it's just ibuprofen." She holds out the bottle as if it were a collective olive branch from all of us.

Costanza finally breaks from his aggressive posture and grabs the bottle.

"Thanks," he says, popping the cork top off and rattling two white pills into his black gloved hand. He then turns around to face the corner, pulls up the bottom of his mask, and tosses the pills into his mouth.

"You know, technically, there's a chance it could have heroin in it," Landon says.

"What?" Costanza demands.

"They're probably just ibuprofen, like Kiki suggested. I'm just saying that back in the early 1900s, the most common pain medications doctors prescribed were morphine and heroin. Arthur is well-documented as having dosed guests at the hotel to make it easier for him to experiment on them. He even drugged some people just so he could tie them up and make them watch him experiment on others."

"Cool. Thanks for telling me all that *after* I've already taken the pills," Costanza says.

Shawn has spent the last five minutes trying not to be noticed in the hallway, and was doing a pretty good job, considering his size. "Maybe while we wait for those pain relievers to kick in, we can get started on the next phase of the game." He waves his rolled-up parchment in the air. "I found a clue."

"You did? What's it say?" Kiki asks with excitement.

"I figured we could all open it together."

"Well, come on! The sooner we solve these clues, the sooner we get out of here."

I'm impressed by how delicately Shawn uses his clubbed thumb to peel back the red wax seal without damaging the paper underneath.

"It looks like a diary entry of some sort."

Landon asks, "Do you mind if I read it aloud? I think the fans would appreciate the consistency of the character's voice,"

"Be my guest." Shawn seems all too happy to turn the room's attention over to someone else.

Landon clears his throat, rolls his shoulders back, widens his stance, then tucks his chin to make him appear slightly taller. When he speaks, his voice is an octave lower than normal, and his enunciation is exaggerated to the point he might as well be performing Shakespeare in the park.

"February the twelfth, 1911. Another accident in the mine has left one man with a compound tibial shaft fracture. Due to the bone's protrusion from the skin and the filthy conditions of the mines, I was called to assist father in performing an amputation of the leg. This was the single detail from the day in which the two of us saw eye to eye. Once again, I suggested using my new pitch-perfect concoction to seal the wound, instead of father's conventional method of wrapping the stump in antiseptic dressing. I explained to him that, if used properly, once the caustic agent in my recipe burns out any surface infection, the pitch will harden into an airtight shell to prevent any further risk of disease. Father, of course, refused, citing an incident from several years ago in which the wound did not cauterize properly, and therefore, a toxin from the resin seeped into the patient's body. Father rather dramatically called the result a 'drawn out and unnecessarily painful death.'

"The way he casually dismissed my invention as cruel forced me to bite my lip with such force that I tasted my own blood. I wished to point out the hypocrisy coming from the man who created a town built specifically to suck the last drop of life from anyone unfortunate enough to visit. Father claims that, as a doctor, it's his sacred oath to do no harm, to value all lives. And yet, he knowingly sells provisions to prospectors who do not know the mines have all but dried up. He owns the gambling den, where those poor miners slowly lose what little they've retained. He owns the saloon, where they drink to forget the families they've left behind in order to take their shot at forging a better future. I cannot think of another person in my life who has done more harm to this community than he.

"As father loves to frequently point out, I am not a licensed doctor. Therefore, I am not under the illusion that I must operate under any such medical code. In order to push forward the world of medicine, sometimes, one must do harm. In a way, it's quite amusing that, in the end, father's failure to recognize his own monstrosity has only served to feed mine. By creating a system which turns civilized hopefuls into derelict wretches, he has created for me an unending supply of patients in which to perfect my craft. While father continues to eat the town alive by pretending to do no harm, I am doing great harm in order to rapidly accelerate the boundaries of science and medicine.

"I wish I could tell father that I have tested *twenty-four* new pitch recipes on fresh amputees in one of my personal operating rooms, and I have all but mastered the process. My most recent subject survived the removal of his arms and legs, using my pitch concoction for over two months. It was only when I attempted to use my method to seal an eviscerated eyeball that the subject perished. Though admittedly, the concept of using this treatment for head wounds was outside of my scope from the beginning."

As soon as Landon finishes reading the letter, his body recedes back into his scrawny curled frame.

"Okay, so that was pretty fucked up," Kiki says.

"I don't want to sound stupid, but how is that a clue?" Britt asks.

Everyone starts talking at once. They're sharing their theories and ideas, while putting others down. It all blurs into a sort of dim background as my attention shifts sharply to a sound coming from outside the room.

Down the hall, I hear a harsh whistle, the kind only grandfathers these days seem to be able to produce. It licks its way into my chest and grabs my lungs, pulling me into the hall. Even after it's gone silent, its absence creates a specter of itself, ringing in my ears.

I know that whistle.

I've heard it before.

I hold my breath and wait, hoping I'm just feeling disoriented from chimney fumes.

"Did you guys hear that?" My words dissolve into Jell-o as soon as they leave my mouth.

Everyone else's voices are behind me, small and distant. Eventually they're replaced by the thudding of my heart in my ears. Its rhythm crashes into overdrive when two more whistles call out in short, punctuated bursts, followed by the words that have played through my head at least a million times over the last eighteen years.

"Clarence, come!"

Clarence? That's a weird name for a dog.

Distantly, I can smell burning pine carried on an autumn wind. See my little sister running up a grassy hill toward a parking lot. I hurry to catch up with her, my legs burning from the steep incline.

That's a weird name for a dog.

"This is Major Tom to ground control. Tawny, do you come in?"

D-wreck jumps out right in front of my face. I take a step back on instinct, but there's no floor for me to walk onto. I'm falling. My whole body is pure electricity, blowing out every fuse in my nervous system. Then my head is quickly yanked backward as something catches my fall.

D-wreck has his arm curled around my back. Just as quickly as I started falling, I'm now hanging in midair. My senses start to come back to me, and I look around, realizing why my foot had nowhere to go.

I'm halfway up the main staircase in the lobby.

"What happened?" I grab hold of the side rail and steady my feet.

D-wreck slides his hand away from my back but keeps a light grip on my shoulder, in case I fall again. "You tell me. I saw you wandering out of the Cigar Room and followed you up the stairs. I must have called your name a dozen times before you reacted."

"I don't know what happened," I say, still feeling muddy, like I've just been jolted out of a much-needed nap.

D-wreck gives me a smug look. "Seriously? I thought I was the one that was supposed to be messing with everyone."

"I am serious. I have no idea how I ended up here. Why did you follow me anyways?"

"Because I'm here for you," he says simply. "I got your back."

A little spark inside of me reignites, and I push myself away from him. "Oh really? You have my back?"

D shakes his head in confusion. "Yeah? What's wrong?"

I don't want to have to say it out loud. I know it will make me look petty and mean to the audience, but I can't help myself. "You told me before we came here that we were going to be a team. We weren't even here five minutes before you ran off with Britt and left me alone."

"That's why you're mad at me?" he says in genuine disbelief. "Britt Holley asked *me* to be her partner. Britt Holley. What was I supposed to do, say no?"

"Well, I—"

"Honestly, if Paul Rudd were here and he asked you to go exploring with him, would you really say, 'oh no, thank you, Paul Rudd, my boyfriend needs me?'"

My anger dissolves, and all I'm left with is feeling stupid. As always, D-wreck has proven himself to be as clueless as he seems. Why was I feeling so jealous anyways? It's not like we're even a real couple.

"Yeah, of course, I would let Paul Rudd take me anywhere. I'm sorry, I guess I just got a bit too in my head."

"Don't feel bad. This house is stressing us all out. We're cool, all right? I got you."

I nod. "All right."

He looks at me for a good minute with skeptical eyes, like he's trying to figure out if I'm pulling some sort of angle. In the end, he settles on a compassionate look that's impossible to distinguish between a performance or genuine concern. "Hey, maybe you should take a break. I was able to grab a bunch of bedsheets from Guestroom One down the hall. It's got a shower, and I think I even saw some clothes in there. Why don't you go get all this chimney crap off you and take a breather while the rest of us knuckleheads get a chance to solve some puzzles?"

Whether he's sincere or not, his warmth helps me feel slightly more comfortable. I suppose it's possible that the combination of breathing in some atomized death along with the stress of being locked in a giant televised escape room has me a little out of it.

Maybe my head *is* playing tricks on me. This wouldn't be the first time I've heard the old man's whistle when there was no one around. Besides, it's not like this is even a real haunted house.

For one thing, I know, with absolute certainty, the owner of that whistle is not only still alive, but is one of those millions of people currently watching me embarrass myself on TV.

CHAPTER TWENTY-ONE

From: Casting@Krentler.media
To: Board@Krentler.media
CC: Lucy.K@Krentler.media
Subject: Potential Subject #4

Gentlemen of the Board,

I have a potential cast member that I think would fit well into your criteria—former NFL linebacker Shawn Eamon.

I know it's been a few news cycles since he was removed from the league, but I believe the story is still fresh in most Americans' minds, and he would be an ideal candidate to take part in *Slashtag*.

Let me know what you think,

Carol

From: Ron.M@Krentler.media
To: Casting@Krentler.media
CC: Board@Krentler.media

Are we sure he could pull in the numbers we're hoping to reach with our #4 slot? I would think the idea of a Black football player who is also gay cancels each other out in terms of audience appeal...

Ron

From: Casting@Krentler.media
To: Board@Krentler.media

Great question, Ron. Our data shows that the combination of keywords for Shawn will actually work toward our benefit for multiple reasons. He has high polling numbers in the gay community, and a 58% approval rating among blacks. I know the original idea for #4 was to have a professional athlete bring in blue collar males ages 16-65. However, we feel confident that, for as many people that will support him, an almost equal number of conservative white males will tune in just to watch him suffer.

Again, our reports suggest that those who engage in "hate watching" tend to be much more vocal about bringing other members of their community on board, which could lead to a huge uptick in viewership once things start to heat up. Between supporters and detractors, I firmly believe, aside from Britt and Landon, no one will bring in more gross numbers than Shawn Eamon.

Carol

From: Ron.M@Krentler.media

To: Casting@Krentler.media
CC: Board@Krentler.media
Subject: Potential Cast Member #4

Fine, go ahead and make an offer. But if he joins, make sure he's one of the first to go...

Ron

CHAPTER TWENTY-TWO

D-wreck was right. A long shower helps to get my head straight, and I appreciate some time away from having to perform for cameras. I've gotten my clothes as clean as they're going to get, but there doesn't seem to be a good drying solution beyond laying them over the shower curtain.

In the meantime, I found an outfit in the room's wardrobe that looks straight out of the 1920s. The clothes are genuine—it's like the smell of an entire antique store got crammed into one blouse and dress. The top is a white button-up shirt that reinvents the word *modesty*, while the heavy wool skirt runs all the way down to my ankles. It makes it hard for me to walk without feeling like a penguin. It's only to wear until my own clothes dry off, but the humiliation of having any footage of me in this outfit should provide enough entertainment to satisfy even my most spurned fans.

I said I was here to make penance, and this is certainly one way to do it.

I'm relieved to find a vintage makeup set in the bathroom and give myself enough of a powder to hide the scars on my chin and forehead, before re-entering the program. There's a tightness in my chest with the knowledge that every awkward step I take is being broadcast to the entire country. It makes even simple tasks, like walking and breathing, feel forced. I follow a trail of voices through the lobby and down a hall to a grand dining room that feels like it's been pulled straight out of the Overlook Hotel.

The cream-colored walls of the octagonal chamber climb nearly two dozen feet alongside a series of stained glass windows. Each of the windows are covered in intricate designs and patterns, all stemming from a large red circle in the center. Massive velvet curtains hang on the sides of each window and run in decorative pelmets across rusted bars. There are about a dozen tables, each octagonal themselves, complete with off-white linens and silverware that blur the line between authentic and replica.

D-wreck, Britt, Landon, and Kiki are gathered around a table, where there is already an empty bottle of Bordeaux and a second standing mostly full. All four of my castmates stop mid-conversation when they notice me in my creative attire.

"Well gee golly gosh, aren't you quite the dame," D-wreck says, his voice imitating the cheesy announcer in the welcome video.

"Soak it all in while you can, chuckles. You have until the second my normal clothes dry to make as much fun as you want. After that, I don't want to hear another word about this for as long as either of us shall live."

"Who, me? What kind of lout do you take me for? I'm with the times, doll face!" D taps off the ash of a pantomime cigar to really complete the character.

"I for one think you look retro-chic." Britt pours a glass of wine and invites me to an empty seat between her and Kiki.

I join them at the table, grab the glass, and us three ladies have a toast.

"To the Suffragettes!" Britt shouts, then brings the glass to her lips.

I give her a playful sneer, then take a sip of wine. It's strong and heavy. As I swallow, it feels like it dries my mouth out more than refreshes it. The wine hits my stomach with a hot rumble, reminding me how hungry I am.

"Where are the other guys?"

"Costanza's getting started in the kitchen, and Shawn's his sous chef," Landon says. He's the only person at the table with a glass of water instead of wine.

"Oh my God," Britt interjects. "You should have seen Shawn's face when the creepy chef asked him to help cook. It was, like, the cutest thing I've ever seen."

"Did I miss anything good?" I gesture to the yellowed paper sitting in front of Kiki. Her phone sits next to it, the screen filled with notes.

Kiki holds up the clue and shakes it for emphasis. "I've re-read the diary entry a few dozen times now, and there are a couple things that stick out to me. First, this guy had some serious daddy issues. I don't know why that's important, but he talks about it *a lot*, so I figure it must have some form of relevance."

"Fun fact," Landon interrupts, "Arthur's complicated relationship with his father was what drew me to the role in the first place. At its emotional core, it's the story about a boy trying fruitlessly to win the love of his father and, as a result, taking extreme measures to step out from under his shadow. It's a very complex relationship."

"Cool story, bro." D-wreck turns his attention back to Kiki. "What else you got?"

"The second thing is this pitch concoction. From what I remember in the movie, Arthur had dozens of insane inventions that he used to torture people. The thing is, the only creation we focus on here is the pitch. Again, it might be relevant to some puzzle later—it might not—but either way, it's worth noting.

"The third thing—and this is what I think we can actually sink our teeth into—is the number. Aside from the date on the top, which seems a little too obvious, the only other number he gives that stands out to me is twenty-four. He says, 'I wish that I could tell father that, since that last occurrence, I have tested twenty-four new pitch recipes on fresh amputees,' and so on. Twenty-four could be referencing something here in the house."

"Okay, so we need to think of things around the hotel that there could be twenty-four of," Britt says, adding nothing valuable to the conversation, but still sounding like the revelation was hers.

"This *is* a hotel, right?" D-wreck says. "All the guest rooms have numbers on them. What if it's a room number?"

"I must have some rubber stuck in my ears. Did I just hear D-wreck say something useful?" Costanza limps into the dining room, with a server's tray full of food to accompany his sarcastic comment.

Shawn is closely in tow, holding several more plates.

"Even a broken clock's right once per day!" D-wreck says.

"All right, I immediately take back what I said."

We each receive a large plate full of steak, green beans, and potatoes.

"Those are olive oil smashed fingerling potatoes, my mom's recipe," Shawn says with beaming pride.

The meta question of how I have to behave on camera snaps back into my head, just as I am starting to have some fun. I haven't eaten meat publicly in years, and I have to make a decision now whether it's going to help or hurt my reputation by eating a steak.

"I'm actually a vegan," Landon says. "Do you have any grilled portobello steaks, or perhaps a dairy-free salad somewhere in the back?"

"Sure, sure," Costanza says. "We've got a great vegan option, actually. You're welcome to enjoy all the sides of potatoes and green beans you like." He stabs a fork down on Landon's steak and transfers it to Shawn's plate. "Here, bonus for the sous chef."

Landon's made the decision easy for me. I'm going to eat the steak.

It looks delicious, and at this point, it would make me look worse if I didn't. I just have to make sure I do it in a way that doesn't offend my vegetarian fans or sponsors.

"I can't even tell you the last time I had meat," I lie. April and I made tacos last night. "But if I'm going to be able to keep my strength up, I'm going to need every ounce of protein I can get." I want to add a bit about honoring the opportunity to taste Costanza's food, but I don't want to lay it on too thick.

We all dig in, and the meal is incredible. Having something to enjoy lets everyone loosen up a bit. It's as if the game is on pause, and we're just seven weirdly famous people having as normal a conversation as we can manage. Landon tells a story about convincing Bradley Whitford to invest in some new eco-refrigerator company. Britt shares a behind-the-scenes story from *Holleywooed* and dishes on what Kim Kardashian is like in real life. Costanza is getting drunk, occasionally pulling the bottom half of his mask up and draining half a glass at a time.

Kiki is the only one who remains focused on Wilson's letter, occasionally referencing back to her notes app and making additions or edits. She picks at her food, putting away maybe half as much as everyone else. At one point, I see her shuffling around her bag, then popping a couple of pills.

"Are you feeling okay?" I ask her quietly.

"Yeah, just a bit of a headache. I think this is the longest I've gone without a smoke in months."

"How are you doing?" D-wreck asks Shawn, with a mouth full of food. "You've been pretty quiet."

"Yeah, no, I'm good. Just thinking of the last time I made these potatoes for Danny. They're his favorite, so I cooked them as our last meal together before he took off for the season."

"Oh right. Because he's still in the, uh..." D-wreck's sentence trails off. He's clearly realized he's putting his foot in his mouth.

Shawn nods awkwardly. "Yeah."

"Shit, man, sorry to bring it up like that. My bad. I'm guessing it's probably still a sore subject?"

"Getting dropped from the NFL for being gay, while my partner still gets to be a superstar? Yeah, it's definitely a bit raw, but it's also pretty much the only thing people want to talk about these days, so I guess I'm pretty used to it by now."

"But hey," D pushes forward, trying to lighten the mood, "at least now you guys get to enjoy that Cali life. I'm sure you're living in a dope-ass mansion in the bay area, right? And it's not like they can take that Super Bowl ring from you."

Shawn looks incredibly uncomfortable, clearly trying to choose his words carefully for the cameras. "Actually, Danny and I are going full long distance right now. My mom's sick, and I had to move back home to Alabama to take care of her."

D glances wildly around the table, looking for a life raft, but no one is there to toss it to him. "But the ring, right? That's still gotta feel good."

"Sure. Football was a very important part of my life, but honestly, I haven't really even unpacked all my stuff. It's still all sitting in a box somewhere in my mom's attic."

D nods, showing actual embarrassment. "Oh."

There's a lingering silence threatening to become painfully awkward, when Kiki seizes the opportunity to pull us back into the game. "So about the clue, I was thinking D-wreck's idea to check room twenty-four is solid. We should go to the lobby and see if there's a key to get in."

"What, no dessert?" Landon asks, clearly still hungry.

"You wouldn't be able to eat it anyways," Costanza says, waving him off.

Next to me, Kiki's leg is bouncing a mile a minute under the table, and her hand is clenching her napkin.

Britt stands up, signaling dinner is officially over. "Kiki's right. We should probably get back to the game. Unless there really is a dessert."

"Nah, I was just messing with him," Costanza says.

A minute later, we're all back in the entry hall, while Kiki stands behind the front desk and scans the rows of keys attached to hooks on the wall. "Bad news, team. This hotel only has sixteen rooms."

"Oh right, I knew that," Landon says.

Kiki looks at him as if he just said the world was flat. "Why didn't you mention this earlier when I was explaining my theory?"

Landon shakes his head. "I didn't really think about it. You delivered it with such confidence and conviction. I was too caught up in the scene to question it. In acting, the emotionality of the performance is usually more important than the details of the plot."

"But when it comes to a puzzle, details are literally the only things that matter." Kiki slaps her hand against the clue for emphasis, then sighs. "Well, this was a fun field trip."

"Hang on," Shawn says, approaching Kiki. "Can I have a look at that note?" She hands it over to him, and he scans it for a few seconds. "What about this part below? First he says he tried his pitch technique twenty-four times, but then later, he says he did all this, quote, 'over two months.' Twenty four over two."

Britt furrows her brows. "Are you saying we should be looking for the room that's on top of room two?"

Kiki shakes her head. "Twenty four over two, as in divided by two. That would make it room twelve out of sixteen." She grabs a key from the rack and joins the rest of us in the center of the lobby. "I say we give it a shot."

"I agree." Britt snatches the key out of Kiki's hand and starts down a corridor toward the guest rooms.

"Actually, there's only eight guest rooms on the first floor, so we want to go upstairs," Landon says, pointing at the staircase.

"Of course." Britt immediately course corrects without any signs of embarrassment. "Let's get to it."

"Wilson mostly did it out of convenience," Landon continues. "Splitting guest rooms between two floors made it easier to connect all the secret passages and various torture chambers."

"How many torture chambers did this guy hide in here?" D-wreck asks.

Landon turns to D with an almost nostalgic grin. "Oh. So many."

CHAPTER TWENTY-THREE

From: Casting@Krentler.media
To: Board@Krentler.media
CC: Lucy.K@Krentler.media
Subject: Potential Subject #2 or #6

Gentlemen of the Board,

I believe I've found an excellent candidate for Subject #6. Koyuki Suura, aka Kawaii Kiki as she's known on her channel. Originally from Australia, she would be the youngest of our subjects at 24 years of age, which is great for Gen-Z viewers. Her channel focuses on creating costumes and accessories for IP's, then wearing them at large comic and film conventions. Because her costumes impress fans of a wide range of licensed movies and games, her demographic is huge, reaching both men and women aged 10-45. Her fanbase also brings in diversity, thanks to her Australian and Japanese heritage.

Another factor for consideration is her experience with escape rooms and puzzles. Her channel includes over thirty videos of escape room reviews, which leads us to believe she would be a valuable asset in order to keep the team from stalling out during puzzles. This is also where I would like to float the idea of considering Kiki for the #2 position. The other subjects wouldn't suspect her of being a plant if she's already known for her puzzle-solving skills.

Finally, in our research, we found a history of drug abuse and a skeleton in her closet that could be leveraged to make her more cooperative. If the candidate makes it to the next round of screening, I will attach an outline of a potential arc.

Let me know what you think,

Carol

From: William.K@Krentler.media
To: Casting@Krentler.media
CC: Board@Krentler.media, Lucy.K.@Krentler.media

She seems like a good fit for the show, though I'm not sure about entrusting so much responsibility on her. Let's see how things go with our first choice, and if they decline, then we will revisit the #2 discussion.

Either way, let's push her along to the next round.

CHAPTER TWENTY-FOUR

Kiki leads us through a series of upstairs hallways, using her notes app to track based on the notations of certain doors.

"Look at that. Someone else is using your system," I whisper to Shawn.

"I wouldn't exactly call it a system. This is literally what the notes app is for." Even though he's denying credit, Shawn still gives me a humble smile.

"And here we are," Kiki says, looking up from her phone to point to the middle door in a trio of guest rooms at the end of the hall.

Britt glides past her and fits the key into the hole for room twelve. To our quiet surprise, it turns easily, granting us access to a guest room almost identical to the one I visited downstairs.

"All right, so it's a room. What do we do now?" Costanza plops himself down on the bed and checks on his injured leg.

Kiki starts to speak, but Britt talks loudly over her to keep the spotlight on herself. "Now we look for clues. Has anyone here done an escape room before?"

Only two hands come up. Shawn goes first. "We did one once as a team-building exercise. No one was into it except me and Danny. We didn't do so great."

The other is Kiki. "I literally have an entire portion of my channel dedicated to escape rooms."

"Oh," Britt says. "I did one for Kaley Cuoco's bachelorette party once. We got out with twenty-two minutes to spare, but if doing escape rooms is, like, your thing, maybe you could tell everyone what kind of stuff to look out for."

"Thank you," Kiki says, having officially been granted permission to speak. "Everyone look around for something that seems odd, or out of place. Keep an eye out for any specific details, like letters, numbers, odd shapes—they are likely part of a clue. There's seven of us, and it's a pretty small room, so this shouldn't be too hard. Everyone try to split up as best you can, and if you see something, say something."

Everyone gets to work, searching through the bed, drawers, and wardrobe. Having already experienced what the inside of a normal guest bathroom should look like, I figure I might be of some use looking for clues in there. I open the door, and for a moment, I'm once again questioning if I'm in reality or not.

The bathroom looks like something straight out of *Hostel.*

The remains of a woman lie hacked to pieces in the tub; she's just a torso and head lying in a pool of her own blood. Her arms and legs are severed and strewn about the room, and the stubs of what's left are coated in a shell of hardened black slime.

A scream squirms its way up from somewhere deep inside of me, but something cuts it off at the pass. This isn't real. None of it is. For one thing, the room is covered in blood, and yet I'm not even catching a whiff of copper or iron in the air. It's all corn syrup and food dye.

Kiki may be the queen of escape rooms, but I've been doing haunted house mazes with April since we were kids. In a different context, I would actually be having the time of my life right now. I have to remind myself this isn't just a game—it's a performance. I need to play my part of the wholesome lifestyle guru, who doesn't want to examine the wound sites further to see how realistic they are. I make the decision to scream, but by now, it sounds forced and not nearly as urgent as it should.

Even when I'm doing something as simple as screaming at a murder scene, I still have to work to sell a lie.

"Oh my God," Shawn cries, backing away and covering his mouth with his hand.

"What's going on in there? What happened?" Costanza asks.

"It's Lucy," I say. "The host lady. Looks like she's been chopped up with an axe or something."

"Probably not an axe." Landon shows nothing but fascination as he settles into his role of resident expert. "More like a hacksaw. Chopping is messy. These were likely made with precision. Besides, Wilson didn't use axes until the end of his first spree, when he was more of a blood-thirsty maniac and less of a tortured scientist."

"Are you seriously talking about that shit right now? We need to get the hell out of here!" Shawn turns to leave the room, but the door leading back into the hallway is shut. He twists the knob and puts all his weight into it, but it won't budge. "There's no knob for the lock. Where's the key?" He looks over to Britt. "Where's the key?"

Britt is staring at the tub, doing her best impression of looking terri-fied. "I left it in the door," she says, after pausing just long enough to sufficiently heighten the tension.

Shawn shoves his whole body against the door several more times to no effect. "Oh come on, man. This isn't funny!"

His panic is genuine, but I wonder to what degree everyone else is putting on a performance. There's no way any of us truly believe we're in front of an actual dead woman, but the reactions some of my fellow castmates are giving makes me wonder if I even have what it takes to muster up that kind of delivery. Back home, when everyone else would be screaming and jumping at Halloween haunts, I'm always the one who can't stop laughing.

Kiki wastes no time inspecting the room. She leans over the bath-tub, taking a closer look at the body and its severed parts. After spending a few seconds pretending to muster up some courage, I join her, deciding I can make myself useful while also pretending to be scared. Unlike the bathroom I used earlier, there's no toilet or sink in here, just a single porcelain bathtub sitting in the center of a triangle-shaped room. On the wall to the right of the entrance, there's a large mirror with a golden frame that nearly goes from floor to ceiling.

"Do you think this is going to lead us to our next clue, or more of a shock and awe move from Arthur Wilson?" I ask Kiki.

"I think it's probably a little of both. I don't see any pockets on her dress. Try to look around and see if you can find anything she might have been holding."

I search the floor around her severed arms, but aside from a serious amount of phony blood, I don't see anything of note. "Nothing in her hands. I don't even see a phone. I hate to put this out into the universe, but do you think it could be in the bathtub?"

Kiki steps around the tub, hesitant to put her hands in. "I don't see anything. Even if it was in there, it's probably dead by now." She lets out a mousy giggle. "Sorry, poor choice of words."

I give her a smile I hope will convey that I'm starting to have fun too. It's really beginning to feel like I'm in a horror movie...but without the fear of dying. And while I'm absolutely certain there's something horrible in store for me in the future, right now, I have to admit, I'm actually having a pretty good time.

"Hey Kiki, I think I found something," Shawn says from the bedroom.

"What is it?" Britt says, now over her freak out reaction and back into her starring role.

"There's a clock in here that's stopped at twelve. I'm wondering if maybe the time is important."

"Hmm, that's a good clue," Britt says, nodding. We all sit through a pregnant pause, waiting for Britt to elaborate on her thought.

When it becomes clear she doesn't have a follow-up statement, Kiki speaks up. "Do the hands move, or are they locked in place?"

"I think we're definitely onto something. The hands move, but the clock is plastered to the wall."

"Okay. So that probably means we need to find a time from some-where else and then match it up on the clock."

I look down, and the answer is literally lying at my feet. "I think I know where the other clue is. Lucy was wearing a watch."

Even though I'm excited to do it, I still feel slightly squeamish picking up her arm to flip it over and see the watch face. The arm feels heavy and cold, like I would imagine from a real severed limb. I want to test out the fingers, see how realistically they bend, but instead, I choose to let Landon keep the mantle of the morbid one and focus my attention onto the task at hand. The glass is shattered, probably from the implied impact of a real severed arm landing on the ground.

"Try 3:14."

A few seconds later, there's a heavy click behind me. I turn and watch as the wall-length mirror slowly swings open, letting out an aching groan of rusted metal. It's a doorway leading into another room.

"It worked! Hey guys, there's a way out through the bathroom."

Shawn is the first to bolt for the door, beelining it across the bathroom. D-wreck follows close behind, laughing as Shawn nearly falls over from slipping on the bloody tile.

"You sure they kicked you out of the NFL because of the whole bigotry thing and not because of, like, a coordination thing?" he jokes.

"Very funny," Shawn says, with just a hint of actual amusement.

"Maybe you should try ice skating next."

Kiki, Landon and Britt all follow me into what appears to be a study. There are books and papers strewn around a large table. The walls are painted a bright pastel yellow, largely covered by the skeletons of small animals posed behind glass frames. In the center of the room sits a chair facing toward the glass door. It's bolted to the ground and has clamps on the hands and feet.

"Look at all of these," Kiki says, scoping out a bookshelf. "*Traumatic Injuries of Facial Bones: An Atlas of Treatment*. A little light reading before bedtime, huh?"

"I wonder if there are any cannibal cookbooks in here for Costanza," D-wreck says, then looks around for either validation or an incoming punch. "Wait, where is he?"

The door between the bathroom and the bedroom slams shut on cue.

"Uh-oh."

"That seems bad," Shawn says, back on full alert.

I lift my ankle-length skirt, hop back into the bathroom, and try to re-open the door into the bedroom. The knob twists, but no matter how hard I pull, the door won't give. I start to pound on it instead, calling out Costanza's name.

I can hear him on the other side, feel the knob turning from his efforts. There has to be some other trick, maybe a different time he could set on the clock to get the door open. I start thinking of potential numbers, when an ear-piercing scream completely redirects my attention to the bathtub.

Lucy's not dead.

She's awake and shrieking in pain and horror. In fact, she does such a convincing job of conveying pure terror, I almost forget she's an actress. I had just assumed it was a doll in the tub, but I have to commend her for committing to the bit.

Unfortunately for me, her professionalism only serves to highlight my total ineptitude at playing along.

"Lucy, are you okay?" I ask stupidly, feeling like I've been put in the middle of a scripted scene without knowing my lines.

"My arms and legs! That fucker took my arms and legs!"

"What do you want me to do? Should I try and pick you up?" I reach into the tub to grab ahold of her, and she smacks my hand away with one of her stumpy arms.

"No!" she shouts, with a level of urgency that is legitimately startling. "He's coming back. You need to get out of here! Get help!"

The light flickers overhead, and then suddenly, a man is standing in the far corner of the room. There's a hacksaw in his hand. He's wearing a surgical apron, with a medical mask over his mouth and nose. Even behind the face coverings, it's clear that it's Arthur Wilson, given away by his thick, bottle cap glasses and brown suit underneath the apron.

This has to be some sort of trick, a bit of Hollywood magic, but I can't figure out how he just materialized like that. My heart surges in my chest, and I try to rationalize the man who just appeared before me. What's most impressive, and also terrifying, are his eyes. They have a shining, mirror-like reflectiveness to them, something I've never seen in a specialty contact lens before.

This just went from "fun scary" to "actually scary" in the span of about two seconds.

My lizard brain kicks in, and I try to take a lunging step away from the homicidal spirit actor. Instead of making a quick escape, the combination of my restrictive dress and the slick blood on the tile floor causes me to go flying straight to the ground. Worse than the pain of landing on my rear, I'm cringing at myself for being the girl who immediately falls down when trying to run from a slasher. I can already hear April giving me shit about it when I get home.

Wilson takes a step toward me, and I instinctively start to crabwalk away from him. My hands grope for solid ground behind me, but instead, they're slipping against wet pools of red.

A hand grabs me by the arm, and I let out a scream, this time for real. I look up. It's D-wreck.

"Come on, the mirror's closing!"

I hear his words but can't put them together, until I see Shawn and Kiki shoving themselves against the mirror door, which is slowly swinging shut.

"Get me out of here!" I shout as panic grips me. Too many things are happening at once, and it's like my body is just shutting down. I can't be stuck here with Wilson and Lucy. I can't be the first one out. Worse than anything, you *never* want to be the first one to go.

Another hand grabs my other arm. I'm lifted into the air, then pulled into the study just as the mirror door swings the rest of the way home.

"Are you all right?" D-wreck asks.

"Yeah, I'm okay." I try to take a few calming breaths to recenter myself, but another scream from Shawn forces me to look back the way I came.

Instead of seeing a door, or the wooden backing of a mirror, I'm peering through a window into the bathroom. Wilson slowly walks around the tub, redirecting his attention to Lucy, who pleads at the two-way mirror for us to get help. He finally stops circling the tub once he's positioned himself to completely block Lucy's face from our view. Her scream hits one last crescendo, when Wilson raises up the hacksaw, then brings it down in front of him, driving it back and forth in sharp movements. Lucy's scream quickly transitions to a choked gurgling sound.

Within seconds, her voice is cut off, and then there's nothing but the wet splattering sound of jagged metal carving its way through meat and bone.

People around me are having all manner of reactions, but all I can focus on is the rhythmic back and forth of Wilson's arm, until finally, the saw finishes its work. He turns on his heel to face the window, now holding Lucy's severed head. It's far more gruesome than anything I've ever seen in a horror maze. It all looks incredibly realistic. My body recoils on instinct when Arthur lobs the head at the window, sending me jumping back as it leaves a large red, streaking blob in the middle of the glass.

Without giving us a moment to rest, the door to the bathroom flies open. Next thing I know, Costanza is standing in the doorway. His rubber head whips wildly around the room, trying to make sense of the scene.

"What the fuck..." is all he manages to say before retreating into the bedroom and out of our sight.

Arthur stares through the mirror, directly into me. He pulls down his surgical mask and curls his lips into a sneer, revealing a mouthful of crooked rotting teeth. The lightbulb in the room shorts out again, and his body flickers out of existence, only to reappear a second later in the doorway to the bedroom. He takes two steps forward, until he's lost from our view.

Just as we begin to hear Costanza scream, the bedroom door slams shut.

D helps me to my feet, then hands me a blanket on a nearby chair. I can only towel off so much of the fake blood, and what's left is sticky and makes the hairs on my arm stand on end.

"You okay?" he asks.

"I'm fine. Just a little lightheaded from the adrenaline, I think. Thanks for pulling me out."

"Of course, I've always got your back." He puts his hand on my shoulder and gives it a squeeze.

It's one of the few non-verbal signs we've established together for when we're in public. A single squeeze for sincerity, and two squeezes to show you're putting on a show for the audience. It's comforting to get confirmation of a genuine gesture in the middle of this improv marathon.

"I told you those cuts were made by a hacksaw," Landon says.

"And I'm going to go ahead and guess that Costanza's out," D-wreck adds.

"What do you think will happen to him now?" Shawn asks.

"I'm thinking it's probably like a *Legends of the Hidden Temple* sort of deal. Spooky guy pops out of a door, grabs you slightly inappropriately, and then Olmac pulls you from the game. So long, Purple Parrots."

"Wait, so you're saying we only got one meal out of him?" Britt pouts. "I was really hoping he would make us coq au vin."

D-wreck pats Shawn on the shoulder. "And it looks like you just lost your cooking internship."

Shawn shakes his head in disappointment. "There's so much I could have learned."

I still can't believe how incredibly realistic Lucy's death was. My guess is, there was a trap door in the bathtub, and while Wilson was conveniently blocking our view, the real Lucy dropped down and was replaced by a headless prop. But it still doesn't explain how Wilson was able to simply appear out of thin air, or teleport across the room. Everything about him felt so real, it sends a tingle down my spine just thinking about him.

"Guys, I think I found something." Kiki's looking at a table on the far end of the room.

Britt steps forward and puts a hand on her shoulder, eclipsing the small girl in the puffy purple coat. "Hang on, Kiki. Before we go any further, I think we should all have a moment of silence for Chef Costanza. He died so that we could push on."

Britt bows her head. Everyone pretends to take it seriously, except for D-wreck, who touches his fingers against himself in the sign of the holy cross, then bites his knuckle as if fighting back tears. Kiki does her best to remain still, but her heel taps a million miles a second.

Eventually, Britt brings her attention back to us and continues. "All right, what did you find?"

"I think it's a map of the hotel," Kiki says.

I join the others in crowding around the parchment. There are three pages to the plans, depicting the first floor, second, and the basement.

Map of the Propitius Hotel

Much of the building's layout is just as nonsensical on paper as it feels in real life. Corridors turn and fold back on themselves for no reason. There are a significant number of areas left entirely blank. Some of these spaces have been filled in by pencil, creating a series of extra rooms and corridors I can only assume are part of Arthur Wilson's secret house of horrors.

"And look at this." Kiki points at three large red Xs scratched across the house, one on each floor. "I bet you anything, this is where we'll find the parts of the key. I think the best plan is to split up into teams and explore these rooms separately."

Shawn stagger-steps forward, inserting himself as best he can between us and the map. "Hey, uh, I don't want to be a party killer or anything, but it's almost midnight. I'm thinking maybe this seems like a good stopping point for the night so we can hit this with fresh eyes tomorrow morning?"

Kiki looks offended. "You want to sleep now? Especially after this?" She taps her finger rapidly against the map to illustrate her point.

"How about we take a vote?" Britt says. "Raise your hand if you're ready to turn in for the night."

Everyone's hands go up, except for Kiki and Landon.

"Sorry, that's four to two. Everyone, take pictures of the map with your phones, and we'll figure out what to do in the morning."

Kiki places her finger against a spot on the first floor of the map. "It looks like there's a cluster of three guest rooms all together over here. I'd reckon it's a good spot to set up for the night, if we all double up."

"I don't really do roomies," Britt says. "I'm very sensitive to ambient sound when I'm sleeping."

Kiki sighs and points at another room just around the corner. "All right, fine. You take this room. Tawny and D-wreck, I'm guessing you two will bunk together. Landon and Shawn, why don't you take another room, and then I'll solo the third."

"Are you sure you want to stay on your own?" Landon smiles in a way that looks charming on screen, but comes across as kind of creepy in real life.

Kiki tries to give a polite smile back, but it comes off looking more like a wince. "Trust me, I'll be fine on my own."

The Propitius Hotel

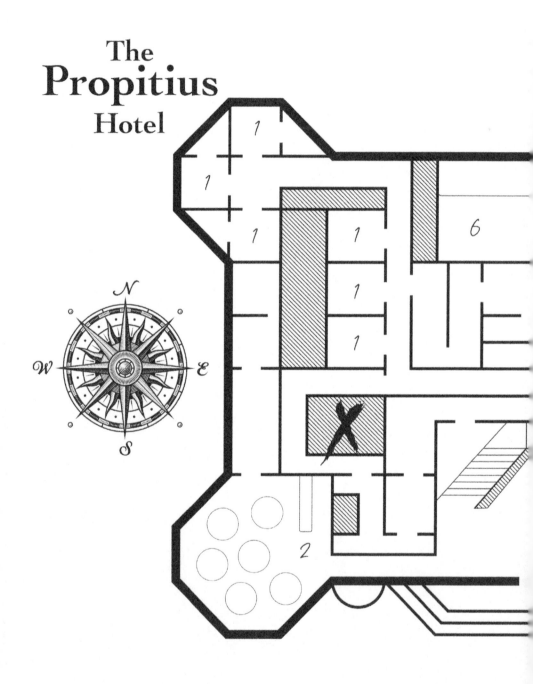

— First Floor —

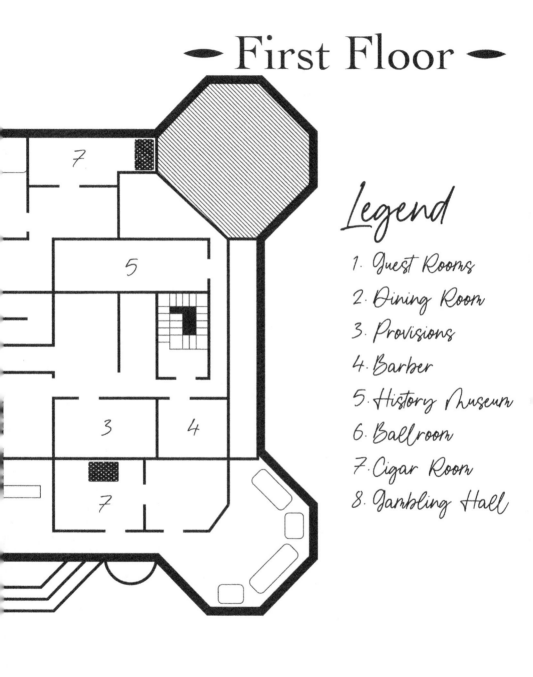

Legend

1. Guest Rooms
2. Dining Room
3. Provisions
4. Barber
5. History Museum
6. Ballroom
7. Cigar Room
8. Gambling Hall

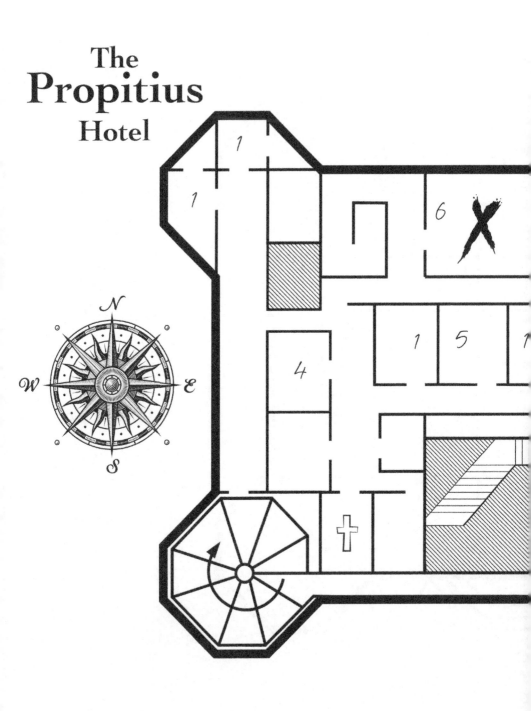

Second Floor

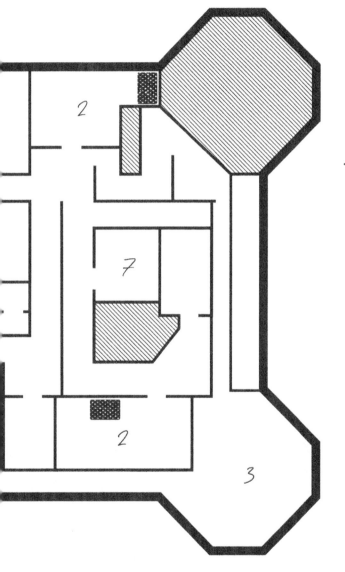

Legend

1. Guest Rooms
2. Cigar Room
3. Apartment
4. Apothecary
5. Library
6. Hunter's Hall
7. Nursery
8. Gambling Hall

The
Propitius
Hotel

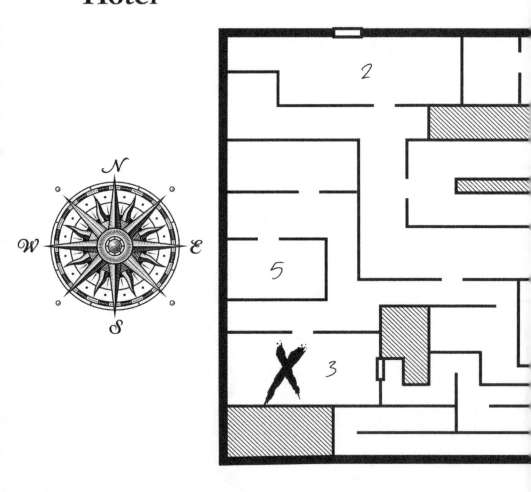

Basement

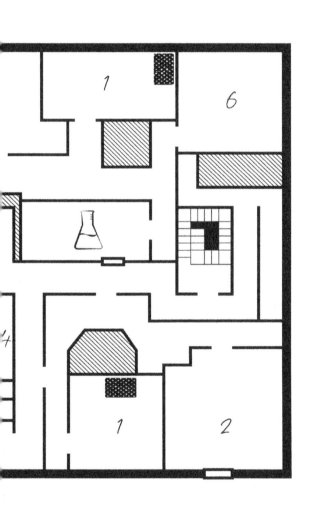

Legend

1. Furnace
2. Distillery
3. Clinic
4. Morgue
5. Storage
6. Electrical

CHAPTER TWENTY-FIVE

From: Lucy.K@Krentler.media
To: Board@Krentler.media
CC: Operations@Krentler.media
Subject: Day 1 Summary

Hello members of the Board and Operations Team,

The subjects have ended their first day of *Slashtag* at 11:29 p.m., within 45 minutes of our projected schedule. Congratulations to our crew on what has so far been a very successful show. That being said, there is definitely room for improvement.

- Because of his size, Shawn's decision to go to the basement during the "power outage" meant we needed to move forward on scenario B to get him out. However, when resetting Wilson's Trophy Room and placing Wilson Letter #1, Todd forgot to remove the Zippo lighter that wasn't supposed to be acquired until the spirit phase. We need the writing team to come up with a fix for this if/when they reach that point of the game. Let Todd's mistake serve as a reminder to everyone that attention to detail is everything.

- Though technically following her arc to a T, Kiki is perhaps overperforming in her leadership role. Our concern is that she may be stealing some of the spotlight from Britt, as seen in the analytics below. In the meantime, let's see how she does with the pills she took from the Apothecary.
- While we had not planned on having Wilson capture Chef Costanza until the end of day 2, I think we can draw out his elimination in a way that actually works better than our original plan. I will detail the new scenario in a separate email.

Analytics brief from Day 1:

- Peak Viewership was from 7-11 p.m., reaching 42 million viewers. This is well within our projected numbers for the first day.
- Currently, the most watched subject is D-wreck, with 37% of our viewers utilizing the Cast Spotlight feature to follow him. Britt is closely behind at 35%, though as stated before, we suspect it's due to the split in female viewers between her and Kiki. Surprisingly, our least-watched subject has been Landon Keating, with only 6% of Cast Spotlight users following him for more than a 10 minute period.
- We are currently at 6% of our target PVI, though I expect that number to increase significantly by the time the night shift is complete.

Finally, I suggest all the dayshift crew get a good night's sleep. We're just getting started, and tomorrow will likely prove to be a very busy day.

Lucy

CHAPTER TWENTY-SIX

"This is for hurting my dog."

His voice wakes me up, the way it has hundreds of times before. It's a strained sound that scratches its way through a worn-out set of vocal cords. My mind is playing tricks on me. It's almost as if I can feel his presence in the room, watching me with his black eyes.

"Like a doll's eyes," April likes to say about Him, which inevitably leads to her reciting Quint's entire speech from *Jaws*.

Somehow, comparing Him to a movie monster always helped us when He would come crashing back into our lives. I can't remember the number of nights we stayed up late, watching horror marathons, so we could have nightmares about *Candyman* instead of Him.

But I'm not asleep now, and the looming presence over my bed doesn't feel like something from a movie.

"Yes, right there. Good for symmetry," he says, repeating the words that are as deeply embedded into me as my scars.

I grit my teeth and start counting my breaths. The smell of mothballs and wet dog floods my senses. My heart is pounding in my chest, and I can feel a panic attack threatening to grab me by the throat.

This isn't real, I tell myself, while continuing to count my breaths.

A streak of pain slices its way down my chin. A warm wetness runs across my jaw and neck.

I open my eyes, no longer able to pretend the threat is all in my head, and try to scream. My panic is so immediate and all-encompassing, I've forgotten how to breathe.

He's here, standing over me. Yellow teeth spread across a malicious grin, coal black eyes staring down at me with gleeful contempt. He's not alone either. Standing next to Him is Arthur Wilson. He's pressing a scalpel into my chin, carving my face up like a pumpkin.

While still searching to find my voice, I thrash as wildly as I can to push the two men off of me. My arms are locked at my side, and so are my legs.

I'm completely helpless, robbed of all use of my voice and body. They're holding me down, somehow grabbing me by my hands and legs, even though they're both hunched over my face.

"There's another one, on the forehead. See it? I gave her that one myself." He's never said those words before, and it causes something in my brain to shatter.

Either I'm now making up new lines entirely, or this is all really happening.

Arthur Wilson tilts his head slightly, staring at the scar on my forehead. His empty eyes look huge, magnified behind a pair of thick round lenses. Wilson looks over to Him and nods, then brings the scalpel down toward my face again.

All my senses burn brightly, and a scream finally erupts from somewhere deep inside of me. The old man's smile grows wider. He breathes deeply, as if inhaling my suffering. The next thing I know, the room goes totally black, and all I can hear are hurried footsteps.

The light comes on. It takes a few seconds for my eyes to adjust. The men are gone, and Shawn and Britt are rushing to my side.

"Holy shit, Tawny, are you okay?" Shawn asks.

"Get them off of me!" I shout, unable to free myself, even though I can't see the ghosts anymore.

"Can you sit up?" he asks, trying and failing to sound like he's not also panicking.

"They won't let me go!"

Shawn throws the bedsheets off of me, and his eyes go wide. "What the actual fuck?"

I lift my head enough to see what's holding me down. My wrists and ankles are shackled to the bed. "Get me out of here!" I shout. More wet streaks run down my face, but this time, they're coming from my eyes.

"Just hold on. We're going to get these off. Britt, can you help with the other side?" The two start fidgeting with my restraints. "Tawny, can you hear me? I need you to stop fighting me so I can get these undone."

I didn't even realize I was still trying to rip myself from the bed. Though I try to calm down and take some centering breaths, my limbs continue shaking, no matter how hard I try to relax. It takes a few seconds for Shawn to undo the belt straps holding my right arm to the bed. From there, I'm able to reach over and work on my other arm, while Britt and Shawn release my feet. Once I'm free, I press my right hand up to the left side of my chin. It comes away red with blood.

"Let me get you a towel," Britt says, rushing to the bathroom.

My mind is spinning. I sit up, but I'm breathing so heavily that I start to feel dizzy and nearly topple off the bed. Shawn catches me, and again, an overwhelming instinct kicks in for me to fight. I don't know this man. I don't know this room. Everything and everyone is a threat. In shoving myself away from Shawn, my hand presses into something cold and sharp next to me in bed.

I lift my hand up.

The blade of a scalpel is embedded in my palm.

I scream, then reach for the handle of the scalpel and rip it out of my hand. Blood gushes from a long slice and further soaks the white sheets in large blotches of deep red. I drop the scalpel, and it clatters to the floor. Using my other hand, I grab hold of some sheets and press it into my wound as hard as I can.

"Oh Jesus." Shawn picks up one corner of the bedsheet and brings it to his mouth. He chews on it until he's made a small V-shaped part at the end of the cloth. He then rips the bed sheet into a long strip as easily as if he were tearing a piece of paper in half. "I need to tie your hand off to stop the bleeding. Is that all right?"

His words come out muddled and distant, but by this point, I've regained my senses enough to understand who he is and what he's trying to do. I nod, yes.

As he wraps my palm in the sheets, I try to piece together all the details. I'm in the Propitius Hotel, being live-streamed to millions of people. This is the bedroom I am staying in with D-wreck, who chose to crash on the couch.

Britt comes rushing back into the room with a damp towel and starts wiping the blood from my chin and neck.

"Where's D-wreck?" I ask.

"I haven't seen him since we went to bed," she says.

"Landon is missing from my room too," Shawn adds.

"What about Kiki?"

Shawn frowns and shakes his head. "We'll go find them in a minute. Can you tell me what happened?"

I have no idea how to answer the question. Frankly, I'm not so clear on the details myself. All I can think is how badly I wish April were here. I don't know what to do without her by my side. She's the one who's always calm under pressure, the one who is never surprised or discouraged when things get bad.

I try to think of what April would say, and it helps me put together a story that has the least chance of making me sound totally crazy. God knows I can't tell them about Him.

"It was Wilson. I woke up, and he was standing over me with a scalpel. He cut my face, and I started screaming. Then you came in, and he disappeared. What did you see?"

"It was dark," Shawn says, with a guilty look on his face. "I just heard screaming, and when I came in and turned the lights on, you were stuck in bed."

"Same," Britt agrees. "I could hear you from all the way down the hall."

"But you didn't see anyone in the room with me? No one standing over the bed?"

"Sorry," Shawn says. "But just because I didn't see anything doesn't mean you're wrong. It's not like you strapped yourself in bed, then cut your own face."

"I can't do this. I have to get out of here."

"Wait, slow down," Britt says.

"You don't understand. This isn't just part of a game. This was a personal attack. Oh God, they're going to kill me."

"Who's *they*?" Britt asks. "I thought there was just one ghost."

"What? I don't..." I stumble over my words, trying to backtrack. His voice still echoes in my ears, and I still see His message across my phone, just before walking into this nightmare.

Good dogs keep their mouths shut.

"I need a minute to clean up," I mumble, hurrying into the bathroom and shutting the door behind me. It takes a full ten calming breaths with my eyes closed before I can bring myself to look in the mirror. Just like He promised, there's a red line on the left side of my jaw, almost exactly symmetrical to the one I keep hidden on the right. A sheet of blood across my neck has absorbed into the already bloody white linen of my shirt.

I swallow back a shock of tears. Eighteen years covering up one scar, and now I've got a new reminder that the whole world just saw. I will never be able to pretend my face is perfect again. For the rest of my life, I'll have people staring at that scar every time they see me. Even if I cover it up, they'll know, and they'll be looking for it, trying to find the exact spot where they saw me get mangled on Social.

My hand rubs against the old scar tissue on the other side of my chin. I can still feel it splitting open as He slammed my face into the seatbelt buckle of his van. I can see my blood drawing lines in the recesses of the brown leather backseat.

Cleaning myself up and practicing my breathing helps me calm down a bit. It almost works, until Britt enters, knocking on the door as a formality after she's already halfway inside.

"You mind if I come in for a little girl's chat?" She shuts the door behind her and points up at the corners of the room, signaling that we're in a camera-free zone. "Off the record?"

I nod, even though I want nothing more than to have a full minute to myself.

Britt shuts the door behind her and takes a seat on the toilet next to me. "I want to ask you something—and you can kindly tell me to buzz right off if it's none of my business—but would I be correct in guessing that you weren't totally thrilled to come on this show?"

Something's different about her voice. She's talking with just the slightest hint of the Texas twang she lost years ago.

I turn to her, pulling a towel away from my split chin to show her the wound. "What gave you that idea?"

"If you can keep a secret, I wasn't too excited by the prospect either. They sure do have a way of making it hard to say no, though, don't they? I don't want to sound like a snob, but I've already got enough fame. I go to parties at Elon Musk's house. Do you really think I'd be having a sleepover at a haunted hotel if I had any say in it?"

Her words come at me like a cocktail of comfort and heartbreak. I'm not alone in being the target of Krentler Media's humiliation.

"I have to do this to help my sister. She's sick. They promised to help her if I came. Now I don't even know if I'll ever see her again."

"Hey, listen to me," Britt commands, in a tone making it impossible for me to do anything but give her my full attention. "It sounds like you and me both know how nasty these old boys can be. They're going to hurt us, degrade us, maybe even make us come out wishing we were dead. But they can't kill us, not for real. That's one of two things they can't do."

"What's the other?"

"They can poke and prod us all they want, sure, but it's up to us to decide how we react. If they get a rise out of us, it only amps them up even more. Shows them that they're onto something. As far as they're concerned, it doesn't matter who makes it to the end. They still win, no matter what. The only thing we can do is try and add a little bitter to their victory. For me, that means playing the well-meaning, slightly dumb, headstrong girl I'm expected to be. If I'm anything but that, my career could be over in a second. Whatever they do to try and make me break character, it's not going to work because I'm not going to let it. Does that make sense?"

Even though I've spent more hours watching this woman on TV than hanging with some of my own extended family members, this is the first time I've ever felt like I'm seeing the real Britt. Her posture makes her seem taller. Her voice is genuine.

"Yeah, and it really does help. Thank you, Britt."

And just like that, she slides right back into character, tapping her hands against her knees as her eyes brighten. "Great! I'll let you finish up. Take your time."

Before exiting the bathroom, I take one last look in the mirror and make sure my forehead scar is covered by my hair. At least I still have control of that.

Back in the bedroom, Shawn is sitting on the couch, looking anxious. "You don't think this could be some sort of elaborate prank from D-wreck, do you?"

I shake my head. "D's an asshole for sure, but he wouldn't physically hurt anyone on purpose. At least not without their consent first. Wherever the three of them are, I'm at least assuming they're together."

"We're going to have to go wandering around this haunted-ass house in the middle of the night, aren't we?" Shawn asks.

"I don't really see another option." I search for my phone at my bedside table.

"What if we just, you know, used the broadcast app to tell everyone to come back?" Britt suggests.

Shawn snaps his finger and points to Britt. "Now, that's an idea. If we can join back up without risking an encounter with a killer ghost? Sign me up." Shawn pulls his phone from his pocket and holds it out in front of his face.

Britt doesn't hesitate to take a seat next to him, putting herself in frame.

"Wow, do these cameras seriously not have any filters? I look scary AF on this thing."

"Wait," I say. "We each only get one of these videos to send. Maybe we shouldn't burn through them unless we have to."

"It's three in the morning. Ghosts are tying people to beds, and half the crew is missing. I'm making the call." Shawn presses a button on his screen. "Landon, Kiki, D-wreck, where are you guys? Bad shit is going down, and you need to get your asses back to the room block ASAP."

He taps his screen, and within five seconds, my phone starts buzzing while playing a little chirping tune. Somewhere on the couch, beneath

Shawn's rear, a second phone is jingling, just slightly out of sync with mine.

"Well, this seems bad," Shawn says, fishing the phone out from between the seat cushions and examining D-wreck's name engraved along the back. "I guess we just have to hope he's with Kiki and Landon."

"Unless they left their phones behind too," I say.

Shawn shakes his head. "Why'd you have to go ahead and say something like that? Fine, we'll check my room first."

Across the hall, it doesn't take but two seconds to confirm my fear. Landon's black jacket and phone are sitting on his bed, and his shoes are on the floor. "Oh, come on, man. What are you doing?"

Kiki's room is the complete opposite. There's no sign of her fluffy purple jacket, white canvas bag, or phone. Her bed doesn't even look like it's been disturbed.

"At least she has her phone," Britt says.

I nod. "Yeah, but I don't think we can count on her being with them. This whole thing is suspicious on multiple levels. Something's going on."

Britt lets out a heavy sigh. "I think we're going to have to go look for them."

Shawn shakes his head. "I knew you were going to say that. What about you, Tawny?"

I look to Britt. She knows that her best move is to play the game. If we don't, they'll only screw with us further until we agree to do what they want anyways.

"Yeah, I think we have to go after them. D-wreck wouldn't just leave without waking me up."

"Just for the record, I'm saying right now that this is a bad idea," Shawn says. "This time of night is when ghosts are always up to no good. Do we even have an idea of where we're going?"

"I know Kiki thinks that the three Xs on the map are clues to the location of the three key segments. It's at least a potential starting point."

We make it around another corner to the main hallway that branches off to the lobby. Shawn has his phone open and is looking at a picture of the map.

"Okay, guys, the nearest X from where we are now is actually pretty close. Though according to the map, the room doesn't have any doors."

"Shh," I say, hearing voices whispering up ahead. I step forward until I get a better look at the lobby to my right. Unlike the halls, which have wall sconces keeping the hotel dimly illuminated, the lobby's only source of light is the chandelier, which is currently off.

I squint and see something moving through the shadows by the check-in desk, barely reading the outlines of three figures, side by side. The one on the right is taller—could be D—while the smallest person stands in the middle. On their left, a figure is bent over, whispering.

"Hey guys," I call out. I barely mean to speak above a whisper, but the vaulted ceiling of the lobby carries my voice, rebounding off corners I can't even see.

The whisperer rears back, stands up straight. Even though it's nearly pitch-black, I can feel them looking at me.

I turn back to Shawn and Britt and wave for them to hurry up. By the time I turn around again, just the backs of the trio are visible, walking away at a harried pace. Part of me wants to run after them, but at the same time, I can almost hear April shouting, "this is how you get yourself separated from the group." I hazard another glance behind me. Shawn and Britt are catching up, but not moving fast enough.

By the time we reach the lobby, I can only see a single pair of legs vanishing around a corner. We cut across the lobby, moving as fast as my ankle-length dress can allow, and follow their path back into a lit hallway opposite the dining room.

It's empty.

This can't be right.

At the speed we're running, we shouldn't have lost them. It makes no sense for Kiki, D-wreck, and Landon to be running away from us in the first place.

We push forward through the hallway, into another large octagonal room filled with lounge chairs and coffee tables.

"I don't want to sound rude, but what exactly are we looking for in here?" Shawn asks.

I start to reply, but my answer is just on the other side of the room.

"Landon."

Standing there, staring at one of the back walls, is Landon Keating. He's completely motionless until I call his name. It's as if I'm waking him from a dream. He rolls to life, filled with a groggy urgency.

"Thank goodness you're here."

"Where's everyone else?" I ask.

"It's Kiki. She went in there and hasn't come back." Landon points at a dumbwaiter set in the wall. Its metal door is slid upward, and there's a small wooden box inside that makes me claustrophobic just looking at it.

"You're saying Kiki went in and rode this thing? On purpose?" Shawn asks.

"She hasn't come back in some time. I don't know what to do. It can only be operated from the outside, but whenever I send it back up, it always comes down empty."

"Wait," I say, putting a hand up to clarify. "I just saw you a minute ago along with two other people. What do you mean, Kiki went up the dumbwaiter? Where is D-wreck?"

"I haven't seen D-wreck," Landon says flatly. "Kiki couldn't sleep and wanted to go searching for clues. I joined her."

"That's not possible. I literally just saw three people in the lobby." I turn to Shawn and Britt. "Please say you saw them, right?"

"If you say you saw something, I believe you. One hundred percent."

"I appreciate your vote of confidence, Shawn, but that's not what I'm asking. Did you see them?"

"I was looking at the map on my phone."

"Me too," Britt says. "And also, everything else he said about believing you and stuff." After a moment of silence, Britt adds, "On the other hand, Kiki did seem pretty fierce about going hunting for clues. Do you think maybe you could have seen Landon's shadow or something?"

"No," I insist. "I'm telling you guys, there were three people standing in the lobby. I know what I saw."

"All I can do is speak my truth." Landon opens his palms to us in a performative show of honest body language. "I haven't seen anyone except the three of you in at least thirty minutes, and I'm beginning to have serious concerns about Kiki."

"Why would she even climb in there in the first place?" I ask.

"She figured out that Arthur's Apartment was right on top of this lounge and wanted to see if she could bypass collecting the keys."

"And you just let her do it in the middle of the night, without talking to anyone else?"

"To be honest, her tenacity makes her a pretty formidable figure. She can be very intimidating, and I've worked with John Cusack before. I know better than to stand in the way of passion."

"What do you think we should do? There's no way *I'm* fitting in there," Shawn says.

There's something very wrong about this situation, but aside from outright accusing Landon of doing something nefarious, I'm not sure what else I can say to convince Shawn and Britt that pursuing this dumbwaiter angle is a really bad idea.

Landon raises his hand. "I'll volunteer. Now that you're here, I just need someone to push the button for me."

The only thing that makes this bad idea seem worse is Landon volunteering to ride the dumbwaiter alone. His whole story feels like it was cooked up to convince us to let him in there. I don't know why he wants this so bad, but I don't like it.

"I should go," I hear myself say, just as much to my surprise as the rest of the people in the lounge. I know better than to go somewhere alone. That's rule number two of surviving a horror movie.

"Uhh, are you sure that's a good idea?" Shawn asks, sounding about as thrown off as I feel.

"Really, I don't mind going," Landon insists.

"I'm smaller than you," I say, even though the difference is miniscule. "And I'm good at puzzles," I add for good measure. "If anything goes wrong, I'll send out a broadcast."

Landon feeds me a grin that feels weirdly genuine, like he just convinced me to paint his own fence. "All right, but do please be careful. And if you need us, we'll be right here."

I climb into the small wooden box, but my constricting dress makes it almost impossible to even get in. Once I've finally gotten my arms and legs safely inside the vehicle, I give one last look to my companions and address Shawn directly. "Keep an eye on Landon, okay?"

"Hey, I'm standing right here," Landon protests.

"I know. If I'm not back in thirty minutes, head back to the guest rooms to wait for Kiki and D-wreck. If I'm not dead, I'll meet you there."

Shawn gives me a nod. "Will do. Be safe." He reaches up in front of me and grabs the metal handle to the dumbwaiter door. It takes a worrying amount of force for him to slide it down.

Almost instantaneously, I feel a screaming sense of regret, and it takes everything I have to resist clawing at the door to pull it back up. I look for a handle or something along the sleek sheet of metal to give my fingers purchase but find nothing.

Before I have a chance to call out, I hear a muffled voice outside the elevator say, "Going up!" before the roaring thrum of the elevator surges to life and I'm jostled around in the little box. It's unbelievably loud, and I have to drop my phone to cover my ears. It's so disorienting that I don't immediately realize the elevator is going in the wrong direction.

I'm not heading up at all—I'm dropping down.

To the basement.

At first, I think my senses are just going haywire, until I lean a little too far to my right and scrape my arm against the outer wall.

By the time the elevator stops, I'm more than ready to get the hell out of here. I pick my phone up off the bottom of the dumbwaiter and point its flashlight at the metal sliding door. Just like the one in the lounge, there doesn't seem to be any grooves or handles for me to grab onto in order to lift it up. I try pressing my sweaty palms against the door, hoping the moisture will create a sticky-enough connection to get some traction.

It won't move, almost as if it's either locked from the other side or rusted shut.

I start banging on the door, desperate for someone above to hear the signal and pull me back up. When that doesn't yield any results, I resort to swearing at the top of my lungs, calling Landon a son of a bitch. It does nothing but increase my own panic tenfold.

In this tiny box, my voice is bouncing back into my ears twice as loud as I'm calling out, to the point where it physically hurts. I then become aware I may be sealed in this box, using up air that may have nowhere to circulate. It might be possible for me to scream myself to the point of suffocation if I don't get out soon. It feels like I'm trapped in a coffin, without the luxury of having room to stretch my legs.

I'm starting to get a cramp in my side, flaring up with every breath I take. The dumbwaiter feels like it's getting smaller, giving the air a sense of weight bearing down on me from all sides. I reposition myself so my feet are pressed against the door and shove as hard as I can. When that does nothing, I pull them back and then kick the door with as much force as six inches of wind-up can allow. I kick it over and over, growing increasingly desperate, until my feet are rapid-firing against the door as I scream.

The cramp in my side is throbbing, and I'm starting to sweat from all the exertion. It's too hot in here, too small. I can't get out, can't cool down, can't catch my breath.

"I'm going to die in here," I say, my heart beating out of my chest.

"Who's going to die in here?" a voice calls out from the other side of the door.

"D-wreck? Is that you?" A surge of hope brings me back from the precipice of a meltdown.

"Yeah, give me a second," I hear him say, followed by the sounds of labored grunts.

Finally, the door slides up. Cool air floods in, and I can breathe again. D-wreck is standing there in front of me, and I've never been happier to see his stupid face in my entire life.

"Tawny, what the hell are you doing in here?"

CHAPTER TWENTY-SEVEN

My phone is blowing up. I'm yanked from sleep, and it takes me a groggy minute to figure out why it's buzzing so persistently. I take a look at the screen and scroll through the dozens of tagged posts.

Holy moly.

At this point in my life, I'm a pro at shifting from the bed to my wheelchair. But in half-waking excitement, my arm slips on the support rail next to my bed, and I come crashing down into my chair with twice the force expected.

It's fine. I'm fine. Just a bonked tailbone.

In the time it takes for me to wheel out into the living room, I've received two more texts from Hector. Rather than texting him back, I go ahead and send a video chat request once I reach my computer. Hector's normally bronze face appears a ghostly white in the glow of his monitor.

"Were you sleeping?" he says, as if it's an insane proposition.

"I *was*, before my phone started going nuts. I'm opening up Social now." I drag Hector's head over to my second monitor, then bring up *Slashtag's* main feed on the other.

Shawn, Britt, and Landon are all arguing in a place that kind of looks like the dining room. Shawn is yelling at Landon, while repeatedly pressing a button on a wall that doesn't seem to do anything. Then I click on Tawny's feed.

"Oh, come on!" I shout at the screen. "Tawny, you dingaling, what the heck are you doing in there?"

"I thought you might say something like that," Hector says. "I don't even watch horror movies, and I know you never go into a tight space like that."

I throw my hands in the air in disgust. "What are these people even thinking? It doesn't matter what sub-genre you're in—slashers, hauntings, monsters, even exorcisms. You never split up, never go solo. It's the second rule of surviving a horror movie! And that's not even touching on the third rule, which again is true of all horror, without exception. Never go out exploring after dark. Seriously, do these people want to die?"

"What's the first rule?"

"Always have a weapon."

"And you're sure Tawny knows all this?"

"Apparently not. Between this and the pratfall in the bloody bathtub scene, she's clearly not getting a Final Girl edit." I shake my head, unable to move past the insanity and stupidity of my sister's actions. "Hang on a second. I need to get some context here. Let me click over to the recaps page...Here we go. This video of Tawny lines up roughly with when my phone started getting alerts."

I click a thumbnail on the side of Tawny's page and travel back a half hour, seeing her sleeping in a bed through a green night vision filter. Over on the couch, D-wreck is curled up in what looks like a fairly uncomfortable position. The video seems calm and quiet for a few seconds, until a pixelated shadow appears on screen. D-wreck calmly sits up and stares forward, slowly nodding as the living darkness hovers next to him.

"Is this some sort of prank to scare Tawny?" Hector asks.

"I don't think so. Look at that weird shape next to him."

D-wreck rises to his feet and shuffles out of the bedroom. After that, things get quiet again, and I have to scrub forward a few minutes through the video's timeline before I see any more action.

Arthur Wilson appears next to another shadow, looming right over

Tawny as she sleeps. I squint to get a better view, but from this angle, I can only see the back of Arthur's head as he leans toward my sister's unobstructed face.

I haven't truly been shocked by a horror movie since *Hereditary*, but what happens next has my hands flying up to cover my mouth. He's holding a scalpel, carving a line down her chin.

Good for symmetry, a voice bubbles up from somewhere deep in one of the darkest recesses of my mind.

In the green light of the night vision camera, the stuff that comes pumping out of her jaw looks black, like oil.

"No way. There's no way."

"No way of what?" Hector asks.

I start to feel lightheaded. Moments ago, I was still pulling myself out of sleep. Now my adrenaline has me on high alert. "Okay Hector, I'm about to tell you something totally insane, and you're probably either not going to believe me or have a bunch of questions. For the time being, I need you to just go with it. Okay?"

I look at him on the other monitor.

He nods seriously. "Okay, sure."

"The cut she just got on her face, it's real. Don't ask me how I know. Just believe me that: A, there's no way she would agree to allow herself to be cut like that, in that place; and B, the fact that it just happened means that she's in very real danger."

Hector pinches the bridge of his nose and squeezes his eyes shut for a second. "Wait, you don't think this is the real ghost of Arthur Wilson, do you?"

"What I'm telling you is that everyone in that hotel's lives are at risk right now."

"And you're sure of that?"

I look at the list of cast members and click one. Kiki is in a nursery, staring blankly down at a crib, completely motionless. It's creepy but not what I'm looking for. I click a couple of others until I reach a video that is so loud, I have to crank down the volume on my speakers.

"You want more evidence? Click on Costanza's feed."

CHAPTER TWENTY-EIGHT

D-wreck helps me out of the dumbwaiter into a sandy-floored cellar that smells like burnt oak. There's a single bare bulb limping out a wavering orange light overhead, but it does little to help me get my bearings.

"D, where the hell have you been?" I demand.

"I got hungry. Went scrounging for a midnight snack and somehow got turned around."

"Bullshit. You abandoned me in there. What really happened?"

D-wreck flinches, and concern flashes across his face. "Honestly? I don't know. I guess I was sleepwalking? I woke up down here. I heard you freaking out and followed the sound. Why were you hanging out in a tiny elevator?"

I want to press him further, but given Landon's recent weird behavior, I honestly have no idea who to trust or what to believe. "I'm looking for Kiki. I was attacked, and everyone seems to have split up." I consider showing him the cut on my face, but a rush of insecurity has me bring up my bloody bandaged hand instead.

"Who did this to you?" he asks, his demeanor shifting suddenly to one of urgency.

"Who do you think? I woke up strapped to a bed, with the ghost of Arthur Wilson cutting into me with a scalpel."

"What the fuck?"

"Yeah. That's why we were supposed to stay together, remember?"

D rubs the back of his neck with his hand, looking guilty. "Holy shit. This house isn't messing around, is it?"

I shake my head. "No. It's not."

"I promise, I would never abandon you on purpose. I'm telling the truth that I have no idea how I got down here." He reaches up and grabs my shoulder, giving it a single squeeze.

I don't know what happened to him leading up to this moment, but that squeeze does more to calm me down than he probably realizes. Even though Landon seemed awake upstairs, his behavior was bizarre. The man standing in front of me right now is one hundred percent D-wreck, and he's catching on that this is more than just an ordinary game show.

"All right. No more splitting up. We'll tie ourselves together if we have to. But first, we need to figure out how to get back upstairs."

I pull out my phone and use my flashlight app to get my bearings. The walls are lined with barrels stacked on top of each other, many of which are broken or black with char. The source of the damage is evident—in the corner of the room sits a twisted pile of metal wreckage.

"Judging by the barrels and the wrecked piece of equipment, I think we're in one of two basement distilleries. My guess is, we're under the southeast corner of the building." I bring up the photos app and point to a marked distillery in the lower right corner of the basement map.

Before I can start to chart a path back to the stairs, a shrill whistle howls through the door at the far end of the room. Despite being over-heated just a few minutes ago, I start to shiver.

"Whoa, what was that?" D-wreck says, to my complete amazement. He even cranks his head in the same direction as me.

"You heard it too?"

"Yeah, it sounded like when my dad used to whistle at baseball games."

I'm not going crazy. I was worried that I was losing my mind, while everyone else was just playing a game. I should feel relieved in knowing I'm not alone, but instead, D-wreck's validation of my aural hallucinations only serves to double the sense of impending dread.

It's not just me Krentler Media seems to be intent on tormenting.

I retreat a few steps from the doorway, but something rolls underneath my foot and I slip. Pain shoots through my cut hand as I shove it out. I expect to brace my impact with the sand, but instead land on something hard and gnarled. I point my flashlight at whatever interrupted my fall and discover I'm lying in a pile of bones.

There is no questioning anymore whether or not they're real. My scream for the cameras is completely genuine. Bones are everywhere, all around me. Half buried in the sand, the grinning face of a skull stares up at me with hollow sockets and a large hole in the temple.

"How many people do you think this is?" D asks, coming to help me out of the mass grave. He freezes in place before he can reach me, eyes growing wide, and lets out a shocked grunt.

Behind me, there's a soft pattering in the sand, accompanied by a low rumbling growl.

I don't want to look; I can't look.

I have to look.

As slowly as I can, I turn my head over my shoulder.

In the corner of the room, far from the feeble reach of the dying bulb, there is a single glowing orange orb. Beneath it shines the wet reflection of a seemingly endless row of white fangs. It's like my own personal Cheshire cat, a disembodied face haunting me from the shadows. Only this one wants me dead.

D-wreck jostles my shoulder with his hand to get my attention. He's telling me it's time to get up and go.

I pull my feet toward me until I can grab the edge of my dress, knowing I can't afford to fall again. As soon as I secure my feet on level ground, the thing in the darkness redoubles its threatening growl. It takes several steps toward us, revealing the features of its black and brown face as it enters the light bulbs aura.

Its right eye is missing. There's just a pink vertical swell where my sister once slashed at it with a knife. That missing eye is one of the reasons I'm still alive today, and the reason she's trapped in a wheelchair.

I suddenly wish that I were just crazy. A hallucination would mean my brain is broken, which is something I've spent my entire adult life attempting to accept. If we're both seeing this dog, it means the world is broken in a way my brain is not prepared to confront.

"Don't run," I whisper, fighting every instinct to do the opposite.

Slowly reaching up and grabbing D's arm, I keep my eyes locked on the ancient rottweiler as I climb back onto my feet. I try to perform a calming breath, but my chest is shaking so hard, it almost comes out as a hushed giggle. Together, D-wreck and I attempt to take a single step toward the door, but the dog feints forward, peeling its lips back over its vicious fangs and letting out a sharp warning bark.

"Good Clarence, stay calm," I say, fighting every muscle in my body demanding I turn and run. *That's a weird name for a dog*, I hear my sister say every time the name pops into my head.

"You know this dog?" D asks, clearly confused.

"You could say that." As I hold my dress up to give my legs some running room, I trace a finger across the imprints from Clarence's teeth, preserved forever on my thigh. "We move slowly to the door, got it? When we get far enough back, grab the door handle, and then we'll shut him in."

"I've got a better idea." D-wreck ignores me completely, bending over and picking up a bone. He rises to his full height, then starts jiggling what looks like a femur in his hand.

"Stop it," I say, punctuating it with a jab from my elbow to his side.

"Who wants a bone?" D-wreck says, in a sing-song voice.

"I mean it, Derek. The dog doesn't care about a stupid bone. Just drop it." I'm hoping that using his real name will get him to understand I'm serious.

It doesn't.

"I've never seen a dog who doesn't love a good bone."

My idiot fake boyfriend then proceeds to hurl the bone toward the far corner of the room. Clarence immediately surges forward, just as I predicted, leaping up and snapping at us. I'm so loaded up on adrenaline that, on pure reflex, I pull back, managing to avoid his razor-sharp fangs by inches.

"Run!" I shout, turning and sprinting for the door.

It's nearly pitch-black in the hallway outside, so we have to feel our way, guided almost entirely by my phone's nearly useless flashlight. Behind me come the frenzied barks of an animal wild with the fury of the chase.

"Left or right?" D pants as we rapidly approach a split in the tunnel. The two paths seem to run parallel to each other, with no discernable difference between them.

"Right," I say, for no other reason than I'm currently to his right, and it's slightly closer for me.

There's no time to do anything but rely on gut instinct. We sprint another fifteen feet or so, following it down a series of twists and turns until splat, we smash right into a wall. It's a dead end.

We turn to face the dog, bracing for it to attack. It comes tearing around the last corner and then skids to a halt. Another sharp whistle cuts through the maze. Clarence just stands there, maybe two feet away from us, panting.

"What do we do now?" D whispers.

"I don't know," I reply, staring at the slashed-out scar where the dog's eye should be.

D-wreck tries to take a slight step toward the dog, testing to see if there's a way of passing him. Clarence growls and bares his teeth. D backs off. As he does, the dog slowly drops its aggressive stance as well. I'm trying to think of some way out of this but am coming up completely blank.

"Oh hey," D-wreck says, in sudden revelation. "Is this why you're afraid of dogs?"

"Now's not really a good time," I say through gritted teeth.

"Some could argue it's the best time," D says. "We currently have nowhere to go, thanks to Clarence."

"Fine. Yes. This is why I don't like dogs. This dog specifically."

"Do you want to tell me what happened? Or maybe why it's here?"

"I don't know. It's been dead for, like, fifteen years."

"Are you saying this is a ghost dog?"

I can feel D's eyes turning to me.

"I said I don't know."

I can't explain why a dog that attacked me in Arizona, when I was twelve, is standing in front of us. Even though I feel like my adrenaline is through the roof, I force myself to think like April, asking what would happen next if this were a horror movie.

If His dog was going to attack us, it would have by now. It means there's something in here for us to do, and it doesn't involve going back the way we came. It means He wanted me down here for a reason. Or something pretending to be Him.

I cast the flashlight around our immediate surroundings. At first, it just seems like we're trapped, but then I notice that two walls are made of concrete, while a third is made of wood.

"I think this wall might be a hidden door. Look for a latch."

D-wreck starts rubbing his hands along the wall, searching for an indent or lever. I take a closer inspection of the seams with the flashlight, glancing over at Clarence every few seconds to make sure he hasn't moved.

You're a good boy, aren't you, Clarence?

"Hey, you didn't by any chance see my phone up in the room, did you?" D asks.

"Yeah, we found it when we sent out a broadcast asking where you were, and it buzzed on the couch."

"You didn't, like, happen to bring it along with you, did you?"

"Does this dress look like it has pockets to you? It's hard enough worrying about tucking one phone into my waistband. And in case you haven't noticed, I have to hold my damn skirt up just to walk straight."

I'm running the flashlight along the corner of the wall, and somewhere above me, I catch the reflection of something metallic jammed into a crack. "I think I found something." I pick at it with my nail until I'm able to pry out a small gold ring attached to a bit of string tucked along the corner of the wall.

With three meditative breaths, I try to prepare for whatever horrible thing is going to come next. When I'm as ready as I'm going to be, I loop my pointer finger through the ring and give it a pull. Behind the wall, there's a *click*, followed by a crack of vertical blue light cutting a line between the wood and concrete. We push the wall. It's heavy, but eventually we have it angled far enough out that we can squeeze ourselves into the next room.

It takes my eyes a few seconds to adjust to the bright blue lights bearing down on a small medical clinic. There's a metal instrument tray on a stand in front of a large white curtain, and sitting amongst the medical tools is a carved piece of brass in an ornamental design.

"D, do you see that? I think it's part of the key!"

"Holy shit, you're right." D hurries over to the table and snatches the rounded end piece of the key before I have time to warn him that this might be a trap.

The moment he picks it up, the curtain behind the table drops, along with my stomach.

Chef Costanza is held to a chair via a set of three leather straps tightened around his midsection. His torso, as it turns out, is the only thing he has left that can be secured. His left arm is missing entirely. The socket where his shoulder should be is instead coated in a large malformed blob of hardened black goo. On his left, he's been amputated at the elbow. One of his legs is missing, along with his other foot. All of them are sealed off with obsidian.

It's hard to imagine his chef's jacket was white at one point. At present, it's a mix of black char from the chimney and red-soaked splotches. His armpits are stained a pale greenish-yellow, and running from his front lapel down his chest are several trails of orange, with little bits of brown stuck to it. My guess is that it's the steak from dinner.

Somehow, the idea of him throwing up in his mask feels almost as horrifying as the other tortures he's endured.

"Oh my God, Costanza!" I run toward him.

His head is wilted forward, though at the sound of my voice, it weakly raises to look at me.

"Tawny? Is that you? I can't see you." The mask has fallen forward on his face so that the eye holes only point to a pair of cheeks.

"I'm going to take your mask off, okay?" I reach forward and grab the rubber mask by the bulbous red nose and the top of the bald head.

When he gives me no protest, I go ahead and pull the whole thing up and off. The first thing I notice when lifting it is the smell—the amount of sweat, vomit, and pure fear trapped inside the mask all comes pouring out like a sour stink bomb, almost making me retch. I have to drop the mask to get it away from me.

What's underneath is a thin-faced Latino man in what I imagine to be his early forties. He's got short dark hair, pockmarks on his cheeks from teenage acne, and a couple days' worth of scruff around his chin. The veins running up his neck are almost as black as the pitch covering his amputated limbs. I imagine he'd be quite handsome under different circumstances, but right now his face looks more undead than alive.

"Wait, who are you?" D-wreck asks, almost sounding disappointed.

"What?"

"Sorry, dude. I'm just a little surprised that you're not a celebrity under there."

"I think we have bigger concerns right now," I say to D.

"Please. Kill me," Costanza says. "He's going to come back. You have to do it now."

"We're going to get you out of here, bro. Don't worry," D says. "But seriously, who are you?"

"That doesn't matter right now," I snarl to D, before turning back to Costanza. "Let's get you out of these straps."

"It's Miguel, all right? And I don't want out. Please, just kill me."

"Why do you want us to kill you?" I ask, searching his eyes for something other than hopelessness.

His body shudders in a convulsion of pain. "I'm already fucking dying. I can feel that black stuff inside of me. It's like my insides are on fire."

D-wreck looks around the room, noticing the white medical cabinets lining the walls and a tray full of surgical instruments sitting next to Miguel. "What would you even have us do?"

"I don't know. Just please, do it before he comes back. I can't handle this anymore."

It takes a few seconds before D-wreck starts reaching over to the instrument table.

"You aren't seriously considering doing this," I say. "This is a real person."

He turns to me, looking like a lost little child. There's no way I'm about to allow D-wreck to murder a person on live television. If he makes a move for any of those weapons, I'm prepared to do everything in my power to keep him from hurting Miguel.

"Don't do it," I say, in my most commanding tone.

The lights flicker overhead, and all around us comes a cascade of voices. There's so many of them, I can't make out what they're saying, only that they're full of hate...and directed toward the man tied to the chair.

Miguel starts to whimper. "Oh God, he's coming." He looks D-wreck in the eyes. "Please, man, just do it."

D takes a step away from the table. Miguel's pleading seems to be scaring him away from the act more than pushing him into it.

"No, no, no, come on, man, please." Miguel lowers his voice to almost a whisper. "He knows things."

Once again, D-wreck takes a hesitant step back from the begging man. I reach out and grab his hand, pulling him toward me, needing to hold onto something familiar. But this isn't a place where comfort lives.

To our right, a door swings open, and standing in its frame is the pale visage of a real life monster. His brown tweed suit is replaced with full white medical garb, tinged an eerie blue in the cool light of the medical room. Something about his smile feels unnatural, stagnant, like I'm looking at a photograph that's partially come to life.

Miguel fights against the restraints in his chair with what little force he can manage. His screams for us to kill him are so loud and insistent, I start to wonder if I made a mistake by stopping D-wreck after all.

D lets go of my hand and lunges for the instrument table next to Miguel. I shout for him to stop, terrified he's fighting the same thoughts of possible regret. His hand lands on a rusted saw, and my breath catches in my throat.

What if Miguel *is* an actor and this actually is all still just a show? What if this is their attempt at getting D-wreck to ruin his own life on live TV?

I'm about to shout for him to stop, when he moves past Miguel. He's not going to kill him. In fact, Derek's placing himself between Miguel and Arthur.

"Don't come any closer," D-wreck warns, holding the saw out as if it were a sword.

Arthur reaches into his apron with two fingers and delicately pulls out a scalpel with the reverence a famous painter might use when selecting their brush. He takes a single step into the room; everything about his movement feels disjointed and unnatural, almost as if someone had recorded him walking backward and then played it in reverse.

D swings the saw through the air. He's nowhere near Wilson, but his intent to defend himself is clear. "I mean it, bro. I don't care if you're an actor or what. You take one more step, and you're gonna get D-wrecked."

Wilson regards him for a moment, sizing my companion up, before pulling his lips into a mocking grin. The lights shudder. In the moment between darkness and light, Wilson blinks out of existence, only to reappear moments later standing directly behind D. Before I have a chance to warn him, Wilson brings his blade to the side of D-wreck's mouth, carving a curling line up his cheek like an overextended grin.

D-wreck screams and spins around with the saw, then leaps away from his attacker. The blade goes through Arthur's midsection as if there was nothing there at all.

There's no tricks of the light, no special effects that could allow a person to both hold a knife and be a projection. There's no mental gymnastics I can perform to convince myself this is just a group of actors making an edgy TV show. I'm standing in a room with the actual ghost of Arthur Wilson, and before this weekend is through, he's going to kill us all.

"Tawny," D-wreck says, his voice shaking as he backs up toward me.

"I know," I say, frozen against the wall.

"I'm pretty sure he's a real ghost," D-wreck says, spelling out the obvious.

"*I know,*" I repeat, with less patience.

"Well, what do we do?"

I just keep standing there, waiting for a plan to materialize, but come up with nothing.

Arthur's ghost stands by the instrument table, grinning at us with his mouth full of scraggly teeth. As terrifying as it is to feel his hollow eyes peering into me, a chill runs down my spine when he finally turns his attention over to Miguel. He picks up a rusted contraption from the table that looks almost like a vise but with grooves on either side of the end, as if to prop something open instead of closed. I've seen it before in the welcome video, though at the time, it was used to hold a man's sternum open during surgery.

Miguel is shaking his head back and forth, while Wilson dangles the retractor in front of his face. It doesn't take more than a few seconds before Wilson becomes visibly agitated and plunges his scalpel into Miguel's side. Miguel screams in pain, and Wilson seizes the opportunity to shove the retractor into Miguel's mouth, clamping it open. He attaches leather straps to a pair of metal bulbs on the sides of the chair so Miguel's head is locked in position, staring at the ceiling.

"We have to do something," I say, more to keep myself tethered to reality than anything else. I need to hear my own voice to know I haven't completely lost my mind.

"Oh no. No fucking way," D says.

Wilson reaches once more into his pocket and pulls out something that looks like an oversized red gumball. D-wreck starts to visibly tremble at the sight. He runs his free hand through his short hair, while his feet shuffle nervously in place.

"No way. Don't you fucking do it, man."

"What is that?" I ask.

Wilson holds his hand over Miguel's face, dangling the red ball inches above his propped-open mouth.

"Put it down!" D-wreck yells, charging at the surgeon.

Wilson does nothing to brace himself. He doesn't need to.

D should already know how this is going to end, and yet he still chooses to throw all his weight into swiping his hacksaw at Arthur while running at full speed. Of course, D runs right through Wilson and is unable to stop himself from crashing into the instrument table.

I'm about to swear at D for being reckless, but I catch a look of dismay on Wilson's face. Passing through him had no effect, but D-wreck connecting the saw to the gumball did. I watch the red ball soar across the room, bouncing several times, then rolling across the tile. I don't know why, but I'm sure that getting that ball is the key to saving Miguel.

Making a run for it, I pray Wilson isn't paying attention to me. It's only a few feet, but each step feels like playing a game of Russian roulette, when I know the ghost can travel at the speed of light. By some small miracle, I make it to where the ball is lying, and as soon as I bend over to pick it up, I feel a sharp pain thrust into the shoulder blade of my outstretched arm. It throws my world off-balance, and the next thing I know, I'm rolling sideways to the floor.

The pain in my right shoulder explodes when I hit the ground. Whatever was plunged into me is still in there, and by hitting the tile, I've only served to bury it further. I'm almost too blinded by pain to see a set of fingers reach down in front of me and pluck the red ball off the ground.

In his disjointed way, the surgeon walks back over to Miguel. D-wreck is screaming something from across the room as Wilson finally drops the gumball into Miguel's mouth.

The chef's body starts convulsing violently, and he makes this horrific gagging sound. A red foam bubbles up past his lips, and what looks like streams of blood run down the sides of his mouth. I know there's nothing I can do for him; I don't even know how to protect myself. Miguel is stuck staring at the ceiling, choking to death, and all I can think at this moment is that if somehow he and I could look each other in the eyes, I could at least help ease his suffering. Let him know that someone was with him in the end.

"Come on!" a voice shouts. It's D-wreck, bringing me once again back into the moment. He's standing in the doorway.

A wave of disorientation passes over me. I can't tell how long I've been staring at Miguel. A look around the room tells me Wilson isn't even here anymore. Miguel's not making any sounds. Pink bubbles continue to rise and pop out of his now still mouth.

"Where's Wilson?" I ask, feeling lightheaded.

"I don't know. We have to get out of here while we can." He's holding his hand against his bloody cheek.

I nod, half registering what he says, but a twinge of pain hits me as soon as I put my hand on the ground. Reaching up and over my right shoulder with my left hand, I find the metal handle of something sticking out of my back. A single firework of pain explodes when I pull a scalpel out of me.

Second one today, I think to myself. I try to get up, but my knees get caught on the edges of my dress, and I once again trip forward onto my injured hand.

"Come on!" D shouts.

I pull up my dress and run with him as fast as we can through the basement maze, making random turns until we find the staircase. We don't allow ourselves to slow down until we're all the way back to the lobby.

We grasp at the front doors, shaking and twisting at them with all our might, knowing of course, they will be locked. Eventually, exhaustion overcomes both of us, and we collapse on the floor.

"What do we do now?" he says.

"We need to find the others and figure out how to get out of here," I say, once I can manage enough saliva in my mouth to get words out. Suddenly, I realize I've still got the scalpel in my hand. "But first, I need to do something."

I've had it with this stupid dress. Spreading my legs as wide as the skirt will allow, I stab the scalpel down between my thighs. The knife cuts into the fabric, and I shove it downward as hard as I can, until I've cut a seam large enough to let me move freely.

"Feeling better?" D asks.

"It was the dress or me," I pant out, feeling my tired body sink against the door.

D stretches on the floor next to me, also clearly out of gas. "So hey, guess what? Ghosts exist."

I nod. "Yeah, looks like they do."

"Also, ghost dogs exist, and apparently they're here to haunt you specifically?"

Clarence is the last thing I want to talk about right now. "Seems like," is all I say, hoping he'll leave it at that.

Of course, he never does. "Why couldn't you have been afraid of sloths? Or sharks?"

"I don't know. Why are you afraid of red balls of bubblegum?"

He doesn't answer. I look over to him and see a renewed sense of fear, along with a deep sense of loss. I immediately regret what I said, even though he started it.

"I'm sorry," I say. "That wasn't cool."

D shakes his head. "It's fine. It's just not something—"

"I know," I say.

He doesn't have to explain it in front of all of America. For the first time, I consider telling him the real story behind Clarence, the whole thing. But I can't do it here. Not while He's watching.

"How about we take a trip to the bathroom?" I say, staring pointedly into his eyes and hoping he catches my drift.

He nods slowly, and the two of us start to stand up. A flashlight appears on the balcony of the second floor, glaring down at us. It's so bright, I need to press my whole forearm across my eyes.

"What the hell happened to you guys?" Kiki says.

Mission Log

- ~~Restore Power to the Hotel~~
- Destroy Arthur Wilson's Body Totem
  - Unlock Arthur's Apartment
    - ~~Find the key's knob~~
    - Find the key's shaft
    - Find the key's bit
- Destroy Arthur Wilson's Mind Totem
  - Unlock the door to Sutter's Sanctum
    - Destroy the Greed statue
    - Destroy the Sloth statue
    - Destroy the Wrath statue
    - Destroy the Envy statue
    - Destroy the Lust statue
    - Destroy the Pride statue
    - Destroy the Gluttony statue
    - Destroy the Disobedience statue
- Destroy Arthur Wilson's Spirit Totem

SOCIAL

CHAPTER TWENTY-NINE

Dripfeed *Presents: So* THATS *How You Get Eliminated in* Slashtag.

It's been almost 24 hours since Social's most anticipated new hybrid horror movie/reality competition has begun, and boy, do we have a lot of questions. How much of it is real versus scripted? What exactly is a ghost totem, and how do they find them? And what the heck is in that black goo that Arthur Wilson's cooking?

At least we've finally gotten the answer to one of the most burning questions: what actually happens when a player is eliminated? The show has been incredibly tight-lipped on how the fictional deaths of these real players would pan out in the game, something that has been a constant topic of conversation online leading up to Slashtag's *launch yesterday. Many Social users voiced concern that if players were just captured and removed, it would defeat the whole purpose of creating a horror series in the first place. The question was always how far the show was prepared to go both in its production values and cast participation to make an on-screen death feel believable. Now that we've had our first official elimination, the answer is clear—the showrunners at Krentler Media are willing to go far and above what anyone expected in terms of commitment to creating something truly terrifying.*

For those watching the primary stream, Costanza's death scene would have come as a shock after his disappearance earlier in the night. For others, it was the culmination of hours of torture at the hands of the evil spirit of Arthur Wilson, the deceased owner of the infamous Propitius Hotel. That's one of the most interesting—or depraved, depending on how you look at it—aspects of Slashtag. *Viewers tuning in via the livestream on Social have the choice at any time to follow any player of their choice. For those wanting to watch a* Saw *movie unfold in real-time, all they have to do is click over to Costanza's page. Viewers who may be looking for a more gentle ride can tune in to reality royalty Britt Holley's feed, which has been decidedly more tame. And for those who want to focus on the puzzling mysteries of the Propitius Hotel, viewers can switch over to the ultra-ambitious Kawaii Kiki, who has been solving riddles like it's going out of style. The point is, whatever your preference, there seems to be a subplot for any kind of viewer out there.*

The biggest question we have now is, how are they pulling it off? We assume there is a fair amount of pre-recorded footage that's been run through special effects teams, like the slow torturous death of Chef Costanza, but what about some of the other scenes? We're constantly guessing whether what we're seeing on screen are real reactions from clueless participants, or a meta masterclass in acting for fake reality TV.

Be sure to let us know your thoughts in the comments section and keep voting in the polls for who you think should be eliminated next. Our first poll wrapped up with the woman who's almost universally being called "Tawny Toilet" in the lead, with 30%, just ahead of multi-Razzie winning actor, Landon Keating, at 27%. Our second round of polling ends in just a few hours, so let us know who you think is going to be given the axe next!

CHAPTER THIRTY

Kiki rushes down the stairs to join me and D-wreck by the front door. With her flashlight out of my eyes, I can see natural light from the sun starting to push through the stained glass windows in the lobby. They cast a pair of red circles into the floor, making it feel like the hotel itself is staring at us.

"Are you hurt?" she asks, kneeling by our sides.

Now the adrenaline has worked its way out of me, I mostly just feel numb. She reaches into her shoulder bag and pulls out a rudimentary first aid kit.

"Here's a PSA for all the kids out there. Don't play with knives," D-wreck says, speaking to every household in America as he points to the forced smirk etched into his cheek.

Kiki soaks some white cloth in a glass bottle full of clear liquid, then gently rubs it against D's torn up skin. He hisses in pain, and the smell of pure alcohol hits my nostrils and makes me a little dizzy. Once she's finished with him, Kiki takes a pass at the cut in my back and properly dresses the slash on my hand. The sizzling pain of antiseptic is almost worse than getting the injuries themselves.

"Is this all from the Apothecary?" I ask, as she pops the cork top of a brown bottle and shakes out a few pills to feed to me and D-wreck.

"I doubled back for more supplies last night. Figured as long as I have the bag, I might as well make good use of it. I found a bunch of other interesting things while I was at it too."

I frown. This kind of proactivity could get her killed. "Kiki, we were supposed to all stay together in groups. Why would you go off with Landon in the middle of the night?"

Kiki looks at me in complete puzzlement. "I haven't seen Landon since you lot went to bed. I couldn't sleep, so I decided to get a jump on the next set of clues."

"Wait, so Landon never sent you into a dumbwaiter?"

"Why on Earth would I do something as dumb as that? To be honest, Landon skeeves me out a bit."

I was hoping having Kiki back would help piece things together, but instead, I'm only getting more paranoid about these people and their motivations. "All right, well now I'm thoroughly baffled. Landon sent me down to the basement based on a story that you were trapped, and as a result, D and I just watched Miguel get murdered by an actual ghost."

"Who's Miguel?"

"Chef Costanza," D clarifies. "Turns out, he was just some guy, not even a celebrity."

"Not really the point either," I say. "In any case, long story short is that Arthur Wilson is, in fact, a real ghost with a real appetite for blood, and you're going to want to trust me when I say you *really* don't want to get eliminated from this game."

Kiki looks at me like I'm a moron. "Yeah, the ghost is supposed to be real."

"No, you're not listening. I mean Arthur Wilson's *really* real."

Kiki nods her head as if she were listening to a drunk toddler. "Of course he is."

I don't have the energy right now to keep trying to convince her. "So nothing weird happened to you while you were alone all night?"

Kiki shrugs, then plays off a look of slight discomfort. "I mean, I've heard some spooky sounds here and there—honestly, it's more annoying than anything—but in the meantime, I think I made some progress on solving the Wilson mystery. Check this out." Kiki rummages through her bag again and pulls out another rolled-up piece of paper.

"I'm glad you were able to make some progress, but—"

I want to tell her to hold off until we regroup with the others, but Kiki starts talking excitedly over me.

"I sure was! I took pictures of some notable things that might come into play."

She pulls out her phone and starts swiping through photos. A flash of anger boils over me when I see an orange alert banner across the bottom of her screen.

"Wait, you've been using your phone this whole time? Did you not watch the broadcast we sent out?"

Kiki crooks her jaw to the side. "I guess I was kind of in the zone when that happened, and I must have forgotten to check it."

I force myself to stand back up, feeling my hand and back groan with pain. "We need to find the rest of the group *now*. Kiki, have you been back to the guest rooms at all?"

"No, but that's a good idea because it'll probably be easier to catch everyone up together and—"

"Okay, then let's start there."

I can't help but cut her off. She's too deep in game mode to recognize the very real wounds she just cleaned. I turn to D and put out a hand to help him up. He's still sitting with his back pressed against the door, but he waves my hand off and slowly pushes himself to his feet, clearly in a similar level of pain as me.

"You good to go?" I ask him.

He nods. "Hunky-dory. Let's do it."

Kiki puts her hands on her hips, clearly annoyed at our lack of enthusiasm. "Are you guys sure you don't want me to just run and grab everyone else real quick? In your state, I feel like I could be back before you even make it down the hall."

"No!" we both shout simultaneously.

"I just needed a minute to get myself together. It's been a long night, okay?" D-wreck complains.

"Okay, grandpa," Kiki says sarcastically, as we pass under the staircase heading into the hallway.

"Hey, that's not funny," D-wreck says. "I'm just barely in my thirties."

I check my phone. It's almost six. Back home, April will still be asleep for another hour and a half. I'd be up by now, applying makeup and reviewing a grueling schedule built to make me look like I have an effortlessly perfect and carefree life. Instead, I've probably sweat off all the makeup on my chin, and just when I think I'm almost too tired to care, I notice my hand rising up and sweeping the edge of my hair forward to cover my forehead scar.

I wish seeing Kiki would have brought me more comfort, but without her experiencing what we just went through, I don't know how we're going to be able to convince her this isn't just us pretending to be afraid of ghosts. Furthermore, she's shoved a wrench in my plan to sneak off into one of the private bathrooms with D and explain myself to him.

Familiar voices can be heard as we approach our room pod. In the bedroom opposite mine, Shawn and Britt are talking on the couch, while Landon lies in bed.

Shawn jumps when he sees us in the doorway, and my joy at seeing him almost counters my anger at seeing Landon.

"Hey Landon, what the hell was that about?" I say, a newfound energy shoving me toward him. "What happened to 'Kiki's up in Wilson's room?' You sent me down to the basement!"

Landon scrambles into a corner by the head of the bed, putting his hands up in a defensive position. "Please don't hurt me!"

"He says he doesn't remember any of it." Shawn rests a hand on my shoulder, stopping me from assaulting the little turd. His heavy fingers land right where Wilson stabbed me, and I flinch away from him in pain. "What happened, Tawny?"

"I almost got murdered, thanks to him. Seriously, Landon, start talking."

"I must have been sleepwalking. I'm so sorry. I have no memory of doing any of the things they told me."

I turn back to D, remembering that he gave me a similar excuse. Even though his story matches, I'm unable to let go of the anger. "And you were sleep-talking as well? We had a whole conversation. You seemed pretty coherent to me."

"He *was* acting kind of out of it," Shawn says grudgingly. "Once we got him back to the room, it was like he woke up and started behaving totally differently."

Britt speaks in short clauses, trying to figure out choice phrasing along the way. "I think that maybe, there's a chance...there are unexplainable things happening, and we should all figure out a calm way of talking about it. For instance, Tawny, didn't you say you saw Landon with two other people?"

I nod, feeling my wave of anger crash against a dam of logic. "Yeah."

"And neither D-wreck or Kiki were with him last night, right?"

"Right," Kiki says.

D-wreck confirms the same. "I didn't see anyone until I rescued Tawny from that little elevator thing in the basement."

"All right." Britt nods. "So then you agree there's something unexplainable surrounding the elevator incident. Maybe instead of blaming Landon, let's try and see if we can—"

I jump in, unsure of how to lay out the groundwork to explain a real ghost is going to pick us all off one by one. "Look, there's a lot more than just the elevator. We have a much bigger problem that we need to talk about."

Landon jumps in, completely missing the point as he scoots forward with newfound confidence. "Yeah, where were you two last night?" He points a finger of accusation at D and Kiki. "Check my wiki. I'm a well-known somnambulist. What are *your* excuses for wandering off?"

Kiki holds up her phone. "I was hunting for clues."

"And what about you?" Landon casts his finger toward D-wreck. "How did you and Tawny meet up?"

"I don't know. I just sort of found her."

Landon upgrades his gesture from a single finger to two full hands pointed strongly in D's direction. "You just happened to find yourself in the exact spot of the basement where Tawny was stuck?"

"You're not listening, bro," D says, getting defensive.

As much as I hate to admit it, Landon has a point. This is twice now that D has abandoned me after promising to have my back, and it's the second time D-wreck has conveniently appeared to my rescue, right when something weird is happening. At this point, I have no idea if Landon was in control when he put me in that dumbwaiter. Britt's already admitted almost everything she says on camera is a lie.

I think back to the secret message on my phone—*good dogs keep their mouths shut*—about Britt explaining she's not here of her own free will, about the red ball that seemed to terrify D down in the basement. Whatever's in this house has a way of getting into our heads. Why wouldn't it know that a shoulder squeeze is just what I would need to trust him?

"What were you *really* doing down there when you found me?" I ask D-wreck.

"You too? Come on, I told you I woke up down there."

"You woke up exactly outside of where I was trapped at the exact moment I was there?"

D looks at me pleadingly and then to the rest of the room. "Hey, I'm not the one who sent you down there. If it weren't for me, you'd still be stuck in a tiny box in the basement. Why are you all looking at me all of a sudden?"

"Because I know you deflect when you're lying. What aren't you telling us?"

D huffs like a fourteen-year-old who's just been caught with a back-pack full of cherry bombs. "I stole your clothes, all right?"

"You *what?*" A familiar flash of anger whips over me. He's not evil, he's just an asshole.

"I really did wake up outside of the room, but when I did, I was back in the lobby. I don't know. I was embarrassed and a little freaked out, so I decided to make it look like I was just pulling a prank. I took your clothes, hid them down in the basement, and that's when I heard you banging against the door of that mini-elevator."

"Dumbwaiter," Shawn clarifies.

"What did you just call me?" D says, stepping up to Shawn with a sudden outburst of masculine energy that reignites the room.

"It's what the tiny elevators are called, dumbass," Shawn retorts.

"Well I thought it was an insult!" D shouts. "It's a stupid name for a little elevator!"

"No more stupid than a grown-ass man calling himself D-wreck."

"Hey!" Britt claps her hands together until everyone goes quiet and gives her their undivided attention. To illustrate her point, she continues to clap to the rhythm of her words. "We. Are. Supposed. To. Be. A. Team. Look, I can see everyone is tired and hungry. Why don't we all take a minute to move this conversation to the dining room and discuss this like adults over some breakfast?"

I look around the room. The mere mention of food immediately softens everyone. It's the one thing in this moment we can all unanimously agree on.

I'm the first to enter the dining room, so I grab a bottle of wine from the bar and a fresh glass.

"Do you think maybe drinking isn't the best idea right now?" Shawn asks.

"After the night I just had, I think I've earned it. Anyone else want some?"

Britt steps forward. "I wish we had champagne for mimosas, but I bet I could make some sangrias work." She looks at the bottle and frowns. "I'd rather have a bold Spanish Tempranillo, but this'll do. Hey Shawn, do you know if there's any fruit in that kitchen?"

"I'm sure there is. This place is fully stocked."

Britt grabs the bottle and my wine glass, then leads Shawn toward the kitchen. "Since we're on the buddy system, how about I play sous chef while you whip us up some breakfast."

The two push their way through a pair of swinging doors heading into the kitchen. Shawn quickly returns, propping both doors open with a couple of bags of flour.

"Even though I'm cooking, I still want to hear what's going on."

The rest of us gather around the table closest to the kitchen. D-wreck, Landon, and I pull up seats, while Kiki stays standing, taking on the role of meeting director.

"Okay, so how about we each take a turn telling our version of what happened to us last night, and maybe we can learn something or find some sort of a connection."

Landon swears he doesn't remember leaving the room. Instead, he recounts a dream in which he was in a casting room as a child. His father told him he either needed to win the role or else he would be walking six miles home by himself. As he drones on, trying to garner pity, I take a minute to think about some of the grander implications of what's happening here.

At this point, there's no question in my mind that Krentler Media has put the seven of us in an extremely haunted house with the intention of killing us all. If that's true, there's no way they could actually televise this. It doesn't matter how rich or famous the board of directors are, no one could actively commit such a heinous crime in plain sight of the whole country and expect to just get away with it. That means there's likely no prizes either, which means the whole story of promising April new kidneys was a lie.

"We have to get out of here." I accidentally cut Landon off mid-story, not even realizing I'm vocalizing the thoughts growing too urgent to keep to myself.

"That's what we're trying to do," Kiki says, like she's talking to a child. "The whole point of this is to escape."

"You're not listening. It's not a game. Arthur Wilson is an actual ghost, and he's coming for us all. We have to find a way out of here right now."

Kiki and Landon stare at me as if I've gone insane.

"It's true," D-wreck backs me up. He shares our story, focusing on the death of Chef Costanza and our encounter with Wilson, leaving out the personal details about Clarence the dog and the red ball.

Shawn pokes his head through the door and calls out, "So who was he under the mask?"

"He said his name was Miguel," D-wreck replies. "I didn't recognize him."

"Hang on," Kiki says. "You're saying neither of you knew who he was? I thought he was supposed to be, like, some celebrity chef in disguise."

"So did we," D says.

"And that doesn't strike you as odd?" She bites at the cuticle next to one of her fingernails.

"Like, is it weird he could get so popular without being famous first? I don't really see how that's relevant."

"No," Kiki says, in an unmistakable tone of condescension. "What if he isn't the real Chef Costanza? You're saying that you saw him in basically the same situation that you found Lucy, right? I mean, I know I'm not supposed to be saying this, but we all know that whole thing with her was fake, right? Nobody actually thinks Lucy is dead IRL."

Britt appears from around the kitchen corner with a large pitcher full of red liquid and tons of cut up slices of oranges, strawberries, and ice, then places it on the table. "All right everyone, who wants a nice, refreshing sangria?"

Everyone grabs a glass and pours themselves some except for Landon and Kiki. She's too focused on making a point.

"You guys didn't say you actually saw Costanza, or Miguel, die, right?"

"I watched him choke to death right in front of me," I say, baffled at how Kiki could still be arguing this.

"But you didn't check his pulse or anything, did you? All you saw was some foam coming out of a guy's mouth. Who's to say that guy was even the same person that was with us earlier? Because of the mask, there's no way to know anything for sure."

"I know what I saw!" Tears well behind my eyes. I fight them back, afraid it will come across as a sign of weakness or hysteria to only further hurt my credibility.

"You've watched a lot of people choke to death then, yeah?" She says it as a question, but the accusation is clear. "So in that case, he could have been an actor, just like Lucy. Someone planted here to make it seem like any of us could actually die, when in reality, it's all just part of the experience."

D-wreck points to his bandaged face . "Did this not look real to you when you were cleaning it?"

"You've gone to further lengths," Kiki says.

"What's that supposed to mean?"

"I've seen your channel, guy. It's not like you haven't filmed yourself jumping into a kiddy pool full of Legos before, or detonated a car's airbag under your ass. I saw your cut. It wasn't very deep."

"Are you fucking serious right now? It's on my face! I was attacked by a friggin' ghost!" D shoots to his feet and knocks his chair to the ground. "The guy wasn't just pretending to be incorporeal when I tried to chop him in half."

"And after he killed Costanza, did he come after you? Did he chase you through the basement with a knife?"

"He disappeared," I admit. "We had a chance to escape, and we took it."

Kiki shakes her head. "So this ghost attacks you, makes you watch him kill someone, then just lets you go? To what end?"

"Pacing, probably," Landon chimes in. "The show's not much fun if everyone just dies at once. You have to space them out, or else you don't have a compelling narrative."

"Hey guys, are you sure we should all be talking about this kind of stuff?" Britt says, trying to lead the discussion in another direction. "Remember in the rules it says we're not really supposed to question the realness of stuff?"

Kiki peels off another cuticle with her teeth. "I don't know. Not being able to metagame kind of feels like playing with one hand tied behind our backs, you know? Especially if they're going to pull these kinds of tricks on us."

Britt stares blankly at Kiki for a second, clearly upset at being undermined. "Well, if that's how you're going to act, I don't want to have any part in it. I'm going back to help with breakfast." She takes a large sip of her sangria, tops it off with the pitcher, then hurries back into the kitchen with her drink in hand.

Kiki continues with her theory. "So first off, I think we can all agree Lucy was an actor. For the sake of my argument, Costanza is an actor too. Look around. Aren't we all actors here, in one sense or another? Sure, it's easy to put any random guy in a mask, but how hard would it really be to hire any of you to pretend to be scared like the rest of us, while secretly having your own side agendas? Britt stirs up insane drama for a living. D-wreck has literally been fucking with people's perceptions of reality for over a decade. Landon is a professional actor. Hell, he's even played this guy before. What's to say he's not just doing a role to make us all believe he's this creepy in real life?"

"Fine, what about me then?" I say. "What's my line?"

Kiki studies me for a second before her face turns to something resembling pity. "You're either an accomplice to some plan D-wreck has to scare us, or you're too dumb to know the difference between fiction and reality."

My fists clench. I've never been in a fight before, but this bitch is getting on my last nerve. Before I say, or do, something I'll regret, Shawn starts shouting for all of us to get into the kitchen ASAP. I'm grateful for the distraction, even though I dread whatever's coming next.

The first thing I notice upon crossing the threshold is just how large the kitchen is. There are prep stations and ovens placed in seemingly random areas in a room that twists and turns beyond where I can see.

A few feet down the line, Shawn is holding Britt by the shoulders and shaking her, shouting her name. Britt either doesn't hear him or doesn't care. She's got a tub of butter clutched tightly to her chest with one hand, while her other is busy taking savage scoops of the stuff and shoving it in her mouth. Her face is gleaming with fat smeared around her cheeks. It's run down her chin and neck. Yellowy streaks shine across her forehead, punctuated by little lumpy chunks of butter rubbed off from her hand while presumably pushing her greasy dark hair out of her face.

"What are you doing?" D-wreck shouts, sprinting toward Shawn and Britt. "Get it away from her!"

Shawn's eyes are wide with fear. He reaches a hand down from Britt's shoulder, toward the tub. She buckles down on it, hovering her face only inches away as she quickens the pace of stuffing her mouth.

D comes at her from underneath, trying to pry her arm away from the metal tub she's got tucked so tightly into her. She's too slippery to grab by the wrist. Britt wriggles away and tucks herself down until she's in a defensive ball on the ground.

"I need your help, man!" D shouts to Shawn, who has been all but useless at separating Britt from the butter.

"I don't want to hurt her," he says, while half-heartedly trying to pry his fingers between her elbows and her hips.

"Just pick her up already!"

Shawn grabs Britt by the elbows and starts to pry her apart. Even though he's finally putting in real effort, she's still maintaining her grip on the metal tub. After some struggle, he manages to pull her scooping arm out, at which point she buries her face into the bucket itself, slathering her tongue around the sides for any lingering globs and moaning in a sick ecstasy. With only one hand left to secure the tub, D is finally able to grab hold of it and rip it away with a firm yank. He tosses it toward me. It bounces and clatters across the floor, slinging large pats of butter across the cupboards and tile.

Britt twitches in Shawn's arms, and D-wreck helps hold her down. After several futile struggles to escape, her head lulls forward, and her body goes limp. Shawn slowly lays her on the ground and then lets go.

"What the fuck just happened?" D asks.

"I don't know. I asked her to get me some butter, and the next thing I saw, she was eating it by the handful."

Once both of the boys' backs are turned, Britt springs upon all fours and scrambles in my direction. Shawn notices her just in time, barely managing to grab her by the ankle. She comes to a sudden stop, her hand outreached in desperation, groping for a mound of butter on the floor. Britt's trying to pull herself forward, closer to the tub, but she's so greasy she might as well be on ice. Shawn keeps her held steady as she tirelessly reaches for the tub. Unable to make any forward progress, she scoops what little is sitting on the tile in front of her into her mouth.

I can't stand watching any more. Kneeling, I grab the bucket, hoping to remove the temptation, but notice something poking out from the butter. My fingers slip against it when I try to excavate the thing from inside. I finally get a grip on whatever it is and pull it out.

It's a figurine of a pig made out of pink glass. I try to hold it up to the light to get a better look, but it slips from my butyraceous fingers and shatters on the floor.

"Oh God," Britt moans by our feet. Her face is full of horror and confusion. She tries to push herself up, but her hands slip out from under her, and she falls back forward onto her face. "I'm going to be sick."

Shawn lets go of her leg. Britt manages to grab hold of a cupboard handle and pull herself up. She just barely makes it to her feet before vomiting several times into a nearby sink.

I turn to Kiki. "You think *that* was acting?"

Mission Log

- ~~Restore Power to the Hotel~~

- Destroy Arthur Wilson's Body Totem
  - Unlock Arthur's Apartment
    - ~~Find the key's knob~~
    - Find the key's shaft
    - Find the key's bit

- Destroy Arthur Wilson's Mind Totem
  - Unlock the door to Sutter's Sanctum
    - Destroy the Greed statue
    - Destroy the Sloth statue
    - Destroy the Wrath statue
    - Destroy the Envy statue
    - Destroy the Lust statue
    - Destroy the Pride statue
    - ~~Destroy the Gluttony statue~~
    - Destroy the Disobedience statue

- Destroy Arthur Wilson's Spirit Totem

SOCIAL

CHAPTER THIRTY-ONE

From: Lucy.K@Krentler.media
To: Board@Krentler.media
CC: Operations@Krentler.media
Subject: Night 1 Summary

Hello Members of the Board and Operations Team,

The subjects ended their Night 1 of *Slashtag* at 7:26 a.m., which gives the day crew two and a half hours to prep for the events of Day 2. Overall, things were much smoother than Day 1.

I believe this is thanks, in large part, to Dr. Pollard, whose psych evaluations so far have been accurate down to a 3% margin of error. Without his insight on our subjects' psyches, traumas, and reaction to fight or flight stimulus, we would be flying blind.

Our night crew was successfully able to facilitate the evenings events without major incident, and Renshaw's work with Arthur Wilson has indeed been exemplary. We are particularly pleased with how easily our cast members fall into a suggestive state when sleeping or separated from the rest of the group.

Of course, nothing is perfect, and there are a few notes for us to either improve our performance or keep of note of moving forward:

- Tawny and D-wreck have already taken advantage of Wilson's inability to interact directly with biological material. While this doesn't change any of our scheduled events, we may need our day crew to put in a little extra effort into separating our subjects, in order to ensure Arthur Wilson can perform his tasks properly.
- Considering the discovery made re: Wilson, we may want to hasten how quickly the subjects collect the remaining keys. We suggest unlocking the History Museum in order to allow for the subjects to move to the mind phase more quickly.
- Distrust between cast members is high. While dividing them was one of the goals for Night 1, we need to make sure that their paranoia doesn't reach a point where anyone veers too far from their planned arcs.
- While it's our hope that the subjects will continue along the key assembly storyline, we've gone ahead and activated the first wave of possession statues, in case any subjects go astray. This will also ensure the Pain Volume Index increases at a steady rate.
- As a reminder to props, be sure to remove clues leading to specific statues if the subjects find them organically
- I know the directive was to eliminate Tawny next; however, given her unexpected leap in viewership, we feel it's best to push her down the list a point or two. Fans love a comeback story, and public opinion is quickly shifting back in her favor.

Now for some analytics from Night 1:

- While there was an initial dip in viewership past 11 p.m. PST, things picked up again at 3 a.m. when east coast viewers began to tune in. At present, our viewership is even higher than yesterday's peak daytime hours, thanks to an aggressive sharing campaign on Social. We are currently reaching 50 million households, 8 million more than during the peak of Day 1. Of course, we also have to consider that today is Saturday, which should allow for a much higher number of binge watchers.

- From the moment of capture, right up to his death, Chef Costanza became the most popular Spotlight character for white males ages 16 and up, making him the second most watched subject of the night overall. This is an excellent sign, and we believe we can only grow those kinds of numbers for Wilson's next victim.
- We were surprised to find Tawny was the most watched subject at 35%, likely due to her uncharacteristic display of bravery in the dumbwaiter and basement encounter with D-wreck.
- PVI is at 24%, just slightly over our projected numbers by this point.

Again, great work, everyone, and a massive thank you to our board of directors. It is my great honor to be trusted with the responsibility of managing this revolutionary event.

Lucy K.

From:Ron.M@Krentler.media
To: Lucy.K@Krentler.media
Subject: Night 1 Summary

Lucy,

As long as Tawny doesn't win, feel free to do whatever the hell you want with her. We just want a good show.

Keep up the good work...

Ron

CHAPTER THIRTY-TWO

We're back in the dining room, and thanks to Britt's butter incident, most of us have lost our appetites. Shawn, D-wreck, and I are munching on dry toast. Meanwhile, Landon keeps mentioning that he's craving scrambled eggs, despite being a vegan. Kiki fishes around her bag, pulling out a clear bottle and shaking out a pill into her hand. She swallows it with a big sip of water, then nibbles on some bread and stares at the hall leading back to the lobby.

"Still have a headache?" I ask.

Kiki almost jumps at my intrusion. "Yeah. Right now, I'd kill for a smoke too."

Britt wanders back into the dining room after having a shower. Her skin still looks shiny, and she's got a trash can in her hand, just in case. She's managed to find a replacement dress that's similar to mine, but of course, it looks infinitely better on her.

"All right, so are we all on the same page now?" I ask. "We're all leaving?"

"You know I am," D says.

Shawn nods. "I've been ready to go since the lights first went out. Let's get the hell out of here."

Kiki shakes her head. "Nah, I'm still in."

"After what you just saw? There's no way that was an act."

"I don't know what you people are capable of. So far, the only thing I've seen that's out of the ordinary is a person eating a lot of butter. It's weird, sure, a little crazy, but you don't have to be supernatural to eat heaps of food."

"Fine. You want to get yourself killed, go right ahead." I stand up from the table. D and Shawn join me, but the rest stay seated. "Britt?"

"I've given this some thought...," she says, her words slow and measured.

"Oh, come on, not you too. How could you possibly think this isn't real?"

"That's just it. I do believe it's real. I just ate more butter in the last ten minutes than I have in the last ten years, and I don't have a single memory of doing it. What do you think is going to happen if I try to smash out a window? I could end up stabbing myself with a piece of glass or something and not even know I'm doing it until it's too late."

"So we die trying to escape, or we die wasting our time with a bunch of stupid riddles. You don't think that's a chance worth taking?"

"I don't think any of us are meant to die. Wilson could have made me do anything when he was in control, but all he had me do was eat butter."

"We have to play the game," Kiki says. "The only way out is through."

"And what if you're wrong? What if there is no end to the game?"

"We have to believe there is," Landon says, staring out into nowhere in particular. "Hollywood hates a sad ending. It's terrible for ratings. We're here to put on a show, and what's more entertaining than a group of celebrities coming together to send a real ghost straight to hell?"

"I take it you're going to stay here and die with the others?" I ask him.

"If I die, it will be in front of millions of my fans, at the hands of a monster I once brought to life. I honestly can't think of a better way to go."

I'm flabbergasted by how flippantly these people are treating their own potential demise. "Fine. Good luck, I guess. We're getting out."

"Do you even have a plan?" Kiki asks.

"We're sure as shit not going to head toward any more of those Xs," D-wreck says. He plunges his hand into his pocket, then slams the end piece of the key on the table. "Here, a little parting gift."

"I think you're making a big mistake," Kiki shouts as the three of us exit the dining room.

Maybe we are, but at least we're doing it on our own terms. We reach the lobby, where the only idea I had was, in fact, to break the stained glass windows. I thought maybe we could shatter a few panes and squeeze through, but upon further inspection, we realize the windows are held together with wrought iron that runs intricate patterns through the glass. I can't imagine squeezing through without seriously injuring myself, never mind the two large men beside me.

"Okay, let's think. Are there any other windows or possible ways out of here that we haven't considered yet?"

Shawn pulls out his phone and opens his notes. He scrolls through a seemingly endless wall of text and, upon reaching the bottom, zips his thumb back up a few times. "Come on, where is it..." He slows his scrolling, then excitedly taps his finger against the screen a couple of times. "Okay, I think I got something. Check this out."

He taps his way out of his notes app and brings up the picture of the map, pinching his fingers together and then spreading them so the phone zooms in on the eastern wall just past the basement stairs.

"All right, so this may be a little out there, but follow me on this. We already saw that some mirrors in the building are more than what they seem, right? I got to thinking about some of the other large mirrors in the hotel. Remember when we went searching for the basement during the power outage?"

"Of course."

"All right, so before we found the map, I took notes of everything that seemed interesting along the way. Down this area, I've marked the provisions store, the barbershop, and a huge mirror at the end of the hallway."

"Oh, you mean like the one from that bathroom that turned out to be a door?" D-wreck asks.

"Yeah. And check this out." Shawn points to a spot on the map which seems to correspond to what he's describing. If he's correct, there's an empty space behind the mirror that looks like a hallway running along the edge of the house. "It could just be a rough drawing not done to scale, but what if there's something on the other side of the glass?"

"It's as good an idea as any," I say, trying to force down the excitement welling up in this new plan.

According to the map, there's only one way in or out of the building, and that's the front door. Shawn's making a number of assumptions here that could pan out to be nothing, but if there's even a chance of finding an alternate way out of here, I'm ready to try it.

We make our way back to the basement doors. Sitting right where Shawn described hangs a giant gold-leaf-framed mirror, almost identical to the one found in the bathroom. Shawn inspects the filigree surrounding the mirror carefully, fingering any cracks or pieces that look like they could be manipulated. At the risk of looking like more of a fool than I already do, I start tugging on the wall-mounted electric candelabras, hoping one of them will crank down, like some sort of secret lever.

After ten minutes of meticulous searching, Shawn and I share a moment where the same thought is running through both our heads.

"This isn't working," he says with a heavy sigh.

D-wreck, on the other hand, is grinning in a way that makes me nervous. "You guys are kidding, right? All that monkeying around was just the lead-up to the real plan."

"What's he talking about?" Shawn asks.

"He's going to 'D-wreck' the mirror," I say, using air quotes.

"Oh no, I don't know if that's a good idea."

D-wreck nods in eager defiance. "I think it's the only idea." He reaches up and grabs the red and white striped barber pole bolted to the wall. It only takes a few good yanks for him to rip the fixture right out of its ancient hinges. He palms the rounded metal head and pats it a few times.

"Yeah, this'll do just fine. Protect your eyes, ladies and gentlemen. D-wrecking to commence in five, four, three..."

I watch him wind up to throw his makeshift torpedo, then turn away, shoving my eyes into my elbow and waiting for the crash. Despite all efforts to prepare myself, my whole body flinches when the barber pole smashes into the glass.

"Holy shit, dude. Holy shit!"

I pull away from my elbow, finding D-wreck bouncing off Shawn's shoulders, jostling him around like they're old football buddies.

"You fucking nailed it, bro!"

I can't find the candy cane striped pole D threw. It's hidden in a darkness lying beyond the mirror. I turn my flashlight on and peer inside. The only thing I see is the flat reflection of the light bouncing off a black painted wall only a few feet ahead of me.

"What do you think it is?" Shawn asks.

"Looks like a hallway, painted black. Could be a crew access path, could be another part of the game." I creep forward and poke my head through the hole, being careful not to touch any of the shards of broken glass lining the frame. To my left, there's a staircase leading upward. To my right, I see a door just a few feet away, also painted black.

"Guys, there's a door."

"I'm on it." D-wreck leaps over the threshold, barely avoiding a large shard of glass, then jogs down the hall to the door. "You ready to taste freedom?"

Even though there's no side doors drawn onto the map, I still want to prepare my eyes for the sudden overwhelming brightness of the sun. Since the hallway hugs the outside wall of the building, the only logical place this door could lead is outside.

D grabs the knob. He turns it and pulls. Even though I feel like I'm prepared for the possibility of failure, I still end up bitter and disappointed when nothing happens.

"Son of a bitch," he swears, kicking the door once for emphasis.

"I guess it's the stairs, then," I say. "Just because this door's locked doesn't mean it's part of the game. This could still be a crew passage that leads to a way out." I don't believe a word of what I'm saying, but seeing as I led this exodus, I feel responsible for the morale of the people who chose to follow me.

Shawn nods, then takes the lead heading up the stairs. The ceiling is surprisingly low, and he has to crouch in order to make the climb. I'm short enough to make it without hitting my head, but the pure painted blackness of it makes me anxious, and I can't help but hunch a little, just in case. We're a few steps in when Shawn stops abruptly and turns off his flashlight.

"What is it?" I ask, unable to see past his wide frame.

"Candles at the top of the stairs. Real ones, I think."

"Anything else?"

"Another door."

We resume our climb, but I can feel Shawn's growing hesitation with each passing moment. As we near the top, I'm finally able to see the erratic flickering glow of the candles sitting on either side of the door. I lean over to the wall to get a better look; there's a large red hourglass etched into the center of the door.

"I think I know where we are," I say. "D-wreck, guess what we found?"

"Don't you get my hopes up," he says from behind.

Shawn pushes the door open, leading us into a small octagonal room with a chandelier in the center. It's shaped like a spider's web, with each point facing one of the eight corners of the room. There are eight doors, none of which are numbered, but each instead has etched carvings of different types of spiders.

"Oh my God, it's the secret spider whorehouse," D says with amazement.

If I do manage to get us all killed, at least I can die knowing I fulfilled one of D-wreck's wishes.

Shawn, on the other hand, doesn't seem quite as impressed. "So this is still part of the game, then. Not a way out. Maybe we should go back and tell the rest about this."

He's one hundred percent correct. Continuing down this path on our own is risky. Turning around is what a normal person should do. It's what the Tawny Howlett with nearly twenty million subscribers would do. But what happens then? We go searching for another mirror to break? I have to find a way to come to grips that, whether I want to believe it or not, I'm actually stuck in a horror movie right now. Unfortunately for me, the vegetarian organic lifestyle guru doesn't usually make it too far once the killing starts.

I need to find the Slasher-obsessed, haunt fanatic Tawny. I have to think like Sydney Prescott, who is only able to beat the game by knowing which rules to break. "We should keep going. At least see if there's anything in these rooms that can help us."

"Sweet, I'm gonna look for antique dildos." D-wreck throws himself into one of the rooms along the right wall.

Shawn considers me for a second. "Are you seriously suggesting this?"

"I don't know where else to go. It's our only lead. I feel like we should at least fully check it out before turning back. If we don't find an exit, maybe we can discover something useful. We clearly weren't supposed to be in this room yet. Maybe there's some sort of shortcut to destroying his spirit or something."

Shawn's look of trepidation finally breaks. "Fine. We'll look around here for now, but if we're going to do this, we're going to do it right. We take the rooms systematically, together." He points to a door on our left, a depiction of a spider with long spindly legs engraved on it. The bottom two fold back against the end of its abdomen, forming the shape of a heart. "D-wreck, come back in here. Let's not get separated."

"In a minute. I'm searching for clues in a very important underwear drawer."

Shawn and I step into a small, pink-wallpapered room, with a rusted metal bed, a vanity with a mirror, and a chest of drawers. Next to the bed sits a metal bucket, the purpose of which I'd rather not think about. Shawn starts searching around the bed, while I volunteer to check out the bathroom. Last time I did this, there was a hacked-up body in the tub, so I can only guess what fresh hell I'll discover this time. Upon first glance, the room looks normal. It isn't until I step inside that I notice the faint smell of sweets. It grows stronger the further I go, taking on an almost sour twinge that turns my stomach.

"Wow, that's strong."

"What is?" Shawn asks.

"The smell of this bathroom. It's like a Starburst sat in spoiled milk."

"Ooh, I want to smell it!" D shouts from another room. He steps back into the atrium at the center of the web. As soon as he does, the door behind him slams shut, completely on its own. D turns on his heel to investigate. While he's facing the other direction, our bedroom door flies shut as well.

Shawn runs to the door and pulls at the knob, but it remains solid. D-wreck is pounding on the other side, yelling our names.

"Go find the others and get help!" Shawn orders.

D shouts something back, but his words sound dreamy and distant.

Something in the room is changing, or maybe it's something in me that's changing the room. Even Shawn's no more than a whisper to me now.

The sickly sweet smell overwhelms me with such intensity I start to feel dizzy. I head over to the bathroom sink to wash my face, but there's something sitting inside the porcelain bowl.

A small red spider, made of glass.

I look up at the bathroom mirror. Standing next to me is an old man dressed in black robes with a priest's collar. His withered face looks like a skull loosely covered by thin drapes of pale liver-spotted leather. Even though he's wearing the guise of an old man, I can see his hollow silver eyes and his crooked grin.

I watch helplessly as Arthur Wilson bends over and whispers horrible things into my ear.

CHAPTER THIRTY-THREE

"Come on, girl, you know better than this."

"What's she doing?" Hector asks, now on hour six of our video chat.

"So far, Tawny has done pretty much everything that should get you killed in a horror movie. The most recent trope she's indulged in is that of the idiot who gets the notion that they're just simply going to leave. As a rule, anyone who says, 'I'm getting out of here,' is not getting out of here. Whether you're in *Cube, Saw, Cabin in the Woods,* heck, even *Jurassic Park*, the only way out is to see it through. When the abyss is already staring at you, the only smart choice is to stare back." I watch the screen as they wander into a bedroom. "Look at this. Even though she knows this isn't an exit, she's just poking around, instead of going back to saddle up with the group. Has she seriously learned nothing from all our years of research?"

"You call watching horror movies research?"

"I do, when it can help you stay alive. See! Right on cue—all the doors slam shut, singling out D-wreck. This does not look good for our generic wise-cracking leading-male type."

"What do you think's going to happen to him?" Hector asks.

"Probably nothing good...Wait. Actually, he's running away to go find the others. Okay, maybe he isn't so dumb after all."

The main feed cuts back from D-wreck's escape to Tawny and Shawn. That's when it hits me. They weren't targeting D-wreck; they were trying to get him out of the scene.

I want to shake the monitor. Tawny slowly approaches Shawn, who has his head pressed into the door. She then gently runs her fingers down his back. He spins around in shock.

"I'm confused," Hector says. "Is she possessed now?"

I stare in horror as my sister suggests to Shawn some of the most sexually explicit things I've ever heard. It's absolutely mortifying and, thank God, clearly not effective.

"Oh Tawny, you can't say that on television." My forehead is hot, and suddenly, I don't feel so comfortable being on a video chat with my closest male friend.

Shawn tries to excuse himself politely, but Tawny reaches behind her back and produces a small metal blade.

"Is that a scalpel?" Hector asks.

I throw my hands out in exasperation. "Of course, the one time she does follow a rule of survival, something like this happens. Son of a B, this is bad, Hector. This is really, really bad."

Shawn notices the blade, realizing his rejection of her advance has escalated toward hostility. My sister makes a sudden thrust with the knife, pointed straight at his genitals. He partially deflects it, saving his manhood and reducing the damage to a slash across his thigh.

"Come on, Shawn, search the dang bathroom. It has to be in there!" I scream for my sister's sake, but she leaps forward with another strike.

Shawn catches her arm this time and throws her to the ground. I wince when I hear the *thud* her body makes. He tries to grab the knife, but Tawny shoves a thumb into the wound in his thigh. He howls and tips backward. I'm overwhelmed at the scene unfolding, rooting for my sister to lose a fight, while simultaneously terrified of what will happen to her if she does.

My lungs nearly leap out of my chest when there's a sharp knock at the front door of my house. I quickly grab the knob on the speaker and crank down the volume. My computer is angled in front of the window in such a way that, if I lift the blinds, I can see who is outside. I lean forward and gently lift up one of the slats.

Two people I've never seen before are standing at my door. One of them is a beefy man in a black suit, his posture like a hitman with his hands over his groin. The other is a scrawny guy with messy hair and an expensive-looking oversized suit.

Mission Log

- ~~Restore Power to the Hotel~~
- Destroy Arthur Wilson's Body Totem
  - Unlock Arthur's Apartment
    - ~~Find the key's knob~~
    - Find the key's shaft
    - Find the key's bit

- Destroy Arthur Wilson's Mind Totem
  - Unlock the door to Sutter's Sanctum
    - Destroy the Greed statue
    - Destroy the Sloth statue
    - Destroy the Wrath statue
    - Destroy the Envy statue
    - ~~Destroy the Lust statue~~
    - Destroy the Pride statue
    - ~~Destroy the Gluttony statue~~
    - Destroy the Disobedience statue

- Destroy Arthur Wilson's Spirit Totem

SOCIAL

CHAPTER THIRTY-FOUR

I come rushing out from a place of catastrophic emptiness, and the first thing I realize is I can't breathe. There's a hand around my throat, squeezing my newfound light right back out of me. The last thing I remember was a putrid saccharine smell, then falling for an eternity, like Alice drifting down the rabbit hole to Wonderland. Now, there's a dark-skinned man with bloodshot eyes screaming at me and holding me against a bathroom wall.

I open my mouth to speak, to beg for him to back off, but all that comes out are a series of stilted squeaks and a sound that reminds me of Miguel choking to death. Though I try to swing my arms and legs around to find any point of leverage, my body has no strength in it. I've exhausted everything I have to try and get him off of me, and all that I have left are my eyes. I try to catch him with mine, pleading for him to stop.

His eyes are unfocused and wild, darting like there's danger all around him. Why can't he see I'm the one in danger? I can feel myself fading away again. My vision narrows to a tunnel lined with sparkling white fireworks. Finally our eyes lock, and I do my best to convey as much urgency as possible, while mouthing what I hope will read as *help me*.

His grip loosens, and a flood of air surges back into my lungs. The tunnels around my eyes ease off into small vignettes, and the fireworks display peters out. Soreness takes over as I get reacquainted with my body. It tells me stories of all the injuries I've sustained so far, and I can feel a few mystery wounds begin to swell around my neck and sternum.

Shawn backs away from me, looking as scared as I feel. I stumble out of the bathroom and collapse on the bed, feeling my ribs violently protest to the force. As Shawn takes a seat on the floor next to me, I notice he's not doing so hot either. His thigh is bleeding, and his cheek has a few scratches on it.

Feathers are everywhere, strewn around the room, and the vanity is tipped over. Embedded in Shawn's free hand, I see small red shards of broken glass.

"Wilson's statues. He got to me, didn't he?" My voice croaks out like a frog. I open and close my mouth a few times, probing my neck gently with my fingers and searching for the tender spots.

Shawn's looking up at me, his eyes squinted as he focuses on my lips.

"What is it? What's wrong with my mouth?"

"Your teeth. I can tell it's really you."

I'm already confused, but this is the last thing I expect him to say. "What's that supposed to mean?"

"When you attacked me, your breath took on this really strong smell, like old candy."

"I smelled it, just before things went dark."

"But it wasn't just that," Shawn continues. "Your teeth got all messed up too. Crooked, like you'd never been to a dentist in your life."

There's something familiar about what he's saying. I remember when Arthur Wilson was grinning at me, his teeth were a mangled mess. I try to stand up, but my body isn't ready for it, and I ease back on the bed.

"What happened? Did I hurt you?"

"Well, you tried to cut my dick off and called me some names I haven't heard since high school."

"Oh my God, I didn't—"

"You missed, thankfully. Though I'd be lying if I said words can't hurt."

Guilt overtakes me. "I swear it wasn't me in there. I don't even remember what happened. I don't know what I said."

Shawn nods slowly. "I hear you. I believe it. But also, you just came at me with some of the most specifically hurtful slurs I've ever heard. It was like you actually got in my head, found the things people have said to me that keep me up at night, and broadcasted it out to the world. It really sucked."

"I'm so sorry. I would never—"

"I know. At least, I think I do." Shawn sits in silence for a minute, and the least I can do is give him that time to collect himself. "I know it wasn't you, but it's also kind of hard to look at you now and not get filled with some, uh, strong feelings."

My heart hurts. It seems that no matter how hard I try to be a sister, role model, or friend, it always ends in disaster. "This is all my fault."

"I didn't mean it like that," Shawn says. "You and I are okay. I just need a minute to sort of deal with my shit."

I shake my head. "I should have known better than to think I could find a shortcut out of here, and I dragged you along with me because you trusted me."

"At least you made a choice to do something, instead of just blindly following what you're told."

"So what? I make bad choices all the time. Believe me, I've got a real doozy of one sitting and waiting for me back in the real world."

"Yeah, but at the end of the day, you still made a choice. You remember when we were down in the basement, and you and Costanza asked why I came on this show?"

I nod. "Yeah. It was right after you told us you don't like the dark, small spaces, or horror."

He lets out an exhausted laugh. "I've been thinking about it a lot. In the moment, I didn't really have an answer. But I think I know now. Can I tell you a story?"

"You sure you want to, in front of all the cameras?"

"Not trying to guilt you, but you kind of spoiled half of it already for the audience. I figure I should at least get to tell my side."

I feel like my face is turning into a tomato. I nod for him to continue before I die of embarrassment and shame.

"When I was a kid, eighth grade, there were basically two high schools you went on to. I grew up in the poor side of town, so pretty much all of us fed into the public high school. Then, for the kids who had enough money or talent, there was this private school. I wanted to go there more than anything, even though they only gave out like five scholarships per year. I spent my time in school working my ass off, keeping my head down, and getting good grades. I applied to every scholarship program I could find.

"But here's the thing. I was always big, and by the time I turned twelve, I was already taller than some high schoolers. To make my folks happy, I joined the football team. Every night after practice, dinner, and homework, I would sit down and write essays for these scholarships, sometimes staying up 'til two in the morning to get them done. One day, I came home from school, and my dad had found my scholarship applications. 'No, son,' he said. 'If you want that education, the only way you're going to get in there is with your God-given talent.'"

"Let me guess," I say, "He wanted you to go for a football scholarship."

"The coach didn't even ask me to try out. He took one look at me and said that, as long as I stayed on the team and kept my nose clean, there was room for me at the school. Which again, I'm not complaining. It's what I wanted. It's just that..."

"It wasn't the way you wanted."

Shawn nods. "He took away my choice to do things my way. Maybe I could have done it on my own, you know? And with football being such a huge commitment from that moment forward, I never had the time to focus on the reasons why I wanted to go there in the first place. Straight from high school, I got a free ride to University of Alabama, again for football, so I had to go there. After four years of nothing but football, I got recruited straight to the New Orleans Saints. That should have been the happiest day of my life, but instead, I just felt like a fraud. There's so many people who have worked so hard, would kill to be in my position. I felt like I was living somebody else's dream.

"But then I met Danny. He wasn't like all the other guys on the team, and pretty soon, we figured out we both had feelings for each other, you know? Finally, there was something in my life that felt like it was mine. Something other than making my parents, or my hometown, proud. But Danny's not like me. He lives for football. He's the MVP, and he's white, so when he decides that he wants to announce our relationship after winning the Super Bowl, there's nothing I can do to convince him it's not a good idea. You know what happened next. Just like every other time in my life, I let someone else decide for me."

"So, coming on here is like your way of making a choice?"

He laughs again, but this time it's full of irony. "You'd think so. While I was playing in the NFL, my dad passed. He left a lot of debt behind, and my mom's not doing so good without him. I had to move back to my hometown, where it turns out, I'm not the most popular guy anymore."

My stomach turns as I guess where this story is going. "Oh no."

He nods. "Yeah. A few months back, I'm walking home from a bar, and I get cornered by a group of guys I played ball with back in high school. They're getting up in my face, calling me basically everything you just said to me. They pushed me into an alley. I could see where things were going. I got scared, and when one of them pulled out a knife, I hit him in the face, just once. Ended up fracturing his nose, and when he fell back, he hit his head on a curb and ended up in a coma."

"Jesus, I'm so sorry that happened to you," I say.

"I thought my life was over. The family was getting ready to press charges, and there were these five other guys there, all ready to corroborate some bullshit lie that I started the whole thing. Forget about losing all my NFL money. They told me I could go to jail for this. And then all of a sudden, some lawyers from Krentler Media show up at my door one day, telling me that if I go on this show, they'll make sure my case gets dropped and keep the story out of the news."

"So you didn't have a choice after all."

"At least this time, I'm choosing to come here as myself, or at least I'm trying to. Sometimes, I get a feeling like this house wants me to be nothing more than a human wrecking ball." He pauses to consider his next words, but before he can get them out, there's a little chime coming from Shawn's pocket.

In the bathroom, I hear mine play somewhere on the ground. He pulls out his phone. It's a broadcast from Landon.

"Well, this can't be good," Shawn says, pressing play.

The first few seconds of footage are a dizzying affair, the camera swings wildly around a dark room. It finally settles on Landon, strapped into a chair. He is sweating, shirtless, and staring in terror at something behind the camera. His hands are clamped to the arms of the chair.

Whoever is holding the camera is not Landon.

"H-Hello, my name is Arthur Wilson. I hope you have been enjoying your stay at my lovely hotel," Landon says, stammering over himself.

A man's voice cuts him off, barking out a single word. "Again!"

The call is immediately followed by the cranking sound of a machine somewhere offscreen, and then a tiny object falls from somewhere above Landon and lands on his lap.

"Oh spirits, please," Landon begs, staring at the thing in his lap.

At first, I can't tell what it is, but once it starts to climb up his heaving stomach, I realize it's a scorpion.

"Again!" the man calls out a second time.

"I recognize that voice," Shawn says.

"Hello, my name is Arthur Wilson. I hope you have been enjoying your stay at my lovely hotel," Landon repeats with a little more vigor. "We have a variety of amenities available to our— Ow!" He recoils as the scorpion jabs its poison-tipped stinger just above his belly button. Landon's sudden flinch only serves to drive the scorpion skittering further up his body.

Meanwhile, a machine clinks once again, and another scorpion drops from above, this time landing on Landon's bony shoulder.

"Again, you talentless little pissant!" the offscreen voice barks.

"Okay, this time I definitely know it. That's the voice of Great Scott Keating!" Shawn beats me to the punch, even though I had it on the tip of my tongue.

Behind the camera, screaming at Landon, is the unmistakable guttural voice of the actor so legendary that, back in his day, he formally became known as the "Great" Scott Keating. He also happens to be Landon's father, and at least five years deceased.

Landon tries to sit up straight, but his whole body contracts as he gets stung again. "Hello, my name is Arthur Wilson. I hope you have been enjoying your stay at my lovely hotel. We have a variety of amenities available to our guests, including a full provisions store, a barber, even—" He flashes his teeth and fights back a grunt of pain as the second scorpion stings him in the neck. "Even a full clinic for those in need of aid. Or, learn all about the great town of Dire in our history museum."

"You call that drivel acting?" Great Scott shouts from behind the scenes. "Reset, then start again!"

"Please, no," Landon begs.

"Once more, with feeling!"

There's another click, and a third scorpion drops into Landon's lap.

He twists and jerks several more times in his seat, the growing gang of scorpions continue to sting him. "Hello, my name is Arthur Wilson. I hope you have been enjoying—"

And just like that, the video ends.

"What the actual fuck," Shawn says.

"Looks like you've finally got a choice to make," I say, looking at Shawn. "Do we go back in and try to help him, or do we look for another way out?"

"No choice there." He stands up and tilts his head from side to side, the bones in his neck popping like a burst from a machine gun. "We have to help him."

For once in this hell house, a behind-the-scenes operator actually does me a favor. There's a click on the far wall of the room, then the bedroom door slowly creaks open.

CHAPTER THIRTY-FIVE

Hollywood Variety Cover Story, An Interview with Landon Keating. Issue #562

Landon Keating has been a household name since long before he even started acting. In fact, he can be seen on the June 1980 cover of Hollywood Variety Magazine, *as just a baby being held by his father, Oscar- and Tony-award-winning Hollywood legend, Great Scott Keating. Since that time, we've grown up with him as the star voice of the '80s cartoon,* King of the Creepies. *He's landed an Oscar nomination for his portrayal of Pharma bro Martin Shkrelli in the biopic* Wu-Tang for One *and topped the billboard charts with his rock band, Copycat. Now he's preparing for his greatest acting challenge yet—playing himself trapped in a haunted hotel. Even stranger, he will be facing off against the very character he played in the 2014 box-office bomb,* Murder Mansion. Holly-wood Variety *sat down with Landon in his Calabasas home to talk about being a part of Social's biggest experiment.*

Hollywood Variety: *Thanks for meeting with us today, Landon.*

Landon: Thank you for coming all the way out to my house. It's always so hot in those press junket rooms, with all the lights and no ventilation. People are walking in and out of the room constantly. Viewers at home don't know this while watching those interviews, but it's extremely distracting trying to thoughtfully answer questions, while PA's and producers are shuffling around behind the camera.

HV: Speaking of comfort, you're getting ready to rough it in what's said to be one of the most famous haunted houses in America. How exactly do you prepare for a project like this?

Landon: In a lot of ways, it's harder to play yourself than other people. Normally, when I get a script, I have some time to learn about a character and step into their skin. For instance, when I was shooting the detective thriller *No More Bones*, I was able to spend a few weeks tailing an actual homicide detective. I learned what it's like to get into that frame of mind, always keeping aware of the dangers they could face at any minute. I consider myself a very method actor, so it's been hard to find any substantial way to prepare for *Slashtag*, largely because I've been given so little material going in.

HV: With live TV being such a large departure from your normal method of work, what made you consider the project in the first place?

Landon: I like challenges. I always say, if you're not pushing yourself forward, you're sliding backward. When preparing to shoot *Murder Mansion*, I spent hundreds of hours researching Arthur Wilson, as well as a number of other serial killers. At this point, I think it's safe to say there's no one out there with a better understanding of Wilson, aside from the man himself. I then had to remain in the mindset of a murderer and torturer for months during filming. In *Slashtag*, it's like we've flipped the whole experience on its head. Now I have to put myself into the headspace of one of his potential victims, which forces me to really explore the opposite side of that character's story, from a new perspective. I think, in the end, it'll really bring the whole thing full circle for me.

HV: Having played Arthur Wilson, do you think that you will have any advantages moving into this competition?

Landon: Again, it's hard to say, given how little I know about the actual project. But yes, I think if I were confronted with the *actual* Arthur Wilson today, I'd be pretty good at managing to keep the target off my back.

HV: And how would you accomplish that?"

Landon: The thing you have to understand about Arthur is that while he was a monster, he was at heart an opportunist. The vast majority of his early crimes were committed under his father's nose, preying on the desperate. You know, drunks, gamblers, poor people. I don't party, I don't gamble, I'm a vegan, and I have people all around the world giving me support. My plan is to keep myself out of his crosshairs entirely by playing against the very lures that draw him in. In his later years, he seized on the gullibility of the ultra-religious and conservative crowd to lure them to their deaths. I'm neither of those things either, so again, I think I'll be okay.

HV: The film, Murder Mansion, *ended up underperforming at the box office, though it did spawn a series of popular internet memes featuring you in character. Do you have any concerns in revisiting a property that gave rise to so many jokes at your expense?*

Landon: You know what they say, any publicity is good publicity. I know [the picture] you're referring to, but I would argue that meme culture is less about lambasting and more a forum for celebrating art in a creative way. People don't go through the effort to create content unless there's passion there. Because of the meme, potentially millions of people gained interest to go see *Murder Mansion*, whether it be out of irony or genuine curiosity. Either way, they're going to walk away from that experience with an emotion that's going to resonate with them, and in the end, that's what art is all about. It's making you feel something, which for me is an honor in any form.

HV: One of the most outspoken critics of the film was your own father, the late Great Scott Keating. What do you think he would say about you participating in Slashtag?

Landon: To be frank, I don't care much what he would think about it. I know it sounds horrible to say. Of course, I have only the most respect for him and everything he taught me. To put it gently, my father came from a different era, and I don't think he would understand the significance of a project like *Slashtag*. We had very different definitions of art in the modern age.

HV: In what ways?

Landon: I don't want to belabor the subject or speak ill of the dead, but I'll just say this, and then we can move on: It's a good thing he passed before the cultural shift in Hollywood occurred over the last few years. The "Great" Scott Keating, as you all like to call him, would not have fared well in the age of on-set accountability. He was a man firmly rooted in the past, for better or worse, and I'm looking to the future. I think that's enough about my father. Let's talk about something else.

CHAPTER THIRTY-SIX

Shawn and I hurry down the black staircase as quickly as we can, heading back toward the dining room. We're no more than two steps beyond the broken mirror, when I hear our companions shouting from somewhere down a hall to the right. There's an open door with a golden plaque reading *Dire Museum of History*.

The majority of the museum is made up of a miniature replica of the town in its early days. It takes up most of the floor space, and it leads to a scale model of the Propitius Hotel pressed against the back of the room. D-wreck and Britt are looking at the walls, while Kiki, who seems to have lost her fuzzy purple jacket, examines the miniature town.

"D-wreck, what happened to you?" Shawn demands. "You were supposed to get help."

"I don't know if you saw the video, but help's sort of in short supply right now," he says. It takes him a second to notice the bruises on my neck. "Whoa, are you okay?"

I nod, even though it hurts to do so. "I'll be fine."

"Look who's back," Kiki says, with palpable disdain. "How'd the escape attempt go?"

"Could have been better," I say, trying not to give her the satisfaction of outright admitting I was wrong. "We destroyed another one of the sin statues."

"What do you want, a cookie?"

"We saw Landon's video," I say, ignoring her jab. "Can you just tell us what's going on?"

Kiki inhales deeply, then begins recounting things so quickly it seems like she's trying to get it all out in one breath. "Okay, so we found our way into the sealed room with the X, which turned out to be a gambling hall. Inside the gambling hall there was this slot machine—but none of us had any coins to make it work. At first, we thought we were out of luck, but—" Kiki finally takes a breath, though it's only so she can step to the side and shout out into the hall, "Would you shut up!"

Everyone in the room collectively looks out into the empty hallway, searching for whatever Kiki just screamed at. We all come up blank. Before anyone has a chance to comment on it, Kiki picks up right where she left off.

"Sorry about that. It's just really distracting, you know? Anyways, there was this whole roulette table with chips, and we figured out this puzzle where—" Kiki squeezes her eyes shut and runs her hands down her face, hard enough they leave temporary white streaks behind.

"Kiki, are you okay?" I ask.

"I'm fine. Just a little tired." She fishes around in her shoulder bag, shakes a little white pill out of a clear glass jar, and swallows it dry. "Long story short, Landon found the coin, and as soon as he pulled the lever on the slot machine, the whole fucking wall spun around and swallowed him up. Then we got that video, where he seemed to emphasize the history museum, so now here we are, standing around with our proverbial dicks in our hands, trying to figure out what the fuck we're supposed to do next. And it would be a hell of a lot easier to do if we could have some peace and quiet around here for a goddamn minute!" She diverts her attention once again to an implied sound in the hall that I can't hear.

I lean over to Shawn and whisper if he's catching something I'm missing. He shakes his head.

"So are you going to help us find the next clue, or did you just stop off to say hello?" Kiki asks.

"We're here to help."

Kiki gestures around the room with open hands. "Do you need me to spell out what to do, then?"

Not wanting to get any further on Kiki's bad side, I make my way in and start looking carefully at the different displays around the room. The walls are filled with pictures of construction, miners, and the hotel. On one wall, there's a series of blueprints to The Propitius in various stages of development, all of which massively contradict each other. There's also a series of maps of the mining tunnels, which, according to these documents, were primarily located to the north of town so that all miners had to pass by the Propitius on their way to and from work. I take pictures on my phone of all of these, just in case.

After a minute of staring at the different maps, I see Britt confer with Shawn, then approach Kiki. "Hey Kiki, I just wanted to check in with you. See if everything's going all right?"

"I told you I'm fine." Kiki dismisses her without looking away from the model town. "Let's keep working."

"It's just that you seem to be having some difficulties right now, and I want to make sure you're fully feeling like your best self."

"I'm not possessed, just irritated."

"I think maybe everyone here would feel a bit more comfortable if we could take a look in your bag and just make sure there's nothing weird inside."

Kiki pins the bag to her side with her elbow. "I already said I'm fine. Back off."

Britt doesn't relent. "If that's true, then you shouldn't mind showing us what's in your bag."

"Seriously, this is the last time I'm warning you to fuck right off." Kiki glances around the room like a cornered animal.

Shawn is standing right behind Britt, looking unsure of whether or not he should intervene. I catch his attention by pointing at my teeth, reminding him of the mark of possession. He nods quickly, then carefully inserts himself between the two women without managing to touch either.

"How about we take it down a little?"

"How about you both get out of my face?" Kiki says.

Shawn glances over to me and gives his head a quick shake. She's not under the influence of a statue. Aside from her clearly hallucinating some sound from the hall, it doesn't seem like she poses a threat right now.

Shawn seems to agree. "Sorry about that, Kiki. Britt, how about we go look for clues over there?"

As Shawn and Britt distance themselves from Kiki, she eases up and gets back to searching the room. Meanwhile, D-wreck meanders over to me, pretending to study some photographs on the wall.

"Hey, you want to tell me about those marks on your neck?"

"I got possessed by Lust, I think, and apparently tried to have sex with Shawn. Upon failing that, I went straight for attempted murder. All told, this is probably the best-case scenario. Shawn could have done much worse if he'd wanted."

D-wreck nods seriously. "Sounds kinky. Should I feel threatened?"

I give him a smack on the shoulder, then move on. "How long has Kiki been hearing things?"

"This seems like a new development, and to be honest, I don't love the manic look on her."

"Well, she's definitely not possessed right now, so I think it likely leaves one option."

We're already talking in hushed voices, but D brings it down even further. "You think it has something to do with the, uh, things we saw in the basement?"

"I think Wilson has a way of getting into our heads. Once we figure out this room and—fingers crossed—save Landon, I think we should have that private talk we've been meaning to. About dogs, and red balls?"

D-wreck chews his lip, looking overtly uncomfortable. "Yeah, I guess so."

We both stare at the set of three hotel blueprints as if it's a spot-the-difference puzzle from a children's magazine. After a minute or so, Kiki calls us all over to the scale model of the town in the center of the room.

"Take a look at this." Kiki reaches for one of the buildings on the model and picks it up off the table. In its place sits a small pressure plate. "The buildings are removable. I'm wondering if they're in the wrong order, and we need to rearrange them, or something. Does anyone remember anything from the town when we first drove in?"

Everyone shakes their heads. "I didn't even know what the outside of this building looked like until I saw this model," Britt says.

"I don't want to sound like even more of an asshole than I already am," D-wreck says, "but aren't we literally in a room full of pictures of the town? Wouldn't this be the best place to find out what it looks like?"

Kiki nods, then pulls the other four buildings out of their squares. The remaining empty spaces have pressure plates that alternate from black to white, like a set of checkers. "Everyone search for pictures of the town, particularly how the buildings were arranged. Looks like there's five we need: dry goods, barber shop, pharmacy, saloon, and doctor's office. Focus on finding those."

Everyone scatters, working to follow Kiki's orders. She stands over the model town, like a general formulating a battle strategy, studying every aspect of it as she bites her cuticles. D-wreck and I abandon the maps to scour the pictures on the walls. There's dozens of framed photographs featuring an assortment of buildings, though none of them seem to give any indication of their relative geography to the hotel.

"I see the dry goods next to the doctor's office!" Shawn shouts from one end of the room.

Kiki grabs two out of the five model buildings, checks the names, and sets them next to each other off to the side.

"Here's a picture of the hotel, with the saloon slightly in frame," Britt says. "I think that means it's the closest, right?"

"Good catch," Kiki says, grabbing the corresponding model and placing it in the square closest to the Propitius.

Something inside the table makes a mechanical grumble, quickly followed by a blaring klaxon ringing throughout the room. The lights briefly turn red.

"What the fuck?" Kiki says. "It's literally in the picture. How could I be wrong?"

Loud metal gears crank behind a giant painting of Arthur Wilson in the middle of the wall. The painting slides upward, as if it were a roller curtain covering a window. There's a small operating room behind a pane of glass. Arthur Wilson is inside, wearing his surgeon's clothes and staring out at us with a malevolent smile buried beneath his mustache. Next to him stands none other than the Great Scott Keating. He looks exactly as he did in the movie *Sacrificial Road* back in the nineties, down to the black suit and purple ascot. This is before he lost his hair but after it had gone gray enough to finally age him out of playing young handsome leads. His mouth is comfortably set in a permanent scowl, and his eyes have a vacancy to them, giving him an aura of cruelty.

The two dead men hold such a commanding presence, I don't even notice what's behind them, until they both take a step back. Landon is still strapped to the chair from the video. This must be where it was filmed. He's covered in large purple welts. His face is hanging in pure misery, and he's breathing in rasps. His blonde man-bun has been undone and hangs in lank tendrils from his head.

"Holy shit," D-wreck says. "He looks like death."

Britt runs up to the glass and pounds on it, rousing him from his daze. "Landon, hang in there! We're going to get you out of there. I know a guy in Beverly Hills that can take care of all of this. You'll look good as new."

"No distractions, boy. This is your big chance in front of a live audience." His father gestures toward us. "Say the line."

Landon takes several heavy breaths, staring at us with pure panic in his eyes. Eventually, he closes them and nods his head slightly, as if rehearsing to himself. As he does this, he straightens up his spine, arches his shoulders back, and tucks his chin. When his eyes open, there is barely a trace of the terrified man from a few seconds ago. What sits before us now is a facsimile of the horrific entity beside him.

"Hello, my name is Arthur Wilson. I hope you have been enjoying your stay at my lovely hotel. We have a variety of amenities available to our guests, including a full provisions store, a barber, even a clinic for those in need of aid. Or, learn all about the great town of Dire in our history museum, which details the founding of this town during the gold rush, all the way up to—"

Kiki is gnawing deeply at her cuticles and lets out a little yip when she bites off more than she can chew. It's enough for Landon to lose focus for just a second, tripping over one of his words.

"Cut!" Great Scott shouts. He nods to Arthur Wilson, who gleefully brings a butcher's cleaver down onto the midsection of Landon's pointer finger.

Landon hollers in pain as half his finger rolls off the edge of the chair's arm. His hand pumps out powerful spurts of blood that travel right through Wilson's surgical apron.

Great Scott turns to face us. In his unmistakable gruff tone, he says, "What are you schmohawks doing? Get to work, or this little piggy's going wholesale to market." He points to a clock timer on the wall behind him, which makes a mechanical fluttering sound as it ticks away. "Next performance is in one minute."

"Who else has any ideas?" Shawn asks.

We all quickly gather around the table, trying to ignore Landon's sobs behind us.

"I've got an idea," Britt says. "Maybe it's backward."

"I wonder if the colors of the holes have anything to do with it," D-wreck adds.

"What do you think, Kiki?" I ask.

Despite all the chaos, Kiki is staring at the empty hallway she was shouting at earlier. I try again to grab her attention. "Kiki, what do you think?"

'Yeah, sorry," she says, pinching her eyebrows together in either confusion or concentration. "What was the idea? Backward?"

"Yeah, like, maybe it's in reverse order, as a twist or something," Britt says.

Kiki picks the saloon model out of its space on the board and moves over to the opposite side.

"Wait!" I say. "Don't just try it. There's always more to these puzzles, an extra step."

"So what's your idea, then?" Kiki asks impatiently.

On the other side of the glass, there's another scream of pain. Wilson has a set of clamps inserted inside of Landon's finger, digging around until he gets a firm grip on the bone inside. He then gives it a yank. The bone comes ripping out of Landon's finger and slips from Wilson's tongs, clattering to the ground.

"You want to keep letting him do that, or do you want me to try and solve this?" Kiki demands.

"That's not right, I'm telling you." I need to give her a reason, literally anything else to go off. "What about the line?"

"What line?"

"The line Landon's reading. The one about the hotel. Do you think that could have something to do with it? He lists three places. The provisions, the barber, and uh..."

"The clinic," D-wreck says obviously, as if we could have forgotten our encounter with Wilson in his private operating room.

"But that's only three places," Kiki says. "What about the other two?"

"Maybe they're decoys. That's why there's three black spaces and only two white ones. Try placing provisions, barber, clinic on the black spaces, starting closest to the hotel."

Another scream comes from behind us, so piercingly loud that it makes my ears hurt. I can't help but look and immediately regret it. Wilson has shoved a scalpel into the hollow socket of Landon's finger and is pouring a smoking black goo on the spot where skin and scalpel meet.

Kiki doesn't even seem to notice and instead gathers models on the table. "Provisions is probably dry goods. Barber is the barber. For clinic, you think they mean this one that's the doctor's office or the pharmacy? There's two different models."

I should be falling to pieces, but instead, I can feel myself moving into gear, refocusing on the task. "My guess is the doctor's office, but let's start with the other two first."

Kiki grabs the model nearest to her, which is the barber, and places it in the middle black square.

Somewhere in the table, there is the sound of metal latching into place, but aside from that, nothing seems to happen.

"That's probably a good sign," I say. "Try another one."

Next, she goes for the dry goods and places it in the space closest to the hotel. A loud electronic wail blares through the room, and the clock stops.

"All right, boy, here's your second chance. Let's hear the line, loud enough for all to hear. Don't forget to enunciate, and speak from the diaphragm."

Landon is drooling as he weeps. A thick line of spit hangs from his mouth. He looks about as far from a pretty-boy movie star as someone could possibly get. "Dad, please. I can't. I don't want to."

"He doesn't want to!" Great Scott calls out, as if quoting Shakespeare to a crowd. "Of course, you don't, and that's because you're nothing but a pathetic little weasel. You've always been a weasel, allowing yourself to be content frolicking in the garbage."

"But Dad," Landon whines.

Judging from my earlier experiences in this house, I get a strong feeling these are words he's heard before.

"A professional never quits, no matter the cost. Cut!"

Wilson's cleaver severs the middle finger next. Landon's entire body writhes in explosive desperation. His legs jerk wildly in their restraints, with nowhere to go.

"Reset the clock!" Great Scott calls, while dramatically spinning his finger in the air. The timer resets to one minute, then starts over.

"So that was your idea," Kiki says, looking at me as though I were the one who just cut off Landon's finger.

"Well, the barber is clearly right," I argue in my defense. "I think that means we were onto something. Hang on, there was something else about the barber shop that I remember."

"Was it me throwing the pole through the window?" D volunteers. "I don't know how helpful that's going to be right now."

"It actually might be." I open up my phone and look at the pictures I took of the floorplans of the house.

"Look at this," I say, putting my phone on the table in a place where everyone can see it. "There are three floor plans on the wall, each from different drafts of the hotel. Everything changes from picture to picture, except for one thing—there's a shop just behind the lobby. In version one, it says clinic. Version two, it's a barber shop. And, look, in version three, it just says provisions. It's the exact words Landon uses in the line. Even though he said provisions, barber, clinic, the right order should be clinic, barber, provisions."

"Wait," Britt says. "So it is just reversed?"

I nod. "Basically. This is it, I know it."

Kiki takes a step back from the table. "If you're so sure, then you can put them in yourself this time. If he loses another finger, I don't want you lot blaming me."

"Thanks for your vote of confidence." I grab the dry goods model and place it on the furthest black square. There's another small mechanical sound but no alarms. Another good sign. Finally, I take the doctor's office—certain Wilson would choose his own father's practice over some competitor's pharmacy—and place it in the space closest to the hotel.

Over in the operating room, there's the sound of a bell dinging, followed by the end of the ticking timer. I look into the room, where Wilson is securing a second scalpel by pouring another mixture of molten pitch over Landon's middle finger.

Great Scott stares at his son. "It was always my hope to just once see you rise to the occasion." He shakes his head and lets out a dramatic sigh. "It seems we still have work yet to do." With that, the painting of Arthur Wilson slides back down, hiding the entire room from view. There are several more clanks and whirrs, then Landon's screams suddenly cut out.

"Are you fucking kidding?" Kiki says. "We do all this work, and we don't even get him back? What was the point of all this?"

Over by the model of The Propitius, a light comes on just inside the front door, casting soft blues, reds, and greens out from its stained glass windows.

The front door then creaks open, and a small brass tube slides out.

Mission Log

- ~~Restore Power to the Hotel~~
- Destroy Arthur Wilson's Body Totem
  - Unlock Arthur's Apartment
    - ~~Find the key's knob~~
    - ~~Find the key's shaft~~
    - Find the key's bit
- Destroy Arthur Wilson's Mind Totem
  - Unlock the door to Sutter's Sanctum
    - Destroy the Greed statue
    - Destroy the Sloth statue
    - Destroy the Wrath statue
    - Destroy the Envy statue
    - ~~Destroy the Lust statue~~
    - Destroy the Pride statue
    - ~~Destroy the Gluttony statue~~
    - Destroy the Disobedience statue
- Destroy Arthur Wilson's Spirit Totem

SOCIAL

CHAPTER THIRTY-SEVEN

"Hi, I'm Todd." A boyish-looking man stands at my door, holding a large tablet in his hand. He's a skinny guy, probably around Tawny's age, wearing an expensive looking, but ill-fitting suit that stands at complete odds with the rest of his vibe. The tie is loosened, top button exposed. His socks don't even remotely match, and his hair is a disheveled mop that looks like he just got out of bed. "You must be April. It's nice to meet you. This is Grimes." Todd points a thumb at the large goon behind him in the black suit. "I'm the assistant day shift coordinator for *Slashtag*, and have I got an exciting offer for you!"

The way he speaks sounds like he's rehearsing lines for a middle school play. I stare at him, waiting for him to finish his clearly pre-written introduction.

"Do you, um, do you want to hear the offer?" he finally says, after an extended pause.

"Sure."

He nods, then jumps right back into his little speech. "I *could* tell you myself, but here's someone you might recognize, if you've been watching the show." He brings up his tablet and presses a few buttons, then flips the screen around.

I'm greeted by the face of a blonde woman in an expensive-looking red suit.

"April, hello! Tawny's told us so much about you. I'm Lucy Hodge, the host and director of programming at *Slashtag*. Sorry I couldn't make it there in person. Lots to do around here! I hope Todd hasn't said anything weird. He and Grimes were the only bodies I could spare."

"He's fine. Looks like you've made quite the speedy recovery," I say, referencing her decapitation yesterday.

Without missing a beat, she laughs and bobs her head from side to side. "That's movie magic for you! Do you mind if my team comes inside for a chat?"

Alarm bells go off in my head. Never let strangers into the house. Especially ones who are trying to kill your sister on live TV.

"Actually, the place is a real mess right now. Tawny would kill me if anyone saw the house like this."

Lucy purses her lips, like she's sucking on a lemon. "You sure you don't want to find somewhere a little more comfortable? They won't judge the state of the house, will you, Todd?"

"No, ma'am," Todd says, shaking his head emphatically.

I gesture down to my wheelchair. "I'm not getting any more comfortable than this. Whatever you want to talk about, we can do it here."

Lucy's face blooms in frustration, but she manages to keep her voice light and pleasant as she talks to me like I'm a four-year-old. "Well, I'm sure you've been watching the show, rooting for your sister, like so many others out there. She tells me you're quite the horror fan, so I thought you might like to come see how we make the show?"

This kind of condescension is shockingly common when I meet new people. Any time someone sees a person in a power chair, they immediately assume there's something wrong with our heads. While it usually irritates me to no end, in this instance, I might be able to use her ignorance to my advantage.

At this point, she has to know I can recognize my own sister in distress, and if her company can be brazen enough to kill real people on TV, they won't hesitate to take me out if I give them a reason. Todd, the man-boy, doesn't look like much of a threat, but the Kane Hodder impersonator behind him could snap me like a twig. I have to play along, at least until I can figure out what Lucy actually wants with me.

"You're inviting me to the Propitius?" I ask, trying to sound excited enough to seem genuine.

"The hotel itself is a live set, so we can't let you directly in, but we are going to be doing a series of segments with loved ones and friends in the control room later. If you like, you could possibly be featured on the show!"

There it is. She wants me to go on TV to reassure anyone who might be concerned that it's not all just fun and games. After that, they'll probably shoot me in the back of the head and cremate the remains. At least in that scenario, I survive longer than being gunned down in my own doorway.

"You want me to be on *Slashtag?*"

"If Tawny doesn't get eliminated before you arrive, absolutely. And if she does, then you'll be right there to cheer her up once she wraps shooting. Sorry, wrap is an industry term. It means finished."

Or in this case, dead.

I've seen this movie before. *Eden Lake, Get Out*, heck, even that one episode of *Black Mirror*. Never let them take you to a second location. Then again, I don't see how I'm any safer here in my first location.

"You know, I was supposed to have dialysis later this afternoon, but this opportunity only comes once in a lifetime. Why not? Let me just grab my phone and a few things—"

"Actually," she cuts me off, "you'll have to leave your phone behind for legal reasons. We can't have you secretly recording any behind-the-scenes footage. It would break immersion if it leaked online." She finishes her spiel with a half-hearted what-can-you-do shrug, implying she's just one small drone in a strict corporate hive.

"What about a change of clothes and some snacks?"

"We have plenty of food, and you shouldn't be gone long enough to warrant a costume change. This is just a day trip. We should have you home before bedtime."

"What about my chair? I can't get around without it."

"Todd, tilt me down," she commands.

He points the tablet's camera at my electric wheelchair.

"Can the battery be removed? There's a lot of complicated technology going on behind the scenes, and any unapproved electronics could affect it."

The excuse makes about as much sense as when I was a kid and the airlines would force me to turn off my Gameboy. I point to a black box tucked into a side compartment. Grimes yanks it up and out of the chair, leaving it just inside the doorway of my home.

"Perfect. Well, I've got to run, but I can't wait to see you in person." Lucy smiles and waves, then the screen goes black.

"All right, then. Let's get to it, I guess." Todd looks expectantly over to Grimes. "Could you, um..." He points at my chair, indicating he wants the goon to push me. "I would, but you know, I've got to hold onto this tablet. They said if I break another one I have to pay for it."

Grimes walks in silence around behind me, grabs the bar on the chair, and pushes me toward a large black van parked on the street. Once he loads me into a seat, he spends some time at the trunk, figuring out how to store the wheelchair properly.

I take this opportunity to have a few words in private with Todd. If there is any way I'm going to make it out alive, he is the one clear weak spot I could potentially use. "Just so we're both clear on this, you know that I'm fully aware Lucy sent you to kidnap me, with the intention of murdering me and my sister, right?"

"What?" Todd's voice raises to a falsetto, and he lets out a nervous breathy laugh. I can almost see the sweat beading on his forehead.

"Honestly, it's going to be a long ride to Dire. If I'm going to die, I'd rather not spend the next four hours sitting with you, pretending like I'm a clueless rube. It's awkward, you know?"

"I, um...We aren't...," Todd stammers, struggling to be even a fraction as competent as his boss.

The trunk slams, and the guard comes around to slide my door shut. As he does, I raise my eyebrows at Todd and conjure up the most carefree-looking smile I can muster.

"Good talk."

CHAPTER THIRTY-EIGHT

After an exhausting deliberation and a vote of four to one against Kiki, we decide it's time to take a breather. No one wants to go back to the dining room. Instead, we shift our base of operations to the lounge. It's one of the most well-lit rooms in the house during the day, which lets us at least pretend there's safety in sunlight.

While Kiki insists on working in the far corner by the dumbwaiter, D and Shawn are fast asleep on sofas near the windows. Britt is staring at her phone and typing what I can only guess is a memoir. I'm lying down as well, in a weird state where I'm almost too tired to sleep. It doesn't help that my last attempt to get some rest resulted in my face getting mutilated by a psychotic ghost.

Eventually, my mind starts to wander as exhaustion seeps in. I'm starting to drift off, just in time to be jolted back awake by Kiki kicking over a chair in frustration.

"Can you stop?" D-wreck moans, curled up in the red velvet lounge chair. "I'm going to call the manager if you don't knock it off."

"I'm so sorry my attempts at getting us out of this alive are disturbing you," Kiki says. "Would you prefer it if I saved you all a little more quietly so you can get some beauty sleep?"

"That would be great, thanks." D-wreck rolls over to face the back of the sofa.

I try to close my eyes again, but there's a tension in the air keeping all my fears buzzing around me, like a swarm of flies. The more I try to calm down, the more unwanted images flash across my eyelids. I see Him, sitting on top of my sister, a bloody knife in his hands. She's bleeding from her side, right where it turns out her kidney is located.

One for symmetry, He says, before plunging the knife down into her other side.

I rub my eyes, trying to shake it off the sounds of my sister screaming in my head. I'm held in the moment as Clarence the dog bites down on my leg like a vice grip, keeping me from crawling to April.

Screw it. If I'm not going to get any more sleep, I might as well get up.

Across the room, Kiki's leg is bouncing faster than ever as she studies her phone. At least now she seems to have accepted the fact this isn't just a game and our lives are at risk.

Each time I sit up, it gets just a little bit harder. My back, face, and hand hurt from getting stabbed and sliced with the scalpel. My ribs and throat are bruised, possibly broken from a fight with Shawn I don't even remember. The pain in my chin plays as a constant reminder that He is watching, and probably loving every minute of my suffering.

I've been running on maybe two and a half hours of sleep for the last two days, but I still manage to drag myself across the room to join Kiki over by the dumbwaiter.

"You mind if we sit down for a second and talk? I promise I won't make a move for your bag," I add, hoping a little light joke will help disarm her.

I feel like I can see her fighting a cringe, but she humors me, and I join her on the couch pressed against the far wall. In addition to her nervous leg, her pointer finger is digging along the cuticles of her thumb. She's catching hanging pieces of raw skin with her fingernail and picking at them until they peel back, revealing bright red blossoms of blood underneath.

"What do you want to talk about?"

"Just checking in to see how you're doing. It doesn't seem like you've slept at all since we got here, and I want to make sure you're not pushing yourself too hard."

"I'm fine," she says, before I even finish my sentence. "I'm used to working an eighty-hour week at the very minimum. I once pulled three all-nighters in a row, just to get a costume perfect in time for an E3 announcement of what turned out to be a mobile cash grab game that nobody even wanted. Believe me, I don't need much sleep to function."

"But you do need some. You know that we're all in this together, right? You don't have to be the one to solve everything on your own."

When she responds, her voice is an entire octave higher, as if she's about to cry. "But if I don't do it, no one will. D-wreck can't take anything seriously, Britt's a mouthpiece with nothing to say, Shawn's only useful when he feels like it, and you...You've already tried to lead a mutiny once. So that leaves me. I mean, seriously. We just saw Landon get several of his fingers cut off, and everybody's immediate reaction is to take a three-hour break? Do you guys even want to save him?"

"Of course we do." I put a hand over hers in an attempt to get her to stop picking at her fingers. It fails, and I pull back when she just keeps tearing at them underneath my hand. "These puzzles are extremely demanding, and I don't want us getting run so ragged that we make a careless error that ends up causing somebody to get hurt worse than they are."

Kiki's eyes burn with impatience. "But in the meantime, we're just allowing them to do whatever they want to Landon. By the time we all decide we're refreshed and ready, he could be dead."

"Something tells me he'll be okay until we're ready to move on to the next puzzle. You made a great point earlier that Arthur could have easily killed me and D-wreck last night, but he let us go. They don't just want to kill us off. They want us to watch it happen."

Kiki has peeled back a long strip of skin on her thumb. She brings it up to her mouth and pinches it off with her front teeth. "Do you think anyone's trying to save us out there? Hell, do you think anyone even believes this is real?"

"I don't know. They billed it as the ultimate reality horror experience. If I were watching this at home, I'd think this is like a *Cannibal Holocaust* kind of thing."

"What the hell's a *Cannibal Holocaust?*"

"It was this documentary-style movie about these people searching for something in the Amazon, and they all get killed in these hyper realistic ways. The filmmakers actually showed the killing and dissection of real animals during the production to sell the authenticity, and it worked so well that the director actually had to bring the cast members into a courtroom to prove that they were still alive."

"So you think everyone watching believes this is fake?"

"I'm still questioning whether or not this is even airing at all. But if it is, yeah. Every generation has a horror event where the point of the production is to fool the population into thinking it's real. Before *Cannibal Holocaust* it was *War of the Worlds* on the radio. In the nineties, we got *The Blair Witch Project*. In England, they did a fake news special on Halloween called *Ghostwatch*, where they pretended guests were calling in supernatural occurrences from all over the country. One kid was so convinced it was real that he committed suicide, truly believing he'd return as a spirit. I think, to the average horror fan, *Slashtag* is just the next logical step in metastorytelling."

"So you're saying it really is just on us to save ourselves." Kiki sends her bouncing leg into overdrive and leans to peer at something around the corner I can't see.

"Can I tell you a secret?" I say, trying to get her to focus back on me.

"Uh huh." She bites down on a piece of cuticle and pulls her thumb away, revealing a wet red spot more than twice the size from when it first went in her mouth.

"I'm a huge fan of scary movies. Both me and my sister, April, grew up watching almost nothing but horror films. My management team doesn't think that particular personality trait is helpful to my brand, so they made me pretend to be this positivity-focused health queen."

"Okay," Kiki says, half listening.

I move my hand to firmly place it on her bouncing leg, pinning it to the ground so she has to pay attention to me. She tightens her mouth and forcefully removes my hand from her leg, but at least now I have her focus.

"Fine. What's your point?"

"My point is that you know puzzles, but I know horror movies. And right now, we're basically living in the horror movie version of *Big Brother*."

"If this is supposed to be some sort of a pep talk, I gotta be honest, you're really doing a shit job of it right now."

"There are rules to surviving a horror movie, just like there are rules to a puzzle. If we combine our knowledge, I think we stand a better chance of getting out of here alive."

With one thumb cuticle thoroughly destroyed, Kiki moves on to fidgeting with her next finger. "What is there to know? This guy has traps all over the house, and even though he can't touch us directly, he can just possess us to do his dirty work for him. How do you plan against that?"

"For one thing, we could arm ourselves. That way, we have protection if Wilson comes after us again."

Kiki scoots closer to me and starts to whisper. "And how does that help us when Shawn gets an idea to start smashing skulls? You really think giving the Hulk a sword is a good idea?"

Shawn's been nothing but an ally to me, even when I tried to kill him. It hurts to think about having to fight him in order to stay alive.

"If it comes to that, we outnumber him three to one. That's when it matters to have weapons."

Kiki nods. Now that we're in planning mode, I finally have her attention. I want to ask her about the thing that seems to keep distracting her, let her know she's not the only one. I just have to do it carefully, or else I may lose her. It's so easy to forget that every moment of our torment has potentially been live-streamed for the world to see, and the extremely personal nature of what I want to ask might be a bridge too far for her. I have to frame it just right.

"Okay, I have a proposal for you. I've got some more ideas of how to keep us alive, and I'm guessing you have some plans for what we should do next. I'll collaborate with you right now to come up with a gameplan of how to make our next steps, but afterwards, you need to try and get at least an hour of rest. Does that sound fair?"

I put out my right hand in a gesture of goodwill, despite it being wrapped with a piece of gauze in desperate need of changing.

Kiki eyes me skeptically. "I'm not touching that. But yeah, you have a deal. What else do you know?"

I know that the only way to get her to trust me is if I put something out there first, but the thought of voluntarily bringing it up makes me lightheaded. And though I promised April I wouldn't share our story without her, she's not the only one I have to be worried about.

After all, *Good dogs keep their mouths shut.*

I center myself with three calming breaths, feeling my heart relax ever so slightly, then pull my slashed dress to the side and show Kiki the scar on my thigh. "When I was twelve, I was attacked by a dog, and it left this scar, along with a few others. I don't tell this story to anyone. I don't show this to anyone. But I need you to believe me when I say I saw this very same dog down in the basement, and so did D-wreck. This thing was real, and it chased us straight to Arthur's clinic."

I cover my thigh, not letting it sit exposed any longer than it has to.

"This was the worst thing that's ever happened to me, and it's been haunting me since the minute I arrived. Arthur's using my own personal ghost to attack me, and he could use it against you too."

I pause for a moment, hoping Kiki will take the hint and volunteer some information on her own, but the moment goes on too long, and I find myself having to ask the question anyway.

"I've noticed there's something that seems to keep distracting you. Something that no one else is seeing. Can you tell me what that is?"

Her head jerks back, and her eyebrows crunch together as if I've just punched her in the gut. "What the fuck are you asking me?" she says, raising the volume of her voice for the first time since we sat down.

"No, listen. I'm not trying to get you to explain anything. I'm just letting you know that for me, I started out hearing things, and then they escalated into something more real."

I look around the room to check on the others. Shawn and D-wreck both seem to be asleep, and Britt has finally put her phone away and shut her eyes too.

"These things from our minds could become dangerous. If there's something you're seeing or hearing that might be a threat, we need to know."

Kiki hunches down and manages to whisper even more quietly than me. "It's not going to become a threat. I swear. It's just a little thing that's really persistent, and annoying, and won't let me get any sleep."

"What is it?"

Kiki brings up her hand and starts again on her cuticle. Out of the side of her mouth, she whispers, "It's the sound of a baby crying."

CHAPTER THIRTY-NINE

From: Lucy.K@Krentler.media
To: Operations@Krentler.media
Subject: The Gauntlet.

Confirming details for the final key challenge and subsequent confrontation with Arthur Wilson. We're all about to be very busy, so I'll keep this brief.

- After a minor diversion, the subjects have managed to acquire 2 out of the 3 key parts.
- The Hunter's Hall is ready to go, and Renshaw has updated our new priority target.
- Landon is ready, and on his mark.

Good luck everyone. At the conclusion of Arthur's Apartment, there will be cupcakes in the breakroom.

Lucy

From: Todd.M@Krentler.media
To: Operations@Krentler.media

Lucy, can you save a cupcake for me?

Todd

From: Lucy.K@Krentler.media
To: Operations@Krentler.media

Todd,

Fuck your cupcake. Do not reply-all unless it directly pertains to the events of *Slashtag*.

Lucy

CHAPTER FORTY

I'm somewhat shocked that, after going through plans with Kiki, we managed almost seventy-five minutes of silence, before a parade of doors slamming somewhere else in the hotel jolts us awake. I don't know if Kiki managed any sleep. By the time I open my eyes, she's already on her feet and peeking out the door.

Judging by the state of her hands, I'm guessing not. Most of her fingers are now spotted red with cuticle cuts.

"Sounds like we've been boring our audience long enough. Time to get this show on the road." She claps and rubs her hands together to further hustle the preparations of everyone else. "While the rest of you were sleeping, Tawny and I came up with some ideas moving forward."

Britt is still groggy from her nap but clearly still feels the need to pretend she's in control. "Good thinking, everyone. We should all have a meeting to get on the same page."

Shawn rubs his eyes and sits up. "I know we just had a break and all, but my stomach is killing me. Is anybody else hungry?"

Kiki points an excited finger at him. "Then get ready to stuff your face, my friend, because the kitchen is actually the first stop in our plan."

Five minutes later, we're all gathered in the dining room, shoving peanut butter and jelly sandwiches down our throats. I didn't even know I was hungry until I took my first small bite, and then it was like some ravenous beast took over, wolfing the whole thing down. After the brief meal, Kiki pulls out the physical map of the house from her bag, along with the two key parts—now assembled—and sets them on the table.

"It looks like the last part of the key is located here." She points to a room on the second floor that we've all been purposely avoiding until now. "The Hunter's Hall."

"And we're sure that's the only way?" Britt asks. "Doesn't a room named *Hunter's Hall* kind of sound like an obvious death trap?"

"You know, I was going to suggest going through the nail salon, but Hunter's Hall just had such a better ring to it."

Britt pushes back on Kiki. "I'm just trying to offer helpful suggestions. If you all think it's a good idea to go into a room where getting hunted is the theme, who am I to stand in your way?"

"I don't love it either," I say, "but it doesn't really seem like we have much of a choice. One more thing, there's a bunch of knives and stuff in the kitchen. I think everyone should have something with them, just in case."

"Are you sure that's a smart idea?" Shawn says, more as a statement than a question. "What good's a knife going to do against a ghost?"

"We already know Arthur can put the whammy on people, make them do things they wouldn't normally do. I think it's in our best interests to be able to defend ourselves if that happens."

"I think it's a great idea," Britt says, turning my suggestion into a decree. "I know I'd feel a lot more comfortable with some sort of accessory. That's good thinking, Tawny."

Just like that, it's settled. We follow Kiki into the kitchen, where there's a wide assortment of cutlery sheathed in a large wooden block. I pick a kitchen knife that comes to a sharp point, the largest one I can wedge between my hip and my skirt without feeling like it's going to slice me by accident. Kiki goes for a butcher's cleaver with a rounded edge and stuffs it in her bag. It makes sense for her—with the number of goodies she has hidden in there, the last thing she needs is to reach in and get poked by the tip of something sharp. D-wreck grabs a frying pan. It's a pretty on-brand choice for him, so I don't question it, but he manages to get a few stares from the others.

"Hey, I've already fought this guy once. I know what I'm doing."

Britt grabs a paring knife with a handle she says goes great with her outfit. Shawn opts for a meat-tenderizing hammer, which actually gives me a moment's pause. Maybe Kiki did have a point before. He was already dangerous enough, but now with the addition of a hammer covered in spikes, I feel like he'd become a much deadlier threat if he did start swinging at us.

We make our way back to the lobby, up the stairs, and through a network of corridors, until we find a room with a mounted pair of antlers hanging over the door. Kiki rushes ahead and already has her hand on the knob by the time Britt calls out some safety tips.

"Remember, everyone, let's take our time before making any drastic decisions. Try to stay calm, and don't touch anything unless we need to."

Upon first inspection, it is indeed a hunter's trophy room, displaying a wide variety of taxidermied animals. Wolves, coyotes, and other desert wildlife crowd the floors and assorted pedestals around the room. There's even a bear standing in the corner on two legs, reared up and permanently stuck in the midst of a vicious roar.

The walls are covered in plaques with the heads of elk and horns of various other types of animals. In addition to the displays of death, there are also large areas of the walls dedicated to the various tools of destruction used to take their lives. A series of antique rifles hang from one large wooden rack, while next to them, at least a dozen different types of hunting knives are on display. Photos and paintings are also scattered around the room, showing off Arthur Wilson, along with various other older white men either in the act of killing or in celebration of their recent domination of nature.

"And here's the fucked-up twist, ladies and gentlemen." Kiki gestures to something on the wall just behind the head of a moose.

I have to take several more steps before I see the newest addition to the room.

Miguel's head has been severed and mounted on a plaque hanging from the wall. His mouth is gaped open, and his eyes have been replaced with glass balls straddling the uncanny valley. Unlike the animals all around us, which have been posed to look ferocious and like they're on the verge of attack, Miguel's face is fixed to a dopey look of surprised horror. The way they have him posed, it almost feels like it would be more respectful to keep the mask on.

"Who is this guy?" Britt asks.

"That's Miguel. Chef Costanza," I say.

"Should we say something? Like a memorial?"

Before anyone has time to answer, the door behind us slams shut. None of us need to check it, the self-locking door trick is old hat by now.

"I think we have more pressing issues," D-wreck says, the first person to break off from the group. "Check this out."

D points to a set of three wooden bas-reliefs taking up almost the entirety of the far wall. The first one is the face of a roaring bear looking head-on, the second is a pig in profile with an apple stuck in its mouth. The third is of an elk, its head turned to show off its massive antlers. Above each of these massive carvings, an unlit light bulb protrudes from the wall.

"Okay, so it looks like there's three different animals in the room that we need to do something with," Kiki says, shoving a finger in her ear and trying to force a yawn. "Everyone know what to do?"

At this point, we're all quite familiar with the process of moving quickly but carefully on the search for anything out of the ordinary. I'm inspecting the head of the elk, when I notice a large gash in its neck.

"Is anybody else checking animals? It looks like there's a stab wound here. I don't know much about taxidermy, but don't you usually want to hide the method of death when mounting them?"

"I got one too!" D-wreck shouts, with more enthusiasm than feels natural. He points to a small hole in the bear's chest. "Looks like this one was shot."

"Okay." Kiki nods, putting things together. "So, it seems like the goal could be to recreate the target animals' deaths. There's guns over here, knives over there."

"But which one is the right one?" I ask.

"Also," Britt notes, "I don't see a pig anywhere, and that seems like one of the three animals we need to interact with."

"I got a picture," Shawn calls out from another wall.

It's a framed photo of Arthur Wilson standing over a dead bear with a rifle in his hands. He's got a foot propped on the beast, and unlike most of the photos and paintings around the hotel, he actually has a look of joy in his eyes.

Shawn squints and leans closely at the picture. "Looks like an old Winchester repeater."

D-wreck scans the rack of rifles, finally pointing to a gun matching the one in the picture. "Miss Kiki, can I play with the gun, please?"

Kiki double-checks between the photo and the weapon, then nods. "Just be careful with that thing. Don't be an idiot."

"Of course I'll be careful," D says, pulling the rifle from the wall. "Weapon safety is no laughing matter and should always be handled with care. I'll have you know, I have excellent trigger discipline." He points the rifle at the bear, aiming at the hole in its chest. "Okay, everyone, cover your ears. This could be loud."

He pulls the trigger.

The rifle makes a dinky little sound, like a hotel service bell. Just like that, a green light comes on right above the bear carving's head.

"Holy shit, I actually figured one out. Guys, I think we have this room nailed."

Several voices all shout over each other, calling D-wreck out for obviously jinxing us.

"What?" he says, spinning around and inadvertently pointing the nozzle of the gun at each of us. "I think we're getting better at this, we deserve a little pat on the back. What's wrong with that?"

In my mind, it only counts as a jinx if there isn't an entire crew of live people, and one sadistic dead person, just waiting to jump on cues like this.

The gun goes off again, this time with a deafening roar, and the room lights up with a flash. Kiki screams and crumples to the floor, blood pumping from her calf.

"I didn't do it!" D-wreck shouts, dropping the rifle to the floor. "Let me help." He rips his red hoodie off his back and kneels to tie it to her leg. As soon as he squats in front of her, the pain in her face turns to panic.

"Get away!" she yells, trying to shove him off of her.

"Just let me slow the bleeding." The harder he fights to wrap her leg, the more desperately she tries to fight him off. "Would you quit it? I'm trying to help you."

"Holy shit," Shawn mutters, seeing something I clearly don't. He leaps at the pair on the floor, tackling them both to the ground only moments before another gunshot rings out.

Huge splinters of wood explode from the exact spot Kiki's head was resting only a moment ago. D-wreck's gun lies inert on the floor, not even remotely facing the direction of the last shot.

I scan the wall again, looking for holes or any other hidden compartment someone could point a gun through. My search stops when I re-examine the picture of Wilson and the bear. While he was once posing proudly on the animal's corpse, he now stands at the ready, his gun pointed directly at the camera. It takes my brain a second to catch up with what my eyes are seeing, especially after the figure in the photo moves his head slightly toward me and winks.

"The picture. He's in the picture!" I point at the photograph on the wall, where Arthur has pumped the lever on his rifle and now has it pointed at me. I throw myself against the wall next to the photograph, hoping he can't hit me from here. When I look around, everyone else has scrambled to find cover from the living photograph.

There's a pregnant pause. Everyone catches their breath and tries to figure out how to cope with the fact that even photos now have murderous intent.

"What if we get him to waste all his ammo? Throw a stuffed coyote into the line of fire until he's empty," D suggests.

"He's using a photograph of a gun to shoot at us. You really think ammunition is going to be a factor here?" Kiki snarls through gritted teeth.

"Okay. What if I smash the picture? That should probably do it, right?"

"It's worth a shot," Kiki says. "Just be careful."

"Yes, mother," D says from the other side of the stuffed bear. He ducks his head and prepares to sprint toward the photo, but just as he does, the lights in the room go out, stopping him dead in his tracks.

Somewhere in the darkness, there's a gagging sound, like someone trying to force down an entire can of sardines in one wretched gulp. Or, like they're choking on an oversized red gumball. It's carrying a sense of urgency, the unbelievable all-consuming panic of when you're suddenly robbed of the one thing you need to survive, along with the desperate crushing knowledge that you're absolutely helpless to do anything about it.

The lights flicker back on.

Crawling on his hands and knees just below the picture is something resembling a child no older than six. Everything about the boy is wrong. His eyes are bulging out, so bloodshot there's almost no white to be seen. His mouth is locked open in shock, and what feels like gallons of blood pump out of it in rhythmic heaves. Between his lips, there's a pink foam bubbling up and dribbling down his chin, reminding me of Costanza's final moments. His neck is purple and rotted. A creeping black mortification is climbing up along his face in dark wicked streaks.

"What the hell is that?" Shawn screams.

The boy reaches out an arm, clawing at us, begging for help. Even if it weren't some sort of twisted trap, I still wouldn't know what to do.

"What does this have to do with hunting?" Britt says. "I don't get it."

"Somebody figure it out," Kiki says, taking back command. "Britt, you find the knife for the elk. D-wreck, you're still on smashing duty."

"No, no, no," D-wreck mutters, backing away from the boy and scraping his fingernails along the sides of his head.

"D-wreck, hey. Over here. Do you know what this is?" she demands, snapping her fingers to try and pull his attention to her.

D just keeps repeating himself, backing up until he hits a wall, then slides to the floor. He curls up into a ball, scratching his hands back and forth along his scalp. I lean forward to see about finding a clear path to him. The gun goes off again, sending a bullet whizzing just inches past my face.

Meanwhile, Britt is safe on the other side of the photograph, taking turns grabbing each knife from a display on the wall and stabbing it into the stuffed elk's neck. Each time, she checks the lights over the bas-relief's head to see if it's lit up, before dropping that knife to the ground and trying again.

"D-wreck, can you hear me?" I call his name several more times, before he finally looks at me with unfocused eyes. "D, I need you to talk to me. Who is that?"

He shakes his head. "No. It's not my fault."

"What's not your fault?"

"It was an accident."

"Come on, talk to me."

"Blood balls!" he shouts, as if it were the explanation to everything, then goes back to scratching the shaved sides of his head.

"What the hell are blood balls?" I ask, as a vague memory comes to me.

There was a candy that was popular about five years ago. They were essentially gumballs but filled with a red juice inside that looked like blood.

I glance back over at the young boy, gushing blood from his mouth like it's a fountain, and it hits me all at once. He's choking on a blood ball. That's what Wilson dropped into Miguel's mouth to kill him, and that's why D-wreck freaked out so much.

Several pieces fall into place all at once.

The carved picture of the apple in the pig's mouth is not an apple, and the pig is not a pig.

"Okay D, I need you to listen to me. You have to pull it out."

He looks at me like I just asked him to walk into a burning building. "What?"

"It's the solution to the puzzle. There's a blood ball in that boy's throat, right?"

Tears run down D-wreck's face as he nods.

"You need to pull it out."

"I can't," he mumbles.

I want to scream at him to take responsibility for his own trauma, but I know as well as anyone, that's not how it works. I can shout at him all day, but if he isn't ready to confront something, there's nothing I can do to force it.

"All right, that's fine. I'm going to go for the ball, but I need someone to cover me." I look to my right, where Shawn is pressed up against the same wall as me. "Can you distract Wilson for me?"

Shawn hazards a look into the rest of the room, then nods. "I think I can do you one better." He shimmies himself away from me along the wall until he reaches the far end of the room, then takes a few deep preparatory breaths. "Ready?" he calls out. "Hut-hut!"

From the back wall, he bursts into a full-on sprint, dashing across the room as fast as possible. Wilson takes the bait, firing a round and missing by a long shot. In the brief time it takes for him to cock the repeater on the rifle, Shawn turns and hurls his tenderizer mallet at the picture, shattering the glass. I look at the picture to see if there's a gun pointed in my direction. Even though the majority of the photo is still intact, Arthur is now missing entirely.

I want to be relieved, but I know it's just a matter of time before Arthur reappears with some horrible new trick. Without wasting any time, I approach the red-and-purple-faced child and feel my heart pound even faster. His eyes plead with me. I can't help but wince, extending my uninjured left arm and reaching for the boy's bloody, foaming mouth.

The bubbles are oily, they pop and fizz against my fingers pushing between his lips. My knuckle grazes the top of his teeth, and his lower jaw clenches on the meat of my hand below the thumb. His tongue lashes against my hand, sliding around at it from all angles, trying to force my fingers out of his mouth. I have to look away to keep myself from getting sick, but I'm able to squeeze just a little further into his throat. Eventually, I connect with something round and hard.

I wedge my first two fingers between the ball and the boy's throat. My fingers inch forward little by little, like a soldier crawling through trenches. His windpipe has almost no give, but eventually, I'm able to feel my finger come out on the other side of the ball. From there, I curl my finger into a hook, and with a quick yank, the ball comes sliding right out of the boy's throat.

He falls to the ground, eyes still bulging like a bullfrog, but at least he's no longer making that gag-inducing sound. My arm is covered in blood all the way up to the elbow, but there's no time to worry about that now.

I rush over to Miguel's severed head and shove the blood ball in his throat. There's another ding, followed by a green light turning on over the pig portrait's head.

Not to dwell on my accomplishment too long, I hear the cocking sound of a gun next to me. There's a painting of a group of men in tan suits standing next to a dead stag in the forest. In the middle of the painting is the animated form of a black and white Arthur from the photo. He's smiling as he points his gun straight at me.

As frayed as my nerves are, my reflexes activate just in time. I drop to the floor before Wilson blasts another bullet across the room.

I'm fine, but behind me Britt screams. Her upper arm is bleeding. The bullet must have missed me and hit her instead. Even worse, the rack of knives is empty, and there's still no light above the elk's portrait.

Britt stands frozen in fear while Arthur cocks his rifle and takes aim. At the last second, Britt looks up at the elk's antlers and grabs the end of one. With a quick pull, the antler splits, revealing itself as the handle to a hidden blade inside. She stabs the knife into the elk's neck, illuminating the third light. A buzzer rings out across the room, and the next moment, we are all plunged into absolute darkness.

After a few seconds of heart-pounding silence, there's a series of clicks, then the lights come back on. A small brass bit comes tumbling from out of the bear's open mouth, onto the wood floor, then the door to the room swings back open with a groan.

Everyone is panting, everyone is bleeding. No one makes a move for the door or even attempts to stand up. Even Kiki seems too worn-out to move.

Shawn is the first to finally speak. "So D-wreck, still think that room was super easy?"

He looks over to him for some sort of comeback, but D doesn't even seem to hear. He's still balled up on the floor, looking no different than he did a minute ago.

Kiki doesn't quite have the same sense of gallows humor about it and instead seems almost insulted. "Seriously, man, what *was* that thing? What did you do to create *that*?"

"It's not my fault," D-wreck mutters. "It was an accident."

"But, like, what was it? What happened?" Kiki persists.

For someone who has been so unwilling to share her own story, it aggravates me more than a little that she's coming this hard at D, mere moments after confronting whatever that thing was. I want to call Kiki out for keeping her own secrets, but I've just worked up some trust with her, and I'm not sure making further accusations will help the situation.

Instead, we need something to lift us back up, keep us going. I decide a little bit of the old Tawny Howlett trademark positivity is in order, to at least try and encourage the team.

"Britt, that was an amazing find with the antler knife at the end. You saved our lives."

"Thanks," she says.

"Yeah, how the hell did you find that—" Kiki's words get cut off as all of our phones simultaneously buzz in our pockets and play that irritating little jingle.

Confusion passes around the room when an alert pops up reading: *A Very Special Message from D-wreck.*

"D-wreck, did you just butt broadcast this whole thing out?" Shawn says.

I press play on the phone. The footage is outside, on the deck of a restaurant. The place is mostly empty, save for a table with two adults sitting under a giant plastic swordfish hung from an awning overhead. The diners don't seem to notice the camera, pointed at them from at least thirty feet away.

"What is this?" Kiki says. "When did you sneak off to a seafood restaurant?"

The camera then drops down behind a table, pointing at a young blonde boy. It's hard to recognize him without the black gullet and bloodshot eyes, but it's the same young man whose throat I just shoved my hand into.

We hear D-wreck's voice behind the camera. "All right, Mikey, you ready to prank the H-E-double-hockey-sticks out of your parents?"

The little boy gives a big toothy grin and nods enthusiastically.

In the corner of the Hunter's Hall, D snaps out of his fetal position. He's frantically searching for the source of the sound. "No. Stop it." His voice is full of urgency. "Turn it off."

In the video, D's hand appears on screen, passing the headless body of a small fish to Mikey. The little boy starts to giggle.

"Shhh," D-wreck hushes the boy. "Do you have the blood ball?"

Mikey reaches his hand into his shorts pocket and pulls out a red ball nearly the size of his fist.

"Dope-asaurus rex. Remember not to pop the blood ball into your mouth until you're, like, halfway to your parents' table. You bite down, show them the fish, say 'I think I swallowed a bone!' and then just let all the fake blood run out of your mouth. Got it?"

The boy nods, brimming with excitement.

"Give me the line again."

"I think I swallowed a bone," Mikey repeats.

"Fantastic, kid. You're a natural. Now count to fifty while I get in a better position, and then you go for it."

The camera cuts, then resets from the other side of the restaurant. It's now facing the same diners, but the background is a deck overlooking a marina full of sailboats.

"Oh shit, here he comes," D-wreck whispers from his new vantage point, catching the two adults at their table in frame as the little boy walks toward them.

We see him pop the blood ball into his mouth, but he only makes it a few more steps, until his little feet stop. The headless fish falls to the floor. Mikey has to grab onto the backside of an empty chair to keep himself from falling. Red and pink stuff is starting to bubble out of his mouth. The boy leans backward, pulling the whole chair with him as he crashes to the ground.

"Oh shit, oh fuck," D-wreck says on video. The camera gets up and runs toward the boy, along with his now-panicked parents.

"Michael! What's the matter? What happened?"

The boy's parents scream as their child convulses on the floor. He's making the wet choking sound, identical to what we just heard in real life.

"Oh God, somebody please help him! What's happening?"

Several waiters and waitresses in nautical-themed outfits come running up to check on the commotion. Though I can't see their faces, it's clear from their voices and body language that they're panicking too.

The camera rushes to the family huddled over their boy. The father turns and looks in shock at the lens, before addressing the man behind it.

"Derek, what the hell did you do?"

"It was just a prank. I didn't do anything."

"What did you give him?"

"I-I just gave him a blood ball. It's only candy."

"Goddammit, Derek. He's allergic to red food dye!" The man looks up to a waitress nearby. "Call 911. He's going into anaphylactic shock. Sarah, do you have his pen?" He shifts his attention to his wife, who has already dumped her purse out onto the floor and is sifting through the contents.

"I'm so sorry. How can I help?" D-wreck says.

"Just leave!" the father shouts, glaring at the camera, then returning his attention to the boy violently coughing up pink foam.

The wife finally finds a long orange pen, lifts up the boy's shirt, and stabs it into his chest. "Oh God, Michael. It's going to be okay, honey. We're here. Mommy and Daddy are here."

"Is he going to be all right?" D-wreck asks, his voice shaking, on the verge of tears.

The wife shoots her head up at the camera, mascara running down her face. "Just get away from us, Derek!" she screams. "Get out!"

The camera continues to back away from the horrific scene for a couple of more seconds, before the screen goes black.

"I didn't know he was allergic," our D-wreck whimpers.

"Who was that?" I ask.

"Mikey. My nephew. They were able to get him to the hospital, but he could have died."

"How come none of us have ever heard of this?" Britt asks. "When did this happen?"

"It's my brother Colin's kid. I thought it would be funny. I swear I had no idea that would happen. Colin made a deal. He wouldn't tell the press as long as I promised never to talk to him or his family again."

"How long ago was this?" I ask.

"It's been four years. Not a single member of my family has spoken to me since."

Mission Log

- ~~Restore Power to the Hotel~~
- Destroy Arthur Wilson's Body Totem
  - Unlock Arthur's Apartment
    - ~~Find the key's knob~~
    - ~~Find the key's shaft~~
    - ~~Find the key's bit~~

- Destroy Arthur Wilson's Mind Totem
  - Unlock the door to Sutter's Sanctum
    - Destroy the Greed statue
    - Destroy the Sloth statue
    - Destroy the Wrath statue
    - Destroy the Envy statue
    - ~~Destroy the Lust statue~~
    - Destroy the Pride statue
    - ~~Destroy the Gluttony statue~~
    - Destroy the Disobedience statue

- Destroy Arthur Wilson's Spirit Totem

SOCIAL

CHAPTER FORTY-ONE

In the car, Todd attempts to feed me several "fun facts" about *Slashtag*, but most of them involve long, rambling stories that end nowhere near where they began. A story about location scouting ends up mostly being a tale of misadventure Todd had at a nightclub in Barcelona.

After sitting through more hours of this than any sane person should ever have to bear, the van pulls onto a dirt road. Dozens of people are pressed up against tall metal gates, and fans of the show are waving signs proclaiming their love for their favorite contestant. I'm pleasantly surprised to see someone holding a sign that reads *Go Tawny!* until I see that underneath it they've written *Don't shit the bed!* A contingent of armed security guards stand at the liftgate, which provides the only access into Dire.

Grimes nods at a guard in a booth, and a few seconds later, we're through the gate and driving past a small strip of buildings. Dead ahead looms The Propitius Hotel. The building is much larger than it seems in pictures. I want time to soak in the magnitude of mayhem that's taken place here, but the car barely slows down as it drives around the hotel. We end up parking in the dirt a few hundred feet behind the building, next to four other vans sitting by the entrance to a mining tunnel.

"Don't go anywhere," Grimes says with a smirk. He opens the door and steps out of the vehicle.

"Hey Grimes, I don't know that we need that kind of humor in here," Todd says, though by the time he's finished, Grimes has already shut the door and walked halfway around the van. Todd cranks his head around to me. "Sorry about that. Some of us didn't take sensitivity training as seriously as others."

"So to be clear, you're okay with kidnapping me, but you draw the line at ableist jokes?"

"I already told you, you're not being kidnapped, silly. Think of it more like winning a golden ticket to visit Willy Wonka at the chocolate factory—only the factory is super haunted, and there's no chocolate... And Willy Wonka is the ghost of a serial killer."

The trunk pops open, and I hear Grimes wrestle with the heavy wheelchair. I hope in his rough manhandling, he doesn't accidentally press any buttons near the joystick. If he did, he might realize the thing he removed earlier was not the battery. It was, in fact, just the box to a drone kit I had sitting in a side storage compartment.

He opens the side door, then reaches out a hand to help me into my chair. I make a point of doing it on my own, even if my legs can barely support my weight. Once I'm fully situated in my chair, Grimes pushes me into the mouth of the mine, while Todd walks next to me.

The tunnel is rounded and about seven feet tall, with wooden support arches frequently supplemented by modern-looking metal attachments. A cluster of cables run across the ceiling, and lights hang every few feet to keep the space almost uncomfortably bright.

We're no more than twenty feet into the tunnel, when I notice a sudden drop in temperature that makes my shoulders shake.

"Sorry about the cold. There's not really much we can do about it," Todd says. "That's pretty much just how caves are. This one time, my whole family went on vacation to New Mexico to see Carlsbad caverns, and even though it was summer, they told me to bring a jacket. But then when we got there, I realized I had forgotten to pack one, and oh my gosh, my teeth were literally chattering. I thought it was just an expression but—"

"Todd, that's enough," Lucy's voice echoes from ahead. She's dressed in a red pantsuit and high heels, which seems like a brave choice given the rough terrain. Lucy glares at Todd like a pet owner ordering their cat off the kitchen counter. When her attention moves to me, her demeanor shifts entirely to that of a cheerful hostess.

I almost want to thank her for getting Todd to shut up, but I have a policy against complimenting people who intend to murder me.

"You must be April. It's so good to meet you. I'm so glad you could make it."

"How could I say no?" I try to fake a smile, but that's really more of Tawny's skillset.

"I'm sure you're excited to see how the show is run from behind the scenes. While I'd love to give you the full tour right now, we're at a really critical part of the show that demands my attention. Can't step away from the story for too long, can we?"

"I suppose not," I say, not having much room for debate.

"In the meantime, I'm sure Todd would love to take you to his office and show you whatever it is he does here."

"Wait, you want me to look after her?" Todd complains.

"Somebody has to. You didn't think I would have time to handle this, did you?"

Todd clicks on his tablet and glances at the home screen. "It's just that my shift is actually supposed to be ending in, like, twenty minutes, so..."

"I guess it's a good thing this isn't a union production," Lucy says, in a tone that clearly ends that conversation.

"What about the others?" I ask. "You said that other players' loved ones and friends were here to record segments too. Why don't I just hang out with them?"

Lucy narrows her eyes at me, like she would snap my neck right now if she could. "Would you believe you're the first one here?" she says, sliding right back into her perfect hostess persona. "Though, when they arrive, I'll be sure to send them to Todd's office to keep you both company. Now, if you'll excuse me, I really do have to get back to the show."

She hurries off around a curve in the tunnel, then I look over to Todd.

"So how much longer do you have to babysit me before I get called in for my close-up?"

"I don't know. I wasn't briefed on this part," he says, openly bitter now that Lucy's gone. "Come on, let's go."

Todd leads while Grimes pushes me down a twisting passage that splits off several times, occasionally breaking into three or four different tunnels. Metal walls have been constructed in front of some of the tunnels, turning them into rooms with signage—like *Costumes* and *Sound Mixing*—on the doors.

"You all work in a literal underground lair?" I ask, almost laughing at how trite it seems.

"We had to work with what was here. There just happened to be a bunch of prohibition-era tunnels down here, so they built a little studio out of it."

We pass a room simply labeled *Renshaw*.

"What's a Renshaw?" I ask.

"He's our Spirit Wrangler," Todd says. "That is to say, um, he's like a VFX director for the ghost footage. He's kind of weird, though, so I mostly try to stay out of his way."

We follow a few more twists and turns, until we reach a room labeled *Assistant*.

Todd opens the door to his office and ushers in me and my chauffeur. There's a bank of monitors stacked along one wall and a single metal table in the center of the room, where he sets down his tablet. Aside from that, it's a fairly cramped space that has the slightly sour smell of BO. I'm rolled over to a far corner, after which Grimes relocates himself to stand at attention in front of the door.

"So what exactly would you say you do here?" I ask.

"I'm the Assistant Day Shift Coordinator. That means I help make sure everything runs smoothly, no matter what. It's kind of like a script supervisor, if you know what that is."

I nod. "I do know what a script supervisor is. It's a very important position on film sets. What you just described sounds a lot more like a Production Assistant, which is one of the least important roles on film sets."

"Well it's not. My job is absolutely critical," he insists.

"Hey, you make the movies. I just watch 'em." I point over to the tablet on the table. If I can get my hands on it, maybe there's something it can do to help Tawny, or call the outside world for help. "You got any games on that?" I ask.

Todd sneers at me. "No, it doesn't have games. It's a serious piece of technology that has a lot of classified stuff on it. Okay, and yeah, it also has *Candy Crush.*"

"Can I look at it?"

"No." Todd's clearly still in a huff over having to stay late.

He may be a pain in the ass, but I don't get a threatening vibe from him. If I'm going to be able to make any progress toward saving Tawny and myself, I'm going to need to get Grimes out of the picture first. I know, easy stuff for a girl who's built like a soggy stalk of asparagus. The scariest thing is that I'm about ninety-nine percent sure the guy has a gun on him. Just the way he's standing makes him look like he's waiting for Hans Gruber to give the signal to start shooting up Nakatomi Plaza.

I have two tricks up my sleeve, and I'm going to need them both to work perfectly in order for me to survive the next few minutes. First, I flip the switch next to the joystick. I have to make a careful point of keeping my hand over the little red LED that lights up so no one can see my chair power is on.

That was the easy part.

Next comes the wildly irresponsible plan that I'd wager gives me about a fifty-fifty chance at being shot in the head. I shove my hand on the joystick, pushing the chair around the room in jerky, wild motions. This whole time, I'm pretending to be shocked, as if the chair has come to life on its own. I make sure to get myself caught in the leg of the table, then turn the chair so the whole thing starts to spin awkwardly with me.

"Hey, knock it off," Grimes commands.

"I can't! It must be possessed by a ghost!" I shout with as much melodrama as I can muster. Again, this is really Tawny's thing. I'm doing the best I can, here.

Grimes shoves the table out of the way, closes the distance to me, then smacks my hand away from the chair's control stick. He does all this while pulling out a gun from a shoulder holster with his other hand.

While his attention is focused solely on the left side of the chair, he doesn't see me slip the stun gun out from the custom-built sleeve under the chair's right arm.

First rule of surviving a horror movie—always have a weapon.

I lunge forward in my seat, shoving the metal prongs against his shirt just under his armpit, and press the button. Every muscle in Grimes's body contracts. Without the use of his fingers, his gun falls conveniently into my lap. The moment I let go of the button, he crumples to the ground, like a ragdoll. With my left hand, I grab the pistol and aim it at Todd, who has not moved a muscle, aside from his jaw dropping nearly to the floor.

"Don't move," I tell him, for good measure.

"I won't!" he squeaks, slightly shaking his head.

On the ground, Grimes groans and starts to push himself up on his elbows. I lean over and press the metal balls of the stun gun to his neck.

"Wait," Todd says. "He's already down."

"Sorry, I need him out." I don't want to do it either, but I press the button and count to ten before releasing. By the time I bring it away, there's a bald smoking patch on the back of the guard's head.

"Oh my God, please don't kill me," Todd begs, his arms now raised over his head, tears and snot starting to run down his face.

I turn the chair to face Todd, then rest my elbows on the metal table, keeping the gun trained on him. "I guess that all depends on how much you can help me."

CHAPTER FORTY-TWO

Britt's gunshot wound turned out to be a graze at best. However, Kiki's leg is a different story.

"I think we should take another break," I say, cleaning and wrapping the wound using the medical supplies from her bag.

"We can't stop now. We finally have the key assembled," Kiki says.

"You've been shot in the leg!"

"Then I guess I'll just lead from behind." She pulls the bag to her, grabs a small handful of pills from a clear bottle, and swallows them with the help of the vodka we've been using as antiseptic. After that, she slings the bag over her shoulder and winces, using the wall to climb back up to her feet. She's barely able to put any pressure on it but nevertheless hobbles across the room toward D, who is still curled up in a ball in the corner.

"What about you, D-wreck? You gonna sit around and feel sorry for yourself, or what?"

"Hey, take it easy," I say.

"Why, has he just been shot? Because unless he just got shot, I don't think anyone has an excuse to tap out right now. Britt, I recall you having been shot recently. Do you want to tap out right now?"

"No," Britt murmurs, suddenly uninterested in being the center of attention.

"All right. How about it, then?"

"I'm fine," D-wreck says softly. He grabs his frying pan and slowly climbs to his feet. "Do you guys think that maybe from here on out you could just call me Derek? I think it might be time to retire the old name."

"You sure?" I ask, knowing how deeply his brand is tied to his name.

He's wanted to drop it for years, but his entire reputation is built on being D-wreck.

He nods. "Yeah. I'm done with it."

"See? He's all right," Kiki says. "Let's get going."

She doesn't waste another moment limping to our next goal. We have no choice but to follow. We make our way back across the second floor, using the map to guide us towards Arthur's Apartment. His door is at the end of a long hallway covered in huge paintings of Arthur Wilson in his signature brown suit, standing next to his father, traditionally seen in blue. In every one of these pictures, Arthur's father is featured prominently, with Arthur standing behind him, always smaller.

"Just in case anybody needed another reminder of Arthur's daddy issues, this is how he chose to decorate his own private hallway," Kiki says.

"Do you think that's why he snatched Landon?" Shawn asks. "Seems like they kind of got 'living in dad's shadow' in common."

I feel a chill run down my spine. If that's why Landon is here, it only reinforces my worst fear regarding my intended fate.

At the end of the hall, there's a wooden door with an ornate brass lock. Kiki pulls the fully assembled key from her bag and slides it in.

"Here we go."

The lock slides with an echoing clack. She then twists the knob and pushes the door. Arthur's apartment is in the southeast spire, just above the lounge. Almost every wall on the far end of the room has floor-to-ceiling stained glass windows.

Dead ahead of us, Landon lies shirtless, tied by his hands and feet to the four wooden posts of a bed. He's covered in sores. His head moves slightly when he hears us open the door.

My first instinct is to run to his aid, but the apartment is filled with a tentative silence that I'm positive will shatter the moment I cross the threshold.

"Look," Shawn whispers, pointing to the far right corner of the room.

There's a large black cabinet standing roughly five feet in height. The entire thing is covered in etches and symbols. Each one gives off a red glow, the brightest of which surround a window in the center of the cabinet. Inside sits a skull that must belong to Arthur Wilson.

Kiki soaks it all in, pausing for only a moment before doling out orders. "That must be the body totem we have to break. Britt and Tawny, you two work on getting Landon free. You boys work on destroying that skull. Shawn, you're fastest. Maybe you can get there before Arthur springs any traps?"

The lights all around us black out, signaling that either Arthur or the directors of *Slashtag* are bored with us trying to come up with a plan. When they come back on, Arthur is standing between us and the bed, in full surgical gear and holding onto a rusty hacksaw.

"Everybody get to your stations. I got him," Derek says, bouncing nervously between the balls of his feet.

"Be careful," I say.

He grabs me by the shoulder and gives it two squeezes. "I will," he lies.

My heart surges in my chest, and true fear comes crashing through my veins. "Please, don't do this," I beg.

"Don't worry about me. Just get the job done." He gives me a wink, then turns back to the psychotic apparition standing before us. "Round two, you four-eyed bitch. Show me what you got!" He charges at Wilson, aiming his frying pan exclusively at the ghost's hand. He swings it hard, surprising the specter and sending the hacksaw flying. "Oh shit! Was that yours? Looks like I got you pegged, bro." Derek taunts the ghost, backstepping further into the room to draw Wilson's attention away from us.

He's going to need help, but I can't waste time right now. Britt and I run to Landon, where his metal shackles are held together by a series of complex knots that look like they've been taken straight from a challenge on *Survivor*. These knots will take minutes to undo. At least, it probably would, if I hadn't talked everyone into carrying weapons on them.

I pull out my kitchen knife and start slicing back and forth at the base of the lowest knot. The rope is thick, but it's going to be much easier than doing it their way. I instruct the other ladies to do the same. Kiki is late to the bed but makes up for it by chopping at the ropes with her cleaver.

"My knife's too small," Britt complains after a few seconds, then switches back to untying.

It might not matter. At the rate Kiki and I are going, we may be able to move onto Britt's knots and still be done in half the time it should normally take. My concern is, it still may not be fast enough.

"Oh shit," Derek says.

I look up from the rope to see my boyfriend looking crestfallen. Wilson grins, pulling a wooden handle out of his front apron's pocket. At first I think it's a hammer, but the handle never seems to end. It's as if his pocket were an empty hole into the universe, upon which anything in the hotel is just an arm's-length away. Finally, the wooden handle gives way to a large, gleaming triangle.

Contrary to what Landon said earlier, it seems Arthur Wilson has no aversion to using axes after all.

"That's cheating, you asshole!" Derek repositions the frying pan in his hands so that it's braced against his forearm like a shield. "Hey guys, I'm gonna need you to hurry this up after all. How's it going there, Shawny?"

Shawn's made it to the cabinet, but he seems confused by how to get it open. "There's a mechanism here, some way to open the box. I'm just trying to figure it out."

"Figure it out faster!"

Arthur winds up his axe, holding it over his head as he advances on Derek. The blade comes down, and while Derek's able to deflect the blow with the pan, the impact sends him staggering backward into a desk chair.

"I think I got it!" Shawn calls out.

There's a sound like a rusty faucet getting turned on, immediately followed by an ear-piercing shriek of pain. From where I'm standing, it almost looks as if Shawn's hand just melted into the box itself.

"Go help him," Kiki calls to me. "I got this." She's already finished chopping through the first rope and is limping over to finish mine.

I nod and make it no further than one step toward Shawn, when Arthur turns his focus away from Derek and onto me.

"Hey guy, don't look at her. Look at me. I'm just getting warmed up." Derek's words don't seem to do anything to distract him.

Wilson's shining eyes are burning into me. I look on either side of him to see if I can find a way to squeeze around. With the added range of the axe, it feels like there's no direction I could take that won't end in getting hacked to pieces.

"You have to go!" Kiki shouts, eager to keep Wilson away from herself as he moves toward the bed.

At first I think she's being selfish, but she's right. The only way this doesn't end in us all dying is if we destroy that skull.

Wilson brings the axe over his head, ready to swing, so I make a split-second decision to tuck my head down and sprint to his right. I'm not fast enough, and I know it. In a moment, I'll feel the impact of razor-sharp steel splitting my spine in two, forcing me to live my last moments paralyzed as he finishes the job with a second blow to the back of my head.

I can feel it coming, the sudden pull of air from the force of his swing. Something slams into my back and sends me reeling forward. It hurts, but I'm still standing. There's no blade buried in my back, no fresh river of blood cascading down.

I catch myself on a desk, and a twisted hunk of metal comes crashing down next to me. It's the remnants of the pan. I look back, and Derek seems just as shocked that he was able to deflect Wilson's blow, even if it did cost him his weapon. Now that he has nothing in his hands, he's completely helpless against Wilson and his axe.

Though I want to find another way to help him, I have to make his sacrifice count.

I run for the black box at the end of the room, where Shawn is on the floor, screaming in agony.

"It burns! Oh God, it burns!"

At first glance, it looks as if a piece of the box melted onto his hand, like a sentient evil virus trying to take over a host. Then I notice the steam rising, and the overwhelming smell of chemicals hits me.

I realize what's happened.

His hand's been covered in Wilson's pitch concoction. The molten black sludge is quickly hardening, creating a shell around the remaining pieces of his hand. Whatever he did to try and open the box was a trap, just like everything else in this house.

"I'm going to stop this," I say, having absolutely no idea what to do about his arm, other than recognizing it's yet another thing I can't worry about right now. I step up to the box and upon closer inspection, see it's covered in knobs, clasps, and latches. Each one seems to be associated with a glowing red carving on the box.

It's another puzzle. I'm sure there's a sheet of paper in this room, or a picture on the wall that will give me the answer.

I look behind me. The girls are still working on the knots, while Derek is holding a wooden chair in his hands, trying to deflect blows from Wilson. He seems to be keeping the ghost at bay for now, but I need to figure this out fast. I look over to the wall, hoping to find a drawing of a rune matching the box.

There are dozens of papers pinned to the wall, each with an insignia drawn on it. None of them seem to have any special feature that differentiates one from the next, until my attention is caught by a pink folding card pinned amongst them that says, *Happy Sweet Sixteen*. There's a picture of a glitter-covered cartoon dog on the front, with a big black X drawn over one of its eyes.

I remember finding this, left by Him, in the glovebox of the car my parents had given me as a birthday gift.

I already know what's written inside, but I rush over to it and open it anyway. The ink is as fresh as it was fourteen years ago. It reads: *Happy Birthday, Tawny. You're almost a woman now. Enjoy your big day, but remember, good dogs keep their mouths shut.*

Your special friend.

My revulsion to the card is just as strong now as it was when I tore it up in my parents' driveway, but just as I suspected, it also holds the key.

On the backside of the card, there is a charcoal drawing of a series of wavy lines with a spiral in the center.

Before I have time to search for the matching insignia on the box, the lights flicker out. When they come back on, Wilson's standing behind Derek, the axe primed to swing. I want to call out a warning, but Derek's ready for him. He spins around, catching the axe's blade in the leg of the chair.

"That's right, guy. I know all your tricks now. You already fooled me once with the backstab. You think I didn't see that coming?"

Wilson rips the axe out of the chair, shearing a leg off in the process. He winds the axe up again, his grin wider than ever.

"Bring it on, man! Second verse, same as the first!"

Arthur begins to swing with all his might, but just before the axe connects with the chair, he blinks out of existence again. When he reappears, the axe is already in full momentum, delivering a blow into Derek's right shoulder. He cries out in pain, drops the chair, and then falls to his knees.

I'm out of time. I have to do something. The swirls from the card are an easy shape to look out for, and it doesn't take me long to find it on the box. There's a small lever just to the side of it.

I give it a pull.

The red lights covering the box swell with an audible hum, and then the glass pane covering the skull slides away. I've done it. I solved the puzzle, and now I can finally be the person who saves the day. After reaching in and grabbing the skull, I slide two of my fingers into the eye holes and my thumb on the bottom of the jaw. As soon as I spin around, I intend to throw the skull on the floor as hard as I can and smash it into dust.

But suddenly it's not in my hand anymore. The jawbone's snapped off, wedged between my thumb and forefinger, as the rest of the skull goes soaring away from me. Time slows to a crawl, and I wonder why this is happening, why there's a blast of wind coming up from beneath me, why I'm getting smaller.

I'm falling.

The floor has opened up beneath me, and I'm dropping into some body disposal chute that probably ends up in a furnace down in the basement. With what little reaction time I have left, I throw my hands out and grasp wildly for anything to keep myself from falling. My hands slap against the hardwood floor, giving me nothing and sliding uselessly toward the pit.

And then something drags against my forearm.

I make my fingers into a claw the best I can and latch them onto Shawn's foot. He's too blitzed out in pain to notice me. I clutch onto his shoe for dear life, gravity fighting to feed me to the hotel.

It takes almost everything I have just to hold on, but my will is invigorated when I see the skull connect with the ground. Teeth go scattering everywhere, and a huge portion of the cheek splinters off. The lights strobe overhead, while Derek shouts obscenities at Wilson.

When the lights come back on, Arthur is nowhere to be found.

"A little help," I call out, feeling my second wind fading as fast as it came on.

Derek comes shambling over and gets on his knees. He reaches out with his good arm. "Going up?"

"Thank you," I say, taking it. He pulls me up enough to where I can start to climb out on my own. "Even when we get the answers right, we're still set up to fail."

"Yeah," Derek agrees. "It's almost as if the game was rigged in order to make the show more entertaining. Falling down bottomless pits is so hot right now." He stands over the trap door, staring down into a pit of darkness. "I wonder where it leads." He leans forward, but in a funny way, like he's doing a bit where he pretends to take a dive.

But then he just keeps bending over more and more, until he's actually falling headfirst into the pit, and I realize this isn't a joke at all. There's a scalpel sticking out of his back, and standing behind him is Arthur Wilson, his face full of triumph.

I blink. It's all I can do as I try to process what I've just seen. I broke the skull, and he disappeared. We won. I look down the hole and see infinite nothing. I don't even hear Derek land.

Wilson winks out of existence with a trick of light, then appears again right in front of me, a fresh scalpel pressed against my throat.

"Fuck off!" Kiki screams.

Arthur's face turns from smug victory into what looks for the first time to be real pain. He stumbles backward, clutching at his head, and then I see why. Kiki is smashing the remains of the skull with the butt of her cleaver, until it is nothing but a pile of broken shards.

With each blow, Arthur's face grows more distorted and fouler. It bends and twists in impossible places, slowly becoming translucent. Wilson's skin and clothes melt as if they were all made up of the same gooey substance. It seeps into the floor, a puddle of shiny slime reminding me of the victims from the eighties remake of *The Blob*, except it's clear instead of pink.

At a certain point, the gelatinous mass just can't hold its shape anymore. Arthur stares up at me, his look of horror shifting into one of grim delight, and he winks at me one last time before liquefying, like a popped water balloon.

Mission Log

- ~~Restore Power to the Hotel~~

- ~~Destroy Arthur Wilson's Body Totem~~
  - ~~Unlock Arthur's Apartment~~
    - ~~Find the key's knob~~
    - ~~Find the key's shaft~~
    - ~~Find the key's bit~~

- Destroy Arthur Wilson's Mind Totem
  - Unlock the door to Sutter's Sanctum
    - Destroy the Greed statue
    - Destroy the Sloth statue
    - Destroy the Wrath statue
    - Destroy the Envy statue
    - ~~Destroy the Lust statue~~
    - Destroy the Pride statue
    - ~~Destroy the Gluttony statue~~
    - Destroy the Disobedience statue

- Destroy Arthur Wilson's Spirit Totem

PODCAST ALERT!
Episode 2 of **Talking Tag** is now live at
www.slashtaginsider.com

SOCIAL

CHAPTER FORTY-THREE

From: Lucy.K@Krentler.media
To: Board@Krentler.media
CC: Operations@Krentler.media
Subject: Day 2 Summary

Hello Board and Operations Team,

The subjects have officially destroyed the body totem for Arthur Wilson, closing out Day 2 at 5:23 p.m. The team solved each of the 3 mandatory puzzles and found 2 of 7 possible secondary clues. This falls well within our predictions. Well done, everyone! Of course, there are still some things to point out:

- D-wreck was supposed to be a low-priority target for Wilson, and now he's been stabbed in the back and thrown down trapdoor 3. Renshaw, what happened? This is the biggest deviation from our plan so far and could affect viewership among young males. Please upload the new elimination order in the attached file to Wilson's "Spirit."

- I'm concerned Britt is starting to fade into the background a bit due to Kiki's overuse of amphetamines. We knew it would be a gamble for such an important role, but it's now reached a point where it could be an issue for the quality of the show and cost us viewers. Notes on how to get her back on track can be found in the attachment.

And now for the numbers. Analytics from Day 2 are as follows:

- Viewership has steadily climbed all day, only suffering a dip when the subjects were resting. As we planned, having Arthur's Apartment take place directly after the Hunter's Hall gave us time for viewership to pick back up before the big confrontation.
- Peak viewership was 68 million viewers, reached just before the contestants entered Arthur's Apartment.
- Current most-watched subject is Kiki, with 39% of spotlight viewers tuning in to her feed. Since capture, Landon's feed has risen to 26% of viewers. This data is frankly astonishing —even for our projections—and may be enough to disrupt D-wreck's early departure. The current least-watched subject has become Shawn, with only 12% of spotlight users focusing on him.
- Thanks to Landon's uptick, we are up to 47% PVI, 6% above estimated numbers at this time.

Before signing off for the evening, I'd like to once again thank everyone for their incredible contributions to the Krentler Media family. We all knew that running a show like this would be damn near impossible, and yet so far, it seems to be an even greater success than we imagined. As long as we can manage to avoid any more missteps like the Derek situation, I believe we are well on track to meeting our PVI quota by early Day 3.

Lucy.

CHAPTER FORTY-FOUR

"We have to go after him!" I hear myself shouting through tears. I know what I'm asking is not only a terrible idea, but also probably pointless. It's extremely unlikely Derek would have survived plummeting into a booby-trapped pit, especially after already being so critically wounded.

Now he's dead, and it's my fault. I should have known that one little chip on the skull wouldn't be enough to stop Arthur. Every time you think the killer is dead, he's ready to come back at you for one last strike. Rule four of surviving a horror movie. If I had held it together for just a few seconds longer, I would have had Derek go for the skull instead of me.

Britt wraps her arms around me. "I'm so sorry, but he's gone."

I don't care if it's real or for the cameras anymore. I hug her back, squeezing as hard as I can, wanting to press my face into her shoulder and break down into big, heaving sobs. The kind of crying where you're so pushed to the limit with rage, fear, stress, and guilt that your whole body convulses from the power of the crumbling dam.

I can't allow that to happen. Not yet. If I fall apart now, I'll never pull myself back together. I break off the hug with Britt and compulsively move my hand up to fix my hair. Normally, this motion makes me feel safe, gives me a feeling of control. This time, I feel a hysterical laugh bubble up inside of me that I have to tarp down. Here I am, a walking collection of cuts and bruises, and yet I'm still fixated on covering up a tiny eighteen-year-old scar on my forehead.

"We have to keep moving," Kiki says, having chewed her way through most of the fingers on her right hand, resorting to shredding the edges of her pinky finger. Her eye is twitching, just slightly, like when there's a sharp buzzing in your ear physically forcing you to cringe.

Everyone seems to ignore her, focusing on their own issues.

Shawn has finally stopped screaming and is staring at a lump of pitch where his hand should be. It's finally hardened and looks like an oversized obsidian raisin coming out of his wrist. Thankfully, he was smart enough to keep it raised. If he'd set it against anything while it was hardening, I'm not sure how we'd be able to get him out of this room.

I ask him how he's doing.

"I can't feel my fingers," is all he says. His face is ashen and hollow, like the life's been sucked out of him.

"At least we were able to save Landon," Britt says.

We turn, expecting to see the man damaged but alive on the bed. Instead, he's all the way across the room, half obscured into the wall. I take a few wobbly steps and find that Landon has squeezed himself inside the dumbwaiter. Before I can reach him, Landon slams his hand on the button next to the machine and pulls the sliding metal door down. As soon as it shuts, an electrical whirring noise I remember all too well spins up as the tiny elevator takes him down to the lounge.

"Seriously? After all that, he's just taking off?"

Kiki shakes her head and arches her eyebrows. "Who knows what psychological torture they put him through while we were all cooling our heels in the lounge. My guess is, he's properly fucked in the head by now. At this point, I'd reckon we're better off without him."

"How can you say that? He's in trouble and needs help," Britt pleads.

"Shoulda thought of that before you decided nap time was more important than getting things done."

"We can't save anyone if we're all too exhausted to do anything," I say, feeling attacked for pushing so hard for the break in the first place. "Kiki, you may be used to pulling multiple all-nighters or whatever, but the rest of us need time to process some of this hell we're all going through."

Britt nods. "Thank you. So, you agree we should go looking for Landon?"

I want to say that yes, of course we should go help our teammate in need. But I know that's not the right answer. "I don't think that's a good idea."

"Whoa, what?" Shawn says, clearly on Britt's side.

"We have to stop pretending we don't know what show we're on. If the four of us in this room want to survive, we need to focus on the best way to keep ourselves safe. Landon made a choice to run off by himself into the hotel, and we have no idea why. There's no point in searching for someone who may not want to be found." I look back down the hole by my feet. "At least we know he's still alive."

Shawn looks troubled by the direction of the conversation, but he reluctantly nods in understanding.

"All right, then. Let's do it," Kiki says, shaking out a pill into her hand and popping it in her mouth.

"Hey Kiki, do you think maybe you should cool it on the pills?" I ask, quietly enough that I hope Britt and Shawn don't hear.

"I don't know. Do you think maybe you should worry about yourself?" Kiki says, shaking me off. "One totem down, two to go."

We head through the newly unlocked door into the longest single hallway we've seen yet. A line of stained glass windows on the left wall leads me to believe we're pressed up against the front of the house, just above the lobby. Kiki's still walking with a heavy limp, but at this point, she's refusing anyone's assistance. At the end of the hallway is another door, which Kiki doesn't even bother slowing down to open.

I follow her into one of the spires of the house. We're just above the dining room now, only there's no windows in this perfectly octagonal room. In fact, there's almost no lights or decoration at all—just bare wood and a spiral staircase hugging the wall leading up to a tower known as Sutter's Sanctum. From here, I can see the wood-and-stone door shown in the intro video, with six of the eight sin crests glowing on them.

As soon as we've all congregated in the middle of the room, there's a whine-click sound as a projector comes to life, casting the words *Recorded April 12, 1965* onto the wall. Below it, another projector bleats out a sepia-soaked photograph of Arthur Wilson standing solemnly in the midst of a raucous gambling hall. We hear Arthur's voice crackle over a speaker, the raspy voice of an old man who sounds nothing like the person we see projected on the wall. He speaks slowly and with deliberation, as if he were giving a lecture to a classroom.

As far as I know, there are no known private audio logs from Arthur in existence. However, I don't have a doubt in my mind that this tape is one hundred percent genuine.

"When I was young, still convinced that I was, above all else, a man of science, I had a curious incident at the Propitius that I've never shared with anyone else. I was working on one of my designs, some ghastly device to which I've long since forgotten the intended purpose. I had just disposed of a failed test subject, and needing a replacement, I naturally made my way to the gambling hall to find another poor wretch down on his luck. The moment I set foot on the casino floor, it was as if the room were suddenly cleared of all patrons, save for me and this one fellow. He had thick and unruly hair, filthy from head to toe, as if he'd been living in the tunnels for weeks. I approached him with the offer to provide a comped hotel room, a trick that frequently allowed me to walk my subjects willingly into their own experimentation chambers. However, before I could even proposition this man, he attacked me without provocation. He produced a knife and attempted to stab me in front of the entire hall. Thankfully, with the aid of several employees, we were able to fight him off. To this day, I swear I don't know how the knife ended up in his chest, but as he bled out on my floor, his eyes burned bright as he clutched at his coat pocket and repeated the same words to me again and again. 'You can't have it.' The man perished before I could make sense of his argument, but that would all change once I discovered the trinket he was carrying."

Another picture is projected against the wall—this time a close up photo of the golden amulet with the red gem in the center. Now that I can get a good look at it, what I thought at first was simple filigree carved into the gold housing are actually the same runes which were covering the box containing Arthur's skull.

I'm shocked to see this. Everyone knows the amulet story was just a legend, given credence by a wildly inaccurate film adaptation. If this recording is real, it confirms Arthur Wilson really did believe in the supernatural.

"It called out to me, told me its name was Duriel. Once in my hands, it spoke silently, granting me knowledge to things beyond the laws of the natural world. It explained how our destinies intertwined, how my terminally failed attempts at medicine were not follies, but in fact the foundation for a much greater cause that we would build together. It urged me to continue my work, not in the name of science, but in his name instead. Duriel demanded I not only provide him with bodies, but enforced that each of my victims had to have an audience to their demise. Entire rooms in the hotel had to be converted into viewing studios for future victims to witness what was about to happen to them. While the work was gratifying, it was also exhausting and caused me to make mistakes that nearly led to my demise."

There's another whine-click of a projector, and the photo of the once-young Arthur is replaced with an old man in priest's regalia, wearing the amulet around his neck.

"It's been nearly forty years since I was forced to flee from the Propitius, and even though I've had a prolific career since then, I've always known it would one day call me back home. It's my belief that the time has finally come. I've been working as a priest for a number of years. It's gained me access to poor houses, junkie rows, allowed me to do my work without suspicion or reproach. However, my body has grown old and tired, and with each passing year, I fear that Duriel will grow bored of me and seek out a new vessel, just as it sought me all those years ago."

The photo of Arthur clicks over to one of him standing in front of a huge congregation in a church. While he looks almost unrecognizable to the man he once was, the smile he wears is unmistakable and makes my stomach churn.

"Under the name Sutter, I built up a congregation filled with the most extreme zealots I could find. I traveled the country searching out the poor, the uneducated, and most importantly, the pious. I taught them all of an eighth sin, which they could not bear to ignore. Disobedience to God. Disobedience to me. Once I had gathered my flock, I brought them back to my old home to start a new community, where their faith would be tested but also rewarded."

The photo of the amulet disappears into blackness for a second and is replaced by a leather book with eight insignias forming a circle around the center. I recognize two of them as the pig and spider that possessed me and Britt. Next to the book sits a red glass dagger, which matches another insignia.

"Duriel has helped me devise a new way of continuing our work that still feeds his desires yet spares me from any mortal danger. These stat-ues, when imbued with the right energies—"

"Yeah, we already fucking know this," Kiki says, her leg tapping on the ground as she chews her fingers. "He hid the possession statues all over the house, and now we're all going to kill each other while enacting the embodiment of those sins. We've all seen *Murder Mansion*. Why rehash all this shit now?"

It suddenly occurs to me that *Murder Mansion* may not be as far-fetched a story as it seemed. I've seen ghosts. I've seen possession and conjurations of the dead and the living. How can I say with any confi-dence that Arthur Wilson wasn't a supernatural serial killer?

"This isn't for us," I say. "It's a 'previously on,' to catch up viewers at home. I bet they're also advertising this as a great time to jump into the show if they've missed any of us getting murdered so far. They're prob-ably cutting to Landon right now, wherever he is, or showing clips from the movie to show everyone what to expect."

"You think there will be any clues?"

I shake my head, trying to stay in the moment, while struggling against the weight of realizing the Amulet of Duriel is real. Something I thought was a joke could actually be a powerful force of true evil that's coming to kill me.

"I don't think the clues matter anymore. Wherever we go, the show's going to find a way to make sure the story keeps moving forward. At this point, it's more like a scavenger hunt than anything."

"So maybe we could look for Landon while we search?" Britt asks.

"If we find him, great," I say, trying to stay diplomatic.

"Then it sounds like it's settled," Kiki says. "Let's get smashing."

CHAPTER FORTY-FIVE

"And that's why there's the option to follow each person in the show. Because they found that keeping fans engaged on just one story instead of a bunch can oftentimes be more compelling from a narrative standpoint. I don't know that I necessarily agree. I feel like the directors are there for a reason. They're here to cut together only the most interesting stuff so you don't have to watch all the boring parts, but that's just my opinion. And then there's a whole subset of viewers who just want to watch people getting tortured for hours on end, which I guess is technically the point, but I still think it's a little gross."

Todd's now spoken at length about every possible answer to every question I haven't asked.

"I'm going to stop you right there, and please be straight with me. Is your evil plan just to have people watch other people die?"

"I'm not evil," Todd whines, clearly taking offense. "Stop calling me that."

"You work for a film crew that's literally torturing and murdering my sister and six other celebrities. What would you call it?"

"I mean..." He grasps for an explanation that will paint him in any other light but quickly gives up the ghost, so to speak. "Look, I didn't ask to be assistant coordinator on *Murder Mansion* two-point-oh, okay? I have feelings too, you know."

"Then what the heck are you doing here? You're clearly not suited for the corporate villain lifestyle."

"My grandpa's on the board of directors. It's a family business. I don't really have much of a choice."

The gun's been sitting in my lap since Todd and I started talking. I can tell from his body language that there's about as much chance of him growing a spine as my kidneys spontaneously healing. But once he mentions the board of directors, I can't help but point the pistol at him again, letting a kindling of rage ignite into a small flame.

"Which member? Who's your grandfather?"

"Charles Menuscha. He's a bigshot Hollywood producer. That's the only reason I'm in TV production in the first place. He actually produced the first *Murder Mansion* movie."

Todd has the ability to talk endlessly about nothing, but I've quickly learned his capacity for deception is about on-par with a two-year-old trying to cover up a spilled bowl of spaghetti.

"Okay Todd. This is very important. I need you to tell me the plan."

"Didn't you watch the video? There's these statues hidden around the house—"

"No. I mean the overall plan. What could the Krentler Media board of directors possibly have to gain by murdering a bunch of celebrities on TV?"

"Oh, *that*," he says, his demeanor shifting to one of almost boredom. "You know that demon amulet that they keep going on about in the show? That's, like, a whole thing. Mister Krentler found it forever ago, and he's been using it to make him and his buddies rich and powerful. Actually, my grandpa kind of got in trouble for having it included so much in the movie. Luckily, no one really believed it was true."

The gun feels heavy in my hand and starts to shake. I drop it back onto my lap. "Are you kidding me?"

Todd nods. "I know, accepting that there are supernatural forces outside of our human understanding can be a lot to take in."

"What? No, that all makes sense. Demons, ghosts, vampires, I'm all-in on that. I just can't believe how unoriginal the plan is. They couldn't come up with something more interesting than old white guys making a deal with the devil for money and influence? And what, the demon feeds on suffering, or something like that?"

As he explains, Todd's eyes point at the ceiling to help him concentrate. "Every time a person watches something violent happen to another person, Duriel gains power that he can use to aid the amulet-bearer to do stuff like mind control, or...more violence. Mister Krentler says it's why the Colosseum was built, but I think that's just a story he made up to sound more important."

My temples are starting to throb. "You're telling me, he bought every social media platform and a TV network so he could force half the country to watch my sister die in order to feed a demon?"

"Well, he already had the TV network. They were actually doing pretty well when they got into politics ahead of 2016, but it turned out that re-shares of violent videos had really diminishing values."

Even more than hearing this insane information, what's boiling my blood is his casual disinterest in it. "How is it that you get amped up talking about a trip to Carlsbad Caverns, but your involvement in murder and domestic terrorism is a boring topic of conversation?"

Todd shrugs. "I didn't actually do any of that stuff! It's just something that's always been around me. The time I didn't pack my jacket was very real to me. You have no idea how cold it was, and we were down there for like five hours."

"I can't believe I'm saying this, but let's forget the big-picture stuff for now. I need you to help me put a stop to this."

Todd gestures around the room with his hands. "I don't know if you've realized this, but I was sort of lying about how important my job is here. There's not much I can do."

I pick up the tablet again. "Is there anything useful you can show me on this? Any way for me to call Tawny?"

"Not really. Because of the tunnels or something, nobody can call each other down here. Not even radios work. It's weird. We can broadcast a signal to every TV and computer in America, but we can't make a simple phone call. I mean, I guess you *could* use the messaging app on the tablet to send a text to her phone, but she wouldn't be able to respond back, so I don't know how much use that would be."

I point to the monitors behind him, where we can see and hear my sister talking to Britt as they wander down a hall.

"Oh, right," Todd says, embarrassment blooming on his cheeks.

Now that I know I can talk to Tawny, I need to find something worth sharing. "Are there solutions to the puzzles on here? Maybe a map that shows where all the statues are?"

"Technically, yes," he says, leaving the rest of an implied sentence out.

"Just spit it out already."

"I'm really not supposed to," Todd says, looking at the floor.

He has no problems explaining the demonic influences behind America's most influential men, but this makes him clam up? I place the gun on the table, then leave it behind as I push my chair toward him. "Whatever it is, you can tell me. I promise I won't shoot you." His shoulders relax a little until I pull out the stun gun and shove it against his throat. "The sound of gunshots would definitely bring a lot of attention to this room, and then I'd be done for. I'm not above tasing the crap out of you, though." I cock my head over to the passed-out guard. "You know I'll do it."

Whatever tension he had let out immediately tightens back up, even worse than before. "Okay, fine. I'll tell you everything. Just don't hurt me," he says, tripping over his own words to get it out.

"Jesus, you really are feckless, aren't you?"

"I don't know what that means, but I'm going to assume it's something nasty. You're really mean, you know that?"

I shrug. "Yeah, and you're part of an organization bent on world domination. I think it's justified. Now tell me about the statues."

Todd takes a second to recompose himself, then leans in and presses a few buttons on the tablet, bringing up a map of the hotel. "Okay, so here you can see all the statues' locations. It's a toggleable layer in the floor plan app that gets updated automatically as things change to accommodate the state of play. The problem is, they need to break eight statues to unlock the door to Sutter's Sanctum, but there's only seven statues in the house."

"What?"

"There's no eighth statue."

I feel a pressure continue to build behind my eyes. "Of course there isn't. Leave it up to a group of rich dudes to create a game that nobody can win, except for them."

"I mean, it's definitely possible to get up there. It's actually pretty clever. See, the reason there's no statue for disobedience is because it's not really technically possible for them to break the rules, but once they get seven of them, there's a whole string of clues that leads them to a secret back entrance."

I want to smack him, but I'm afraid he might start to cry and alert guards to the room. "Why didn't you just lead with that?"

"If you have them just skip everything, that's kind of cheating."

I shake my head. "You have a bizarre set of morals. Show me where the passage is."

He points to a room on the map, then glances at the bank of monitors behind him. Tawny and the others are headed down a hall toward the lobby.

"Though just a heads-up, if you're going to warn her, you're probably going to want to do it sooner than later. They've activated the rest of the statues, which means the lobby's not really a safe place right now."

CHAPTER FORTY-SIX

Kiki has decided we should start our search in rooms we haven't visited yet, so she decides our first stop will be the Ballroom.

"I don't get something," Britt says, as we venture down the twisting corridors of the second floor. "If we are supposed to destroy these three totems of Arthur Wilson, why start with us destroying the body? Doesn't that basically mean we've pulled the bad guy from the story?"

I shake my head. "The story was never about him. This isn't *Friday the Thirteenth*. The cast aren't just a bunch of cannon fodder waiting around to get mutilated by Jason. There's a reason Krentler Media went through the trouble to bring celebrities on this show, and not just regular people. This story's about us humiliating and ultimately destroying ourselves."

"Or each other," Kiki adds.

"But why would anyone want to watch that?" Britt asks.

"Because as much as they like to watch us win, they *love it* when we fail," Shawn says.

We're almost to the bottom of the stairs, when I feel a buzzing on my hip. I wait to hear a chime or for anyone else to react, but none of them seem to get the alert.

"Hey, did anyone else's phone just buzz?"

Britt checks her phone, then shakes her head, and Shawn does the same. Kiki doesn't even slow down as she limps into the lobby.

"Kiki, wait. I think I got a message."

She stops and leans against the check-in desk, while rubbing a finger deep into her ear canal. "So what? It's probably just *Slashtag* screwing with us. Ignore it."

I pull out my phone and tap the word *MESSAGE* that's covering half the screen.

> This is April. I'm alive, but being held captive under the hotel. Get out of the lobby. Do not go to the ballroom.

My legs almost give out when I see her name. Opposing tides of relief and worry crash over me. I've spent this whole time trying to get to her, and now she's managed to get trapped in here with me. I remind myself April's basically been pretending she's in a horror movie for the last eighteen years. I'm guessing she figured out this was all real probably around the same time I did. And also like me, she has massively overestimated her resilience and thrown herself into danger.

"Guys, I got a message from my sister, April. She's here, and she says to stay away from the ballroom."

Kiki throws her arms out in a dramatic gesture. "Come on, that's a load of bullshit, and you know it. You're smarter than this."

I look to the others for confirmation.

"I mean, it does kind of seem like a trap," Britt says.

Shawn remains silent, weighing his options.

I'm about to turn around and head back upstairs, when I hear several more buzzes trickle across each of their phones.

"It's from Danny," Shawn says in a tone of urgency. "He says they have him too, but he is being held in the ballroom."

"Oh my God," Britt says, in total shock.

"What is it?" I ask.

"It's from John Stamos. He says he forgives me, and he's waiting in the library."

"Well that just proves it," Kiki says. "These are all fake as fuck. Let's keep moving."

I take a step toward Kiki. "What does yours say?"

She shakes her head. "Nothing but a heap of bullshit. Come on."

"I see it!" Britt says, leaning over Kiki's screen. "It says it's from her mom. What does she forgive you for? Who's Shoko?"

"Would you just back the hell off! I already told you, it's not real, All of this isn't real!" Kiki hurls her phone as hard as she can across the room. It smashes into the wall and falls to the floor in pieces.

"Kiki, would you just calm down for a second, and we can figure this out?" My phone buzzes again.

> This is REALLY April. Don't move, I'm working
> on a solution.

My whole body is humming with confusion. "I agree that they're probably not all real, but April's original text came through like a minute before everyone else's. Maybe they messaged the rest of you to throw us off."

"So, what do you want to do? Are you saying we just give up on trying to get out of here, all because your sister says it's dangerous?" Kiki's face is turning red. "News flash, we're all fully aware this place wants to kill us by now!"

Another buzz.

> Head to the Library

"Now she's telling me to head to the library."

"You think she's with Stamos?" Britt asks.

Buzz.

> NO! Do NOT head to the library!

Buzz.

> Stay put while I find a more secure channel. Do
> not leave the lobby under any circumstances.

Buzz.

Kiki lets out a yelp of pain and presses her hand against her ear. It pulls us all away from the torrent of messages flooding all of our phones. Her eyes are squeezed shut, and her mouth is wide open. It's like she's trying to yawn out the pressure on an airplane. I run to her side, and she nearly hip-checks me when she flinches away.

"Kiki, are you okay?" I ask.

"It won't stop!" she screams. She shoves her finger into her ear and shakes it until blood starts to run from the hole.

"Is it the crying?" I ask, in as low a tone as I can.

"It's this whole fucking house. Everyone just put your phones down, and let's stick to the goddamn plan." She reaches into her bag and pops another pill, the third I've seen her take this hour.

"Are you sure the ibuprofen is helping?"

"It's fine," she says.

I keep pushing. "What if it has some weird ingredients? Maybe we should take another look at the bottle and see what's—"

"I said it's fine," Kiki snaps at me, now clutching at her shoulder bag. "Let's just go already."

"Wait," Britt says, tucking her phone into her waist and grabbing Kiki by the arm. "I want some."

"Fuck off." Kiki tries to pull away, but Britt holds her grip tight, yanking her back. "What for?"

"Why won't you just give me a damn pill? What are you, the medicine gatekeeper now?"

The room freezes as the two women stare each other down, fighting once again over Kiki's bag.

"All right, fine," Kiki says, digging through and pulling out a dark brown jar.

"That's not the same bottle," Britt says.

"What? Yes, it is."

Britt shakes her head. "The bottle you've been using this whole time has been clear. What else have you got in there?"

"I've been taking care of the essentials. I've got all the clues, the map, medical supplies, my *cleaver*." She makes a point of emphasizing that last word, like she's not afraid to use it.

"Well, who says you should hold the bag all the time? I don't remember anyone voting for you as the leader of the group."

"Nobody voted for you either, Britt! Just because you're more famous than the rest of us doesn't automatically make you in charge. I've seen you on TV. You couldn't lead a team to Taco Bell."

"Maybe we should all just calm down for a minute," I say, looking over to Shawn to help me diffuse the situation.

But he's not even paying attention to what's happening. Instead, he's pacing nervously, reading the stream of messages on his phone.

"Why won't you just show me what's inside? What are you hiding in there?" Britt makes a move to snatch at the bag.

Kiki twists as much as she can to play keep-away, but Britt has a good six inches on her and has a much longer reach.

"Get away from me, you psycho!"

"Give me the bag!" Britt screams, then seizes Kiki by the throat.

Within a second, she's moved both hands around the girl's neck and has shoved her all the way against the lobby wall. Kiki's slapping her hands against Britt's arms. She doesn't have the reach to go for her face.

I rush in to try and help pull the women apart. As soon as I get close, Britt snarls at me, revealing a mouth full of crooked teeth and sending out an almost visible cloud of sweet stink. I barely get my hands on her before she brings her elbow back at lightning speed, smashing me in the nose and sending me stumbling backward.

Shawn has finally put his phone away, but he's having almost as little effect as me. For one thing, he's only got one working hand, and he's trying to find a way to separate the two women without hurting either of them.

Kiki's eyes start to flutter. Her flailing becomes simultaneously more desperate and less effective. I think Shawn sees it too, because he takes a step back, tucks his shoulder, and body slams Britt so hard, she's thrown off her feet. She lands on the ground with a hard thud.

Everything goes silent.

I make my way over to check on Britt, but as I do, my vision blurs. There's a warm tickling sensation running down my lips and chin. When I wipe my sleeve against my mouth, it leaves behind a large, red smear. I'm seeing double. There's two bodies on the floor. One of them is Britt, squirming in pain. The other is a man I've never seen before. His face is covered in blood, and his nose is crooked and purple. His face is so swollen that it's hard to see what he's supposed to look like under a head of blood-soaked blonde hair. There's another guy kneeling over him, staring at Shawn with shock spread across his square-jawed face.

"What did you do?" the stranger asks.

Shawn stares in horror at the two men in front of him. "I'm sorry. I wasn't trying to hurt anyone."

"I don't think he's breathing!" he cries.

"I didn't...I'm sorry..." Shawn backs up, shaking his head.

On the floor, Britt starts to rise. She's panting like a wild animal, pulling herself on all fours toward Kiki, who is sitting against the wall, recovering from the fight.

"Shawn, it's not real. It's a trick," I say. "I need you here, right now."

"I'm so sorry," Shawn keeps repeating, tears streaming down his face. "I was just trying to get home—"

Shawn's lost in the past, and I don't have time to deal with that. "Kiki, I think Britt's possessed by Envy! We need to find the statue now!"

"I'm a little busy right now," Kiki says, pulling her cleaver from her bag.

"Try not to hurt her!" I beg.

"If this bitch comes at me, I'm going to do whatever it takes to survive."

I know she will, too, and that scares me almost as much as Britt's feral influence.

Without Shawn, there's no way I'm going to be able to stop these girls from seriously hurting each other. I need to find the statue possessing Britt.

I scan the room, looking for anything that feels out of the ordinary. Since this is the lobby, I'm guessing it's likely hidden somewhere by the check-in station and am hoping it's not in the chandelier.

I run behind the desk as Britt makes another dash toward Kiki. Just as she promised, Kiki swings the cleaver. Britt catches Kiki's arm, but not before the blade connects with the side of her head, sending a chunk of white-blonde hair falling to the ground, along with a small cube of flesh. Britt rolls her whole body into Kiki's arm, slamming her wrist against the wall and forcing her to drop the knife.

Meanwhile, I'm searching frantically under the desk, but all the cupboards and drawers are completely empty. It isn't until I spin around and look at the key rack that I notice all the keys are missing. Just below each numbered square is a small drawer handle. I reach for the drawer labeled *one* and pull. At first, there's no give, but as I tug at it, I find that, with a combination of strength and some fiddling, it starts to give. It takes maybe ten seconds to get the drawer fully open, but each of those seconds draws on like an eternity between the sound of Shawn dealing with the ghosts of his past and Kiki and Britt's battle to the death.

With one final tug, I yank the drawer out of its hole, and sitting inside is a green glass figurine of an eyeball.

That's it.

I throw it down on the ground and feel a swell of victory in my chest as it shatters spectacularly into a thousand pieces. No half measures like the skull. I make sure this thing is completely destroyed. Taking a step toward the lobby, I ready myself to help the women deal with their fresh injuries.

They haven't stopped fighting.

If anything, their attacks have intensified. Now without a weapon in hand, the girls are pulling hair, scratching, even biting each other. My heart sinks. I turn back and see fifteen other drawers, each of which I'm now sure contains a glass statue. I try to think of any hints Arthur may have left behind. The only number I can think of with any significance to him is the number of sins his cult centered around. I work on drawer eight, moving it inch by agonizing inch, jiggling the poorly fitting wooden box out of its hole.

Inside is yet another eye. With a greatly diminished amount of confidence, I throw it on the ground, watching it shatter. It also does nothing to stop the rapidly escalating situation.

The square-jawed man's sorrow has now turned to anger. He's left his buddy on the ground and is stalking across the lobby, shouting insults and slurs at Shawn.

"It's not like that," Shawn pleads. His eyes are shut, and he shakes his head back and forth.

There's no way I'm going to have time to open all of these drawers. Without any clues, I might as well just pick a random number. With so many options and no direction, I'm wasting time just staring at the wall.

Even if I do pick a drawer, what do I do if it fails? Do I just keep going until I get lucky, or someone dies? It's hard to think between the fight, the haunting, and the constant buzzing on my hip.

I need help. Once again, I grab for my phone, hoping April can find some way to cut through the chatter.

> It's number two, trust me

Buzz.

> This is April! Open number ten!

Buzz.

> Seven, eight, better stay up late.

Buzz.

> Envy is the fourth sin in the bible!

There's dozens of messages listing every possible number with every possible reason, but there's only one of them that truly feels like something my sister would send. Our favorite horror series growing up was *Nightmare on Elm Street*. There's a nursery rhyme in every movie, where these little girls count to ten while singing warnings of Freddy's imminent attack.

I scroll up on the phone to see if this is a part of a sequence I'm missing, but there's no "One, two, Freddy's coming for you," to be found. She's leaving me a message only I will know. I've already tried drawer eight, and so my guess is it's either seven, or I'm meant to add them together.

I go for fifteen.

Behind me, the chaos amplifies once more. Britt has Kiki pinned to the ground. She's slamming her head repeatedly into the floor, shouting the words, "you can't have it!" over and over, while Shawn's ghost has nearly reached him cowering in the corner.

If this isn't the right box, I'm not going to have time to try another.

I grab the handle for fifteen, brace my foot against the wall, and yank so hard that the drawer comes shooting out of the hole, sending the glass eye flying across the room. The statue hits the ground and shatters into dozens of pieces.

Two heartbeats later, Kiki is shoving a sobbing Britt off her, the ghosts are gone, and I'm ready to collapse.

Mission Log

- ~~Restore Power to the Hotel~~

- ~~Destroy Arthur Wilson's Body Totem~~
  - ~~Unlock Arthur's Apartment~~
    - ~~Find the key's knob~~
    - ~~Find the key's shaft~~
    - ~~Find the key's bit~~

- Destroy Arthur Wilson's Mind Totem
  - Unlock the door to Sutter's Sanctum
    - Destroy the Greed statue
    - Destroy the Sloth statue
    - Destroy the Wrath statue
    - ~~Destroy the Envy statue~~
    - ~~Destroy the Lust statue~~
    - Destroy the Pride statue
    - ~~Destroy the Gluttony statue~~
    - Destroy the Disobedience statue

- Destroy Arthur Wilson's Spirit Totem

SOCIAL

CHAPTER FORTY-SEVEN

From: Lucy.K@Krentler.media
To: Operations@Krentler.media
CC: Security@Krentler.media
Subject: Security Breach, All Hands On Deck

This is not a drill. For reasons unknown, Todd Menuscha has turned his back on us and is actively attempting to derail the production. He's hiding in the tunnels with the secondary subject and helped her gain access to the messaging program.

All on-site personnel not actively part of Command or Spirit Wrangling are instructed to immediately track down this traitor and his accomplice. If found, make sure to restrain the secondary subject at all costs. While it's the board's preference to keep Todd alive for interrogation, he is considered expendable if it ensures the secondary subject is captured unharmed. If apprehended, she is to be sent to Renshaw immediately for processing.

Regarding the messaging issue, unfortunately, we cannot deactivate one device without disrupting our entire network down here. Our team has come up with a temporary band-aid by flooding all of their phones with messages. However, until these two are apprehended, the entire project is at risk.

Get it done.

Lucy

CHAPTER FORTY-EIGHT

"Fuck all of you. I'm on my own from here on." Kiki storms off toward the ballroom before any of us even has a chance to process what just happened.

Shawn hasn't opened his eyes yet, and Britt's crying quickly turns to screaming once she sees pieces of her hair on the ground around her. She pulls out her phone and turns on the selfie camera app.

"Oh my God, what did she do?" She then pulls back what's left of her hair to reveal the missing part of her ear, and her scream almost triples in volume.

I look around for the medical bag, then remember Kiki took it with her as she stormed off. "Britt, we need to follow Kiki. Can you walk?"

"Screw her. She just tried to cut my ear off!" Britt wails.

"We need her medical supplies to clean and bandage your wound."

"I know where the Apothecary shop is. I can get more."

"But what if she hurts herself out there alone? We need to go after her."

Britt turns to me, her eyes bulging and full of spite. "Kiki made a choice to run off by herself into the hotel," she says, spitting my argument against searching for Landon back at me. "There's no point in searching for someone who may not want to be found, right?"

"This is different," I argue, though I'm not entirely sure how yet. "Kiki's just freaked out. We don't know what Wilson did to Landon."

"Well go on, then. I won't stop you." Britt breaks eye contact with me to stare at herself on the phone.

I try Shawn next. "Hey man, I need you right now. Those guys, they're gone."

Shawn shakes his head. "They're always here. I didn't mean to hurt him like that. I didn't have a choice."

I check back down the hall. There's no time for this. Even though Kiki's got a wounded leg, it barely seemed to slow her down.

"I'm coming right back, okay? Stay here."

I hope that wherever April is, she's not watching this part. Once again, I'm about to blatantly break the second rule of surviving a horror movie.

I hurry toward the ballroom alone. As I approach, I start to hear the sound of big band music. It swells behind the door, like a stereo that's playing inside, growing like air in a balloon just about to pop. I push the door open and can feel the saxophones and snare drums rattle in my chest.

Flickering against the backdrop curtains of the stage plays a huge video of the very room where I now find myself. It's shot from a high angle, probably up by the projector displaying the film. The ballroom is full of people, ninety-eight to be exact. They're pressed up too tightly to dance to the music. Mist is swirling around their feet. Some of them are swaying, but it's without any joy or rhythm.

It's not long before they start grasping at their throats. Some try to throw themselves against the door, but it doesn't budge. The fog gets kicked up by their frantic movement, which only seems to hasten their desperation. They're climbing the stage, searching for escape and finding none. I've never seen this video before, but I know what it is. It's well-known that when Reverend Sutter—aka Arthur Wilson— decided it was time for his cult to end, he gassed them all to death. It was never disclosed that it was in this room. Nearly a hundred people perished right where I'm standing now.

Movement flashes across the space. In the shadows under the film, Kiki is climbing up onto the stage and heading toward a podium set up in the center. Sitting atop the podium is a red glass dagger, about twelve inches in height. Kiki stares at it, transfixed.

For just a moment, I see someone standing next to her, hunched over and whispering into her ear.

She nods.

"Kiki, wait!" I shout.

The whispering man whips his head to look at me. In the darkness, all I can see are his mirrored silver eyes, staring into me and filling me with dread.

An old man sends out a sharp whistle behind me. There's a dog barking, and I can smell burning pine carried across a crisp autumn breeze. I turn around and the ballroom melts away, along with Arthur, the Propitius, and everyone in it.

I'm standing in a park. It's been a beautiful day, full of mostly blue skies with just enough clouds to keep my skin from feeling hot. But now it's getting late, and most of the blue has shifted into a dreary gray.

I hear a second whistle, and then something soft nuzzles against my leg. A brown and black dog presses his cold wet nose into my thigh, wagging his short tail.

"Doggy!" my kid sister says, running up to meet the animal. After a few pets, she leans down to hug it, and the dog licks all over her face.

I think dog slobber is gross, but April just laughs and scratches behind its ears. She's only ten years old. That makes me twelve. Her cheeks and nose are pink and starting to burn. It's all right, though. There won't be many more days where it will be this warm again until after winter. A little sunburn won't hurt.

There's another sharp whistle, the kind only grandfathers seem to be able to make. "Clarence, come!"

The dog looks over at his master, an older man who is standing by the sidewalk.

"Is this your dog?" April asks the old man.

"Why, yes he is. Don't worry, he's friendly, if you can't already tell. Come here, boy, let me get that leash on you."

The dog whines once, then pulls himself from my sister's affection and trots over. The man slowly crouches and fixes a little clasp onto the dog's collar.

"Sorry if he bothered you. He knows better than to go around sniffing strangers when he's off the leash. He just gets excited, don'tcha, boy!" He scratches the dog behind the ears.

It squints its eyes and pants with appreciation.

"He's no bother. We like dogs," I say. My voice is surprisingly high. It feels off. I look around, suddenly noticing it's later than I thought. The park is empty, save for a couple of cars and a green van.

"Can I pet him some more?" April asks. She's already running back up to the dog.

"Well sure! I'm just getting ready to leave, but I suppose a few minutes with some new friends won't hurt. This boy here is Clarence."

"Clarence? That's a weird name for a dog," April says, raising one eyebrow so high she might as well be a cartoon.

"He's named after our Supreme Court Justice, Clarence Thomas. He's a good boy, isn't he?" The old man intensifies his affection on the dog. "Yes he is! He's such a good boy! And you can call me Mister Rogers."

"Like the man on TV!" my sister shouts. "I'm April, and this is my sister, Tawny."

"Yes, just like him." The old man tips his head of short gray hair toward us. "It's nice to meet you girls."

"We should get going. Dad's expecting us for dinner," I say.

"But he likes me!" April is on her knees with her arms around the dog.

"No, no, your sister is right. It's time for me and Clarence to be off as well."

While standing back up, Mister Rogers lets out a sudden gasp of pain. It's surprising and a little scary. April squeals in fright. He turns away from us and takes a couple of hunched steps over to a green van, leaning his upper body over the hood.

"Are you okay?" I ask.

"I'm sorry. I don't mean to scare you. It's just my back. It goes a bit funny sometimes. I'll be all right, though. Don't you worry about me. You girls have a nice night." He takes several deep breaths while slumped against the car, wincing with each inhale and hissing out each exhale.

"Do you need any help?" April asks, still petting the dog.

"No, I think I'll be all right. If you could just hold onto Clarence while I get the door for him." It takes Mister Rogers a great effort to push off the hood and lean against the side of the car. He slides along the vehicle for stability, taking tiny steps until He makes it to the rear door and slides it open. "Oh, actually, there is one thing you could do to help."

"What is it?" April asks.

"Clarence likes to ride with the windows down so he can stick his head out and sniff. But in order to keep him from jumping out of the window, I need to tie his leash to the center neck holder. I just don't know that my back is up for the task right now. Do either of you girls happen to know how to tie a knot?"

"I do," I say, before April gets the opportunity. I know I'm supposed to stay away from strangers, but it's just one old man, I tell myself.

"Thanks, Tawny. I'm sure grateful for the help, and I know Clarence is too."

I grab the end of the leash and climb into the brown leather interior of the van. There's a metal rod sticking out of the middle seat between the chair and the headrest. I scoot along on my hands and knees until I'm ready to loop the leash around the rod.

As I reach up to tie off the leash, I see a man peering through the window. He's in his mid-twenties, Black. I recognize him, but none of this is right. This isn't what's supposed to happen.

"Tawny?" he says my name, then reaches in through the solid side of the car and grabs me by the shoulder.

As soon as I feel his hand touch my skin, the whole world goes dark, and suddenly, I'm standing in a ballroom in front of Shawn and Britt.

CHAPTER FORTY-NINE

www.cryptidsciencereadingroom.fanwiki.com/demons/duriel

Duriel

Also searched terms: Dureel, Dolor, Algae.

Companion to: Amulet of Duriel, Amulet of Dorozus, Goblet of Duriel.

History

Duriel is a demonic entity who feasts on pain and suffering. Its origin is hotly contested amongst demonologists. Many believe the name *Duriel* comes from Roman roots, referring to Dolor, an ancient Roman personification of pain and grief. Another possibility could come from Dolus, the spirit of treachery and deceit.

The demon could also have ties to ancient Israel, as the name Duriel comes from the Hebrew word, meaning *Heaven is my dwelling, God is my home.* While not present in any known volumes of the Bible, there are other books that tell of a fallen angel named Duriel, whose deeds were so wicked his name was to be struck from history. As a punishment for his crimes, God cast him into a prison within an amulet, to be kept secret and safe by a select few.

The most common theory regarding the amulet's appearance throughout history starts in 70AD, when soon-to-be Roman Emperor Titus besieged Jerusalem. It is theorized that during this attack, he found and claimed the amulet for himself. Afterward, Titus rose to power and completed construction on the Colosseum in Rome. Furthermore, statues of Emperor Titus always show him wearing a pendant with a gem at its center.

It is said that any place the Amulet of Duriel is found, there is always death and destruction in its wake. There are many tales and depictions of the amulet being seen throughout history, from carvings in Mayan temples dated around 300AD, and later the Incas in the late 1500s. There are drawings of it during the Salem witch trials, and even possible connections with the disappearance at Roanoke.

Duriel in Popular Culture

In modern day, Duriel is most widely known thanks to the film *Murder Mansion*. Duriel is also a boss character in the video game *Diablo II*.

CHAPTER FIFTY

"He was here," I gasp, searching desperately around the room for Him. The music around me is blaringly loud, like turning on a car and remembering the hard way you had the volume cranked all the way up when you'd parked.

"Who? Wilson?" Shawn asks.

"Good dogs keep their mouths shut." The words come tumbling out of my mouth, but I'm not the one saying it. I throw my hands to cover it up before I let Him say anything else.

"It's okay. You don't have to talk about it. Are you all right?"

I nod, though I'm struggling to come to grips with where I even am right now. A part of me keeps waiting for a rag doused in chemicals to come out of nowhere and cover my mouth. The smell of it burns my nostrils. I can faintly hear my sister screaming, until she steals the knife from His pocket and saves my life. I'm so caught up in that nightmare, I had almost forgotten all about the one I'm stuck in right now.

"Did you find her?" Shawn asks.

Find who? April? What was I just doing? The room goes dark for a second as the film reel resets itself and begins again. A still pile of bodies are suddenly all back on their feet, waiting to repeat their deaths over and over. There's a podium underneath. Something used to be on it.

"Kiki. I saw her. She grabbed one of the statues. I think it was Wrath."

"Great, sounds just like what that girl needs right now," Britt says, her ear completely white in bandages.

"Did you see where she went?" Shawn asks.

I shake my head. "No. I got a little preoccupied. You didn't see her in the halls on your way over here?"

They shake their heads. I don't even know how long it's been since she left. She could be anywhere by now.

There are two doors along the back wall of the ballroom with emblems of a gentleman and a lady, but a quick check of those doors by Britt reveals them to be locked. I climb up onto the stage, searching along the red hanging curtains for a side door.

"Guys, I think I know where Kiki went, but you're not going to like it."

At the end of the side wing, there's a black metal ladder running up at least twenty feet to a small square of light that must be a room above.

"Are you going to be okay climbing with just one arm?" I ask Shawn, once he and Britt have joined me at the base.

"I'll manage."

I take the lead, pushing away any thoughts of the vertigo I'm already experiencing. Grabbing onto each rung, I keep my eyes only on the next bar above me, scaling the wall as quickly as I can. Every time my right hand reaches a bar, it gives me a nice little zing of pain—a reminder of my first encounter with Arthur Wilson's scalpel. After what feels like hundreds of steps, I can finally start to see the immediate space above me with a little more light. I hazard a look up and scream, seeing a monstrous face glaring down at me from the room above.

My right hand slips. It's bleeding again. I fall backward, and one of my feet slides out from a rung. Suddenly, a hand and a foot is all that separates me from falling to my death.

I hug the ladder with my remaining arm, and the rest of me searches wildly for purchase. After I make it back on the rungs, my whole body clenches up with adrenaline, and I take a few deep breaths, forcing myself to look up again. The face is still there, frozen in the exact same position as it was before.

It's a bear, mid roar.

"Holy shit, you guys. It's the Hunter's Hall."

I never thought I'd feel comforted by seeing this room again, but just about anything is better than being on this ladder right now. Pushing past my vertigo, I keep my eyes on the bear and scramble the rest of the way up.

Britt comes next, and below her, I can hear the slow and steady clunking of Shawn carefully climbing.

"Any idea where she went?" Britt asks.

I look for any sort of evidence of her through the door. "No. And from this room, it's possible that she could have gone almost anywhere. I have no idea where we would even start looking."

If only there was someone who had access to the cameras, they could help us find her.

"Where's Kiki?" I shout, looking up and toward a random corner, hoping there's a camera hidden somewhere. I turn to another corner. "We need to find Kiki. Where is she?"

"Who are you talking to?" Britt asks.

"April. If she's really watching this, then she might be able to find her."

My phone starts blowing up in my waistband. I open the screen, and there's already a stream of messages to sort through.

> She's in the kitchen

> Ask Britt, she killed her!

> Kiki's with Damien

> She's in the bathroom in room 4

> This is April! Get to the Barber shop

> She's on top of a pile of bodies

"Damien!" I shout, knowing the message is from her but unsure what to make of it.

"Did I miss something?" Britt asks.

"Damien. The kid from the *Omen*. I think April might be using a code of horror movie references."

Buzz.

> Beep Beep, Tawny!

Shit. This one's definitely from her, and I realize my mistake instantly. She's telling me to shut my damn mouth.

It's too late. They've figured it out too, and a new round of messages come pouring into my phone.

Buzz.

> Three more days til Halloween. Silver Shamrock!

Buzz.

> I know what you did last summer

Buzz.

> Kiki's on a date with Art the Clown

Buzz.

> Left to die under the sun. The hive never spared anyone.

Buzz.

> What's your favorite scary movie?

Buzz.

> Ade Due Demballa!

I've ruined her code. Any attempts to help out in the future is only going to result in a random smattering of horror movie references.

I can kick myself later. April knows where Kiki is right now, and I'm going to have to make her last clue count.

"You said Damien's a kid, right?" Shawn says. "Because I'm looking at the map here, and I'm seeing a nursery nearby. You think she could be there?"

That must be it. I nod. "Lead the way."

At first, he's careful to make sure we take the right turn with each junction, though it soon becomes clear we don't need it. I can hear Kiki shouting something in the distance. I run to catch up with her, hearing another sound over her shouting and swearing.

It's a baby crying hysterically.

I round the corner and find Kiki standing over a crib, holding an infant in her hands. It almost looks like a ragdoll, with Kiki shaking it violently back and forth while screeching obscenities. I run up to her, shouting her name while I try to pull her away from the crib. As soon as I touch her arm, I'm sprayed in the face with something warm.

Kiki's face changes. She stops screaming and looks at me in total confusion, before coughing up a mouthful of blood.

The baby has stopped crying, and when I look down, I can see why. There is no baby in her hands, only the red glass blade of Wrath.

Kiki's dress is polka-dotted with red spots. There are at least a dozen stab wounds focused around her chest and abdomen. She drops the blade, and it shatters as it hits the ground. Her legs give out, and she crumples to the floor. Her breathing has turned into a series of quick shallow gasps with a bubbling rasp underneath.

I hold her, at a complete loss of what to say. Her eyes land on mine and surge open for a second.

"I don't hear her anymore," she says, almost smiling. She then makes a sound like a wet hiccup and goes silent.

Mission Log

- ~~Restore Power to the Hotel~~

- ~~Destroy Arthur Wilson's Body Totem~~
  - ~~Unlock Arthur's Apartment~~
    - ~~Find the key's knob~~
    - ~~Find the key's shaft~~
    - ~~Find the key's bit~~

- Destroy Arthur Wilson's Mind Totem
  - Unlock the door to Sutter's Sanctum
    - Destroy the Greed statue
    - Destroy the Sloth statue
    - ~~Destroy the Wrath statue~~
    - ~~Destroy the Envy statue~~
    - ~~Destroy the Lust statue~~
    - Destroy the Pride statue
    - ~~Destroy the Gluttony statue~~
    - Destroy the Disobedience statue

- Destroy Arthur Wilson's Spirit Totem

SOCIAL

CHAPTER FIFTY-ONE

Todd and I are hiding in a server room. His office stopped being safe the moment I started sending messages to Tawny. I had him take me here because I figured it has valuable collateral, in case we get caught.

"Well thanks a lot, April," Todd says, kneeling next to me behind a large glowing server box. Apparently, Lucy has sent out an email putting us on blast. "Because of you, Lucy's labeled me a traitor. Now I'll be lucky if killing me is the worst thing they do!"

"Even with your grandpa on the board?" I ask.

"Loyalty is everything in these families. If they even think you've flipped on them, they will throw you under a bus faster than you can say *macaroni salad*. This one time, my cousin Barry stole my great aunt Mimi's Bolognese recipe, and they pulled out all of his teeth and cut off his tongue so he could never enjoy food again."

"On that lovely note, I don't want to jinx us or anything, but shouldn't we be swarmed by, like, twenty armed guards by now?"

"Nah. Aside from Grimes, the only real security we have inside the complex are a couple of ex-military guys. But their only job is to protect the head honchos on the lower level. The rest of the guards are all the way at the edge of town, keeping fans and protestors out."

"Doesn't that seem weird to you?" I ask, unable to stop looking a gift horse in the mouth.

"That people would drive all the way here just to stare at a house?"

"That there's only two security guards in this whole complex."

"Not really. They don't even have security cameras down here. This whole show pretty much runs on nepotism, so we all have something to gain by doing our jobs."

"Even Lucy?"

"Especially Lucy! You really think her last name is Hodge? Try Krentler. Girl is the top branch of the nepotism tree. Imagine if Ivanka was competent, capable of murder, and really wanted to be a gameshow host."

"Hang on, let's go back a second. You said the guards inside the complex are looking after the head honchos. Does that mean the board of directors are here?"

Todd looks exasperated just by hearing them mentioned. "Yeah, they have this super-secret mini boardroom setup with, like, a magic cup they're filling. I know how stupid it sounds. It feeds back into the whole amulet thing. The hotel is built on a nexus of power, or conduit of realities, or whatever. Something magicky sounding. It gives them extra juice to the mind control spell they're doing."

"You really have no interest in the immense supernatural forces at play here. Do you even care why you're working to kill these people?"

Todd starts to whine again. "I don't know what you want me to say. This may seem weird for you, but this is just how my life has always been. During company picnics, all the kids get together to play games and eat barbecue, while the old guys sacrifice a virgin in a barn. When literally everyone in your family and social circle is killing people on the reg, and they're saying it isn't a big deal, you just sort of go with it."

I nod, trying to understand what this guy's life must be like. "So why are you working as an assistant coordinator instead of sacrificing virgins to demons?"

Todd's head bobs, as if he's reciting a quote from a movie. "Because grandpa says I'm not so much a shark as I am a goldfish. Which is fine by me, most of the time. Everyone around here are just a bunch of jerks.

I bet a lot of them are excited about the idea of killing me now that they basically have permission."

Because he's proved at least half a dozen times that he doesn't have a deceptive bone in his body—or a spine, for that matter—I wonder if there's a way to leverage his excommunication.

"How about I make you a deal? You help me get Tawny out of here, and we'll do everything we can to keep you safe from these guys."

"I mean, if I could make it out of here and get to my dad, I'm sure he'd help smuggle me out of the country or something. He's still a shark like my grandpa, but deep down I'm, like, seventy-five percent sure he loves me. Plus, I've always wanted to go to New Zealand."

"All right, then. It's settled."

Todd doesn't look very enthused. "I wouldn't get my hopes up. The odds of getting your sister out of here are practically zero, even if you do seem weirdly badass."

"I don't care. We're still going to try. Now help me figure out another way to get Tawny where she needs to go."

CHAPTER FIFTY-TWO

"Oh my God, Kiki!" Shawn shouts, hustling into the room with Britt. Kiki is lying in a pool of blood on the floor. "What happened?"

"It was already too late by the time I got in here. She did it to herself."

"But wasn't she under the possession of the Wrath figurine?" Britt asks. "Shouldn't she be trying to kill one of us instead?"

I shake my head with no clear answer to give. "I don't know. I guess the person she was most angry with was herself. I tried to get her to open up to me, but it was like she just didn't want to deal with it. The only thing she ever told me was that she'd been hearing a baby crying in her ear basically from the moment she arrived. That's why she was so obsessed with taking those painkillers. I guess it was giving her a headache."

"Speaking of, maybe we should grab her bag before everything inside gets ruined with, you know...blood," Britt says.

Shawn and I both look at her in disbelief. Even at a time like this, she's still more concerned with the bag than Kiki. Britt seems to pick up on it pretty quickly and stumbles over her words to correct herself.

"I'm not possessed. Shawn told me what I did. It's not like that. You guys can hold on to it. I just think it's important that someone has it, in case of medical emergencies, or clues."

I don't know that I would have called Kiki a friend, but it doesn't make her death any less devastating. Still reeling from what I just saw, the last thing I want to do is pull a shoulder bag from under the arm of her body.

"I can't do it alone," Britt says, pressing the issue.

"Fine," I say, in maybe too harsh a tone. "Can we at least try and do this respectfully? It just doesn't feel right, disturbing her now that she's..." I don't want to say the word *dead*. Instead, I close her eyes for her, and finally let her rest.

We work calmly but quickly to lift her arm and head and slide the bag out. As soon as I have the bag, I lead Shawn and Britt into the hall, shutting the nursery door behind me. It feels like I've been holding my breath since I walked in there, and only now can I let it out. I sit on the carpet and finally take some time to inspect the bag. There's a large red spot along one side, but it looks like we retrieved it before it could soak through to any of the contents inside.

I dig through the bag and find a brown bottle of pain pills, along with some gauze, a bottle of high-proof vodka, her cleaver, a Zippo lighter, and a set of papers all neatly folded together. It's only when I've removed everything I realize there's a side pocket, and tucked away inside is a clear glass bottle of pills.

Even though Britt had been under Sutter's influence when she called Kiki out, she wasn't wrong about Kiki lying.

"This bottle isn't ibuprofen. It's something called Forced March, made primarily out of cocaine and caffeine. Jesus, no wonder she didn't sleep. This stuff is enough to make anyone go nuts, especially at the rate she was downing them. What was she thinking taking these?"

"She always seemed unstable to me," Britt says. "But if she didn't want to tell us about it, then she probably wouldn't want us talking about it now. We should keep moving."

I hate to admit it, but she's right. Ditching my kitchen knife in favor of the cleaver, I thread the bag over my head, pointed bloody side out. "Where do we even go from here?" I ask. "April, got any more ideas?"

Predictably, our phones all start to hum to life again with a series of buzzes.

> Sometimes dead is better.

Buzz.

> Head to the office. You are the caretaker.
> You've always been the caretaker.

Buzz.

> Come on down to the basement. You'll float.

Buzz.

> Evil dies tonight!

"Huh," Shawn says, reading his messages. "I just got a weird one."

"Join the club. What's yours say?" I ask.

"Most of my texts are claiming to be Danny. He's begging me to go in all sorts of directions, but I just got one that says, 'There seems to be an alien pubic hair in my drink.' What the hell is that supposed to mean?"

I know this one, easy. Checking my list of messages, I find the same one buried between a bunch of other nonsense. "I have it as well. It's from *The Exorcist*, but it's just a weird line thrown in there by a drunk party guest." This must be how she's trying to cut through all the misleading messages, by sending the same line to all of us. "Britt, how about you?"

She shakes her head as she scrolls through her phone. "I've just got a bunch of messages from Nick Lachey, asking me to be on *Love is Blind*."

"Okay. So two out of the three of us got the same message. I feel like that's good enough for me. What about you?" I ask Shawn, hoping he will validate what feels like somewhat shaky logic.

"I guess so, but I still don't know what this is supposed to mean."

"Well," I say, before I actually have any ideas. "At its core, *The Exor-*

cist is a movie about a priest getting rid of a demonic possession. Wilson both became a priest and is possessing us, but I don't really know where that's supposed to lead."

"Do you think maybe it's just *Slashtag* finding a new way to mess with us?" Britt asks, casting further doubt on the notion.

I sigh. My brain is churning through ideas, but my body is so tired that it's hard to keep focused on any one thread for more than a couple of seconds. "I guess it could be another trick, but it's just such a specific and deep-dive line from the movie, I feel like it has to be April. Are there any chapels in here?" I look on my phone and find a blank room on the second floor with a drawing of a cross on it. "That has to be it."

"I don't know. That sounds like more of a coincidence to me," Britt says. "I feel like you guys are reading too much into this mystery text. If Arthur has hidden these statues all over the hotel, doesn't it seem a little too obvious that he would hide one in his own chapel?"

"I don't see what we have to lose by checking it out. It's a room we haven't explored yet. Unless she wants us all to go enjoy a bowl of pea soup, this is the only thing that I can think of that possibly ties back to *The Exorcist*."

Shawn nods. "I'm game to try it."

Britt is wearing her frustration on her sleeve, but she's outnumbered. "Fine. Lead the way."

According to the map the Chapel is located right next to the spire leading to Sutter's Sanctum. It's a short walk to a closed door that has a small gold plaque reading: *Chapel*.

I jiggle the handle, but it won't turn.

"Well, so much for that idea," Britt says. "Where should we try next?"

"Hang on, let me give it a go," Shawn says.

"Every other locked door we've come across has been impossible to open. Do we really need to go through this again?" she says.

"To be fair, I didn't have this before." With a little effort, Shawn lifts up the black rock engulfing his left hand.

"Oh God, please be careful," she says.

He nods, then brings his clubbed hand over his head, already wincing. Shawn takes a few quick breaths to pump himself up, then brings the hand down with his full might. The ball of pitch connects with the doorknob. There's a clattering sound, and the entire door handle falls to the floor, along with a series of little black shards chipped off of the pitch.

Shawn clutches the ball with his other hand and moans in pain.

"You okay?" I ask

"I'll be all right," he says, though his face indicates otherwise.

"The good news is, it looks like it worked." There's a hole in the door where the knob used to be. I try to push it and immediately eat my words. It still doesn't open.

"Son of a bitch," Shawn mutters, massaging his forearm.

"It's locked."

"So all that was for nothing," Britt says.

"Hang on. We can't give up now. If April told us to go here, then there must be a way in." I know I sound naïve. At this point, we should expect nothing but pain and misery at every turn. I just can't stand the idea of letting Shawn down again, like I did in the whorehouse.

Down on my knees, I peer through the hole in the door. It does look to be a small chapel inside, with several rows of pews facing a statue of Jesus on the cross. Nothing seems out of place, but also, there's nothing that gives me any sort of hint of how to get in, or what to do.

"Maybe there's a deadbolt or something on the other side that we can twist. I think I can get my hand through the hole if I give it a good squeeze."

Both of my companions look at me like I'm crazy. I don't remember which number this is, but it's definitely on the list of things you should never ever do in a horror movie. Shawn and Britt aren't even horror fans, and they know better than to stick your hand through a hole in a haunted house.

I wish I could take it back, but now that I've pitched the idea, I feel like I have to go through with it. I shake out my arm, if for no other reason than to stall having to execute my own plan, and take a few calming breaths. With one more look through the gap to make sure there's no ghost priests or one-eyed dogs, I squeeze my hand through. Once I make it past the wrist, I flatten my hand against the back of the door, sliding it upward and hoping to find a knob. For once, I get lucky.

A metal bulb attached to a rail slides inward, ending with a satisfying snap.

"I got it."

Making sure not to jinx myself, I pull my hand back through the hole as fast as humanly possible. The door swings in, and we step into the chapel. Upon first inspection, there's not much more to the room than I could see through the door. The pews are wood paneled and painted white. There's a podium between the seats and the Christ statue, and all of the walls are draped in red curtains.

"Do you want the pews or the walls?" Shawn says, now a seasoned pro at this game.

"I'll take the walls. Britt, you want to look at the statue?"

Britt is staring at her phone, at this point seemingly completely disconnected from the game. "Sure."

Starting with the right wall, I peel the red curtains back along the golden rod running above. Aside from a few crosses nailed to the wall, there's nothing that seems out of the ordinary.

"I found something," Shawn calls. "I think it's a Christmas card."

My heart lurches in my chest. "Don't open it!" I shout on reflex.

Before I can spin around, in my mind I have already envisioned the white outline of a nativity scene played against a sparkly blue background. By the time I actually see it, Shawn's pinching it with two fingers and holding it away from him, like it's a bomb about to go off.

"What's wrong with it?" Shawn asks.

"Everything," I say, rushing to the note, already knowing every word inside. Once I've snatched it from his hands, I immediately set about tearing it into little shreds.

"What the hell are you doing? That could have been a clue!"

"It's not," I lie, taking the ripped pieces, stacking them on top of each other, then ripping them again.

"How do you know?" he says, starting to sound aggravated.

"It's a personal attack to rattle me. Can we just leave it at that?"

Shawn shakes his head. "Not if it could help us get out of here. They could have written anything in there! If it was a hint on how to move forward, it shouldn't be up to you whether or not we just destroy something."

Back in Arthur's apartment, nobody but me noticed the first card that contained a clue. Even if they had, there's no way I'm letting the whole world see the photo He took of me and April asleep in our beds on Christmas eve.

"Look," I say, trying to give him a breadcrumb, "at least we know we're on the right track. The fact that there's something in this room means it's part of the game."

"But without reading the clue, how are we supposed to know where to start?"

"We don't need it!" I hear my voice rising to a shout. "We've got April now. I don't need to see another thing from Him again."

Shawn shakes his head in confusion. "Who is He? Arthur Wilson?"

My heart is racing so fast I'm starting to feel dizzy. I need to get Shawn to move on from this. "I'm going to get us out of here. We just have to find a door or something." I double-time it back to the far wall and start yanking on curtains until they pop from their rings.

"Can you slow down for a second, Tawny? I'm worried about you."

"Yeah," Britt chimes in. "You're looking kind of manic. Are you sure you didn't take any of Kiki's pills?"

Their persistence only serves to make me work faster. I've ripped all of the curtains down behind the Jesus statue and am making my way to the other side of the room.

"Ha!" I shout, as one of the fallen curtains reveals a wooden staircase leading up to what looks like a trap door in the ceiling. From my side, there's no levers or locks to muddle through—just a simple wooden cut-out. "There. I've solved the room, okay? Now we can all just forget about the card and keep going."

An impossibly strong hand grips my arm when I start to climb the stairs. I try to yank it out, but my strength is nothing compared to Shawn's.

"Forget about the card, Tawny. You're freaking me out. What's going on?"

"Check her teeth!" Britt says, half-hidden behind the statue. "Maybe she's possessed."

"I'm not possessed!" I hiss back, flashing her my teeth, like *I'm* the snarling dog for once.

"Hey, forget about her," Shawn says. "Talk to me."

It's not just that I don't want to talk about it; I can't talk about it. I made a promise to April that I wouldn't tell our story without her. And besides, there's still the invisible elephant in the room.

Good dogs keep their mouths shut.

"Look, Shawn, I'm sorry that I blurted out all of your trauma on camera when I was under Wilson's influence, but that doesn't mean I'm obligated to reciprocate just because you want me to."

His confusion turns to hurt. "What? That has nothing to do with this. I'm concerned because I care about you, and whatever's happening right now seems to have you on the edge of some sort of breakdown. I don't know if you've noticed, but losing control in this hotel never seems to end well."

A cracking dam is holding back a waterfall of tears held just behind my eyes. I regret everything I've just said. Shawn's been nothing but an ally to me this entire time. He doesn't deserve the way I'm lashing out at him. Guilt sloshes into bitterness as I think about Him watching the monitor with glee, knowing he still holds this much power over me.

I'm going to explain everything to Shawn. I just can't do it yet. "I'm sorry for snapping at you. Look, I found the way out of the room, and April's still looking out for us from the outside. Can we please just keep moving for now and chalk this moment up to temporary madness?"

Part of me wants him to keep pushing, to chew me out for being rash and insensitive. I deserve it. But like always, he shows himself to be infinitely more emotionally mature than me and releases my arm.

With a nod and a sad smile, he just says, "Okay. Let's keep going."

Britt lets out a guttural sound of surprise. "Are you serious? After that temper tantrum, you're just going to let her keep calling the shots?"

"Whatever was in that letter was clearly something personal to Tawny. If she's not ready to share it, that's her choice. All we can do is respect her decision."

Britt throws her hands up in frustration and joins us by the stairs. "Fine, what do I know? Let's just wander blindly up here, I guess."

We climb the stairs, with Shawn in the lead. He pauses before pushing on the door, adding a bit of tension that I'm not sure I need.

"Moment of truth," he says, then places his single free hand against the edge of the trapdoor.

He pushes.

Nothing happens.

He takes a step up to rearrange his hand position, then tries again.

Nothing.

"Seems like it's locked," Britt says. "If only we had some more information on how to get it open..."

"Hang on. I don't think it's locked. It just feels like there's something on it. Let me try something else." Shawn turns around to face us, then backs up two stairs, angling his shoulder and upper back against the door. He grits his teeth and pushes.

Sure enough, the door slowly starts to rise. At first, there's nothing but darkness above and a scratching sound all around the door. Once he has it about halfway open, he turns himself around to face forward and pushes with his one hand. The trapdoor moves quickly after that, and light floods the passageway as what turns out to be a large rug is cleared from the floor above the trap door.

"Always lift with the legs," Shawn says with a smile, before climbing the rest of the way into the room.

I follow him into an octagonal spire with stained glass windows covering the majority of each wall, save for one, which has a stone fireplace complete with a crackling fire. Each piece of glasswork is intricately arranged to form a picture representing one of the sins. In the center of the fireplace wall is a tapestry of a man, his head cast away from a pair of eyes staring down upon him with contempt. I assume this one represents disobedience.

The sun must be setting. Intense light pours through three of the glasses, making one half of the room much more colorful than the other. Opposite the fireplace, there's a curving staircase along the wall, leading to a thick wooden door with four glowing insignia carved into stone. There are another four interspersed among them, which have all gone dark—a pig, a spider, an eyeball, and a knife.

"I think we just came in through the exit, like for after we destroy the mind totem," Shawn says, noticing the door as well. "I mean, it's not like we solved any sort of riddle to get in here. We just used brute force and your sister's clue. I bet that lock was meant for us as a path back into the hotel afterwards."

Beneath the blindingly colorful windows, the walls are lined with desks filled with books, papers, crosses, dozens of old packets of Now and Later candies, and a few dozen replicas of the sin statues. The only thing missing in the room is Arthur himself.

I head to one of the desks, searching for anything that looks out of the ordinary, my hands nearly shaking at the prospect of finding another of the dozens of letters He's sent me over the past two decades.

"His mind totem is a book, right?" Shawn stands next to a stack of maybe twenty leather-bound tomes.

"Yeah, this'll definitely be easy to find," Britt says.

"Maybe you deserve a little challenge, since you all cheated to get here," Shawn says.

I turn around and see Shawn hunched over so that old man Arthur can whisper into his ear.

"I had such wonderful games planned."

"Shawn, if you can hear me, you need to get away from Wilson right now."

"Shawn's not here," he says with a grin, revealing a mouth full of rotten teeth.

I glance over at Britt, who is sifting through books near the far end of the room.

Right now, Shawn's attention is on me. I figure the best plan is to keep it that way while Britt locates and destroys the totem.

"Arthur," I say, trying to appeal to the spirit inhabiting my friend. "You're more creative than this. What's the fun in just beating us to death?"

"Ha!" Shawn barks out a laugh that's like no sound I've ever heard him produce. It's malicious, condescending, threatening—all the things Shawn isn't. "Do you know how many decades it's been since I've been able-bodied enough to do the work myself? It will be my pleasure to take you apart piece by piece."

Shawn takes a heavy step toward me. Floorboards creak beneath his weight. I match his stride, retreating but still keeping his attention.

"So you're going to kill us, and then what happens? Your spirit's still trapped here. What if we could free you from this place?"

He laughs again, driving home the point that Shawn isn't home right now. "Where would I go? I spent forty years trying to get back here. This is my home."

Shawn takes another heavy stride in my direction. I once again step back but feel myself press up against a desk. He slowly raises his stoney hand over his head, ready to bring it down over me. I know I don't stand a chance against his physical strength, but as long as he telegraphs his moves, maybe I can keep away from him long enough for Britt to make more progress.

When he brings his mutilated fist down, I leap to the side, though it turns out he's faster than I expected. I only just make it out of his way before he smashes his hand into the desk behind me. Wood splinters fly everywhere as the table collapses under his force. I land on my hands hard and feel the wound in my right palm split open again.

I try to shake it off, pulling Kiki's cleaver from the bag with my good hand. "Please, Shawn, I don't want to have to use this against you."

Shawn laughs. "Against who? I can feel your friend inside. He knows you're too weak to finish the job, even if you had the chance."

Against the right person, I absolutely *could* kill. I could even enjoy it. Against Shawn? I honestly don't know.

Shawn holds both of his huge arms out to his sides. His full span takes up almost half the room. It reminds me of Freddy Krueger in the first film, with arms stretched out so long they fill an entire alleyway.

Without warning, Shawn charges at me, taking up as much space as possible to prevent me from getting away. I try to duck under him, but a knee comes out of nowhere and knocks me back. He then wraps me up in a giant bear hug, lifting me off the ground and squeezing until I feel my back, ribs, and everything in between crack and compress.

I'm face to face with him now. His eyes are dull and blank. His rotten-candy breath makes my stomach lurch. The white fireworks dance around the edges of my vision, and an involuntary hiccup escapes my lips as he finds one last pocket of air to squeeze out of me.

The both of us jerk hard to the side, and the immense pressure releases when I fall to the floor. Britt is standing over Shawn, meat tenderizer in hand.

"I think I found the totem," she says, as Shawn fumbles around on the floor, pressing his hand against the back of the head. Britt runs to a desk and grabs a book. "This is it!"

Shawn shoots back to his feet in an instant and grabs her by the neck from behind. He climbs up onto one of the desks, easily dragging Britt up along with him.

"Britt Holley," he spits into her ear, as if it were some sort of derogatory term. "Of all the treats provided to me in this offering, no candle will be as sweet for me to extinguish as yours." He then drives her head forward, smashing her face through one of the stained glass windows. She shrieks in pain and drops the book to the floor, her hands flying up to brace her impact.

Much like the rest of the windows in the hotel, each piece of glass is housed in a frame of wrought iron, twisting through the picture like a set of spiked prison bars that have taken on the life of a vine. One of the iron tendrils comes to a sharp point just beneath Britt's chin. She's got her feet pressed against the bottom of the window and is doing everything she can to keep her head from being impaled on the spike.

It's do or die.

I scramble to the book, groping at it with my wounded hand while keeping the cleaver ready to strike. There's only one chance for me to stop this now. I wind my arm back and hurl the book at the fireplace as hard as I can.

My hand is so slick with blood that the book slips from my fingers. It's flying through the air but not at the speed I had hoped. It hits the floor only a foot shy and slides the rest of the way home. It only barely breaches the fireplace threshold before bursting into bright blue flames.

A raspy voice cracks out of Shawn. "No, no!"

Britt seizes on the moment, shoving backward and freeing herself from his grasp.

He stumbles off the desk, spinning like a puppet with its strings all knotted up. When he falls to the ground, old man Arthur remains, contorting in agony on his feet. He coughs out little belches of black smoke, then stumbles forward onto his knees. The loose hanging skin on his face begins to melt, turning white and then eventually clear as it drips to the floor in thick ropes of goo. Just like when we destroyed his body's totem, he eventually reaches a point where he can no longer hold his form and simply pops like a water balloon.

The three of us lie on the floor, without enough energy to even call out to each other for what feels like at least five minutes.

Mission Log

- ~~Restore Power to the Hotel~~

- ~~Destroy Arthur Wilson's Body Totem~~
  - ~~Unlock Arthur's Apartment~~
    - ~~Find the key's knob~~
    - ~~Find the key's shaft~~
    - ~~Find the key's bit~~

- ~~Destroy Arthur Wilson's Mind Totem~~
  - Unlock the door to Sutter's Sanctum
    - Destroy the Greed statue
    - Destroy the Sloth statue
    - ~~Destroy the Wrath statue~~
    - ~~Destroy the Envy statue~~
    - ~~Destroy the Lust statue~~
    - Destroy the Pride statue
    - ~~Destroy the Gluttony statue~~
    - Destroy the Disobedience statue

- Destroy Arthur Wilson's Spirit Totem

PODCAST ALERT!
Episode 3 of **Talking Tag** is now live at
www.slashtaginsider.com

SOCIAL

CHAPTER FIFTY-THREE

From: Lucy.K@Krentler.media
To: Board@Krentler.media
CC: Operations@Krentler.media
Subject: Day 2 Summary- Updated

Members of the Board and *Slashtag* Crew,

I'll be the first to admit we had some hiccups in the mind totem phase of the program. Due to an unforeseen outside intervention brought on by our own team member, Todd Menuscha, the subjects were able to destroy the second totem by 8:48 p.m. They only found 4 of the 7 statues and made their way into the chapel without finding any of the 5 clues that were supposed to lead them there. At least we had one confirmed death, with Kiki ending herself in a PVI positive manner, and between the Envy possession and the fight in Sutter's Sanctum, we have nearly made up for lost time regarding the Pain Volume Index. Instead of nitpicking things to improve, let's head straight to the analytics:

- In the last 3 hours, there has been a sharp incline in viewership, most recently coming in at 74.6 million.
- Much of the viewership uptick actually came from viral buzz regarding April's communications with Tawny. #hacktag became the top trending hashtag on Social, bringing in over 5 million new viewers. We had initially predicted the meta angle had potential to be a draw, but we had no idea our viewers would be this engaged by contestants breaking the fourth wall.
- The most watched player has bounced around, shifting from Kiki to Britt, and then finally Tawny with 39% of Spotlight viewers tuning in to her feed.
- Due to the particularly violent nature of our brief second phase, we have reached 71% PVI, despite only one subject death during this time. This still puts us well on track to reach our target within the next 5-14 hours.

I wish we could say this leg of the production was more of a success, but we feel confident that we will still clear our target PVI and then some. Let's not let a few ants spoil the picnic. In the meantime, Todd and April are still unaccounted for, and until they are apprehended, everything we're working for is still at risk.

Let's tighten up this ship and steer us into the final act with a bang.

Lucy

CHAPTER FIFTY-FOUR

"I'm confused," I say, watching the spirit of Arthur Wilson melt for a second time on screen.

"About what?" Todd asks.

"There were no possession statues in that tower, right?"

Todd nods. "Sutter's Sanctum, right."

"I thought it was implied before that the statues were basically pre-programmed artifacts that had been, like, imbued with magic or something. No one else has been able to talk as Wilson or act like they're directly under his command earlier. Why can he do that now?"

"Oh, that." Todd bites his lip and concentrates for a second, finding his words. "So here's the thing. Ghosts don't really work the way you think they do. It's not like a person has some lingering spirit that just wants to go around messing things up. I don't really know the best way to describe it. It's like they're robots, and as long as you have the remote control, you can make them do pretty much whatever you want."

"So you're saying Arthur Wilson was resting peacefully until Krentler dug him up and turned him into a dancing murder puppet? Wilson isn't even in control of his own actions?"

"Technically, Renshaw is the Spirit Wrangler. He does all the actual programming. Programming is a weird word for it because their essence is still there and has some input, but for the most part, yeah, he has to do whatever he's told."

"That's sick, you know that? Even for someone like Wilson, you don't just go around enslaving spirits."

Todd looks offended. "It's not like we resurrected the spirit of Gandhi to murder everyone. Besides, Wilson's so evil, he'd probably be doing the exact same thing if he had his own choice."

"It doesn't matter how evil they are, it's not cool to just summon up someone's soul and split it up into three totems."

Todd scrunches up his shoulders and scratches the back of his head. "We should probably talk about that."

"Jesus, what now?" I say.

"We sort of made up the totems for the sake of the game. It's more fun for the audience if it feels like there are clear boxes to check off along the way. The amulet is really the only thing that matters."

"You're saying Arthur still has the ability to possess people and chop them up? Destroying those totems did nothing?"

"Well no, that's what I'm trying to explain. We programmed him to stop doing those things after those prop totems were destroyed."

"But you also changed the rules to have him just directly possess people when you felt the story called for it. Who's to say you won't just change the rules again?"

Todd shrugs. "I dunno. Continuity?"

I shake my head and pull up the tablet. "I have to tell everyone this." I open up Britt's phone messenger and type up the first of three warnings I'm going to send to each of them, then freeze as I stare at the last message I sent out to the trio. "There's something else that doesn't make sense to me."

"What else is there?"

"When I gave all three of them the hint to head to the chapel, only Tawny and Shawn said they received it, though I'm seeing right here in my chat log that Britt got it too."

Todd's eyes meander around the room. "Okay, so maybe she missed it."

"I don't think she did. Todd..." I say, doing my best impression of a mother getting ready to scold her child. "Why would she purposely ignore a hint that would get them to jump ahead in the game?"

Todd scoffs like a petulant teenager whose hand just got caught in the cookie jar. "Okay, so she might know a little bit more than the others."

"How much inside information does Britt have?" I ask through clenched teeth.

"If you want to know so bad, why don't you look up her file already. It's right there on the home screen."

I like to think I'm pretty darn good at controlling my anger. But the way Todd keeps drip-feeding me critical information makes me want to jab him with the stun gun. "I didn't even know there was anything worth looking at!"

I find the app he's talking about. It brings me to a list of the participants, and I click on a tab that reads: *Subject #2: Britt Holley*. Inside, there are dozens of files on her background, her many television shows, social media analytics, and so on. I keep scrolling until I find an .mp4 video file, the thumbnail of which shows security footage of William Krentler's office. I tap it, and the thumbnail blows up to fill the screen. Krentler is sitting at a large marble desk in a spacious office. A glass door swings open from the side of the screen, and Britt Holley steps into frame.

"Hi, Mister Krentler," Britt says.

"Britt, so good to see you." The elderly man rises from his chair and meets her halfway around his table to give her a formal hug. "Have a seat, sweetheart." He gestures to a chair on the other side of the desk and returns to his. "How's the family?"

"Everyone's great. My mom says hello."

"Give her my best as well." He shifts in his seat, leaning forward and putting his arms on the table. "I want to thank you for meeting with me, I know how busy you are these days."

Britt replies with an exuberance of enthusiasm. "Aww, of course. I wouldn't be so busy if it weren't for you."

"I'm sure you would have done just fine on your own without any help, but that's very sweet of you to say. I wanted to talk to you today about a new opportunity. It's a groundbreaking new series, a combination of a reality competition and a horror film. The cast is made up of the top celebrities in each of their fields, competing to survive a three-day weekend full of murder and mayhem. That's where you come in. I want you to be the heroine who makes it out alive and becomes the official face of Social."

Britt resettles in her chair, framing her body away from the glass door. "Just to be clear. Is this a regular kind of production, or is it something for *you know who?*"

Krentler nods slightly. "There will no doubt be danger involved, though if we can trust anyone to make it out on top, it would be you. Of course, you would have every possible advantage."

Britt thinks on it for a second, staring at her manicured nails. "How are you going to explain the deaths of the other contestants?"

A smile comes easily to the old man's face. "You let us worry about that. What do you think?"

I turn off the video, having seen enough. "Great. So you're saying this whole thing's been rigged for her to win from the beginning?"

Todd waffles to explain. "That's kind of a hard question to answer."

"It really shouldn't be."

"Yes, it's rigged, but no, she can't win. You know that third totem? The Amulet of Duriel?"

"What about it?" I ask, already knowing where he's going.

"It isn't technically in the hotel. The Amulet's down here. Renshaw actually needs it in order to control Arthur."

"There's no way for them to win the game? You're just going full *Cabin in the Woods* and killing everyone?"

"I mean, it's a priceless artifact. They can't just let somebody come in and destroy it."

"Why did you wait until just now to tell me this?" I demand. I've gotten too loud, lost my cool. I know this because the door to the server room comes swinging open before he gets a chance to respond.

A woman who looks to be in her mid-forties stands in the doorway, a gun in her hand. She has black hair, thick black eyeshadow, black clothes, and firetruck-red lipstick.

"Well, look what I found," the woman says, stepping into the room. "Must be my lucky day. I always knew you were a gutless beta cuck,

Todd, but holy shit, why would you get in bed with a cripple?" Her voice is raspy, full of vocal fry.

"Charlotte, good to see you, as always," Todd snivels. "There's no way I could talk you into pretending you didn't just find us, is there?"

While these two take their time catching up, I think of one last code to send to Tawny.

"Hey Wheels, you wanna drop the tablet?" Charlotte says, pointing the gun in my direction.

I lean over to drop the tablet on the ground, tapping my thumb against where I hope the send button is before letting it fall. As I'm bent over, I grab hold of the pistol on my lap that's obscured behind a bank of servers.

"What are you going to do with us?" I ask.

"Todd's about to get something that's been a long time coming. You, on the other hand, are on reserve for one of the board members."

"I knew it!" I shout. I was never meant to be a correspondent on *Slashtag*, and I'd rather die than go through whatever they have planned for me. I pull the gun up and point it at her, using what little leverage I've just learned I have. "You aren't allowed to kill me, are you?"

Charlotte lets out an irritated sigh. "All right, you want to go down this road? Fine. No, I'm not supposed to kill you. That doesn't mean I can't hurt you."

"So what?" I say. "If you shoot at me, I'll just shoot you back. I'll be hurt, but you'll be dead. I'm not afraid of pain."

She seems thoroughly unamused. "This isn't going to pan out how you think. If you decide to shoot, before you even realize you want to tell your finger to squeeze that trigger, I'll have you nailed in the shoulder. At that point, your shooting arm's down, you got nowhere to go, and Todd gets one between the eyes. Either way, this ends with me taking you to Renshaw. One way's just a whole lot worse for you."

"She means it," Todd warns. "Charlotte's like, the third-scariest person here."

I narrow my eyes at her. "It sounds like you're saying that either way I'm screwed, so why not at least take a shot at killing you?"

"Because I can tell you're a fighter, and you think you've got better chances of surviving if you don't have a bullet in your arm."

She's not wrong. If I let her in close, I still have my stun gun, though given she has a pistol, there's no guarantee she'll ever get close enough for me to use it. I slowly start to bring my gun down but stop once the nozzle points directly at the server in front of me. "Okay, so how about this. I've currently got this gun aimed at the network's central distribution processor." I have no idea what I'm actually aiming at, but I'm hoping she understands this stuff as little as I do. "Without this, your broadcast is canceled, and I don't think your bosses would be too happy if they learned you were the reason for that."

Charlotte smirks. "Well, we can't have that, can we?"

There's a flash from her muzzle, and the small room explodes with the sound of gunfire. It's deafening, so loud I can feel it like a shock-wave through my own body. Next to me, Todd goes down. There's a red hole almost exactly between his eyes. On instinct, I pull the trigger several times, but nothing happens. I aim the gun back at Charlotte and continue to uselessly pull the trigger as she advances, pointing her pistol squarely at me.

"Toss the gun, kid. It's over. I'm only going to say it once."

It all happened so fast, I can barely even understand what she's saying. Reality comes crashing over me.

I'm not playing a hero in some movie. This is real life.

I have a real gun pointed at me, and I'm really about to get shot. Todd is dead.

My body starts to shake as I toss my gun on the ground in Charlotte's direction.

She picks it up, then shows me a switch on the side. "Pro-tip, kid. Always check to see if the safety is on." Charlotte tucks the weapon into the back of her waistband. "You ready to get this show on the road?"

CHAPTER FIFTY-FIVE

After picking glass out of Britts face and consoling Shawn for the acts he committed against his will, we decide we need to put as much food into ourselves as we possibly can. The idea of sleep is still an ongoing debate. We're beyond exhausted, but the thought of putting ourselves in such a vulnerable position seems like a terrible idea.

As we shamble into the kitchen, my phone buzzes one last time.

THERES HIGH TENSION IN HOLLEYWOOD

"What if we take shifts standing guard?" Britt asks. "Two people sleep, and one stays awake."

Shawn opens a fridge and pulls out some deli meats and cheeses to make sandwiches. "I don't know if we can trust any of ourselves to be alone."

I'm barely paying attention to them. Instead, I'm focusing on processing what the message could mean. It's not a quote from any movie I can think of, but the way *Holleywood* is spelled makes me think it has to be about Britt. It was the title of one of her shows. But what about her? We're all in a really high-tension situation. Why point her out specifically?

Maybe it's not about her being tense, but more about the wording. High Tension. There's a French horror movie called *High Tension*, but from what I remember, it's nothing like the scenario we're in. I can't find the connection.

That is, until I remember the twist.

It turned out the heroine of the movie, the small girl getting hunted in the woods while her friends got butchered, actually ended up being the killer in the midst of a psychotic break. She was the bad guy. I replay the last two days through my head, thinking about any situations in which Britt could have secretly been a saboteur. I think about our talk in the bathroom, where she confided in me a story eerily similar to mine, pushing me to keep playing the game.

"Who needs a drink?" I ask as we all assemble sandwiches.

"Now, there's a bad idea I could get behind," Shawn says.

"Hey, Britt, do you think you could make us another round of that sangria?"

"Totally!" she says, her eyes lighting up. "I'll go find us the perfect red. I think I saw a bottle of Garancha yesterday that looked like it could be pretty tasty." She rushes off into the dining room toward the bar.

"Shawn, I think Britt's a spy," I whisper, nervously tugging at my hair.

He laughs. "Come again?"

"Britt. I think she's working for them."

Shawn's look of amusement turns to concern. "Are you being serious right now? Look, I'm all for believing you. If you say something happened, I'm there. But first you rip up potential clues, and now you accuse Britt of being a mole? Are you sure you're not just so overtired and on edge that you're seeing things that aren't there?"

"No, I'm right about this." The more I think about it, the more weird little things pop into my head. "Remember how she was super against going into the chapel? It's almost as if she knew it was a back-door to the mind totem."

"I wouldn't say she was super against it. I'd say that, based on previous experience, she had a reasonable doubt that messing with a locked door would yield anything."

"What about her insisting on having her own room for the first night? Or all the time she's spent on her phone, even before we started getting text messages? And where's her trauma ghost? Everyone else has had some horrible thing from their past that they've had to deal with publicly, except for her."

"I don't know. Maybe she doesn't have any regrets?" Shawn says, sounding unconvinced by his own argument.

"Have you seen *Drama Mamas?* Landon's father was a saint compared to some of the crap Britt's mom said to her on that show."

His face drops, like he just remembered he left an oven running at home. "Shit. What about when she found that hidden knife in the antler of the elk in the Hunter's Hall. She only did it once she became Wilson's target. Like she knew it was there the whole time but was waiting for some reason."

"Waiting to put on a good show," I say, holding my eyes firmly on his to show him my very real concern.

Britt bursts back into the room, holding a pitcher half filled with red wine. "I need some ice and fruit. What's gotten into you two?" Her brow sharpens, clearly seeing the suspicious looks on our faces upon her re-entry. "What?" she repeats, forcing us to say something.

"How did you come to be on this show again?" Shawn asks.

"What do you mean?" she says, looking over to me.

I can feel her silently calling into question the entire pep talk she gave me in the bathroom. "You told me what I needed to hear to re-enter the game and follow their script. In fact, your goal this entire weekend has been to keep everyone on track and playing the game. When Shawn, Derek, and I tried to leave, you stayed, knowing that you were in danger."

"I was right in the end, wasn't I? There was no escape."

"But you actively pushed for people to stay." Shawn takes a step toward her, and whether he realizes it or not, his size can make his approach very intimidating. "Can you be real for one second? Did you know what was going to happen here?"

"Stop it, you guys. You're really starting to scare me." She continues to plead her innocence, but as she backs out of the kitchen, her eyes tell a different story. They're darting around to every corner in the ceiling, as if calling for help from somewhere outside the game.

"So it's true?" He advances toward her again, reading her body language as easily as me. "You were in on this the whole time?"

"I'm feeling very threatened by your stance right now," Britt says, hustling backward to put a table between herself and Shawn.

"You're feeling threatened? I've watched people die in here. I've been stabbed multiple times, by multiple people, had my hand melted in fucking tar, possessed by a serial killer, harassed by actual ghosts from my past, and *you* feel threatened?"

Britt backs up even further. She glances behind her several times at the hallway leading to the lobby, looking like a rabbit about to run. Part of me wants to de-escalate the situation, see if there's a way to get Britt to confess without things getting out of control. Another part of me wants to give chase and see if she leads us to a hidden way out.

"Shawn, let's calm down a little and give Britt a chance to explain herself." I choose the diplomatic approach, remembering what happens every time the final survivors turn on each other in the last act of a horror film. It's not a rule on our survival list, but if we make it through this, I'll be sure to add it.

"I'm not going to hurt her. I just think we deserve an explanation," Shawn says. "How about we all sit down, eat our sandwiches, and talk this out like adults."

Britts eyes keep flicking around the room, signaling for help that will never come.

"They're not going to save you," I say.

The corners of her lips begin to tremble.

"Whatever deal you thought you made, you have to know by now that it was a lie. Let's say, for the sake of argument, you knew going into this that other people were going to die. What kind of future do you think you're going to have with a face like that?" I point at the dozen or more lacerations across her face.

It's overly harsh, I know. I hate using my own biggest insecurity as a weapon against her like this, but it's the beginning of a thread I'm carefully trying to pull.

She reaches up and feels all the cuts, many of which are still leaking blood, despite our best attempts to clean her up.

"Do you know how hard it's been for me to hide two little scars on my face for almost twenty years? You just got carved up in front of millions of people. The only life you have after this is, at best, one of sympathy. That's not who you are. You're too strong for that."

"I can rise above it. Show how resilient a woman can be after surviving something like this. I'll be an inspiration."

I shake my head without breaking eye contact with her. "Not if everyone thinks you signed up for this willingly. Then you're a fraud. A willing accessory to murder. A crisis actor. That is, of course, unless you were *forced* to be a part of this."

Britt instantly picks up on where I'm heading and shifts her demeanor from guilty criminal to victim. "They threatened my family," she says, forcing out a sniffle. "Some network producer called me into his office. He told me if I followed the rules, I would be the sole survivor and that no serious harm would come to me. I told him no, but he said if I didn't do it, he'd kill my family. And then he brought out this man who made Arthur Wilson appear right in front of my eyes. He said he could make Arthur go anywhere, even in my parents' home. I didn't have a choice." Her crocodile tears are perfectly crafted and even seem to roll down her cheeks on cue.

This is why she's the queen of reality TV drama.

I look over to Shawn to make sure we're on the same page. "That sounds horrible. Krentler has my sister kidnapped too. You know it really was her messaging me, right?"

She gives a meek nod.

"Okay, so we need to find our way out of here and get the police to go after them. Do you know a way out?"

She shakes her head.

"What about the spirit totem? Do you know where the Amulet of Duriel is?"

Britt gives more than a moment's hesitation before nodding yes. "There's a secret door in the barber shop. I can show you."

I want to believe she's telling the truth, but it's impossible to know if anything she's said this entire game has been real. Nevertheless, we have no choice but to follow her.

"All right, then. Let's find the totem, then get the hell out of here." We follow Britt down the hall, staying a few steps behind her out of caution.

"Do you think she's really taking us to the amulet?" Shawn whispers.

"I'm banking on her doing whatever's in her best interests, and right now, that's making herself look like a victim to get out of here."

From the lobby, we head under the stairs and take the first right. The barber shop sits on the far right corner of the hall, near the mirror door we shattered on our way up to the brothel.

She looks at the door with concern, then continues down the hallway.

"I thought you said we needed to go to the barber shop," Shawn says.

Britt steps over the shattered glass door, then bends over in the black-painted hallway. When she rises again, she's got her arm wrapped around the barber pole Derek threw into the mirror. With her free hand, she twists the metal cap of the pole until it pops off. "First, we need this," she says, producing a small silver key from inside the barber pole.

For just a split second, I see myself slamming her head into one of the outstretched shards of glass still clinging to the side of the broken mirror's frame. It was one thing hearing her admit to being a plant. Watching how easily she fetches our salvation makes me want to pour every ounce or rage I have into a single act of vengeance.

Deep breaths. Fix your hair. Cover the scar.

"Great." I choke the word out as I swallow back my anger.

Britt returns to the barber shop door and opens it after a quick twist of the key. "I know this sounds shady, but we're each going to have to do this one at a time." She takes a seat in the further of the two barber chairs and reaches for a crank by the feet.

"Hold up," Shawn says, placing his giant hand over hers. "If that's the case, maybe Tawny or I should go first. No offense, but I don't have a whole lot of trust in you right now."

"Rule two of surviving a horror film is you never go alone," I say.

"If this was a trap, wouldn't I want Shawn to go down first?" she says candidly. "Then I could catch Tawny by surprise and be the sole survivor."

"You know this really isn't helping your credibility," I say.

"This'll take me down to the mining tunnels, and as soon as I step off, it'll come right back up for whoever's next. I swear."

Shawn looks over to me for the final word, but honestly, I feel like this could go either way. In my mind, it obviously makes sense for her to do the right thing to help salvage her image, but I have no idea what else she knows that she's not telling.

"It's your call," I say, leaving fate in Shawn's hand.

"All right. I'm going to trust you. But you better be there when I get down."

Britt nods. "I won't go anywhere."

Shawn takes his hand off hers. She pulls the crank.

Nothing happens.

She pulls it again.

Nothing.

"Whoops, it must be the other one." She hops off the chair, climbs into the other, then pulls the crank.

"I don't get it," Shawn says. "What's the punchline here?"

If this is a joke, Britt clearly doesn't get it either. She keeps pulling the lever, growing more frantic each time. "No," she says, shaking her head in disbelief. She hurries back to the first chair, pulling that lever several more times. "No. This should work."

My heart sinks. Either she's putting on the performance of a lifetime, or her usefulness to Krentler Media has reached its conclusion.

"All right." I put a hand on her shoulder. "Let's go back to the kitchen and get those sandwiches."

"No!" Britt shouts, now in full panic mode. "Why isn't this working?" Once again, she looks up at a corner of the room. Real tears stream down her face. "Let me out!"

"Looks like you're stuck here with the rest of us rubes," Shawn says, just a smidge of satisfaction layered on top of his obvious disappointment. "Come on, I'm hungry."

Britt falls forward from the chair to the ground, breaking down. "I did my best," she sobs, hands covering her face.

It's starting to get annoying. While I was willing to be nice to the girl to get out of here, watching her late realization that she's not exempt from the rules doesn't really drum up much sympathy in me. I grab her by the arm and help pull her back onto her feet.

"Let's go. We'll figure out our next step in the dining room."

"You don't understand!" she shrieks, her voice rising to a falsetto as she pulls away from me. "All the rest of the clues in the house point to the barber shop. There is no next step!" She stumbles out of the room, looking completely punch-drunk.

We're about halfway to the lobby, when I see a figure standing down the hall.

"Oh darling, there's always a next step," he says. It's Arthur Wilson. He's young again and dressed in the tweed suit and bowler hat iconic to his look. He's holding something in his hands—the axe from his apartment.

"You gotta be kidding me. Wilson's back now? I thought we destroyed the body totem," Shawn moans.

Arthur advances toward us, though as he gets closer, I can see there's something different about him. His face is covered in sores. The white shimmering light that was in his eyes has been snuffed out. One of his hands isn't holding the axe properly—two of the fingers have been replaced by scalpels.

"Not Wilson," I say. " Landon."

CHAPTER FIFTY-SIX

When Charlotte first ushered me out of the server room, I had hoped she would at some point get close enough that I could use my taser trick to zap her to the floor. Then I could be armed—this time with the safety off—and ready to figuratively bust down some doors and get the jump on Renshaw. With a title like Spirit Wrangler, I imagine I'm going to need all the help I can get.

Unfortunately for me, Charlotte is leagues more clever than Todd ever was. I know he was, at his core, a gutless, evil worm, but that doesn't mean I think he deserved what happened to him. Charlotte, on the other hand, is absolutely ruthless. Ever since we left the server room, she's forced me to lead the way, while she always remains several paces behind, her gun trained on me. It doesn't leave much wiggle room to come up with a plan.

To make matters worse, my wheelchair is not built for off-roading events. As such, guiding it through this carved-out mine tunnel has made for an extremely uncomfortable ride. I was okay when we were primarily going downhill, but the trip to Renshaw's office has been mostly incline on rougher terrain.

An electric wheelchair is different from a hand-operated one for a number of reasons. One that some people may not realize is just how

small the wheels are on mine, as opposed to the huge hand-crank variety. Several of the dips in the ground have been big enough to nearly
jostle me out of the chair entirely. At first, it's just irritating, but then I
wonder if there's possibility in these potholes. The next time my wheel
falls into a hole, I surreptitiously slide my hand across the power button
on the chair. It makes it look believable when I push the joystick
forward and nothing happens.

"Keep moving," Charlotte commands, maintaining at least five feet
of distance behind me.

I push the knob forward several times for show. "I'm stuck."

"I don't care. Find a way to keep moving. Crawl if you have to."

"Look, there's nothing I can do!" Real panic seeps into my words as I
start to worry she may never come within striking range. I allow the
anxiety to pour in, hoping it will help sell the act. "It won't move!" I
knock the joystick in all directions to show there's no way out.

"All right, all right, just cool it already." Charlotte steps around to my
side, inspecting the hole. She crouches down a little and narrows her
eyes, giving me a strong urge to flinch and look away.

I fight it off and stare back until she speaks again.

"So I'm guessing you need a push?"

"I think so," I say, trying to make sure she believes it was her idea.

"Fine." Charlotte stands back up and starts to make her way around
to the back of my chair.

I slide my hand under the grip, grabbing my stun gun, and get ready
to pull it and spin around as soon as she grabs the bar.

My chair lurches forward so violently that I almost faceplant onto
the tunnel floor.

Charlotte has kicked my chair out of the hole. "Looks like you're
good to go."

"Thanks." I tap the power button and push the joystick forward,
frustrated at having been outsmarted by this horrible woman. Still, I'm
not ready to give up and instead search for another way to distract or
gain information. "So what exactly is it you do here?"

"I get things done," she says with confidence.

"I know Todd said he was Charles Menuscha's grandson. Which
family do you belong to?"

Charlotte lets out a single wicked laugh. "I'm one of a very select group of outside hires. Unlike Todd, I actually earned my place here." We roll up to the door labeled *Renshaw*. Charlotte has me wait about ten feet back as she makes her way around and performs a very specific series of knocks on the door.

"Come in," a muffled voice says from the other side.

Charlotte pushes the door open, then circles back behind me and gestures with the gun.

"Inside," she says.

The first thing that strikes me upon entering is this room looks like it could be inside of an actual building. White plaster walls have been erected to cover the stone. There's a tile floor even with the ground. Several large metal tables sit in the center of the room, reminding me of a morgue. In one corner, there's even a metal sink.

Sitting in front of one of these tables is a chubby man in a white lab coat, who I have to assume is Renshaw. He looks nothing like what I imagined. With a name and job title like that, I expected a tall spidery man in ominous black robes, gray hollow cheeks, and deep sunken eyes. Instead, this guy looks more like a pediatrician, or an off-duty mall Santa. He's an older man with a bushy beard, more salt than pepper, and has a surprisingly warm smile as he greets us.

"Hello, I'm Doctor Renshaw. You'll have to forgive me for not standing up. I'm just finishing a little something now, and then I'll be right with you." His sleeve is rolled up, and there's a needle in his arm, sucking blood into a bag on his lap.

From what I can tell, he's getting ready to replace an almost fully drained IV bag that's hanging over a gray tub on the table. I have my suspicions about what's in the tub, but because of my chair, I can't see inside.

"Where do you want her?" Charlotte asks.

"Just one second...and there we are." Renshaw pulls the needle from his arm, then puts a piece of tape over the injection site. "April, is it?"

I nod.

"Why don't you come up and sit here next to me. You're not going to bite, are you?"

"No." I push my chair forward until I can see the inside of the tub.

My pulse pounds. I might as well be looking at the Necronomicon ex Mortis, or the Lament Configuration. This shouldn't be real, yet here I am, less than a foot away from the actual Amulet of Duriel.

There is a steady dripping of blood onto the artifact from the IV bag above; however, the amulet itself looks completely clean. Each drop falling onto the gem causes it to faintly flash red. Then, as the blood runs down the side of the jewel, it gets swallowed by one of the dozens of runic etchings carved into the gem's gold housing. Each one functions like a small mouth, ready to swallow whatever lifeforce it can.

Renshaw looks up from his workstation at the woman behind me. "I think we're all right now, Charlotte." He pulls the empty IV bag off its hook, replacing it with the fresh bag without disrupting the steady flow of blood.

"All due respect, sir. She may be more trouble than she appears," Charlotte says.

"I suspect we're going to get along just fine. Isn't that right, April?"

"Right," I say, fighting back a sudden urge to giggle hysterically. If I can get the girl with the guns out of here, I'm just one quick tase away from getting control of that amulet. Even if I can't figure out how to make it work, maybe I can find a way to destroy it. At least then, Tawny will be safe.

Well, safe-ish.

"See, we'll be fine," Renshaw says.

Charlotte's nostrils flair. "Yes, sir. I'll be up in HQ. Message me if you need anything." She turns to leave, making it halfway through the doorway, when she stops and spins around. "Oh, I almost forgot. One last thing before I go." Charlotte stalks up to me, placing her hands on the arms of my chair and leaning into my face. "You didn't think I missed you reaching for this, did you?"

As she pulls away from me, her hand slides under the arm of the chair and grabs my stun gun. She's just robbed me of my last possible chance at survival. It hits me like a punch in the chest.

"I'll be seeing you around," she says, flashing a cruel smile at me and making the stun gun dance between her thumb and first finger. After she's satisfied with her taunt, she finally turns and leaves the room, shutting the door behind her.

"Was that meant for me?" Renshaw asks, with an amused grin. "Gosh, you really are a clever one, aren't you?"

I stay quiet, still trying to get a read on him, needing to figure out a new plan, find a new weapon. Laurie Strode's been in tougher spots than this. If I stay calm and think this through, I can still do this.

"I certainly don't blame you for trying. If I were in your position, I'd probably do the same thing. Of course, I do have a few tricks of my own."

"What are you going to do to me?" I ask.

"Me? Not much, personally." He swivels around in his stool, completely unafraid to turn his back to me. Renshaw reaches onto a shelf and pulls out an ancient-looking leather-bound book. "It seems you and your sister have made quite a powerful enemy. I'm sure by now you've seen how I'm able to control the dead using the amulet. I'm to perform a ritual on you that works similarly, except without having to put you through the mess of dying first. I'll admit the process can be quite unpleasant. If you like, I can offer to sedate you first. I can't speak to what happens to you outside of these four walls, but in my office, I can promise you this. I'll do my best, as both a spiritual and medical physician, to help you make the transition with as little discomfort as possible."

"Well, when you put it like that, how can I say no?"

Renshaw nods. He's still smiling, but there's a little bit of sadness in his eyes. "I should caution you before we do this. I'm sturdier than I look. I don't want to hurt you, but if you give me cause, I'll have to defend myself in ways you might find quite repulsive. Understand?"

I nod.

"Good. Normally, I'd have you get on the table. Considering your condition, I think it's just as well to do it in the chair. Is that all right with you?"

I nod again.

"Excellent. In that case, I'll just have you pull up a little closer to the table here so I can give you the injection." He turns away again, grabbing a syringe and filling it with opaque brown liquid.

I pull up next to the tub containing the amulet. Just being near it gives me a buzzing feeling, making me deeply uncomfortable. It's like a queasiness fills my whole body and makes my limbs want to go limp.

Renshaw returns to his round stool by the table. "Just put your arm out here, and we'll get started."

I lay my arm palm-up across the table, exposing blue veins running through my inner elbow. My arm is shaking.

"Steady now. You don't want me to miss the vein."

"Sorry," I say, terrified of the risk I'm about to take.

"It's just a tiny prick."

As soon as I feel the needle enter my arm, I shove my other hand forward on the joystick of my chair. The needle carves a deep line of red up my arm as I plow into Renshaw. The narrow legs of his stool don't require much pressure to tip the chair, sending him crashing backward to the ground.

I reach into the tub and grab the amulet, watching a fresh stream of my blood pour into it and wishing that I could be free from this man forever.

The power in the room surges, sending the lights into a strobe.

Renshaw starts to climb to his feet, his soft eyes turned hard with rage. It's short-lived. His resolve breaks into absolute fear as Arthur Wilson appears by my side.

"No, you're not in control here. I banish you, spirit! Ben-daza, kalavector solemnos—"

His words get cut off as Wilson lunges at Renshaw, brandishing a scalpel. He stabs Renshaw repeatedly in the chest. I hear his gurgling gasps as the old man tries to spit out the rest of an incantation, but soon, it fades into wet nothing. Once he is completely still, the lights flicker overhead, and I find myself alone in the room.

"I guess he wasn't that sturdy after all?" I say to no one in particular.

CHAPTER FIFTY-SEVEN

"I do hope you have been enjoying your stay at my lovely hotel." Landon steps under a light, and I can finally get a clear view of his face. He's covered in boils and looks like he left his sanity in the dumbwaiter.

"Landon, it's us. Do you remember me? Tawny?"

"Landon's dead. My name is Arthur Wilson, and this is my home." Even through all of his injuries, he's talking, moving, exactly how he did in *Murder Mansion*. His performance is a far cry from what I've come to know from the actual Arthur Wilson, but it doesn't make him any less threatening.

I grab Kiki's cleaver. Britt seems to have lost her weapon.

"Landon, we've destroyed the body and mind totems, and we're about to eat some dinner. Why don't you put the axe down and join us?"

The three of us are creeping toward the lobby, where, if Landon does attack us, we will have a much wider space to scatter. Unfortunately, he's advancing down the other side of the hall just as quickly. It's a game of inches, and each moment grows more excruciating as we wait to see who will break first.

It turns out to be Britt.

She runs for the lobby, but Landon is faster. Even with his slight limp, he still manages to reach the space before Britt, swinging the axe at her as he charges. She screeches to a stop, realizing early enough she isn't going to make it in time, but the sudden shift in momentum causes her to twist her ankle and fall to the floor.

If she hadn't run without warning, I'd be close enough to help her. But now, she's at least a dozen feet away, and Landon is already bringing the axe over his head for another attack.

It may be an impossible distance for me, but not for Shawn. He bursts into a full sprint, and a scream gets caught in my throat. If he's trying to tackle Landon, he's more likely to end up on the receiving end of the axe's blade before doing enough harm to take Landon out. The axe is already swinging down as Shawn gets into range, but instead of barreling into Landon, he leaps forward, hurling his pitch encrusted hand into the blade's path.

The axe buries itself in Shawn's pitch, which in turn crashes down onto Britt's stomach. She lets out a pained gasp, the ball knocking the wind out of her. At least it's better than being disemboweled.

Shawn, on the other hand, is screaming in pain. The axe blade must have cut deep enough to slice into whatever is left of his hand. Shawn grabs the head of the axe with his other hand and pulls himself backward as hard as he can, stripping it away from Landon. He stumbles into a wall and doubles over, already gassed just from this much effort.

Meanwhile, Britt's managed to scramble onto her hands and knees and is once again trying to make a break for the lobby.

She doesn't see Landon sweep in from behind.

He takes one arm and wraps it around the front of her chest. Landon then brings up his other hand. A pair of scalpels are sticking out, fused to his fingers at the mid-knuckle by dabs of black pitch. The blades stab into the side of her neck, then draw two horizontal lines across her throat. Her scream is instantly swallowed by the blades in her neck. Landon pulls out the scalpels and draws a second pair, moving vertically over the other lines.

"Hashtag you're dead," he says, giggling.

Britt's body shudders in his arms as she bleeds out. Her eyes are searching madly in all directions. They land on me several times, then move on, trying to find something else in the corners of the room.

Looking for a camera so she can connect with her audience one last time.

Landon lets Britt go. She drops to the floor, dead.

"Oh Jesus," Shawn says, then looks at me with feverish fright. He tries to get up, but the combination of the axe and the pitch have just become too heavy for him to lift without extreme pain.

Over in the lobby entrance, Landon is still standing over Britt, admiring his kill.

Shawn looks at me and whispers, "Help get this thing off of me!"

I rush over to his side and grab the handle of the axe. My first attempt to pull it results in nothing but a muffled scream from Shawn, his hand covering his mouth.

"I'm going to need leverage. This is going to hurt," I whisper.

Shawn grabs a handful of fabric from the neck of his shirt, stuffs it in his mouth, then gives me a nod. I set my foot along his forearm, then yank upward with all my might, until the blade flies free from his hand with such force that it almost slips out of mine. It's heavier than I expect, and my shoulders are already burning from the effort.

Shawn squeals into the shirt, and blood starts to pump out of the crack in the ball.

"You know how to use that thing, little lady?" Landon says, blocking the entrance to the lobby and shifting his attention back to me.

"You want to find out?" I'm hoping he doesn't, but something inside of me knows otherwise. I consider turning and running back down the way we came, but aside from the basement, it's nothing but dead ends. I can't come up with a single reason why I would ever voluntarily go back down into that basement, so once again, our best option is the lobby.

I glance back at Shawn. He's made it to his feet but looks like he's in no condition to fight.

I wait for Landon to make the first move. There's no use in expending energy until absolutely necessary, so I fight against my instincts and wait until the time is right. When he begins to make his run at me, I pull the axe back behind my right shoulder like it's a baseball bat, and swing it as hard as I can.

He dodges my attack easily.

That's all right. I never believed I'd be able to hit him with that heavy thing, anyway. Instead, I've embedded it as deeply as I can into the wall. I figure if I can't use it effectively, I might as well try and take it out of commission for a minute.

Because I never meant to hit him with the axe, I'm ready for his low approach and use a trick I learned in my recent fight against Shawn. As soon as he ducks down, I swing my knee up into his jaw. His teeth make an audible clack, and his head flies up and back. I swing not just my fist, but my whole shoulder at him. It's a follow-up that sends him to the floor.

"Come on!" I shout to Shawn, taking the opportunity to kick Landon in the ribs. I don't want to kill him on national TV, but I also need to capitalize on any chance I have to incapacitate him. I get two or three good shots in before he lashes out with his mutilated hand and slices into my calf. It stings, but at this point, my body is so battered and bruised I hardly even feel it.

I run for the stairs, knowing there are more guest rooms and secret passages on the second floor to hide in. Shawn is following, but his movement is uneven. I wait for him to climb the stairs first.

"You hanging in there, Shawn?"

"Yeah, don't worry about me," he says, struggling to catch his breath.

As we hurry, Landon is shouting. "Run all you want. There's nowhere to go! I've got eyes everywhere!"

Once we reach the top of the stairs, we hurry down a series of halls, not making any real conscious decisions other than trying to get as deep into the hotel as possible. We pass the Apothecary and the nursery. The door is no longer closed, and I make a point of keeping my eyes shut until I've passed. At the end of the hall, there's a door with a golden plaque noting it as one of the many cigar rooms located around the hotel. I figure it's as good a place as any to hide.

I burst through the door. The room is almost identical to the one we saw on the first floor. There's a sofa along one wall, with a reading chair, bookshelves, a cigar rack, and a fireplace.

"Help me." I try to pull the sofa to block the door.

Shawn groans in protest as he joins me, basically pulling the entire thing by himself with a single hand. Once we're done, he collapses onto the couch, and I sink into the smoking chair. My heart is pounding, but also, I want nothing more than to rest my head against the leather side of this chair and fall asleep.

"What are we going to do?" Shawn says. "He's going to find us eventually. Either that, or the real Arthur is going to show up with some creative new form of torture."

"I don't know. April, are you still out there? We could really use your help right about now." My phone doesn't even buzz once, which is worrying.

The fact that no one is messaging me means they know April is no longer able to communicate, which probably means she's dead. A new panic starts welling in my throat. It's taken so much for me to concentrate on my own survival, I can't bear to think of making it out of this and never seeing her again. I've survived so many things, but thinking about my sister dying has me stretched to my absolute limit.

"I just wish we could have eaten those sandwiches," Shawn mutters. "At least I wouldn't die hungry."

I don't know why I can't help but laugh. It starts as a low rumble, but I quickly lose control, and everything I've been through comes pouring out of me as a bizarre outburst of giggles I can't turn off. Panic turns into tearful hilarious hysteria, and I wonder if this is what losing my mind feels like. Then Shawn joins in, and soon, we're both gasping for breath, tears drawing lines down our filthy faces.

Buzz.

Followed by a jingle.

I pull my phone out of the bag, and my jaw drops. The message says: *Broadcast from D-wreck.* I click the button, and my heart swells when I see a video of Derek, still alive.

He's sitting in a sand pit, his back up against a large metal drum. His face is bloody, and he's out of breath. "Hey kids, remember me? I bet you thought I was dead. You've all been walking around here, thinking you can only have final girls. Well, I'm here to be the exception to the rule, ladies! I've said it once, and I'll say it again. I am a Final Boy for life!"

He pulls the camera back a bit and then spins it around, revealing one of his feet is pointing almost entirely the wrong direction, and the leg of his jeans is completely black.

"So on that note, I can't feel one of my legs so good. If any of you have some crutches, or maybe a papoose that you could carry me in, that would be great. Looking at you, big Shawnie. All things considered, it could be worse. At least they didn't use up my one broadcast sending you all that video of what's now officially been dethroned as the worst day of my life." He tries to laugh but winces in pain. "Anyways, a little bit of good news for ya. I've been crawling around down here, and look what I found inside of this moonshine machine?"

He produces a large glass yellow coin.

"I'm guessing it's the Greed statue that Wilson's supposed to use to possess me, but the jokes on him because the only thing I want is to get out of here. See ya!"

He points the camera at a wall and throws the coin like a frisbee. It shatters, just like the others, and then he brings the camera back to his face.

"Hope that helps you guys take out Arthur. Of course, you can all thank me in person when you finally get your asses down here to save me." He starts to tilt the camera down, like he's going to sign off, but then quickly brings it back up. "Oh, and if you guys could bring me a bottle of water and maybe, like, some nachos? That would be super dope. Best of luck, everyone. Derek out." He kisses two fingers, flashes a peace sign, and the screen goes dead.

We should still be laughing after hearing the good news, but instead, all I feel is a renewed sense of panic. Derek is alive, and he just told everyone—including Landon—exactly where he is.

"Shit." I rub my eyes, preparing to say something I was really hoping I'd never have to. "We have to get to the basement."

I get up and check the fireplace, then head across the room and lean over the couch to start banging on the door.

"What the hell are you doing?" Shawn asks.

"Getting Landon's attention."

"I thought you just said we need to get to the basement."

"We do," I say, then gesture over to the fireplace. "That way."

Shawn shakes his head. "No way. I already told you, I'm too big to fit in there."

I pause from pounding on the door for a second. "That was when we were trying to pull you up. This time, you'll have gravity on your side."

I start knocking on the door again but rear back in surprise when something heavy bangs against the door in reply. It's sturdier than any hand. Must be the butt of the axe.

Landon calls from the other side, "Little pig, little pig, let me come in, or I'll chop, and chop, and I'll bash this door in!"

I turn to Shawn. "It's either the chimney or Redrum—your choice."

Shawn juts his jaw forward in dismay. "Fine, but you go first. If I get stuck, at least one of us should get out."

"I'll meet you at the bottom."

Once we pull off the metal grate, it takes a little bit of careful footing to get myself angled properly in the chimney. I'm going to be descending two full floors, using only my legs and back to try and control my speed. If I don't pin myself to the chute correctly, I could easily tumble to my death.

I also remember one other critical lesson learned from my last trip through the chimney—I tuck my head entirely into the filthy antique blouse to keep as much soot out of my eyes and nose as possible.

The wall is made of bricks, and each one grinds against my spine during the descent. Once upon a time, I would have considered this nearly unbearable pain, but as of right now, I'd rate it somewhere around middling discomfort. Because my eyes are shut, I don't notice any light when I come upon the ground floor. I'm caught off guard when the wall ends and I free-fall the last five feet to the ground.

Thankfully, the floor in this room is covered in a thick layer of ash and sand, which helps break my fall. Once I'm back on my feet and slightly dusted off, I call up to Shawn to come down. I can hear the echoes of him grumbling and wedging himself into the pit.

There's a breathless moment where the movement in the chimney suddenly comes to a stop.

Oh no, he's stuck, I think to myself.

After an endless span of five seconds, he resumes shimmying down the chimney, not stopping until I see him slide feet first out of the hole and land safely on the ground.

"See, cowardly lion? It turns out you had courage all along," I say, in an attempt to not think about all the charred remains of human beings he's now coated in.

"All right, we're in the basement," he says, shaking ash from his hair. "Where's the distillery?"

I open my phone to the map and see two different rooms with that name. "I've been in one of them, but the still inside had exploded, so I'm guessing Derek's in the other one...here." I point on the map to a room not too far from where I think we are now. It turns out to be a short walk to a set of double doors propped wide open.

"Oh man, am I glad to see you," D-wreck says as we enter the distillery. He's sitting on the floor, looking significantly worse than he did on the video. It seems like he can barely hold himself up in a sitting position. An entire side of his shirt is soaked in blood, and his leg is horrifying to look at in person.

I'm just happy to see him alive.

"I'm so sorry we didn't come to look for you." I give him a hug that feels like the most real thing that's happened to me in the last two days. "We thought you were dead."

"You're good. I'm just glad you're here now. How you holding up, Shawn?"

"I've been better," Shawn says.

"Fair enough. So catch me up. Who else is still alive?"

"Well, Landon is still kicking, but he's kind of gone insane and is trying to kill us all," I explain.

"Cool, cool. What about Britt and Kiki?"

I shake my head. "We're it."

Derek blows out a heavy breath of air. "Okay. Well, hey, at least I have a chance to give this back to you." He points at a pile of clothes stuffed behind the still. "I remembered where I hid your clothing before. I figured if I was going to die, at least I'd get you your Lululemons back."

I smile at the doofus. "Thank you. This is very thoughtful."

"What's the plan, then? How are we getting out of this bitch?"

"I have no idea. The front door is impenetrable. All the windows have spikes on them. April found a way to message me earlier from somewhere under the hotel. She was feeding us info for a while, but..." I trail off, unable to finish the sentence.

"Well, that's it, then, right? Let's just take the tunnels. Where they at?" D asks.

Shawn shakes his head. "No idea. And if there are any, they're probably sealed off."

"Hang on a second," I say, bringing up my phone and swiping through pictures from the Historical Museum. I flick through several floor plans of the hotel, until I get to a rough map of the tunnel system used during prohibition.

Not only are there two tunnels that line up with the hotel, they stem from each distillery. I look up at the wooden wall behind the still.

"Guys, you're not going to believe this. I think we're already at the mouth of the tunnel."

CHAPTER FIFTY-EIGHT

From: Lucy.K@Krentler.media
To: Renshaw@Krentler.media
Subject: Emergency Request

Renshaw,

I need you to send Arthur to the basement ASAP. Target priorities in order are:
   Tawny
   Shawn
   D-wreck

What a fucking mess. At least Landon's conditioning seems to have worked. Thank Duriel for small favors.

Lucy

CHAPTER FIFTY-NINE

I've poured Kiki's bag out onto the sand. If the other still exploded, I'm thinking there could be some way to get this one to blow up too. If it did, we might be able to destroy this wooden wall and get into the tunnels. I have no idea how a still works, though Shawn seems to have a very basic grasp of the idea.

"You need a heat source, alcohol to vaporize, and then something to block the escape of that vapor. Once it gets to be too much, the vaporized alcohol will either find a leak, or combust from heat and pressure. Either way, that much vapor caught by a flame all at once should hopefully make a pretty big boom."

I shove my Lululemons up into the topside nozzle of the still to create a point of blockage. There's a gas line running under the still. I give the valve a twist, then flick the Zippo by it, and a flame sparks to life.

"That's not going to cut it," Shawn says, pointing to the half-empty bottle of vodka we have left. "If it's going to be enough alcohol vapor for an explosion, then we're going to need more."

"Psssst." Derek signals with his hand up to his mouth, like he's whispering in class. "How about that?" He points to a barrel standing on the other side of the room.

Shawn struggles to pop a bunghole from the top, then jerks his head back from the smell.

"Yep, uh huh. That'll do it."

We try to move the barrel of moonshine, but it becomes painfully obvious after a few seconds that it's way too heavy. Instead, we manage to knock it on its side, fill the vodka bottle with moonshine, pour it into the still, then repeat until the base of the tank is full of liquid.

Shawn closes the hatch and seals it, then cranks the nozzle on the gas line all the way up so the fire is burning as bright as it can beneath the still.

"What do we do now?" I ask.

"Well, uh, we wait," Shawn says.

"For how long?"

"Hey, I was just supposed to be the football guy, remember? I'm pretty sure I made up at least half of what I just told you."

I give him a smirk. "I know you way too well by this point to let you get by with that excuse. Come on, give me your best guess."

He shrugs. "Could be five minutes, could be an hour. In any case, we should get some distance from this room. When it does blow, I have no idea how big the blast will be."

A moment ago, the still felt like it would take ages to blow. As soon as Shawn suggests getting some distance, I suddenly feel like I can't get out of the room fast enough. I peer down several of the dark hallways splintering off from our position, knowing Landon could appear from anywhere at any time.

"Let's get back to the chimney room. It's not too far, and there's only one way in."

We pick up Derek—slinging one arm over each of our shoulders—and make our way back out, shutting the door to the distillery behind us. We venture around the corner to the room we fell into and shut that door behind us as well.

Derek looks up the chimney hole. "I thought you said there was only one way in here."

"Okay, one way in from the basement," I say. "If Landon came down by way of the chimney, I don't think he'd stand much of a chance."

"But what about other things? Either of you have a traumatic run-in with bats? If something freaky drops down from there, it could push us right back out toward psycho Keating."

Shawn looks at the door, like he's playing out different escape routes in his head. "This is the only other room in this wing of the basement that we know. I feel like it's not a great time to start exploring."

"Fine," Derek concedes, tossing out his hands at his side. "But if an evil Santa Claus comes popping out of that chimney, don't look at me."

We sit in pulse-pounding silence for five minutes, ten. At first, I'm all nerves. Derek's got me paranoid about the hole in the ceiling now. Whether I'm watching the door or the chimney, I always feel like there's something creeping behind me.

Another ten minutes of silence goes by. The more time passes, the more the tension deflates, until doubt starts to creep in whether our plan is going to work after all.

"Well, this is probably a lot of fun for the viewers at home," I say, when the quiet gets to be too much.

"You know what we should do?" Derek says, like he's had a thought bottled inside until someone else gave him permission to speak. "If we get into those tunnels, we should broadcast everything from that point on with our phones. I'm guessing there's no cameras in there for all our adoring fans, right? If they've tuned in to us for this long, they should at least get to see how it ends."

"Fair enough. I've still got my broadcast available," I say.

He makes a surprisingly good point. If we just wander into tunnels, never to be seen again, Krentler Media can spin this however they want.

"If we record whatever happens beyond the game, maybe we can control the narrative for the first time since we got here."

Shawn looks troubled. "Hang on. This probably *is* really boring for the viewers."

Derek gives a half-hearted attempt at looking offended. "Look man, I know I make it seem like it's effortless to be this entertaining all the time, but it takes work. I'm only entertaining maybe seventy-five percent of the day, eighty at most."

"No, I mean, we're presumably live on *Slashtag* right now, but in the last twenty minutes, they haven't sent any ghosts after us, or clued Landon in on where we're hiding."

"We've had downtime before," Derek says, like it's nothing. "Maybe the audience is asleep, and they're waiting until they can watch us die horribly over Sunday breakfast."

I shake my head. "Shawn's right. We're in the final act—there shouldn't be this long of a break here. We've destroyed two of the three totems, the lunatic is chasing us around the hotel, and we've put into motion a crazy scheme to escape after learning the big twist that the game was rigged. We should be fighting for our lives right now, not biding time."

"So what are you thinking? They shut the gas off?" Shawn asks.

"Maybe that. Maybe Landon's waiting right outside to surprise us. Who knows."

I look back at the chimney, where it's starting to feel weird that some paranormal threat hasn't appeared. Derek nailed that it's the perfect setup for horror, and there's only one reason why I can imagine it hasn't happened.

Deep down, I feel a flutter of hope try to push itself up through the blood and ashes. It's so outlandish, I'm afraid to even say it out loud.

Maybe April's alive, and she's found a way to stall the production. If that's the case, every minute we spend here is wasting whatever opportunity she's giving us.

I was too late to save her from Him when we were young. Maybe I can make up for it now. "I think we should check on the still," I say.

"Tawny, if the pilot light is still burning, it could blow at any second. I don't think—"

"No, Shawn. You were right the first time. Something is wrong, and the more time we spend sitting around, the more time the producers of *Slashtag* have to figure out a new way to screw with us. I'm going to go check on it."

"Then I'm going too," Shawn says.

"Well, yeah. You weren't just going to let me wander out there alone, were you?"

Shawn's face blanches. "Well, of course not—"

"I'm kidding." I consider patting him on the back, but then I remember that the three of us are nothing but walking aggregations of cuts and contusions.

"Well, I guess that's my cue, then." Derek braces himself against a furnace, trying to pull himself to his foot.

I hurry to his side to keep him from falling. "We just got you back. You're in no shape to go out there."

"Look, I know you guys are trying to make sure I stay pretty, and I appreciate it. But I know you've seen this movie a hundred times before. Either you two are going to go out there and I'm going to get murdered offscreen, or I come with you and go out in a blaze of glory. All things considered, I could live with Shawn being the Final Boy." D's mouth crooks to the side when he realizes his poor choice of words. "I mean, I'm okay with my legacy being that I graciously passed the Final Boy baton to Shawn."

"No," I say.

"Excuse me?" Shawn says.

"Sexist." Derek shakes his head while sporting that goofy grin I've grown to love.

"I mean, You're not going to die. There can be two Final Boys."

"Come on," Derek says, not breaking from his positivity act for a second. "I've already just coined the term of a single Final Boy. You want to complicate it already by making it two?"

The more he jokes, the more I feel my heart break. He's right, of course. None of us are in shape to take on an axe-wielding maniac, but Derek can barely even stand without help from both of us.

It doesn't mean I'm not going to try.

"Fine, you can come with us, but you need to be careful. We're all making it out of this."

Derek gives me a salute, like he's a sailor in the navy. "Aye aye, captain."

Shawn and I each take one of D's arms and lift him between us. We open the door and head down the hall. When we reach the distillery, Shawn cracks the door open. The fire is still flickering near the floor, and the air up by the ceiling is shimmering, as if the wall were a mirage.

"Oh shit," Shawn says. "It's leaking too much. I don't think your clothes are stopping the gas from escaping. It's just all lingering around the top of the room."

"But shouldn't it eventually explode once it reaches the flame?" I ask.

"I'm guessing not. If gas is leaking out through the cracks of the wooden wall into the tunnel, it may never get low enough to reach the fire."

"I guess that explains why they didn't need to come after us. Not if the plan was going to fail, anyways."

"This may be a stupid question, but what if we use the lighter?" Derek asks.

Shawn thinks about it, then nods. "Sure. If you ignited the gas it, would probably cause an explosion, but you'd get caught in it too. There's no way you'd survive."

"Say there, chums, you wouldn't know where a fella could buy a drink around here, do ya?"

Landon appears in the doorway from just inside the distillery, swinging his axe up from his waist. Shawn tries to jump backward, but the blade slices a line up his sternum. Suddenly, all of Derek's weight falls onto me. The two of us stumble back against a wall, and Shawn falls to his knees. Landon readies his axe, the blade coated in crimson streaks.

Shawn's sits there in shock. Landon slowly lifts the axe over his head, preparing a final blow.

Derek wastes no time in shoving himself off the wall and limping along on his mangled leg for the three steps it takes to tackle Landon to the ground. No sooner does he have the man pinned to the sandy floor before he's yelling in pain and rolling off, clutching at his side.

Just below his ribs, a large red stain grows, and Landon's scalpel fingers are coated in fresh blood.

I scream, wanting to run to both men's aid, knowing I'll never make it to either without having to confront Landon first.

"Well, darlin', it looks like you and I are the last two left at this party. May I have this dance?" Landon climbs to his feet, his eyes transfixed on mine. He's holding the axe loosely in one hand, brandishing his Freddy Krueger fingers with the other.

I'm sick of having plans. Sick of running, sick of playing other people's games. I'm all that's left, and if I'm going down, I'm squeezing out every last ounce of what I have left.

Catching Landon off guard, I hurl myself at him. I favor the side away from his razor fingers so I can avoid the same fate as Derek. Without any strength left in my arms, I bring my forehead down and ram myself into his nose. It hurts, but pain means nothing to me anymore. All I care about are results, and it looks like I'm off to a good start.

He shuffles backward, catching himself from falling by bracing his clawed hand on the distillery door. I've broken his nose. Blood pours down his face. His teeth gleam red and white as he lets out a maniacal laugh.

I don't stop, and before he can raise his arms, I bring up a leg and kick him as hard as I can in the stomach. He loses his grip on the door and stumbles back even further into the distillery. I can smell the alcohol in the air as I follow him in, throwing a weak punch to his face.

He doesn't bother to block my attacks. No matter how much I hit him, he just won't go down. I move in to uppercut him with my elbow, but he brings the axe up and socks me in the stomach with the handle, knocking the wind out of me. While I'm bent over, clutching at my stomach, he whips his knife fingers across my face, slashing two thin lines along my cheek.

Now, I'm the one retreating. He drops the axe and grabs me by the collar of my shirt, yanking me toward him and thrusting his razor fingers at my throat.

A hand grips me by the waist and pulls me back, just before the blades pierce my vocal chords. Derek is back up on his foot, and he's throwing his entire self onto Landon, sending the two men crumpling to the Distillery floor. Derek punches Landon in the face, doing his best to ignore the extreme pain he must be in. Landon stabs him in the torso, but it doesn't stop D from wailing on him for a good five or six punches, before collapsing on top of him.

Derek starts to crawl away from Landon in the direction of the still. "You're headed the wrong way!" I scream.

"Shut the door!" Derek shouts as Landon rises again to his hands and knees, albeit this time, much more slowly.

It's only now I realize where Derek is headed.

A few feet in front of him is a small rectangular piece of silver.

"We'll find another way!" I shout, but I know better than to argue with Derek once he's made his mind up.

"Just do me one favor," he says, grabbing the Zippo and flicking the head open. "Make sure you get Shawn out alive. He's still got people that care about him."

I want to tell him *I* care about him. That he matters as a human being, not just a brand. I want him to know I really did believe he could have still had an amazing life ahead of him.

Instead, I give him one last pleading look. Upon seeing the resolve in his eyes, I scramble around the corner, shutting the door as I run. There's a sound of a flint wheel grinding against metal, and then an incredible blast of heat throws me from my place in the sand, smacking me into a wall.

CHAPTER SIXTY

From: Lucy.K@Krentler.media
To: Board@Krentler.media
CC: Operations@Krentler.media
Subject: Emergency

There has been a breach into the tunnels, and the subjects are armed. All non-essential crewmembers are to head for the emergency exit immediately, and all available guards head to the boardroom for lock-down. We have reached 100% PVI and must leave the boardroom undisturbed until the ritual is complete.

Lucy

From: William.K@Krentler.media
To: Security@Krentler.media

Belay that order. By the time security makes it to the boardroom we will have completed the ritual and will no longer need their services.

From: Lucy.K@Krentler.media
To: William.K@Krentler.media

> Dad, can I just come to the boardroom and wait this out with you? I can't reach Renshaw.

From: William.K@Krentler.media
To: Lucy.K@Krentler.media

> You have your orders. Make us proud.

CHAPTER SIXTY-ONE

I'm blind and deaf. My head is throbbing, and the only sound in the whole world is a high-pitched ring. It takes me a few seconds for my eyes to adjust back to the dank basement after the flash of blazing light. When I try to stand, the world inverts, and I have to close my eyes to keep from passing out.

What finally rouses me, after the ringing has been reduced to a low roar, is a groaning sound from across the hallway.

I open my eyes, slowly this time, and allow the fireworks display to fully die down before attempting to lift myself. The first thing I notice is that the metal door to the distillery has not only blown itself off the hinge, it's nothing more than a heap of twisted metal partially embedded in the concrete wall opposite the doorway.

Down the path, Shawn is moving slightly and mumbling something to himself.

"Shawn," I call out, though my voice sounds small and hollow in my ears, like it's coming from one end of a very long tunnel. "Shawn, are you alive?"

"I don't know," he says, completely deadpan.

It takes several attempts to find enough strength in my arms to prop myself up and then another few failed attempts to climb back to my feet. Literally everything hurts. There is no single spot on my body where I'm not feeling my own pulse send rhythmic thuds of pain dragging across every nerve in my being.

I shuffle my feet over to Shawn. He's lying on the ground, clutching at his side.

"Where are you hurt?" I ask.

"Everywhere," he says, mirroring my own feelings.

I check his stomach and am shocked to find his cut isn't too deep. "Can you stand?" I consider bending over to try and help him but immediately give up on what is absolutely an impossible task.

"I think so," He sits up, then grits his teeth and clutches his stomach, poking around a few spots and wincing. "Landon really cut me good there. I think he got caught on a rib."

Landon.

My attention shifts rapidly from the pain to fear. For such a lean guy, he seemed to be able to take more abuse than Michael Myers. Then again, that feels about on par for a horror villain. They always get back up.

I shuffle over to the entrance to the distillery. Black smoke is pouring out the doorway, and I have to hunch down to keep myself from coughing up a lung. There's two charred black bodies lying in the center of the room, so badly burned I honestly can't tell which was Landon and which was Derek.

My pain rolls inward. Our romantic relationship may have been fake, but our friendship had become real. Real enough that he sacrificed himself so Shawn and I could have a chance at getting out of here. I don't know which body to mourn and which to spit on. It feels like one last twist of the knife in a series of cruel and unfair tricks this hotel has played on us.

As much as I hate it, we have to move on. The still is nothing but metal scraps, but what's more important is the wooden wall behind it. It's been destroyed, save for some smoldering edges of the wall. Beyond it, a tunnel leads downward and curves to the left.

"How'd we do?" Shawn asks.

I want to smile for him, to show some physical display of the kernel of hope that we may yet survive this, but I simply don't have it in me.

"It worked. You know, if cooking doesn't pan out for you, it seems like you have a promising career in pyrotechnics."

"Still need to get out of here first," he says, finally pushing himself to his feet but keeping low enough to avoid the black cloud of smoke billowing across the ceiling.

"We should be okay to breathe once we get a little lower." Shawn starts to lead us toward the tunnel, but then I stop, remembering something. "Wait. Remember what Derek said?"

"Yeah, though I don't really feel like celebrating becoming a Final Boy. I'm still not entirely clear what that means, and I don't know if I like being called 'boy' under any circumstance."

"I mean the broadcast." I grab my phone and find the app.

I'm startled at first from the image appearing on the screen. There's a ghoulish figure staring into the camera. Her face is a smear of black and red, with two nearly glowing white eyes in the center. Her hair is wild and blown back, like the mane of some sort of feral animal. There are slash marks running all along the side of her face.

It takes me a few seconds to realize the creature staring into the camera is me.

And you know what? I don't care.

I push the red button at the bottom of the screen, and a little red bubble appears in the upper right-hand corner of the phone. White text inside of it spells the word *LIVE*.

"Hello to everyone who's been watching us get beaten, stabbed, possessed, tortured, choked, exploded, and whatever the hell else I'm forgetting to mention right now. You may not be able to recognize me from my usual self, but this is Tawny Howlett, here with Shawn Eamon. Say hi, Shawn." I turn the camera to face him. He gives a limp wave to the camera, then I turn it back to me. "For those of you still wondering, yes, everything that's happened on this show has been real. No, we were not aware we were signing up to be tortured and murdered for your entertainment. This is not a joke. We've been held against our will while, somehow, Krentler Media has managed to send an actual ghost after us.

"If you've been watching, you'll know we're about to head somewhere that they don't want any of us to see. They've kidnapped my sister, who has nothing to do with any of this, and we're going to try to find her, and then get the hell out of here. Shawn, you ready?"

I press a button to flip to the phone's front-facing camera, then the two of us venture into the tunnel. Aside from some damage near the explosion site, the old mine is well-lit, with metal frames supporting the structure and a network of wires running along the ceiling. It spirals down, and the first thing I notice is a chill that, for the first time, makes me thankful for wearing an ankle-length wool dress. We venture deeper through the network of tunnels, making gut decisions at splits along the way.

"Wait," Shawn says, coming to a stop. "I hear something."

Footsteps run in our direction.

"What should we do?"

I pull the cleaver from my side. At this point, the only rule holding in my head is to always have a weapon. "Be ready."

"Oh my God, she has a knife!" a blonde woman in a pantsuit screams when they round the corner. "Stay back!"

It's Lucy. She's clutching a tablet to her chest, and she's accompanied by a trio dressed in black. One is a man with a large video camera slung over his shoulder, another is holding a boom pole with a microphone over his head, and the third is a woman with mussed black hair and blood-red lipstick.

"*You* stay back!" I shout, feeling like a cornered animal. I expected to see guards with rifles, or maybe Clarence the ghost dog. I did not expect to see a camera crew. "What are you doing?"

"Please, put the knife down. You've suffered some sort of psychotic break. It's me, Lucy Hodge. The host of *Slashtag*?"

"Oh my God, are you really going to try to gaslight me right now? We're way past that. You killed Miguel, Kiki, Britt, Derek, Landon—"

"Actually, you killed D-wreck and Landon just now, when you went off-script and blew up part of the set and nearly burnt down a historical landmark. Shawn, can you please tell her?"

He shakes his head, looking so angry he could spit. "No way, lady. There's no way you're turning this back on us."

"Turning this back on you? Shawn, you're an actor in a multimedia hybrid live mega-event. You're not even supposed to leave the set. Now,

I understand it has been difficult for the both of you to participate in this show's challenges, but I'm very concerned that you've lost your connection to reality. We need to get you to a hospital for psychological evaluation." Lucy takes a step toward me, and her whole crew advances with her.

"Stop lying!" I snap, slicing the knife through the air for emphasis.

Lucy leaps backward in an overly dramatic fashion, dropping her tablet to the ground.

"Tell me what you did with April!"

"That's what I'm trying to tell you, Tawny. We haven't done anything with April. Her messages to you were part of your arc. You were even the one to come up with the idea in the first place, remember? You said it would be 'meta' to play around with horror tropes, whatever that means."

"I'm not going to ask again. Tell me where she is!" I swing the knife, this time lunging forward to make my point.

The woman in black reaches into her waistband and produces a pistol, which she aims right at me. "Drop the knife!" she barks.

My hand shakes, and the knife feels heavy in my outstretched arm. My shoulder burns. With a gun pointed at me, it's useless, anyway. I let it fall to the ground, but I keep the camera pointed at the gun.

"If this is just a normal production, why do you have an armed guard with you?"

"Because you were just responsible for the death of an A-list actor and your own boyfriend. Charlotte is here to protect us in case you try to kill us as well." Lucy softens her eyes to look as innocent and convincing as possible. "Don't drag this out any longer than it has to. You've already ruined the show. How about we turn the cameras off, once and for all?"

I knew it. That's the reason I haven't been shot already. As soon as I stop broadcasting they gain control of the narrative. They can edit things however they want to justify killing me.

Lucy makes a small flapping motion with her hand. Behind her, the crew member points his camera down at the ground. "There, see? We've put ours down. Now it's your turn, okay? And then we'll get you the help you need." Her eyebrows perk up with a notion. "You can see your sister."

"No." I keep the camera trained on them. "If you're going to kill me, you're going to have to do it in front of the whole world."

Lucy shakes her head in mild disappointment. Then, after an appropriate pause, her eyes pick up just past me, in urgent terror. "Shawn, what are you doing? Oh my God, he's got a gun!"

I realize what she's doing just a moment too late.

The woman named Charlotte fires her pistol, but it's no longer pointed at me. I jerk the camera over to Shawn. He's standing there, wide-eyed and completely still. Shock is painted across his bruised face.

He doesn't fall. Doesn't stagger backward, doesn't grip his chest. That's because he doesn't take the bullet.

Arthur Wilson does.

I start to shiver uncontrollably at the sight of the ghost standing directly in front of Shawn. I don't know why or how he absorbed a bullet, but he's saved Shawn's life. Arthur then does something even more bizarre.

The ghost turns to me with his shining eyes...and winks.

"Arthur," Lucy says, this time actually surprised. "What are you doing here?"

Arthur tucks his chin, and a disconcerting smile I recognize all too well spreads across his lips.

I'm now thoroughly confused. Why does Lucy suddenly seem more afraid than me?

"What should I do?" Charlotte asks, her voice full of urgency.

"Hold your position," Lucy orders, as if she were a four-star general. "Arthur, we don't need you here right now."

Arthur Wilson takes a step toward Lucy. This time, it's her crew's turn to back off.

"Arthur, we've got the situation under control. Go back to Renshaw. Your character is wrapped for the day."

The man in the brown suit reaches into his coat pocket, then carefully removes a scalpel, holding it as if it were a tea cup.

"I'm serious, Arthur. Stop it right now. Go back to your room. I mean it!"

A phone buzzes. To Lucy's surprise, it's not hers. "What's it say?" she demands when Charlotte glances at her screen.

"Boss wants me down at the boardroom. Sounds like he's getting nervous."

"What's it say about me?" Lucy asks, finally frazzled. She looks back at Arthur.

He's inspecting his scalpel with a look of dismay, no longer impressed with his trademark weapon. It clatters to the floor, and when he reaches into his jacket this time, he pulls out a familiar-looking hacksaw.

Lucy retreats, only to find her legs caught on the lip of a large white bathtub that's appeared directly behind her. She tumbles in, her head slamming into the back of the porcelain rim.

"I think you're on your own." Charlotte holsters her weapon and backs away, along with the film crew.

Lucy struggles to pull herself out of the tub, but her arms and legs keep slipping on the sides. She reaches out for Charlotte. "You get me out of here this fucking instant! You have to take me with you!"

"That's gonna be a hard pass for me. I've been on the wrong end of a botched ritual before. I can see where this is headed, and I'm out. Give my regards to your boss, if you see him again."

Lucy has a meltdown as she watches her only chance of survival turn tail and walk back up the tunnel. "You bitch! When my family hears what you've done, they're going to make you wish you'd died here today! You hear me? I'm Lucy fucking Krentler!"

For all her screaming and scrambling, Lucy ends up in the exact position I saw her last.

Arthur takes his time with a slow approach. When he gets close enough, I'm surprised to see Lucy's flailing arms and legs connecting with a corporeal being. Whatever Arthur is now, he's not following the same rules as before. He grabs her by the hair, and I watch him start to re-enact his decapitation performance, skipping the limbs this time and going straight for the throat.

"Well, that was some shit," Shawn says, after the lights flicker and Wilson disappears, leaving a headless woman lying on the rockbed floor.

"It seemed like a fitting end to me," a voice calls from around the corner, accompanied by the light hum of an electric motor.

My heart nearly explodes when April comes rolling down from around the bend. Her arm is bleeding. Aside from that, she looks better than ever.

I run to her and squeeze my arms around her so hard I nearly pass out from the pain.

"Tawny, I love you, but you smell awful."

I manage to pull myself away from her, and tears are already streaming down my face. "Am I really that bad?" I say, in a combination of laughs and sobs.

"I guess I can let it slide this time, seeing as I'm the one that dragged you into this."

"No!" I cry, hugging her again in spite of her active protest. "I'm responsible for my own decisions. Besides, you saved me. Again."

April smiles. "Well, I figured you'd probably remember most of the rules of surviving a horror movie, but you might need a refresher on a few details. Plus, I managed to hack their ghost system. Arthur works for me now."

I look in amazement at my sister. My hero. "That was you?"

She tries to downplay a proud smile and shrugs one shoulder. "What can I say, I like to tinker."

"Shawn..." I wave at him to come over. "I want you to meet my sister."

"Nice to meet you," Shawn says. "Thanks for saving our asses back there."

"Happy to do it. I'm a big fan," she says. "Oh, not of football, though. More like, a fan of the way you played this game."

Shawn lets out a tired but relieved laugh. "Thanks."

"Please tell me you know a way out of here," I say to April.

"I do, but—"

"But what? Let's go," Shawn says.

"Well, hold your horses. I do know the way out, but there's something else here that I think we need to do first."

I furrow my brow, wanting nothing more than to get out of here and wondering what could possibly convince me to stay one second longer. "What is it?"

"*He's* here."

"Who is?"

April raises her eyebrows in a you-should-really-know-this way. And then I do.

"*He's* here. Along with the entire board of Krentler Media. I guess they needed to be onsite to perform some ritual for mass mind control."

"Wait, you mean every single board member of Krentler Media is in these tunnels?"

"In one room."

She nods, and I'm suddenly filled with a second, third...I don't know...twentieth wind.

"Then let's get going," I say.

Shawn shakes his head. "I'm confused. To do what?"

"To burn this whole fucking thing to the ground."

CHAPTER SIXTY-TWO

The following is a post from Hector Palencia, known on Social as Hectorious B1G:

Since the cops won't listen to me and my family now thinks I'm crazy, I'm posting this here as a last resort. *Slashtag* is real, and I have proof. I work with Tawny Howlett's sister, April, at their house five days a week.

While I was there, I got to see everything that Tawny did before going into *Slashtag*. None of it was rehearsed. She was completely in the dark and didn't even sign up until like two days before it came on.

I was on a video call with April when some people from Krentler Media kidnapped her from her home. I'm literally still on the call now, looking at an empty house that's been connected for almost 20 hours.

I can't sit around and wait any longer while everyone believes this is still just a TV show. I don't know what good I'll do, but I'm leaving now to drive to Dire and see if I can find a way to help my friends.

I'll update this post when I get there.

CHAPTER SIXTY-THREE

Before we storm the gates, so to speak, I take Shawn aside. "Listen, this is me and April's fight from here on out. You can walk away now and be done with it. If you come with us, I can't guarantee your safety."

Shawn grabs the phone from me and speaks directly into the camera. "You don't have to try to convince me of anything. It's my choice to come with you till the end."

"I can navigate," April says. "I've pretty much figured out the tunnel map on this tablet. I can get us there.

"What about that?" I ask, motioning to the blood-sucking pendant. "Is it actually the real thing?"

"I don't want it," April says, her words already spring-loaded in her mouth. "It makes me feel bad."

She holds out her hand, presenting the Amulet of Duriel to me. I still can't believe it's real. My eyes are drawn to the red jewel in its center, which pulses faintly in a hypnotic rhythm that makes my eyes lose focus and forget where I am. The fading light in the jewel tells me it's hungry. It knows what's happening here is wrong, and it needs me to help make it right. If I feed it, it can help me do anything.

I can get us out of here.

I can get April new kidneys.

I can get revenge.

"Just a heads up, it might make you feel a bit woozy." April shakes it in her hand, jarring me back into the moment.

I reach out with my good hand and grab the amulet carefully by its gold shell, making sure my fingers don't land on any of the sharp protrusions where runes have been carved. Inspecting the symbols, I recognize many of them from the box in Arthur's Apartment. While they all range in size and complexity, each rune has at least one sharp point that protrudes, like a needle running along a canal into a hole.

I look at my wounded hand, the one that got sliced open the first night and never really closed. The skin across the gash is puffy and purple. When I look back at the pendant, all I see are a hundred little teeth, funneling into a hundred little mouths.

I press the back of the amulet into my oozing palm and let it drink deeply from me. The more blood I feed it, the better I feel. The lights flicker overhead, and then Arthur Wilson is standing in front of me.

But it's not Arthur, not entirely. I can feel him inside the Amulet, but he's not at the wheel. Arthur's a puppet, a memory that can be rewritten at the whim of its beholder.

Me.

I can feel the spirit of every person who ever held the amulet. More than that, I can reach inside of them, and experience the pain of all their victims. I can see through the eyes of every witness who was forced to watch Duriel's heralds commit some of the most wretched and horrific atrocities imaginable.

"You ready?" April says.

Looking through my own eyes, I see my sister and feel an energy inside of me start to hum. It makes me stand up taller, my senses sharper. It also makes me so deeply hungry. April and I have been starved for eighteen years of a meal we both deserve, and now, it's time for us to eat.

"Yeah, let's go." With a blink of my eyes, I make Arthur disappear. I don't need a boogeyman as a scapegoat for the punishment I'm about to inflict. "Make sure the camera's still on," I say to Shawn.

Just like they did to us, I want the world to watch them choke on the worst moments of their lives. Duriel wants that too, maybe even as much as I do.

We follow April deeper and deeper into the earth, through a winding series of twists and turns, until we finally reach a door with two rifle-clad guards standing in front.

They both immediately raise their guns to us and shout, "Freeze!"

I don't just see two men in front of me. I see pain, and suffering, and trauma, all patched together into little boys playing army.

"Leave one of them alive," I say, squeezing the amulet and feeling my soul catch fire.

"Where's my little Gary?" an ominous sing-song voice echoes through the chamber. "Where's he hiding?"

One of the guards, presumably Gary, turns to face his partner, pointing his rifle at him.

"What the hell are you doing?" the other guard says, as a tall old man with a sleeve of tattoos and a blonde buzzcut appears right behind him.

"I'm waiting for you, Gary. Uncle Marty's here."

Gary squeezes the trigger and fires a burst of rounds into his partner, who leaves a spray of red against the wall as he slides to the ground. Behind him, the ghost is gone as quickly as he appeared.

"Get us in," I say.

The voice continues, this time on the other side of a steel door with a glowing keypad next to it. "I see you hiding in there, Gary. Come on out. Come on out." The guard presses buttons on the keypad, and the door slides open.

He makes it no more than two steps into the room, before several more gunshots ring out and Gary falls to the floor. I don't need to see inside to feel the gunman. I tighten my fingers around the gem and grit my teeth. The pain I feel is nothing compared to the man he killed.

"Come on, don't stop filming," I say, stepping toward the boardroom.

April grabs my arm. "Wait! You'll get killed."

"Trust me. It's finally my turn to save us."

Crossing the threshold feels like stepping back into the Propitius. It's a grand wood-paneled room adorned with paintings, statues, and at least a dozen other expensive-looking artifacts. Only one of them catches my eye. It makes me feel a magnetic pull toward it.

In the center of a wooden round table sits a large golden goblet covered in runes that I can feel pulsing inside of my veins. It's encrusted with red gems, which glow in the same rhythm as the one in my hand. Inside the goblet bubbles the blood of all seven contestants, distilled down into the pure essence of our suffering. The amulet shows me how it turned our pain into a kind of infection, a spore spreading via witness. It's rooted itself in the brain of every viewer who tuned in to *Slashtag*. Every person who watched us suffer and die has fed a piece of themselves into the contents of this goblet. A piece of Duriel now sleeps in those holes, just waiting to be given a command.

"You ruined my fucking life!"

An angry shout pulls me out of the goblet and back into the present. Three old men in suits are sitting around the table with books in their hands, looking like deer caught in headlights. A fourth man has risen out of his chair, pointing a gun across the room. It's Joseph Bartlett, a billionaire whose famous Raconteur hotel line is only eclipsed by his reputation for not paying any of his building contractors. He's aiming his pistol at the person shouting, a man in jeans and a T-shirt, with a bullet hole through his eye.

"I lost my job, my house, my family because of you!"

Bartlett shouts something back, but it's drowned out by the sound of him emptying his clip into the dead man. The corpse shakes his head, unfazed by the barrage of gunfire as he pulls a pistol from the back of his pants.

"Not this time." He pulls the trigger, and Bartlett drops to the floor.

"Jesus, did you do that?" Shawn asks, looking worried.

"Sort of," I say, feeling like I'm half in a dream. I can't stop thinking about the goblet. All my pain, all that power. It's inside the cup. It's what they took from me, and I want it back. I want to gulp it down until there's nothing left and then punish everyone who got their kicks by watching us squirm.

"What do you think you're doing?" an outraged geezer shouts, rising to his feet. It's Charles Menuscha, the film producer behind *Murder Mansion*. "You can't do this!"

I want to laugh. He's so used to getting his way, he doesn't understand that he's already dead. I reach into the gem and pull out a beautiful young woman dressed in white lace. She stands before him with a deep purple bruise around her neck and a look of betrayal painted in her bloodshot eyes. He freezes in disbelief as she leans in, whispers something in his ear. She then wraps a belt around his neck that I imagine fits the dimensions of her bruise. He tries to pull back, but she drags him away from the table, watching his eyes bulge the same way hers did.

As entertaining as it is to watch them suffer, I can't help but feel myself once again pulled back toward the cup full of our blood. If I drank it all, I could reach out to every single *Slashtag* viewer and make the seeds in all of their heads grow until their brains go pop. Or I could control the seed, make them rise up against injustice everywhere. After all, there's more evil in the world than just in this boardroom. If we've come this far, why stop here?

I have to drink it. It's the only way to keep me and April safe from all the others out there who would want to hurt us.

The next thing I know, the goblet is already in my hands. I'm pulling it toward my mouth, ready to receive its gifts.

There's something stopping me. Physically stopping me. Hands on my arms, voices shouting at the other end of a park.

April. She's pulling at me, begging me to stop. I don't understand why. I'm doing this for her. Literally everything I've done to get here is for her.

For April.

She watched the show. The seed is in her. The seed is in my parents, watching from back in Arizona. The seed is in Hector, and Maggie, and probably Derek's family who don't talk to him anymore. The seed is in Shawn's mom.

It's April who pulls me back from the precipice, just like she always has. Even now, she's the one saving me. I turn the goblet over, pouring its contents onto the floor. As I do, there's a scream of rage coming from the amulet in my hand, and within seconds, the intoxicating power I felt melts away, back to exhaustion and a shaking nausea.

"Are you okay?" my sister asks.

"Yeah. I don't know what came over me. It wanted me to hurt people, a lot of people."

"And now?"

I look at the gem. "I don't want it anymore. But we're gonna need it for just a little bit longer. You ready to finish what we started?"

She nods.

"What have you done," William Krentler moans, staring at the empty goblet. He's not sounding accusatory so much as defeated. "It's all ruined."

"Mr. Krentler, it's an honor to finally meet you. We're going to get to you in just a second, but if you don't mind, there's somebody else here that I have been waiting eighteen years to have a little chat with. Hey Shawn, can you do me a favor and point the camera at this withered old asshole over here?" I step in front of the camera myself and point to the remaining old man, still sitting in his chair.

He doesn't look surprised or afraid. He's made of nothing but hate.

"For those of you who don't know, this is former Arizona Supreme Court Justice Ron Morrison, Jr., and boy, do I have a story about Him that I've been waiting to tell." I look to my sister, who is watching me say what we've always been too afraid to.

"Actually, it's a story that *we've* been waiting to tell. April, do you want to head over to this side of the camera?"

She smiles and nods as she comes to sit at my side.

"This is my sister, April. When I was twelve years old and April was ten, we met Ron in a park one afternoon. He lured us to his van with a dog, pretended to be old and weak, then he drugged me in an attempt to kidnap me. I'd be dead if my sister hadn't been quick enough on her feet to steal his knife and stab both him and his dog. In retaliation, he stabbed my sister in not just one, but both of her kidneys. I tried to help her, but his dog attacked me and held me down. The only reason we survived was that a car happened to pull into the parking lot right at the moment he was getting ready to drag me back to his home. Before he pulled away, he looked at me and said, 'good dogs keep their mouths shut.'

"But the story doesn't stop there, does it, Ron? It's just the beginning. See, after my sister fell into a coma at the hospital, I went down to the police station. I gave a description of the man, his dog, including its name, a detailed description of the car, and even the first three letters of his license plate. What was that cop's name?" I ask my sister.

"I believe that would be Officer Davis," she says.

"Officer Davis, that's it. We never heard back from Officer Davis, but let's fast forward six months. By this time, April was awake and back home but wheelchair-bound and forced to do dialysis twice a week because of her kidneys. One night, we're sitting around the dinner table while our parents had the news on. There was this segment about none other than Arizona Supreme Court Justice Ron Morrison, Jr. and what a pillar of the community he was. We both recognized him immediately and went back to our old friend, Officer Davis. Again, we gave him all the information, relived the whole event, and what happened? Nothing. And Officer Davis, who was actually now Lieutenant Davis, said he spoke to Ron, looked at his car, his dog, and found nothing suspicious. Told me with absolute certainty it couldn't be him."

"Who would have known so many people had one-eyed rottweilers named Clarence?" April says.

"That's when I got to researching," I explain. "I looked up Morrison's history. Back in the eighties, he lived in Flagstaff, where I found a string of cases of missing young girls, never found, and no suspects ever charged. The disappearances miraculously stopped as soon as Morrison moved to Phoenix, where, would you believe it, young girls started to turn up missing. Once again, I brought this information to Lieutenant Davis, and once again, nothing happened. Well, almost nothing.

"At this point, we started receiving Christmas cards from Ron every year. Even when we moved, he still found us and continued to send us cards. And not even just Christmas—he'd even send us birthday cards with five-dollar bills inside! We took *those* to the police, where Lieutenant Davis—"

"Oh, don't forget. He was a Captain by now," April reminds me.

"Right! *Captain* Davis said that we needed to stop coming in and picking on poor old Ron, or else we could be arrested for harassment and slander. That if we persisted in our assault, he could sue us for every penny our family had. So there we were, knowing exactly who tried to kill us, and we're watching him get more and more famous, more and more powerful on TV, and we're completely helpless to do anything about it.

"The first time I went viral with one of my videos, it should have been a day of celebration. Instead, my channel got temporarily suspended, and the next morning, there was a Christmas card on my cabinet with a picture of both of us sleeping in our beds, signed 'good dogs keep their mouths shut.' Oh, that reminds me of a fun fact—April has been on the kidney transplant waiting list for eighteen years now. Do you know how long the average wait for a kidney is?"

"It's three to seven years," April answers. "And that's not counting the millions of dollars Tawny's donated to kidney foundations."

As we're speaking, the blood is slowly draining from Ron's face. At first, I think it's because we're doing such an effective job at calling him out for his bullshit, but then I look around and see that the room is slowly filling with young girls, I'm guessing between the ages of eight and fourteen. Each of them is in a tattered dress, covered in cuts and bruises, and staring intensely at Ron.

I don't let it slow me down.

"This man nearly killed me and my sister when we were kids, and then he proceeded to dedicate a portion of his life to making sure that we suffered every single day, that we never forgot what he did to us. And to top it off, he made sure I had to be involved in this shitshow, just so he could share my suffering with an entire nation. You want to know why I signed up for this crappy show? Ron here got Krentler Media to promise that if I participated in *Slashtag*, they would get kidneys for April. Another lie just to fuck with us because, as it turns out, he was planning on killing both of us anyways.

"He's done all of this for nearly twenty years, and, I don't know, maybe he thought it was funny?" I turn back to face Ron. "Was it funny for you to twist the knife on us every chance you got? Or did you ruin our lives because you weren't able to finish the job you started, and it ate you up inside that you couldn't torture and kill me the way you did to all your other victims? Is that it, you just can't stand to lose?" I stare at him, but his focus is now spread to at least two dozen young girls, blinking into existence one by one all around the room. "This isn't a rhetorical question, Ron. Have you got anything you want to get off your chest before you take your final bow?"

Ron finally locks eyes with me once more. His mouth is gaped open in disbelief. It's finally over, and he knows it. "These are all some very creative stories, miss, but you're pointing a finger in the wrong direction. I'm an innocent man, a good person! I don't deserve this."

I shake my head. "You know something, Ron. I've played out my revenge fantasy against you at least a million times, and you want to hear something funny? In every one, even in my wildest dream, I never believed you would ever admit to a single goddamn thing. I was sure that you'd be a lying, self-serving monster right up until the very end. It's fine. I don't need to hear you say it. I got what I came for." I turn to April. "You got anything else for him?"

She shakes her head. "Nah, he wouldn't understand it, anyways."

We turn around and head back to Shawn, finding a narrow path in this now fully packed room of thirty, maybe forty, young women.

"All right, girls, have at him."

Ron rises from his chair once the chorus of girls start to advance in unison on his position. He tries to back away, but only manages to bump into a line of little women behind him. Ron spins around and screams as he gets an up-close look of their rotting faces, their dead eyes, and their hungry teeth.

I lose sight of him once a group of girls climbs up onto the table, obscuring my view, but the sounds of his screams are enough for me. They start out as short bursts of panic but quickly turn into desperate howls of pain.

Little girls leap off the table and grapple onto him, biting at his flesh and ripping him apart. Death by a thousand nibbles. Soon it's a swarm on top of him, and his screams are garbled and wet. It's only after he's been quiet for more than a minute that the army of girls vanish, leaving behind a twisted hunk of leathery meat on the floor.

Next to me, a hand slides into mine and squeezes tightly. It's April. Her eyes are glistening, and I can tell she's thinking the same thing as me.

I feel fifty pounds lighter. I can breathe easier knowing he's not in the world anymore. I don't have to worry about seeing him in the news in the morning or discovering some sick new way of him reaching out to me to show me that, even though I survived, he won.

I'm just about ready to get out of here, find a hospital, and maybe sleep for twenty hours, but there's just one last piece of business to attend to.

William Krentler. The actual man behind *Slashtag*.

"All right, I said I wasn't going to use a prop, but for you, I think it seems fitting." I squeeze the amulet for what I plan to be the last time.

Arthur Wilson appears before me, waiting for orders like an attentive lapdog.

"You were a pretty inventive guy, Arthur. What would you like to do to him?"

Mission Log

- ~~Restore Power to the Hotel~~

- ~~Destroy Arthur Wilson's Body Totem~~
    - ~~Unlock Arthur's Apartment~~
        - ~~Find the key's knob~~
        - ~~Find the key's shaft~~
        - ~~Find the key's bit~~

- ~~Destroy Arthur Wilson's Mind Totem~~
    - Unlock the door to Sutter's Sanctum
        - Destroy the Greed statue
        - Destroy the Sloth statue
        - ~~Destroy the Wrath statue~~
        - ~~Destroy the Envy statue~~
        - ~~Destroy the Lust statue~~
        - Destroy the Pride statue
        - ~~Destroy the Gluttony statue~~
        - Destroy the Disobedience statue

- Destroy Arthur Wilson's Spirit Totem

PODCAST ALERT!
Episode 4 of **Talking Tag** is now live at
www.slashtaginsider.com

SOCIAL

CHAPTER SIXTY-FOUR

Dripfeed presents: What the F* Was That?**

Well that certainly was...interesting. For those who somehow haven't watched the absolutely bizarre, reality-bending madness that was *Slashtag*, where have you been? From the moment Krentler Media announced that its first Social-produced mega-event would not only be a reality competition, but also one that's horror themed, we figured we were going to be in for a bonkers ride.

We had no idea.

Slashtag started out as an elaborate haunted house escape room, then it went full *Saw* for a minute before turning into a possession story, a slasher, and then ultimately, a found-footage spoof of itself. I'm exhausted just writing that sentence. It's been a wild ride, and people all over the country haven't been able to stop arguing whether or not *Slashtag* was a magnificently scripted ruse, a reality show with some heavily plotted elements, or as a vocal minority claim, a televised series of murders by way of ghosts in service of a demonic entity that wants to possess us all.

Even industry insiders are getting in on the debate. Spiderman-ager616 posted, "I work in the VFX industry. There's absolutely NO

POSSIBLE WAY any of that was unscripted. All the fight scenes and ghost effects were too well-choreographed. TOTALLY FAKE!"

Meanwhile, on the other side of the fence, Destiel15 says: "Been working in reality TV for over 20 years, and believe me, this is definitely reality TV. They've absolutely been coached on what to do during certain scenes, and of course, all the death and stuff was pre-recorded, but the drama was 100% real."

People are especially heated over the ending, with some saying the story took a wild left turn once Tawny's sister, April, started texting her from "outside the game." Some are praising the move as refreshing. Social user GhastlyGary86 posted: "*Slashtag* going meta was the best possible direction it could have gone. The story would have gotten stale if they just kept having them solve puzzles over and over. The constant shifts in sub-genre kept me guessing right up until the very end."

Some others aren't as thrilled, with one user, BilboGoggins22 saying: "The whole ending made no sense. Everything after the body totem was stupid and had weird pacing. I was on board with all of the ghost stuff, but then there were magic amulets, demonic possession, and everything got weirdly political. Most disappointing ending since Dexter."

We couldn't finish this article without sharing one of the more fringe opinions, that *Slashtag* was indeed some elaborate scheme to murder celebrities and possess an entire country. HectoriousB1G, a self-proclaimed insider, says everything on the program was real and that he has the proof to show it. Unfortunately, Hectorious' Social account was deleted ten minutes after making that post, so we may never know if there was any merit to his claim.

It also seems like Final Girl, Tawny Howlett, who saw the largest rise in followers throughout the program, has also deleted her Social account at the conclusion of the show, along with her co-star and "Final Boy," Shawn Eamon. Given the nature of the show's conclusion, it remains to be seen if Tawny and Shawn will end up becoming the new faces of Social, as initially promised as part of the grand prize.

We've tried to reach out to the showrunners and rest of the cast for comments, but true to *Slashtag's* ever enigmatic nature, we haven't received word back from any of them at this time. Of course, it's only been two hours since the show wrapped, so we will likely not hear any statements until at least Monday morning.

All right, readers, now it's time for you to tell us. What do you think? Is *Slashtag* a genre-bending masterpiece, a flawed-but-inventive reality hybrid, pure garbage, or a thwarted attempt at world domination by a group of society's elite? Let us know in the comments below!

EPILOGUE

I'm passing through the aisles of Target, though what I'm looking for isn't on the shelves. Nevertheless, it's impossible to miss the hundreds of copies of books covering every endcap. Each one shares the same name as the huge sign on the far wall, advertising the autograph signing happening by the author.

I grab a copy of the memoir, *Cook for Your Life*, by Chef Costanza, and step into the back of the long line. I'm nervous, thinking of what I could possibly ask him if I ever reach the front.

Of course, it's not the real Chef Costanza. I watched him die six months ago in the basement of a demonically charged hotel. But then again, according to the news, I died of an apparent murder/suicide after a gas leak caused me and my castmates to go on an insane killing spree. They even found a scapegoat for Arthur Wilson, citing that a wannabe actor named Todd Menuscha was one of the first to go nuts.

With everyone involved in the production either dead or missing, there was conveniently no one left to be held accountable for the tragedy witnessed by millions of Americans. By a stroke of fortune, William Krentler's son, Billy, was offsite during the filming of the show and has since been installed as the new head of the company. Since his appointment, he's managed to acquire even more businesses, moving from social media websites to buying up streaming services that were competing with Social and the Krentler Media Channel. I don't know what his plan is, but by the end of tonight, I intend to find out.

Though none of this will work if I get caught first.

A security guard monitoring the line of customers looks at me funny, and it makes my heart start to race. Does he recognize me?

I look nothing like the woman I did half a year ago. Without all the fad diets and insane skincare and makeup routines, I'm almost unrecognizable. I've gained twenty-five pounds, my skin is scarred and blotchy, and the long silky black hair I used to have has been bleached nearly white and chopped into a bob that covers my forehead. I've traded designer gym wear with Old Navy sweats.

Still, Krentler Media knows me, April, and Shawn are alive, and they're almost certainly on the lookout.

I bail out of line and head across to the toys and games aisle, trying to look as casual as possible. As luck would have it, the top-selling board game right now is a horror game called *Grind House*, loosely based on the real life events of *Slashtag*. I pick up the box—half to keep my cover and half out of morbid curiosity—and turn it over to read the back.

Designed by Jon Cohn (formerly Menuscha), host of the Talking Tag *podcast,* Grind House *is a party game for two-to-eight players in which you'll be lucky if surviving only costs you an arm and a leg. In Grind House, it's your job to survive whatever the nefarious Host has to throw at you at all costs. Will you be the last one left standing, or will your dreams for survival be slashed?*

It turns out, I didn't need to read that after all. Just another opportunistic leech looking to make a cash grab off someone else's pain. Though maybe it's just me, I seem to have lost my taste for horror films as of late. I put the box down and nearly jump when a security guard is standing right in front of me.

"Is there something I can help you with, miss?" he asks.

"I'm good, thanks," I say, trying to sound as nonchalant as possible.

"I couldn't help but notice you grabbed Chef Costanza's new book.

The signings over there." He points back to the line of customers I clearly just walked away from. "What a story, right?"

"I don't know. I haven't read it yet."

"But you know the basics. Crazy how getting eliminated first ended up being the thing that saved him. I guess the gas leak didn't start until after he left the building."

"Yeah. Crazy," I agree, then wait to see if he wanders back to tending the line.

He doesn't. "So, you gonna get in line for him to sign it?"

I nod, feeling a knot in my chest begin to tighten. "Yes, I just remembered I have to get a gift for my daughter first."

"Don't you mean *sister*?"

His words catch me so off guard, I have to do a double take. "Excuse me?"

"April. You know, I was actually there that day. At the Propitius. I was supposed to look after her, but she damn near killed me."

"I have no idea what you're talking about. You must have mistaken me for someone else." I set the book down on a shelf and turn away from him.

"I don't think I am mistaken," he says, following me as I hurry my steps toward the store's exit. "I'm pretty good with faces, and I've been specifically told to keep an eye out for yours." He grabs me by the arm.

I'm caught.

"If that's the case, you probably know it's not a very good idea to make me angry. You saw what I did to the board. What makes you think I won't make a scene here?"

"Because," he says with a rat-fink smile, "without you, there's no way your sister's going to survive on her own. We don't know how you're still getting her dialysis, but I'm guessing, if you don't come back, she's in for a rough road ahead."

He makes a strong point. "Fine. What do you want?"

"You come in voluntarily, tell us where your sister and Shawn are, and we will make sure you get to live out the rest of your days in a private facility owned by Krentler Media. You'll never have to worry about her health or safety again."

He's not really giving me a chance to make a counterargument. At least not here. "Can we take this outside first? Have the rest of this conversation somewhere less public?"

The guard lets out a single chuckle. "You read my mind, Miss Howlett." He tentatively lets go of my arm, then shoves his chin in the direction of the front door. "Go on, slowly. You try anything funny, and I won't hesitate to plug you with two rounds."

I've seen the gun in his holster, and I believe him. Even without it, he's a big enough guy to snap my neck without breaking a sweat.

Just as he said, I slowly walk to the building's exit, letting him keep close behind. No one's watched me this closely in such a long time. It almost feels exciting to be giving a performance again, even if it is for a perp walk. The front doors slide open, and I'm greeted with a breath of fresh air, something I never take for granted anymore.

"Where to now?" I ask.

"To the right, around back," he says.

Fantastic.

I lead him around to the side of the building. He pulls out some keys from his pocket. The headlights of a silver sedan flash next to a large black van. I can feel his heart pounding behind me. He knows he's won, and he can hardly contain his excitement.

Surely, at the end of this, he'll receive a commendation from Krentler himself, and likely a hefty bonus. He opens the door to the backseat, then gestures for me to get in. "I gotta ask. What the hell were you thinking, coming here in the first place? What did you want with Chef Costanza?"

I smile at him and shake my head. "Nothing. Costanza's dead. I came here for you, Grimes."

The look on his face is priceless as the side-door to the black van slides open. Before he can reach for his gun or radio, April shoves her stun gun into his back, and Shawn catches him by each of his arms. They work together to quickly pull him into the van.

I hop in, slam the door behind me, then signal for Hector in the driver's seat to go.

"What the fuck?" the guard screams.

I nod, letting his soured excitement wash over me. "I know. What the fuck is right, huh? April, can you get the—"

"Already on it," she says, walking hunched over across the van to a box and pulling out some rope and a gag.

"You? How the fuck are you walking?" Grimes asks.

I can imagine there's a million questions running through his head right now, but I'm glad he started with this one. I pull the Amulet of Duriel from my pocket and let a hundred little teeth find their way into the holes in my hand. It hums to life, eager for what's about to come.

"See, I tried to destroy the amulet after we finished off Krentler, but would you believe this thing is damn near indestructible? Turns out, it was all for the best, as it seems like the evil apple doesn't fall far from the tree. It seems we still have a lot of work to do to stop Krentler Media."

As I'm explaining this, Shawn pulls the gun from Grimes' holster and tucks it into a box. Next, Shawn pulls the radio from his belt and stomps it into smithereens, then searches his pockets and ankles for any hidden weapons or transmission devices. "He's clean."

By this point, April's tied his arms and legs together and unbuttoned his shirt, revealing a surprisingly hairy chest heaving with panic.

I nod to Shawn, then bring my attention back to our subject. "The thing is, Billy Krentler is almost impossible to find. As far as we can tell, there isn't even a corporate headquarters listed anywhere. We started small, trying to find low level Krentler Media employees. While their sacrifices helped to heal April of her wounds, it didn't really get us anywhere in terms of finding out where your home base is. We needed to find someone who had been with the company for a while. Someone they knew they could trust."

Grimes shakes his head. I can feel terror coming off of him in waves. It tastes like citrus and makes me feel warm inside.

"Why would you think I know anything?"

"Because, you're a valued member of the Krentler Media family. I mean, you're here to guard the great Chef Costanza, the face of Social. Or at least, whatever puppet you've installed to pretend to be Costanza. As you say, you were at the Propitius. You knew what was going on, and you still decided to remain loyal to the company." I look over to April, who hands me a scalpel.

Grimes tries to act tough, as if I can't see and taste everything he's feeling right now. "You're fucking crazy. If you know that I'm this loyal, then you know there's no way I'm telling you a goddamn thing."

"I was hoping you'd say that," I say, making my first incision in the middle of his chest. "See, I don't need you to tell me a thing. Thanks to Duriel, I can learn everything I need to know about your entire life just from hearing you scream."

And boy, does he scream.

Mission Log

- ~~Restore Power to the Hotel~~

- ~~Destroy Arthur Wilson's Body Totem~~
  - ~~Unlock Arthur's Apartment~~
    - ~~Find the key's knob~~
    - ~~Find the key's shaft~~
    - ~~Find the key's bit~~

- ~~Destroy Arthur Wilson's Mind Totem~~
  - Unlock the door to Sutter's Sanctum
    - Destroy the Greed statue
    - Destroy the Sloth statue
    - Destroy the ~~Wrath~~ statue
    - Destroy the Envy statue
    - Destroy the Lust statue
    - Destroy the Pride statue
    - Destroy the Gluttony statue
    - Destroy the Disobedience statue

- Destroy Arthur Wilson's Spirit Totem

PODCAST ALERT!
Episode 5 of **Talking Tag** is now live at
www.slashtaginsider.com

SOCIAL

ABOUT THE AUTHOR

JON COHN IS A WRITER and professional board game designer based out of San Diego, California. You can follow him on Instagram and Twitter @joncohnauthor. He would also love to give you free stuff like stories, audiobooks, and games by signing up for his mailing list at joncohnauthor.com.

If you enjoyed this book, please take a moment to leave a review on Amazon or Goodreads. If you did not enjoy this book, the good news is, it's now over.

facebook.com/joncohnauthor

instagram.com/joncohnauthor

twitter.com/JonCohnAuthor

ALSO BY JON COHN

Printed in Great Britain
by Amazon

44966445R00235